To AL,

It's Murder, My Son

A Mac Faraday Mystery

By

Lauren Carr

Enjoy Murder at Deep Creek Lake!

Lauren Carr

10/9/11

It's Murder, My Son

With Love,
To Jack,
My King of the Beasts

PROLOGUE

Deep Creek Lake in Spencer, Maryland

The sitcom was senseless. That didn't matter. Katrina was too tense to handle anything with depth. The hot bath and martini had failed to soothe her nerves. She ran the water until steam filled the master bathroom.

The weather channel had predicted that the severe winter storm would hit around midnight and continue through the next day. Spotting storm clouds on the horizon, Katrina anticipated waking to white-out conditions. Buried in a thick white blanket would be her last memory of Deep Creek Lake.

After a long soak in the tub, Katrina slipped into her red silk bathrobe and combed out her long black hair. Tenderly, she rubbed the most expensive anti-aging moisturizer over each inch of her olive flesh.

Her beauty had earned her millions. That made it worth preserving at all costs.

Time for a third martini before bed. She wondered if she would hear from her husband before she fell asleep. He had told her that he would be working late in the city.

Like I don't know what you've been working late on. Go ahead. Get snowed in with Rachel for Valentine's Day. Enjoy it while you can.

After completing her nightly beauty routine, she returned downstairs to the home theater where she got sucked into a verbal exchange between a husband and wife about their teenage son's sexy girlfriend.

A noise outside made her jump out of the recliner.

She glanced at the clock.

Almost nine. Could Chad have decided to come out when I mentioned my appointment with the divorce lawyer? Maybe he does love my money more than he loves Rachel.

She listened. Nothing except the wind signaling the blizzard's approach.

Maybe I should call David? No. It wouldn't look good if Chad found him here. He's already suspicious.

The German shepherd began scratching at the back door.

Not again, you damn dog! When you aren't wanting out or in, you're digging up the back yard.

With a groan, she pulled herself out of the recliner and let the dog out onto the patio. As long as she was up, she poured herself another martini and admired her reflection in the mirror behind the bar before returning to her seat for another sitcom.

Her mind sucked in by the television, Katrina was unprepared to fight when her killer attacked and pinned her down by her throat.

"Did you really think I was going to let you leave?" she heard through the roar in her ears while gasping her last breath.

CHAPTER ONE

Three Months Later

The Valentine's Day blizzard that had paralyzed the East Coast for almost a week was only a memory when Mac Faraday drove between the stone pillars marking the entrance to Spencer Manor.

In the heart of Maryland, the cedar and stone home rested at the end of the most expensive piece of real estate on Deep Creek Lake. The peninsula housed a half-dozen lake houses that grew in size and grandeur along the stretch of Spencer Court. The road ended at the stone pillars marking the multimillion dollar estate that had been the birthplace and home of the late Robin Spencer, one of the world's most famous authors.

While packing up his handful of belongings in his two-bedroom, third-floor walk-up in Georgetown, Mac Faraday envisioned his arrival into high society:

He would pull up to the front door of Spencer Manor in his red Dodge Viper. Then, the front doors would open and Ed Willingham, the senior partner of Willingham and Associates, would welcome him into his new home. Ed was the first attorney Mac liked. He sensed it had something to do with Ed working for him.

Everything happened as Mac had envisioned until Ed opened the front door and released a hundred pounds of fur and teeth that shot like a bullet aimed at the man in the roadster.

"No! Come back here! Stay!" the lawyer seemed to beg the German shepherd, which landed in the front passenger seat of Mac's convertible in a single bound.

Mac felt the beast's hot breath on his cheek while they spilled into the stone driveway. He shoved against the canine straddling his chest to keep him from ripping his throat open.

In a flash, his thoughts raced back to the event that had brought him to this moment.

Mac's twenty-year marriage had ended with the single pound of a judge's gavel. Even though his wife had left him for another man, the judge had awarded their home and everything of value to her. Mac had received the credit card debt that she had racked up after tossing him out of their home. After the hearing, Mac had made an appointment to meet with his lawyer to arrange for the next legal proceeding: bankruptcy.

Ed Willingham had cornered Mac on his way out of the courtroom. Assuming that the silver-haired gentleman had been sent by his now ex-wife's lover to deliver another round of legal torture, Mac Faraday had escaped and hurried away.

After jogging three city blocks in Washington, DC traffic, Mac had felt sorry for the sweaty little man chasing after him. When he had turned around to face him, Mac had noticed that this lawyer wore the expression of a child bursting to tell his secret, which would change his life forever.

The teenage girl who had given him up for adoption forty-five years earlier had grown up to become Robin Spencer. Upon her death weeks earlier, America's Queen of Mystery had left her vast fortune to her illegitimate son, an underpaid homicide detective named Mac Faraday.

Nobody had told him that a man-eating dog was part of that inheritance.

A high-pitched whistle broke through his screaming and the shepherd's barking.

The canine froze.

"Gnarly, get off him!" Mac heard yelled in a feminine, but firm, tone.

The German shepherd paused.

"Yes, I'm talking to you." She seemed to respond to the dog's nonverbal question.

As if weighing his options, Gnarly glared down at his quarry.

Through his fear, Mac noticed that the dog's brown face was trimmed in silver. His fingers dug into Gnarly's thick golden mane. He would have thought Gnarly was a beautiful animal if he wasn't trying to mutilate him.

"Mac is your new master," the woman back on the porch told the dog. "What have I told you about biting the hand that feeds you?"

The dog uttered a noise that sounded like "Humph!" before climbing off Mac's chest and disappearing around the front of the roadster.

Sighing with relief, Mac pushed himself up onto his elbows.

Keeping as far from the beast as possible, Ed Willingham rushed around the rear of the car to help him climb to his feet. "Mac, I am so sorry. I never expected Gnarly to react like that. Your mother always called him a pussy cat."

"That was no pussy cat." Mac clutched his chest where Gnarly's paws had threatened to crush his ribs. He glanced around for the woman who had saved his life. "Who called him off me?"

"That's Archie." Ed led him by the elbow up the porch steps and into the foyer of the manor. "She comes with the house."

"What do you mean she comes with the house?" Before Ed could explain, Mac sucked in a deep breath when the reality of what he had come into struck him with full force.

The front foyer of Spencer Manor stretched up two stories to the cathedral ceiling paneled in cedar. Granite slabs made up the floors throughout the home, including the three steps that led down to the dining room which opened up onto the deck overlooking the lake. Colorful afghans were draped across leather furniture in the living room, which was twice the size of the one in the home Mac's ex-wife had won from him thirty days earlier. Stone fireplaces commanded every room. Every window and door provided a view of Deep Creek Lake.

The scent of leather and cedar seemed to wrap around him like a soft blanket welcoming its lost son home.

Candid photographs of people Mac didn't know and memorabilia dating back generations littered the mantles, walls, and end tables. He wondered what connection these things had in his and his grown son's and daughter's roots.

Outside on the deck, a petite woman with shortly-cropped blond hair set a table for lunch. Even though the season had yet to shake the chill from winter, her skin was golden from the sun. Ankle bracelets jeweled her bare feet. Her white shorts and short-sleeved top contrasted with the jeans and jacket Mac wore for protection against the cool breezes that swept in off the lake.

"Archie was Robin's editor and assistant. She's lived in the guest cottage for years," Edward explained. "She receives a check every month from a trust fund Robin left her; plus, she gets to live in the guest cottage for as long as she wants." He clarified, "She's been taking care of the estate and Robin's dog, Gnarly. He's now yours. Good luck with that character."

"He's going to need it," Mac muttered about the German shepherd following at Archie's heels. With food on the scene, the dog seemed to have forgotten about him.

Inside the living room, Mac stopped before a life-sized portrait hanging over the stone fireplace. The image was that of a man, dressed in stylishly casual clothes, sitting in a wing-backed leather chair. Gray touched the temples of his auburn hair. His facial features included chiseled cheekbones and a strong jaw. His blue eyes seemed to jump out of the painting. A German shepherd sat at attention by his side.

The resemblance between Mac and the man in the painting was striking.

"That's not you," Ed told him. "Robin had that portrait done over fifteen years ago. It's her vision of Mickey Forsythe,

the detective in most of her books, and Diablo, his dog." He added, "Uncanny resemblance, huh?"

Mac felt a chill go down his spine. "Weird."

"Your ancestors founded Spencer back in the 1800s," Ed explained. "They were millionaires by the 1920s when the electric company put in the dam and built the lake. After that, Spencer became a resort town. One of the most luxurious hotels in the country is the Spencer Inn. Robin's grandfather had built it and passed it down to her, but she preferred murder to business." The attorney sighed with a smile. "Robin wasn't interested in anything that didn't involve a dead body."

"Now I know where I get it," Mac replied.

"Lunch is ready," Archie stepped in from the deck to announce.

Claiming he couldn't stay due to an appointment in the city, Ed handed Mac two sets of keys before speeding away in his Jaguar.

"Hungry?" Archie had prepared salmon and salad.

The smell of mesquite filled the air. Mac noticed a fire in the outdoor stone fireplace that took up a corner of the deck. She had cooked the fish on a grill over the open flames.

As if to answer her, Gnarly jumped up to snatch the salmon from one of the plates. Archie turned around in time to see him gulping it down. "Gnarly! Bad dog!" Done with his meal, the dog sniffed along the edge of the table to see if it held anything else worth stealing. "Stop it!" She swatted the dog's rump. "Go lay down."

After backing up a single step, Gnarly sat with his eyes trained on the table.

"He's a bad dog," she said. "But he's really very loveable." She patted Gnarly on the top of his head. She offered Mac her lunch, which he continued to decline until she offered to split it.

On his way to the table, he stopped at the deck railing to take in the view.

Boulders lined the shoreline of Spencer Point. At the very tip of the peninsula, the boulders had been lined up to support a wooden walkway leading to a gazebo housing a hot tub set in the lake. Trees along the lake provided privacy without cutting off the view.

A path off one end of the deck led to Archie's log cottage tucked into the corner of the property. Surrounded by a floral garden, it resembled a grown-up version of a little girl's playhouse.

"Beautiful," Mac breathed.

"Robin loved this place. She had traveled all over the world, but she thought this was the most beautiful place of all. She wanted you to enjoy it the way she did." When Archie turned to lead him to the table, he caught a whiff of her scent. She smelled like the roses in the garden.

Offering him the seat facing the lake, she sat across from him. "I thought that since we're going to be living here together, the least I could do was welcome you with a nice lunch." She smiled. "From here on out, you're on your own when it comes to cooking."

"I was afraid of that." Mac sipped the water. "I'm a rotten cook. I've been living on take out since my wife and I split up."

"That stuff can kill you. You might want to consider hiring a housekeeper and cook. Robin didn't have one because she liked doing that stuff for herself. She had a cleaning lady come in once a week, but that was it as far as household staff. Last summer, the cleaning lady got married and moved to Maine. Robin never got around to replacing her. As big as this house is, you'll need a housekeeper."

"How much do housekeepers cost?" he asked.

Her laughter reminded him that with the two hundred and seventy million dollars Robin Spencer had left him, he could easily pay the going rate for any maid service. In an effort to take the attention away from his goof, he asked her, "What kind of name is Archie for a girl?"

"Archie is what Robin called me. My real name is R. C. Monday."

"R. C. Monday?" Mac asked. "What does R. C. stand for?"

"Nothing," she answered quickly. "Robin loved it. She said I was her Archie. Everyone else took up on it and that's what they call me. Do you remember Nero Wolfe?"

"Who's Nero Wolfe?"

Her smile dropped. She blinked at him in disbelief. "Nero Wolfe. The Fat Man. His mysteries are a classic."

Again, Mac's cheeks felt warm. "I'm afraid I'm not up on murder mysteries. Most of the reading I've done is to study murder cases and forensics. Only in the last month, since I found out that Robin Spencer was my mother, have I been reading her books. It takes a long time to read eighty-seven books, five plays, and watch twenty-eight movies based on her books."

"Plus, her journal," Archie said.

"You know about her journal?"

"Robin and I were close. She was like a mother to me," she said in a soft voice.

"Since you know about it, then would I be correct in assuming that you knew about me before all this happened?"

"I'm the one who found you for her. It took me less than three weeks." One corner of her lip curled up. "But I have to admit that it was Robin's idea to meet you by calling your police department with a story about basing her new detective on Georgetown's top homicide detective. Once she was alone with you, it was a cinch for her to collect your DNA to confirm that you were her son."

Mac shook his head at the cleverness of it all.

Five years earlier, he had felt honored when his supervisor had chosen him to meet Robin Spencer at the Four Seasons to answer questions for her book research. The celebrated author's cutting wit had caught him off guard. They had lunched on burgers and eaten ice cream for dessert. Before he knew it, the afternoon was over and Robin had invited him to have dinner with her as well. Claiming to want to know everything in order to create a realistic character, she had interviewed him about his childhood and family. The next day, she had sent him a basket of fruit and a thank you card.

Ed Willingham had told Mac that Robin took the spoon he had used to eat his ice cream to a private lab to compare his DNA to hers to determine if he was her son. At the time, the thought had never occurred to him that he had spent the day with the birth mother who had given him up for adoption over four decades earlier.

Archie interrupted his thoughts by saying, "I know all about you." She fed her last bite of salmon to Gnarly, who wolfed it down without tasting it.

Mac enjoyed her playful nature. "What exactly do you know?"

"You had the best arrest record in DC, but that didn't matter much after Freddie Gibbons Jr. flew off into the sunset on his daddy's private jet. After that, no one looked good and you were made the scapegoat."

Mac lost his appetite.

She leaned across the table in his direction. "Who do you think gave Frederick Gibbons the heads up that the grand jury was about to indict his little boy of being the Rock Creek Park serial rapist?" she whispered as if someone else was on the deck to overhear their discussion.

"Didn't matter who gave Gibbons the heads up. According to my boss, it was my fault that he got away," he said, even though he knew the fault didn't belong to him.

"Do you mean Harold Fitzwater?"

That startled him. She even knew the name of his supervisor in Georgetown.

"Don't you think Stephen Maguire handling the indictment was a conflict of interest?" she asked. "They were fraternity brothers and roommates at George Washington University."

"You're kidding."

She nodded her head. "Less than a month after Freddie Gibbons escaped to Switzerland, Frederick Gibbons Senior made your boss's home mortgage disappear."

"Fitzwater criticized me for not being a team player." Mac gritted his teeth while recalling, "He kept telling me to look elsewhere for suspects. He and Steve were protecting Gibbons all along." He wondered how he had missed finding out that the assistant district attorney prosecuting the monster who had terrorized Rock Creek Park for months was close friends with the rapist's father. "How did you know?"

Archie answered, "I looked into the players' backgrounds and found that they had both graduated from George Washington University with degrees in political science. They were the same age. So I figured they had to know each other. A check on their previous known addresses proved that they had once been roommates."

"I'm impressed," Mac said. "Now tell me what you know about Patrick O'Callaghan."

For an instant, her face went blank. Then her eyes widened and her mouth opened to utter a gasp. "Pat? Chief O'Callaghan? Why do you want to know about him?"

"I heard the name."

"Where? You read about him in Robin's journal."

"She did mention him."

"He—He was your father?" She gasped again. "I should have known. You look just like him."

Mac responded with, "Should have known? I thought you said Robin was like a mother to you. She told you about me and she told you about the journal, but she never told you who my father was?"

"I never asked. I figured if she wanted me to know that she would have told me."

Mac sat forward in his chair. "Judging by your reaction, I take it that you knew my father."

"I can't believe I didn't see it. Robin was devastated when he died. I knew they were close—" She made a noise deep in her throat. "Duh! She even told me that they dated when they were in high school. It was after Pat got sick that she told me about you and asked me to find you. Now, I know why. She wanted me to find you for him."

"She said in her journal that she told him all about me. He died seven months after I had met her at the Four Seasons." He asked her, "What was he like?"

Archie smiled broadly. "Oh, he was fabulous. Pat O'Callaghan is a legend on Deep Creek Lake. Imagine John Wayne and Matt Dillon wrapped up into one. The police chief Spencer has now is a boob. Pat and Robin made such a good team. I knew she loved him. I guess that's why she never got married after her husband died in Vietnam."

"Pat wanted to marry her when she got pregnant, but her parents refused to let her marry a policeman," Mac explained. "They thought she would end up being a widow. So, they shipped her off to college, where she married an army officer who died and left her a widow anyway."

"Why didn't she come back for Pat?"

Mac cleared his throat. "She did, but by then it was too late. He had gotten married."

"To Violet," she said. "Pat would never have left Violet, even though he loved Robin. He was very loyal. Did she tell you in her journal about…?"

"My brother. Do you know him?"

"David's a good friend of mine," Archie said. "After his father died, he and I started working together to help Robin on her cases."

"Her cases?" Mac asked.

She explained, "Robin was a homebody. She liked her writing and her gardening. She hired me to do her research. I would research on the Internet or go interview people for her. I'd come back with the information and she would write her books. Then, I would edit them. Every now and then, a real case would come up that Robin would take a personal interest in. When that would happen life would get exciting." She grinned.

Uttering a whine, the German shepherd inched toward Mac's plate, which contained one bite of salmon. Archie fed him a crouton from her plate. "She acquired Gnarly while working her last case."

"Gnarly?" Mac reached out to pat the dog's head. Previously, he had concluded that Gnarly appeared so large to him because the dog had been standing over him. In the less threatening setting, Mac could see that he was indeed one of the largest German shepherds he had ever seen.

"It means extreme, and that's Gnarly all right. He can be really good, or he can be really bad," Archie said. "The woman next door was murdered Valentine's Day weekend and her husband didn't want him, so Robin bought him."

"Murdered? Next door?" Mac pushed his plate aside. "Have the police arrested her killer yet?"

"No, Robin was looking into the case when she passed away. I told her to go see a doctor because she had such a bad headache for like four days. She thought it was a migraine. If I'd had any idea that it was an aneurysm…" She looked down at her plate.

When Mac saw the pools of tears in her green eyes, he could see that his mother had meant more to her than a paycheck.

She sucked in a shuddering breath. Her chest heaved before she declared, "I've tried to carry on with it, but it's really hard without her."

"Tell me about the murder."

"You're just like your mother." Archie stacked their plates. "Your face lit up like it was Christmas morning when I mentioned a murder right next door."

She carried the plates into the house with Gnarly prancing at her heels in search of any scraps that might fall into his mouth. After picking up their water glasses, Mac followed her into the kitchen. The stainless steel appliances shone. The granite counters looked like sheets of emeralds.

"In which house was the murder committed?"

Archie stepped out onto the deck and pointed through the trees scattered along the stone wall separating Spencer Manor from the rest of the peninsula. Through the branches filled with fresh young leaves, Mac could make out the corner of a gray cedar house.

"Her name was Katrina Singleton," Archie said. "Three months ago, she was found in the family room with her throat crushed. The police are looking for a stalker that killed her first husband. They haven't been able to find him since her murder."

"Was her first husband killed here in Spencer?"

She gestured up toward the top of the mountain behind them. "Right up there. No one understands this case. Our phone book reads like a listing of who's who among America's rich and famous. Suddenly, out of the blue, this guy with wild hair shows up dressed in an old army jacket. He was threatening her, attacking her—horrible stuff. The police never caught him even once. Katrina swore he was a disgruntled client from Washington, but he always had an alibi."

"If it wasn't him, did she have any idea who else would have wanted to stalk her like that?"

With a shake of her head, she went back inside the house to the kitchen. "She said he had the words 'Pay Back' written on the name label on his army jacket."

Gnarly gazed up at Mac with big brown eyes. His size alone was intimidating.

"Strange that someone would target a woman with a dog, especially Gnarly," Mac said. "Didn't he do anything to protect her?"

"Gnarly was found beaten to a pulp. David took him to the vet before Katrina's second husband Chad got here from Washington. Chad told the vet to put him to sleep. When Robin got wind of it she offered to buy Gnarly." Archie rolled her eyes while adding, "Chad Singleton is such a jerk. He wanted five thousand dollars. He said that if Robin didn't pay his asking price that he would have him put down. Robin was between a rock and a hard place and he knew it. She paid every penny. Bastard." She proceeded to load the dishwasher.

The doorbell rang.

She reminded him, "It's your house."

Mac went to the foyer and gazed through the cut glass window panes. A police officer in a white shirt with a silver badge pinned to his chest waited for his response on the other side of the door.

What're the police doing here?

It took a moment for Mac to recall that his picture had been all over the news—the bankrupt detective inheriting the world's most famous mystery writer's vast fortune. Overnight, he had become famous.

Opening the door, his eyes met those of the officer.

O'Callaghan was the name printed on the label pinned under his badge.

This was the man Mac had come to Deep Creek Lake to meet. The man's eyes were the same color and shape as his. He also had the same height and build. His blond hair seemed to be the only difference in their appearance.

"Mr. Faraday?"

Mac tore his eyes from the name plate. "Yes?"

"I'm Officer David O'Callaghan." He offered Mac his hand. "I came to welcome you to Spencer, Maryland. Your mother was a friend of mine. She and my father grew up together. He used to be Spencer's police chief."

Mac stepped back and opened the door. "Would you like to come in?"

David accepted the invitation. While Mac closed the front door, Gnarly ran in, planted his paws on the officer's shoulders and licked his face.

Apologizing, Mac tried to pull the dog off. "He's a really bad dog."

"Your mother didn't think so." David rubbed the dog's ears. "She loved Gnarly more than anything. He hung out here even before she bought him." He stopped in front of the portrait and gazed up at it before turning back to Mac. "Unbelievable. I always thought Mickey Forsythe was from her imagination."

"She had that painted years before she ever met me."

"A mother always knows her child."

"Did you know about me?"

The officer said, "Robin never mentioned you to me."

"Hi, David," Archie called from the kitchen doorway. "How's Violet?"

David answered with a sigh. "As ornery as ever. She doesn't like the new nurse. But that's okay. The feeling is mutual." He told Mac, "My mother is in a wheelchair and housebound. I work a lot of hours, so we have a live-in nurse. We've been through seven in the last four years."

Archie turned her attention to Mac to explain that she needed to go home to her cottage. She had a short deadline to meet on an editing project. With a farewell wave from across the room, she stepped out onto the back deck and disappeared among the trees between the main house and cottage.

"This sudden change in lifestyle must feel strange to you." David sat on the sofa under the portrait.

"I never imagined it would feel as strange as it does. This morning, I caught myself comparing the price of gas between two service stations before I remembered that I had enough money to fill up the tank at either of them."

After a few pleasantries, David told him, "Mom's health went to hell in a handcart after my father passed away. She refused to go into a nursing home and I couldn't take care of her. Robin set up a trust fund for her. She footed the bill to make sure my mother had a live-in nurse and that her medical expenses would be taken care of." He smiled in spite of the truth about his mother. "Mom's so obnoxious that the nurses keep quitting." David shook his head with a sad expression. "Her mind's not there enough to think about where the money's coming from to pay for the nurse, but it's there enough for her to remember that she hated Robin. If she knew the truth, she'd be mad enough to kill someone, if she could get out of her wheelchair to do it."

Even though he sensed why, Mac asked, "Why did your mother hate Robin?"

"Robin and Dad were close, and Mom was very jealous of their relationship."

After years of investigative training and experience, Mac could easily spot David studying him from where he sat with Gnarly at his feet.

If David had been a murder suspect, Mac wouldn't have the dilemma of what to say next. But he wasn't a murder suspect. He was the younger brother for which Mac had yearned when he was a child.

Murder was a safe topic.

In the tone of one professional to another, Mac asked him, "Archie told me that a neighbor here on the Point was murdered. Have you made any headway in finding out who did it?"

David sat back in his seat. He seemed to relax with the change of topic. "The man Katrina claimed to have been stalking her disappeared from his home in Washington shortly before her murder. He had an alibi for every incident we questioned him about. Yet, we can't ignore him taking off at such a convenient time."

"Washington's pretty far to travel to stalk someone," Mac noted. "Is there anyone local who may have wanted her dead?"

David bent over to rub both of Gnarly's ears. "The Hardwicks, the couple who live two doors up from you. They're kind of..." He cleared his throat. "High strung." Grinning, he embraced the dog. "Gnarly was running loose when he allegedly impregnated the Hardwicks' poodle. They went so far as to file a civil suit for paternity against the Singletons. The judge said that without proof positive that Gnarly was the father, they had no case. The last I heard, they were trying to get his DNA. No judge will waste his time with a warrant. Archie says every time Gnarly goes beyond the wall, Mr. Hardwick is close behind him trying to scoop up anything Gnarly will leave behind. It's been months and he's got nothing. We're beginning to suspect Gnarly knows what he's up to."

"Isn't DNA testing at a private lab—on a dog—expensive? What kind of people...?" Mac burst out laughing when he saw the officer was indeed serious.

"Now you know what I meant when I said they were high strung."

"Plus they have way too much time on their hands. Is that common with rich people?"

"Not really," David said. "They had reported Gnarly to animal control, who said that if they have no proof that he has been running loose, there was nothing that they could do. So, they installed a security camera to try to catch him. We had hoped that they got something the night of Katrina's murder, but they claim someone broke their camera and it doesn't work."

Mac's mind was working. "Where was the victim's husband during the murder?"

"He was in the city. He's an estate lawyer working in DC." David noted, "He put the house up for sale and hasn't been back since the murder. He also remarried one month after his wife got killed."

"That's kind of fast."

"He and Katrina only got married last June." David cocked his head before asking with a grin, "Why are you so interested in the murder of a neighbor you never even met?"

"Murder is my business."

"You told Larry King that you were retired."

"Everyone needs a hobby."

* * * *

Mac felt like a stranger invading someone's bedroom. Located at the far end on the top floor of the manor, Robin Spencer's bedroom suite had two balconies with views of the lake on opposite sides of the house. Even though Archie had replaced the bed in which his mother had died, as well as replacing the floral-printed bedding with masculine royal blue satin sheets and comforter, he still felt awkward.

The movers had delivered Mac's clothes and personal items earlier that week. Archie had hung up his clothes in the walk-in closet and put away everything else. Except for the pictures and mementos of people he didn't know, the suite looked like it had always been his.

Two paces ahead of his new master, Gnarly charged into the room and leapt up onto the bed. He lay down in the center and faced Mac as if to dare him to try to remove him.

"You may be very pretty," Mac told the dog, "but you're not my type. Off the bed." He gestured with a swipe of his hand.

The canine seemed to consider the consequences of disobeying the order before jumping down from the bed and sitting at his feet.

"Good boy." Mac patted him on top of the head on his way into the master bath.

After introducing himself to the steam shower, the satin sheets seemed to embrace his body for his first night as master of Spencer Manor.

Mac had placed two books on the nightstand. One was Robin Spencer's fifth book. He was making his way chronologically through her writings. The second was a thick clothbound journal in which Robin had written her deepest thoughts and feelings. She had started it the day she found her son. He made a point of reading two or three entries each night before going to sleep. When he opened the journal to read the next entry the question crossed his mind, *I wonder what my mother thought about the murder in her own backyard?*

Recalling that the murder was committed on Valentine's Day weekend, he flipped through the pages until he came to an entry near the end of the book:

My darling son – What was supposed to be a quiet weekend on the Point after Mother Nature dumped two feet of snow on us turned into a circus. David found Katrina's body today. Everyone is assuming the psycho stalking her finally did her in. In theory, it makes sense. We've all seen him scaring Katrina to death. It doesn't make sense to me. I was so certain about the Holt case. The necklace proved the worst possible solution. Maybe I'm too old to be doing this anymore. This whole thing has given me a headache. How could I have been so wrong? My doing nothing got that poor girl killed. If David finds out, can he ever forgive me?

CHAPTER TWO

Mac Faraday's first mystery at Spencer Manor was the case of the missing butter.

Before his arrival, Archie had bought staples for the kitchen so that he wouldn't have to rush out to the grocery store. He found his refrigerator stocked with unopened eggs, bacon, butter, milk, and other items that most people needed to get by.

His first morning, Archie took him to McHenry to complete his shopping. When they returned, Mac discovered both the butter and bacon missing from the fridge.

"Maybe you had them for breakfast," she suggested while loading the meat into the freezer.

"A whole pound of butter and bacon for one breakfast?" Mac checked the door leading out onto the back deck. As he had thought, it was locked.

She laughed. "Who breaks into a house like this and steals butter and bacon? I'd take the Monet in the study. You do know that painting is the real thing, don't you?"

As if he thought the butter and bacon would reappear, he opened the refrigerator again to look inside. "It was there when I made my list this morning. Now it's gone. I can't cook without butter. What am I saying? I can't cook with it, either."

Archie offered to lend him some of hers. Still, he wondered who would break into a house loaded with antiques and artwork from all over the world only to steal butter and bacon. He suspected the stalker wanted for killing his neighbor.

Two days later, Mac was still puzzling over the missing food when Archie helped him interview prospective housekeepers and cooks.

One applicant in a form-fitting dress indicated to Mac that she was more interested in a position as his trophy wife than his housekeeper. Archie crossed her name off their list before she sashayed out the door. Another was polite enough, but her satanic tattoos, body piercings, and probing questions about dead bodies the former detective had seen in the line of duty made Mac nervous. Another applicant discovered that she was allergic to dogs. Minutes into the interview, she ran from the house with red, swollen eyes, a runny nose, and hives. The other two applicants were inexperienced in either cooking or housekeeping.

The last applicant was scheduled for mid-afternoon. With the break between interviews, Archie prepared chicken sandwiches and a pitcher of iced tea, which they ate on the lower deck by the water's edge. In the warm days leading into summer, their neighbors were enjoying a variety of water sports in the cove.

Archie referred to her notes after swallowing the last bite of her sandwich. "Cathy Miller comes very highly recommended. She's in her fifties. She had both cooked and cleaned for the Steinbecks for fifteen years. Robin used to know them. They have a big horse farm in Fairmont."

"Why doesn't she work for them now?" Mac refilled their glasses with iced tea.

"She had to quit when her father became ill. By the time he died, the Steinbecks had already replaced her."

"Where's Gnarly?" Mac realized he hadn't seen his dog since breakfast when he'd stolen Mac's frozen waffles. Recalling that his new dog had been the cause of a civil suit against Katrina Singleton, he wondered what antics Gnarly pulled when he wasn't home.

"He's probably casing a cookout." Archie stacked their paper plates. "Would you believe Easter weekend he came home with a T-bone steak? He stole it off the Taylors' grill."

Spencer Court ran the length of the peninsula before curving onto a bridge that crossed the cove to intersect with Spencer Road, which zigzagged to the top of the mountain. A handful of luxury homes resided on the lakeshore across the cove.

A stone and log showplace rested directly across from Spencer Manor. Across the water between them, Mac spied an in-ground pool, in addition to tennis courts and an elaborate garden. A woman with long dark hair sunned herself by the pool. In spite of the distance, he could see that she had a perfect figure.

"That's Sophia Hainsworth," Archie said when she saw him peering across the cove.

Mac felt like he should recognize the name.

"Her married name is Sophia Hainsworth-Turner. She's been in a lot of televisions shows and a half-dozen movies—a couple of them halfway good. She's married to Travis Turner."

"Now that name is familiar," Mac said. "I've read a couple of his novels. They're mysteries, too."

"Robin discovered him," Archie said. "He was born and raised here in Spencer. He went off to Hollywood to be a movie star. A few years later, he called Robin and told her that he had decided to try his hand at writing and asked if she'd read his book. It was excellent. The only thing she suggested was changing the outcome for one of the characters and the title. She introduced him to her agent and Travis Turner became a household name."

"His books aren't as good as Robin's."

"Spoken like a loyal son."

Mac asked, "Why's a famous novelist bringing his movie star wife here for the season instead of the Hamptons? Deep Creek isn't particularly known for being the in place for the Hollywood set."

"Usually they do travel with the Hollywood A-list, but Travis is basing his next book on Katrina's murder."

Beyond the Turner home and up toward the mountaintop, the Spencer Inn was a part of Mac's inheritance that he had yet to investigate. The manager, Jeff Ingle, had invited him to inspect the hotel. Frankly, the notion of owning a five-star hotel and restaurant intimidated him.

Two docks up the cove, Mac spied a couple he had identified as the Hardwicks. They eyed him and Archie through thick black cat-eyed glasses while sipping wine under a deck umbrella. Equally short and round in shape, they were dressed in identical black trousers and white button-down shirts.

Archie whispered, "Do you see them?"

"David told me that they had filed a paternity suit against the Singletons on behalf of their poodle."

"They've complained to the police more than once about Gnarly's barking. If it weren't for David we'd be having a lot more trouble with them than we do." She shook her head slightly. "It's only a matter of time before you get a call from Ed saying that you're being sued for some cockamamie mental stress over Gnarly."

"And I thought that life would be a breeze if I was rich."

"Welcome to the world of the rich and famous, Mr. Faraday. One day about three years ago, the Hardwicks were a couple of middle class nit-picks having lunch at a five-star DC restaurant when the server tripped over a briefcase left out in the aisle. She spilled Gordon Hardwick's coffee in his lap. He got burnt, and—Wham! A jury gave them the ticket to the Point. Not only did they win one, but two lawsuits. Prissy Hardwick filed a separate one claiming that, due to the burn to her husband's family jewels, she suffered mental distress because he was unable to perform his husbandly duty." She leaned over to tell him, "Guess who the idiot—or maybe he wasn't such an idiot—was who left the briefcase out where the server could trip over it."

"Gordon Hardwick," Mac concluded.

Archie nodded her head. "That coffee stunt got them their early retirement. But two point five million only lasts so long when you have money going out and not much coming in.

They've been looking for another million-dollar award to keep them in the lifestyle to which they've become accustomed. Watch your step around them."

"Thanks for the warning." Mac checked his watch. The next applicant wasn't due to arrive for another fifteen minutes.

From their table at the water's edge, he could see over the stone wall up to the Singleton home, where three months earlier its resident had been murdered. "I read about Katrina's murder in Robin's journal." Mac asked, "Can you tell me what happened, from your point of view?"

Archie smiled. "David and I made a bet about how long it would take you to ask for specific details about the case. I bet within one day. He said you'd play it cool and wait." She flashed him a mock frown. "I lose. Katrina was thirty when she married Niles Holt. They moved in two years ago this month. They had lived out here less than three months when Niles Holt was murdered. Katrina went back to the city after Labor Day, and returned in June with a new husband. Eight months later, she's dead."

After pausing to allow Mac to store away that information, she added, "Chad Singleton stayed only a couple weeks before he went back to the city. Within a week or so after he left, we started seeing this bizarre character following her around. Katrina told David that he was a disgruntled client who started his terror campaign in the city before she moved here."

"Where was husband number two while all this was going on?"

"We saw more of her stalker than we saw of him," Archie answered. "It was weird considering that they were newlyweds. Katrina had long dark hair down to her waist and a body that wouldn't quit. She had these exotic green eyes. After the snow storm, Chad called the police because she wouldn't answer the phone. David went to check on her and found her body. Gnarly was behind a flower pot on the patio. He didn't get buried under the two feet of snow. Otherwise, he would have suffocated or frozen to death. David threw him in the back of his cruiser and took him to the vet."

"Did the police try putting the Singleton place under surveillance to catch her stalker before he killed her?"

"Sure, but nothing happened. When they would quit, Pay Back would show up again." She said, "I suspected husband number two. Chad would have known when she was under surveillance. Did you ever see *Gaslight*? The husband was trying to drive his wife crazy for her money. Chad certainly didn't waste any time quitting his job and remarrying after Katrina died."

Mac agreed. "That is suspicious."

"Are you going to continue investigating this case?"

"I'm retired," Mac reminded her. "I now have a career as a millionaire playboy."

Archie grinned. "I can't see you spending your days playing golf and rubbing elbows with the rich and famous any more than your mother."

"Mr. Faraday?" A woman with long straight salt-and-pepper hair tied into a ponytail at the back of her neck waved to them from the corner of the upper deck.

Archie checked the name in her notes before replying. "Mrs. Miller?"

"That would be me." The chunky older woman began a slow descent down the steps to the lower deck.

Seeing the job applicant hobbling toward them, Mac stood up. "No, don't bother coming down. We're coming up." He whispered to Archie, who was gathering the plates and glasses. "Do you have the list of questions for us to ask her?"

After assuring him that she did, she noted, "I don't see any body piercings and I doubt if she's applying to be your trophy wife."

"So far, so good."

The interview went close to an hour, but within fifteen minutes Mac glanced at Archie. Cathy Miller met all of his requirements. She was experienced in everything he needed to run the big house. He saw agreement in Archie's eyes.

"By the way," Archie said to Mrs. Miller, "Mr. Faraday has a dog. He's a big German shepherd."

Mac interjected, "He's very mischievous."

"Oh, I love dogs." The housekeeper went on to tell one long, drawn out story after another about the various dogs she had encountered in her life, from the dog that had been run over by a school bus when she was a young girl to the dog that she raised from a pup for the Steinbeck family, but had to leave behind when her father became ill. When she began her fifth story, Archie interrupted her in mid-sentence with the suggestion that they show her the house.

Mrs. Miller took this as a sign that she had the job. Mac could see that Archie had made her decision also. In every room, Mrs. Miller delayed them with stories from her life.

This woman is going to drive me up the walls. Mac rubbed his aching temples when they returned to the living room. *How am I going to get out of this?*

"Oh, is that your dog?" Mrs. Miller pointed out the doors to the deck where Gnarly was chewing on a dark-colored round object covered with a stringy substance.

"He must have found some kid's soccer ball in the lake." Archie stepped to the door to take a closer look.

"What's he pulling off it?" Mac asked.

"Seaweed?" Archie suggested.

The housekeeper stood between them to peer at the dog and his treasure. "Odd shape for a ball."

"That's no ball," Mac breathed in a low voice while he opened the door.

Grasping the object with one hand, he stopped Gnarly when he tried to carry it inside. It felt slimy to his touch. Two empty eye sockets peered up at him. Mac announced, "That's not seaweed. It's hair." Becoming entwined around his fingers, the slimy strands came loose from the skull.

"It's a head!" Archie shrieked.

Mrs. Miller screamed and continued to scream. Too shocked to form words—Mac guessed it was probably the first time in her life—she uttered one continuous screech while grabbing her purse and running from the house to her car to peel out of the driveway.

"I guess I should cross Mrs. Miller off our list," Archie moaned.

"I guess so." Mac agreed while suppressing a smile.

CHAPTER THREE

"Until the ME tells us otherwise, we can assume this is the COD." Mac pointed out a small hole above the ear on the side of the head.

"Shot on the left side of the head. Looks like a big caliber." With a latex-gloved hand, David O'Callaghan pointed at a larger hole on the other side of the head. "The bullet went through and came out the other side."

Sitting perfectly like a contestant in a dog show, Gnarly watched them and Archie through the French doors. After taking his new toy from him, Mac had set the head on a garbage bag out on the deck. David was the first police officer to arrive.

"Who is it?" Archie asked.

Mac inquired if the head fit the description of any missing persons.

David turned it over. Some long hair hung from bits of scalp. Its eyes and ears were missing due to decomposition or predators. "I can't even tell if it's a man or woman." He looked up at them. "Where's the rest of the body?"

"You've got me," Mac said. "The head is all Gnarly brought back." He quipped, "I guess the body was too heavy for him to carry."

"Where's he been?"

"I have no idea. He's been gone most of the day."

Archie suggested, "Could it have washed up from the lake? Maybe the rest of the body is at the bottom."

Both Mac and David shook their heads.

"Bodies that have been in the water don't look like this," David said. "The body has to be on land." He spread out the hair with his pen. "Look at this."

Mac and Archie leaned over on their haunches to examine the hair. A black powdery substance covered the strands.

"Do you know what that is?" Mac asked.

"Sure do," David answered. "It's coal dust."

Before he could say more, Gnarly let out a howl followed by non-stop snarling barks.

Four men rounded the corner of the house. Three of them wore police uniforms similar to David's.

Wearing a red sweater over a white turtleneck and slacks, the fourth visitor sauntered over to the dismembered head like it was a new game introduced at a neighborhood party. "Hey, O'Callaghan, what've you got?"

David rose to his feet.

"Mr. Faraday?" One of the officers, whose insignias designated that he was in charge, stuck out his hand. "I'm Police Chief Roy Phillips." His uniform hanging on his boney frame, Chief Phillips reminded Mac of Barney Fife on *The Andy Griffith Show*. He could see bald spots on the scalp through his thin, dirty-blond hair.

After giving Mac's hand a limp shake, the police chief gestured at the visitor in the red sweater. "This is Travis Turner, the famous novelist. He's researching Katrina Singleton's case for a book." He glanced at the object on the deck. "We understand you found a head without a body attached."

His dark eyes peering at Mac, Travis firmly shook Mac's hand. Mac noted that, with his broad chest and shoulders, the author's flashy good looks would turn any head when he entered a room. In contrast, he recalled that when he had met Robin Spencer, she had reminded him of his third grade Sunday School teacher.

"We're neighbors," Travis told him with a gesture at the estate across the cove. "I heard the call about the head on the scanner. After everything that's been going on this past year, I thought I'd better see it for myself. Who found it?"

"Isn't it against police policy to allow civilians access to secured crime scenes?" Mac asked David.

Before the officer could respond, Travis said, "I've researched hundreds of murder cases during my career. You may have read some of my books. My first, *A Death in Manhattan*, won the Pulitzer."

"Where I come from, that still wouldn't warrant granting you access to a crime scene," Mac argued. "A defense attorney would have all the evidence collected here thrown out of court like that." He snapped his fingers.

Chief Roy Phillips declared, "Well, we're a small town here—rich—but small, and we welcome any help, especially from someone of Mr. Turner's caliber. Now, who found the head?"

"My dog did." Mac gestured in the direction of Gnarly, who was pressed up against the doors in his effort to get out at them. The German shepherd had been barking so hard that the window was covered with dog drool. "I don't know where the rest of the body is."

"Will somebody shut that dog up?" Chief Phillips yelled before kneeling next to his two subordinates to examine the head. While the chief had been talking to Mac, they had been photographing and collecting evidence from the head.

Excusing herself, Archie squeezed through the doors in order to keep Gnarly from charging out while she went in. Mac saw her lead him by his collar in the direction of the entertainment room downstairs.

"Ah, give him a break, chief." Travis smiled to display a wide mouth filled with straight teeth. They appeared bright white against his dark tan. "Lee Dorcas killed his mistress and beat him half to death."

Standing over the head while looking down at it, Chief Phillips asked, "What do you think, Turner?" He brought the end of his thumb up to his mouth. Mac winced when he saw he had bitten each of his fingernails down to the quick until they were raw.

"Dorcas didn't disappear off the face of the earth like we thought. The psycho offed himself," Travis said.

"Dorcas?" David repeated the name. "We don't know for sure that this is Lee Dorcas."

"He was reported missing a few days before he killed Katrina," Travis said.

"We still don't have any real evidence to prove that," David argued.

The writer said, "You put out an APB and no one has seen him. Why else would he disappear if he wasn't guilty of something? Like murder?"

"What about the petty thefts?"

"What petty thefts?" The theft of his butter and bacon quickly came to Mac's mind.

David explained, "Shortly after Pay Back showed up we started getting reports of stuff disappearing here on the Point. Wallets, purses, cell phones, keys, towels. You name it. So small that some victims don't even bother reporting everything that's been stolen."

"What about food?" Mac inquired. "Like bacon from out of a kitchen?"

"That's our guy's M.O." David nodded his head. "Since Pay Back was clearly unstable and the thefts have been occurring in the same vicinity, it's likely that they're connected. Just two weeks ago, the Holdens reported two wallets and a handbag stolen from their patio during an Easter party. That's almost two months after Katrina's murder."

Travis chuckled. "Did it ever occur to you and the Holdens that one of their caterer's staff had sticky fingers?"

"That was the first thing I checked into," David said.

Chief Phillips asked him, "Are you sure you checked into it thoroughly? Two wallets and a handbag sound more like something some hired help would steal than a psychopathic murderer."

"The staff is clean."

"I appreciate your tenacity, Officer O'Callaghan," the police chief interjected, "but you should leave the investigating up to the professionals."

"I'm a professional," Mac said.

From where he knelt next to the skull, Travis peered up at him.

"Almost twenty years in homicide. I stopped counting how many murders I investigated after my hundredth case," Mac told them. "I suggest before you go jumping to any conclusions about this head being connected to Katrina Singleton's murder that you get a positive ID on it."

Chief Phillips looked down at Travis.

Mac asked, "Do you have any evidence to prove that Dorcas—Is that your suspect?"

"Lee Dorcas," David answered. "He was once a client of Katrina Singleton."

"Do you have any evidence to put him on the scene the night she was killed?"

The police chief responded by sticking the side of his pinkie finger into his mouth and biting down on it.

Mac continued, "Other than the bullet hole where the shot was fired above his ear on one side of the head and out the other, what positive evidence do you have to prove that he, or she since we—you—have yet to determine the sex of this head—inflicted the fatal wound himself?"

While his question was met with silence from the police chief, Mac saw David cover up his mouth with his hand. He guessed that he was covering up a smirk, which he also saw on the faces of the other two officers.

"You need more evidence before closing this case along with the murder of Katrina Singleton. I suggest you start with finding the rest of the body," Mac said. "Of course, that's only my humble and professional opinion."

"That's what I intend to do." Chief Phillips called out, "Okay, men. Let's split up and search the Point. We need to find the rest of this body."

Travis Turner said, "I'd love to help, but I have some writing to do."

The writer, chief of police, and one of the officers went off in different directions. David stayed on the deck while the remaining officer wrapped the head in the garbage bag and placed it in a box for transport to the state lab.

"Where on the Point can we find coal dust?" Mac whispered to David.

"Nowhere," he replied in a soft voice.

* * * *

"What do you think?" Mac blocked a tree branch threatening to stab him in the eye.

While he led Mac up a mountain trail, David explained how coal dust, like that coating the head's tangled hair, could be found in the Spencer Mine. Since it had been abandoned the century before, the mine had become popular with hikers seeking a strenuous trek.

"Think about what?" David called back over his shoulder in response to Mac's question.

"About that head belonging to Lee Dorcas?"

"What does it matter what I think?" the officer answered. "You heard Chief Phillips. He considers the case closed. Lee Dorcas killed Katrina Singleton. If that head proves to be his, then it's a simple case of murder-suicide."

Mac said, "I don't think in all my years in homicide that I've ever seen an investigator close a murder case that fast. How long has this guy been chief of police?"

"A little over four years." David directed him onto a wider path at a fork in the road. The other path went straight up the mountain at a steep incline. "Spencer is usually a quiet little town. All Phillips expected that he had to do was socialize with our rich and famous. The fact that he's old friends of the mayor didn't hurt any. When Katrina's first husband was killed he had to do actual police work." He gestured back at the path they had passed. "He died back there up at Abigail's Rock."

Mac asked, "Is that at the top of the mountain?"

"Nearly. It's a rough trail. Forty-five minute climb over rocks from off this path. The rock was named after your great-

great-grandmother. She and her husband were on their way west when they stopped here. She climbed up to the top of the rock, which has a magnificent view of the area, and decided she didn't want to go any further. They were Spencer's first residents."

"And then Niles Holt took a header off the rock," Mac noted. Seeing no sign of strain in the younger man, Mac sucked in his breath to control his own heavy breathing. After accepting the water bottle David offered, he leaned against a tree to rest.

"Katrina and Niles Holt wanted to see the sunrise from Abigail's Rock before going back to Washington for the winter," David told him. "They were admiring the view when Katrina saw something move out of the corner of her eye. She claimed Lee Dorcas knocked her down. Niles came to her defense, but he was an old man. She was still coming to her senses when Dorcas threw her husband off the rock."

Mac asked, "Why didn't he kill her if she was his target?"

"He told her that he wanted her to suffer."

"What did she do to make him terrorize her like that?"

"Dorcas swore Katrina stole his inheritance," David replied before adding quickly, "but she was never charged with embezzlement."

"That doesn't mean she didn't take it," Mac said. "If Lee Dorcas has an alibi—"

"He and his band were singing at a festival at Rehobeth Beach in Delaware. Witnesses place him there at ten o'clock in the morning. The band went on stage at noon and played for over an hour."

Mac handed the water bottle back to him. "Band?"

"Lee Dorcas was a hip-hop artist wannabee. He took care of his maternal grandmother and expected her to leave him everything. She had a brownstone in Old Towne Alexandria, Virginia—"

"That's prime real estate."

"—plus, hundreds of thousands of dollars that she got from her husband when he died thirty years earlier. But then when she kicked the bucket, he found out that yes, she had left him everything, but it wasn't much. All he got was the house and about twenty thousand dollars—a far cry from the hundreds of thousands that he was planning to use to finance his music career."

"And he blamed Katrina," Mac concluded.

David said, "He charged into her office and threatened her in front of witnesses. He filed a lawsuit, but it turned out he didn't have a case. Katrina said he showed up at her wedding and told her to enjoy her marriage while she could because he was going to kill her new husband. She didn't take him seriously until he killed Niles Holt three months later."

Mac reminded him, "Dorcas had an airtight alibi for Holt's murder. How could he have killed her husband at sunrise and made it all the way across the state to Delaware by ten?"

"No way." David turned to continue up the trail.

The rest break over, Mac followed. "What's Travis Turner's role in all this?"

"He's one of Deep Creek Lake's most famous citizens," David said. "His next bestseller is based on Katrina's murder."

"Why was Chief Phillips conferring with him instead of you?"

"Very observant." David turned around so abruptly that Mac collided with him. "In the beginning, Phillips and I got along fine. I trained him. Then, I spent a year in Afghanistan. By the time I got back, Phillips had decided I was incapable of doing anything right."

Mac said, "This is a murder case in an area not known for murder. Phillips probably feels like this is his only chance to prove himself, and here the son of Chief Patrick O'Callaghan, Spencer's answer to Marshal Matt Dillon, is horning in on it."

"I'm not horning in," David objected. "I'm doing my job."

"Maybe so," Mac said. "But if I were an incompetent like Phillips, I know I'd feel threatened by you simply being on the scene."

David pointed up the path. "It's up that way." The steep trail had previously been used by mining carts to haul coal to trucks at the bottom of the mountain.

"I used to play up here when I was a kid," David explained as if he sensed Mac's question about his familiarity with the secluded area. "I almost killed myself playing in the mine when I fell through a shaft. It was only by the grace of God that I was able to climb out."

They broke through the trail to find the mine boarded up with a red sign nailed across the front: Keep Out, No Trespassing.

David unclipped his flashlight from his utility belt. "I hope he's not too far in there."

Mac glanced around at the coal spread out around the front entrance. "The body doesn't have to be in the mine for it to have gotten coal dust on it.

David noted one of the boards broken off to provide a hole through which to climb.

"This was broken off not too long ago." Mac saw the fresh wood exposed on the break. A set of paw prints led into the cave. "I guess this is where Gnarly went in."

Perching his flashlight on his shoulder next to his head, David crawled through the boarded-up entrance. He stopped to light the ground with a sweeping motion. He found the body sprawled out twenty feet into the mine. While they made their way up to the form, David tapped the button on his radio. "Dispatch, this is Officer O'Callaghan reporting that we have found the rest of the body to the head found at Spencer Manor. It's in the Spencer Mine."

The hands' flesh had been eaten away. Scavengers had torn its clothes to get to the food provided by the body.

The flashlight illuminated the object next to the body. Mac knelt to examine it. "Colt revolver. Forty-five caliber. That could have put the hole in his head."

Both David and Mac noticed the green army fatigue jacket encasing its torso. While the officer aimed the torch on the body's chest, Mac smoothed the material to read the label sewn across his breast. The block lettering read Pay Back.

* * * *

"Can you find any identification?" Chief Roy Phillips asked David during his examination of the body.

David replied that there was none. "And his fingertips have been chewed away. We won't be able to get any prints off this body."

"What kind of person carries no wallet?" the police chief asked.

Mac replied, "Maybe the person who put the bullet through his head took it."

Roy Phillips shot Mac a sharp look before turning his attention to David. "What were you doing up here? I ordered you to search the Point."

David answered in an equally forceful tone. "The head had coal dust on it. This mine is the closest location that he could have picked it up."

The chief exchanged sharp glances with his officer. "Good night, Officer O'Callaghan."

David gestured at his colleagues collecting evidence from on and around the body. "But this crime scene—"

"We don't need you," the police chief said. "Start your first shift at the school crossing in the morning."

* * * *

When Mac invited David to join him and Archie for dinner at the Spencer Inn, he declined because it was his mother's nurse's night off. After Mac suggested he bring his mother, David accepted.

In celebration of Mac's first evening out since his move to high society at Spencer Point, Archie changed from her usual barefoot style into a gold sundress that matched the tone of her sun-kissed skin. The color brought out the emerald tone in her eyes. She accented her ensemble with delicate gold jewelry. For the first time since Mac had met her, she wore shoes: sandals with gold straps that wrapped around her ankles. The bronze polish on her toenails matched the color on her fingertips.

After Mac directed the Viper to the mountain's top, Archie led the way to the Spencer Inn's stone steps. The front of the Inn offered a view of the lake below and the mountains off in the distance. Instead of entering through the front door, Archie turned the corner of the wrap-around porch furnished with cane rocking chairs. Mac followed her to find an outdoor café on a multi-leveled deck that looked out across tennis courts, a golf course, and a ski lift with trails down the mountain. The Inn also offered guests meals and refreshments at tables or in gazeboes while lost among the flora of an elaborate maze.

"My family built this?" Mac breathed.

"I'm surprised you haven't heard about it," Archie said. "There have been articles and pictorials featuring the Spencer Inn in every gourmet and travel magazine."

They stepped through the glass doors on the upper level of the deck and crossed the lobby separating the hotel from the restaurant. Like the Manor, the Inn had been constructed of stone and cedar. Huge windows provided a view of the rural countryside from every angle. Halfway across the lobby, Archie skipped up three granite steps and through another pair of cut glass doors.

A man with dark hair and a thin mustache at the reception desk turned to greet the incoming customer. When he laid his eyes on her, his formal expression evaporated. "Miss Archie, how are you? It's been so long." He rushed around his desk to hug her and exchange pleasantries in a language that Mac recognized as Italian.

Reminding himself that he owned this establishment, Mac gazed at the elegance before him. The servers wore uniforms consisting of white button-down shirts with black slacks and shoes. Black aprons hung down to their mid-calves.

I couldn't have afforded to eat here two months ago.

The touch of her hand on his elbow startled him. "Mac, Antonio is going to take us to our table."

Antonio led them through the dining room until they came to a table in the corner that provided a view of both the lake and ski slopes. "Your mother was such a lady, a true lady. We all miss her. This was her table. Now, it's yours, Mister Forsythe."

"Faraday," Mac corrected him.

Looking in his direction, the servers whispered among themselves, "The new owner is here."

Antonio rushed off to find the wine steward to fill Archie's order for a specific bottle of champagne, which she had ordered in fluent Italian.

A willowy man in a gray suit that matched his slicked-back hair rushed in from a hallway that led back to the kitchen. Lured by his employees' excitement, he located Mac and crossed the dining room while straightening his tie and smoothing his suit.

"Mr. Forsythe?" Jeff Ingle, the inn's manager, extended a slender hand to Mac.

"Faraday." Jeff's hand felt cold and clammy in Mac's palm. He saw that it was covered with red scars on the back that disappeared up his sleeve.

"Excuse me," the manager said. "You look so much like the way your mother described in her books." He rattled on. "It's a pleasure to finally meet you—" He turned his attention to Mac's companion. "—and to see you again, Archie. We haven't seen you since Robin passed away. I hope you know that you're always welcome here—on the house, of course."

"Thank you, Jeff."

Antonio and a server wearing a cork screw on a band around his neck returned to the table. The wine steward carried an ice bucket containing a dark bottle with a white label and two champagne flutes.

"Le Montrachet, Grand Cru," the steward showed the bottle to Mac. "From our—your—private reserve." He extended the bottle toward Archie, who took her time to examine the label before nodding her consent.

While the steward opened the bottle, Jeff explained that it had come from Robin Spencer's private collection. It was reserved only for her and her guests. "We always make sure that we have a case of Le Montrachet on hand," Jeff finished while the steward poured a taste for Mac's approval. "It was one of Robin's favorites."

Mac handed the glass to Archie. "You're the expert."

She sniffed and tasted it. "Wonderful, as always." The champagne approved, the steward poured it into their glasses and left with Antonio.

"Mr. Faraday, any time you're ready to take a tour of the Inn simply give me a call." Straightening his tie, Jeff hurried away to supervise a busboy who didn't appear to be clearing a table quickly enough.

"Nervous, don't you think?" Mac observed the servers. Their manner was formal to the point of bowing their heads before leaving the tables. Only after he had become a multi-millionaire and taken his children to the most expensive restaurant in Washington did he know the meaning of five-star service. From what he saw, the Spencer Inn was in, if not above, that same league.

"Considering that he's had free rein running this place and you're the man with the power to end it all, he should be." Archie explained, "Robin only cared about her writing, but she wasn't stupid. She didn't know about managing a hotel, so she hired Jeff and paid him very well. But she was around enough to keep him in line. If she'd ever caught him in a lie, or cheat, even once, then she'd have buried him. Considering all the people she's killed on paper, Jeff knew that if anyone knew how to bury someone so that no one would find his body, it was Robin Spencer." She studied the champagne in her glass with a smile. "Ed ordered a complete audit after Robin died. The Inn came in as being ten cents off in your favor."

"That's pretty good," Mac said.

"Damn good considering the amount of money that flows in and out of here." She held up her glass. "How do you like it?"

Mac took a sip. Admitting that he didn't know a lot about champagne, he guessed it was one of the best he had ever tasted.

"Should. It costs five hundred dollars a bottle. " She grinned. "It isn't like they're going to hand you the check after we're done eating."

Carefully setting down the glass for fear of spilling one expensive drop, he asked her, "Why does everyone think I'm Mickey Forsythe?"

"Robin Spencer wrote over sixty books about Mickey. She described him as tall, slender, dark haired, blue eyed, and with a fair complexion. He was a cop who had inherited a fortune and now spends his time as a private eye helping people." Archie looked at him. "Don't you get it? You saw her portrait. Robin described you."

"The fact that I look like Mickey is nothing more than a coincidence. I'm nothing like him."

Across the dining room, David followed Antonio, who was pushing a wheelchair carrying a white-haired, frail looking woman clutching a wooden cane. When Mac stood to remove a chair from their table to make room for the wheelchair, two busboys appeared to direct him back to his seat.

"So you're Robin's bastard boy," the elderly woman cackled when David introduced him. "Proves I was right about her." With a wicked grin, she added in a low voice, "Tramp."

"Mom, behave," David ordered. "Mac invited us here as his guests."

"He may be a bastard, but now he's a rich bastard." Amused by her own wit, she cackled again. When their server arrived with menus, she ordered a vodka martini, shaken, not stirred. "And don't forget the olive."

David leaned over to whisper to Mac, "Now you see why I don't go out much."

After the server went to fetch their cocktails, Mac cleared his throat. "David, I was wondering, why would Lee Dorcas shoot himself?"

"We still don't know that the body is Dorcas," he answered. "The only possible motive is insanity. I questioned him once. He was angry with Katrina, but sane. Not only was he sane, but he had strong alibis."

"Which eliminated him as a suspect."

"But Dorcas disappeared the week of Katrina's murder," David reminded him. "His band said he was meeting a big-time promoter. No one has seen him since, nor do they have any information about this promoter."

Archie said, "Sounds like a set up to me."

David agreed. "I thought the petty thefts were connected to this case. But if that was Dorcas's body in that cave, then I was wrong. That body has been dead longer than a couple of weeks."

"Maybe the petty thief is the same perp that shot him in the head and took his wallet," Mac suggested.

"You're not buying the suicide scenario," said David.

"Katrina's murderer beat Gnarly halfway to death," Mac said. "Assuming that Lee Dorcas is Pay Back, and he beat Gnarly in self-defense, why'd he go all the way up to the Spencer Mine to blow his brains out? Why not just let Gnarly rip his throat out if he wanted to die?"

With a raised eyebrow, Archie suggested, "Because a bullet through the brain would be less painful than having your throat ripped out."

"The body in that mine wasn't wearing that jacket when Gnarly attacked it," David said.

Mac smirked. "You saw that, too."

"Saw what?" Archie asked.

David explained, "Except for decomposition and attacks by scavengers, the clothes underneath the jacket were intact."

Mac said, "If Gnarly attacked that body, it would have had defense wounds. The clothes under the jacket would have been bloody and shredded. Someone else wore that army jacket when Gnarly attacked it. Who?"

"I've been thinking about that ever since I saw that body," David said.

"Besides the army fatigue jacket, did our victim look like Pay Back?"

Archie answered, "No one except Katrina got close to him."

David shrugged his shoulders while shaking his head. "Same approximate height and weight. His hair had the long dreadlocks. The jacket and the writing on the label read 'Pay Back' like Katrina stated in her complaints."

Violet craned her neck to look around the dining room. "Where is that waiter with our drinks?"

"We're in no hurry." Discreetly, Archie signaled to a passing server.

In the lounge, she spied a woman sitting at the bar. A glass of wine rested next to her writing tablet. In an establishment that catered to the rich and beautiful of Deep Creek Lake, she stood out in shabby clothes that lacked both color and style, worn to conceal herself and her obesity. Between scribbles in the notepad, she brushed her untamed mane out of her face.

"Betsy's here," Archie announced.

"Who's Betsy?" Mac turned around in his chair to peer into the lounge.

"Travis Turner's assistant," she explained. "Betsy Weaver. Robin used to keep me busy, but not as busy as Travis keeps her. I think she enjoys it though. Look at that. She has the evening off, but she's working away there in that notebook of hers. She's probably editing Travis's latest book. He puts out one a year."

Violet, who had been searching for their server, snapped at Mac, "If you're the owner, then I guess it's you that I complain to about getting some service."

"Mom!" David hissed. "Settle!"

Violet's face brightened when their drinks arrived. "Can I get you anything else?" the waiter inquired before leaving with their dinner orders.

"How about some service?" Violet snapped at him.

David ordered, "Stop it, Mother. You're not going to ruin our evening."

Clutching her drink, she sank into her chair in a pout.

Mac suggested, "You know, if that body was a decoy to make the police close Katrina's case because they believed the killer was already dead—"

"Which is exactly what Phillips intends to do," David said.

"—then the killer might not be a disgruntled client."

"Whoever he is we have his DNA."

"Are you kidding me?"

"Cost me a written reprimand and three days' pay, but we got it." David smiled. "When I left the crime scene to take Gnarly to the vet, I had a state crime scene investigator meet me at the animal hospital to take samples of the blood that had frozen onto his fur. I was right. Not all of the blood on Gnarly was his. His fur had human blood and tissue on it, and it didn't belong to Katrina. They got enough to get the killer's DNA."

Mac wanted to know, "If you got the perp's DNA, why'd you get a written reprimand and docked three days' pay?"

"Because I left the crime scene. I left one of my patrolmen there, but Phillips claimed I was negligent to leave it to save a dog, even if he was evidence and a potential witness." David muttered, "Doesn't matter. We have his DNA. Now all we need is someone to compare it to."

"We do have someone to compare it to," Mac said. "That body in the mine. If it doesn't match with what you collected from Gnarly, then that will be enough to force Phillips to reopen the case."

"Ben, have you met Mickey Forsythe yet?"

Mac was so enthralled in their conversation that he jumped in his seat when he heard Travis Turner's voice behind his back.

"I don't believe I've had the pleasure." A hand slipped in between Mac and Archie to request a shake. "Mr. Forsythe?" Mac turned around in his chair.

An attractive blond couple dressed in matching tennis togs peered at Mac with curiosity. "It's him," the woman breathed with excitement in her tone. "It's Robin's son."

"Mic—"

"Mac," Mac interrupted before grasping the hand offered by the male half of the pair. "Mac Faraday. Mickey was a fictional character in my mother's books."

"Pardon me," Travis apologized. "We were having some drinks before dinner and ran into the Flemings." He wore the same white slacks and red sweater that he had been wearing earlier.

Up close, Mac recognized his wife, Sophia Hainsworth-Turner. He had seen her in a series of commercials promoting beauty products. She wore her long straight black hair down to her waist. Her flawless golden skin suggested that she spent most of her time in the sun or tanning booth. She displayed her taut slender figure in a black sleeveless and backless dress.

"I saw you on Larry King," Sophia said to him through thick lips dressed in dark red lipstick. "Welcome to Spencer." She released Travis's elbow to grasp Mac's palm. The enormous diamond she wore on her wedding finger made for a clumsy handshake. As soon as he released them, she placed her fingers back on Travis's elbow as if he'd get away.

In the lounge beyond them, Mac saw Betsy pause to divert her attention from her notebook to them. When she brushed her unruly hair out of her face, he saw that she wore glasses with lenses so thick that her eyeballs seemed to bulge from their sockets behind them.

"You look just like I imagined," the blond-haired woman gushed at meeting Robin Spencer's son.

Her husband introduced himself. "I'm Ben Fleming, Garrett County's prosecuting attorney. I knew your mother. This is my wife, Catherine." He acknowledged Mac's companions. "Nice to see you again, Archie, David, and Violet."

"I've read all of your mother's books," Catherine interjected while reaching out to caress Mac's fingers as if his touch beheld a magical element for her to treasure. "She was my favorite writer." In her excitement, she failed to notice her insult to the famed author in their midst.

Mac asked Travis, "Did anything you saw this afternoon inspire you?"

"Inspire?"

"For the book you're working on?"

"Oh, that." Travis chuckled while caressing his wife's shoulder. "I'm sure the head the dog dragged in will get quite a reaction from my publisher, especially when it turns out to be the killer's head."

"I wouldn't write that chapter yet," Mac said. "David and I found the rest of the body."

Travis's brilliant grin dropped. "What? No one told me that."

Ben interrupted, "What are you talking about? What head? What dog? What body? What happened?"

"Gnarly brought home some dead guy's head," Archie explained.

"It's got to be Lee Dorcas," Travis said. "He lost his marbles, killed Katrina, and then offed himself."

"When did you find his body? Where was it?" Ben demanded to know. "Why wasn't I told about this?"

"Because Mac and I only found the body in the Spencer Mine a few hours ago," David said.

"It's hard to arrest a dead body," Travis chuckled. "Dorcas was crazy."

"Was it Lee Dorcas?" Ben asked David. "I thought his lawyer and the police in DC cleared him of any wrongdoing."

"We don't have an ID on the body yet."

"When you get it call me." Ben took his wife's arm.

Catherine said, "Oh, this is just like old times when Robin was alive." After another round of assertions that Mac looked exactly like he did in his mother's books, the couple made their way to the lobby.

Travis peered down at David. "Don't you think you're making this a lot more complicated than it needs to be?"

"When did you graduate from the police academy?"

"Every single one of my books has made all of the bestsellers' lists because I've researched hundreds of murder cases," Travis said. "It's simple, especially when the murder victim tells us herself. Katrina told you, and me, and Sophia—last year right over there in the lounge—a crazy ex-client named Lee Dorcas was harassing her. He killed her husband right in front of her and got away with it. The police couldn't—or wouldn't—do anything to help her. He'd been terrorizing her for over a year and she knew that it was only a matter of time before he'd kill her. Don't you remember that?"

David argued, "The evidence says differently."

"And the evidence never lies," Mac finished.

Travis turned to him. "You don't know how things work around here."

"Tell me," replied Mac.

"Chief Roy Phillips is looking for a reason to fire David. Lee Dorcas told her that he was going to kill her. Now she's dead. We have a murder victim—"

"Two," Mac corrected him.

Travis glared at him.

"Are you forgetting Niles Holt?"

"Two," Travis said.

"Maybe three," Mac pointed out.

Travis's dark eyes narrowed.

Mac said, "There was a bullet hole in that head. That makes it a homicide. The death needs to be investigated to determine if the gunshot was self-inflicted or not. That's SOP."

"SOP?"

"Standard operating procedure," David said.

"It seems to me," Mac said, "David is not making this more difficult than it needs to be. Chief Roy Phillips is making it much easier than it really is."

"Very well." Travis stood up tall. "Take my advice, Dave. Keep your nose out of this case. Write your speeding tickets, stay out of Phillips's way, and pick up your pay check."

"Let's go, Travis." Sophia's dark brown eyes had glazed over during their conversation. She was there to be seen and that wasn't happening to her satisfaction.

Travis hissed at David, "Think about it, bud."

Sophia tugged on her husband's arm until he led her outside to the deck where they disappeared down the steps in the direction of the garden.

Neither of them noticed Travis's secretary's eyes following them when they left. Once they were out of sight, Betsy gestured to the bartender for another glass of wine before making another note in her scratchpad.

CHAPTER FOUR

Mac hadn't noticed that his mother's office equipment consisted only of an old laptop and printer until after he received a copy of Katrina Singleton's case file from prosecutor Ben Fleming.

So, he went in search of Robin's assistant.

The guest cottage was a cozy cabin with a great room that featured an enormous stone fireplace and a writer's loft. French doors opened on to a patio with a picture view of the lake. Built-in bookcases crammed with books, including every one of Robin Spencer's books, took up one whole wall.

Robin Spencer's books weren't the only signed first editions Archie owned. During her years of working as the mystery writer's assistant, she had become friends with some of the most famous authors in the country. Another wall was a who's who photo gallery of novelists and other celebrities.

With every inch of bookshelf space filled, Archie stacked other books on the hardwood floor. The rest of the flat surfaces in the cottage held research files. The editor had converted the larger of the two bedrooms into an office with a desktop computer, laptop, printer, scanner, fax, and a wide assortment of other equipment, including cameras, recorders, and every technical toy a girl could want.

After scanning the photographs in the case file, Archie pulled up a chair to study the pictures on Mac's laptop. He could feel her breath on his neck. "What do you see?" She rested her chin on his shoulder to peer at the image on the screen.

Katrina wore a ruby red, floor-length robe. Her dark hair was fanned out behind her. Its shine matched the silkiness of her garment. A dark line marked the width of her throat. Her legs rested to the side, bent at the knees as if she had been practicing sit-ups before taking a break. Her arms lay askew where they had fallen after her last failed attempt to push away the object crushing her larynx.

"It's what I don't see." Mac zoomed in on Katrina's naked fingers. "Where's her wedding ring?"

"Phillips will claim she took it off," she said. "Her husband did have a mistress."

"Either that or her killer took it as a souvenir." He zoomed out on the picture to study the room. The only sign of a struggle was an overturned recliner. "Was there any sign of forced entry?"

"None," Archie answered. "There wasn't in any of the attacks. The security system was on when David found the body. This guy was like a magician, popping in and out of nowhere."

"The woman was being terrorized but she remained here alone." He shook his head. "This case is a mess of contradictions." He moved the mouse in a circle to make the curser rotate around the picture. "If she took off her wedding ring, it would have been in her personal effects."

"It was three carats."

"Sounds like a three-carat motive for murder."

"In all your years in homicide, did you ever see a case where a thief terrorized his victim for months before robbing and killing them?"

"No," Mac said. "I've never seen a case like this one."

* * * *

"Hey, buddy, how's it going?" Travis Turner startled David out of his thoughts about Katrina's murder.

The officer had stopped at the coffee shop in McHenry for an egg sandwich before reporting for duty. He had become so absorbed in mentally replaying the months of incident reports in search of a missed clue that his sandwich had grown cold in the meantime.

Travis snapped him back to the present. "You looked like you were a thousand miles away," he laughed while filling his coffee mug with a special blend.

"Kind of." David sipped his lukewarm coffee.

"Hey, did the autopsy report for Pay Back come back from the ME yet?" Travis sat in a vacant chair across from him at the small bistro table.

"Should be on Phillips's desk this morning." David rose from his seat to warm his coffee with some fresh brew. "Why?"

"I'm wondering what he found."

Before David could respond, a woman at a corner table gestured for Travis's attention. Excitedly, she held forth a hardcover book with Travis's image filling the back cover. "Are you really him?"

Travis's face broke into a wide grin. "Yes, I am."

While digging through her handbag, she hurried out of her seat. "Could you please autograph your book for me?" She extracted a pen from her bag and handed it to him.

David returned to his seat to finish his hot coffee and cold egg sandwich while the woman gushed over meeting a star while eating a muffin in little ol' McHenry, Maryland. He saw that Travis seemed to have the ability to make his usually bright smile even more charming in the presence of his admiring public. By the time the fan left with the now valuable book clutched to her breast, the officer had finished his sandwich and was rolling up the wrapper.

Redirecting his attention to David, Travis stopped him from leaving. "What do you expect the ME to find?"

"ID for one. We got Lee Dorcas's dental records. If it's him, then we can close the disappearance case. But I doubt if the ME's report can answer the real question. How was he able to terrorize Katrina for all those months without leaving any evidence for us to arrest him? How did he get in and out of the house without triggering the security system? I met the guy. He wasn't smart but even with Katrina's eyewitness statements, we could never get enough to arrest him."

"And you think an ME report can tell you why and how Dorcas pulled it off?" Travis chuckled.

"It won't give me all the answers, but enough to point me in the right direction."

Travis sat so far back in his chair that the front legs lifted off the floor. "Listen, Dave. I'm going to give you a piece of advice. Drop it. She's not worth it."

"I can't do that. I took an oath when I became a cop. My father taught me that that oath is worth everything. Our civilization depends on those taking it, keeping it." He squinted at Travis. "Katrina was our friend. Don't you remember? Back in high school? For a while there, it was me and her, and you and Yvonne. The four of us were so tight."

"High school was a long time ago. A lot has happened since then." Travis sighed. "I've seen how the world really is. It's nothing like Spencer. There are a lot of sick people out there who target someone for no reason except for something that makes sense only in their warped minds. If you spend too much time trying to make sense out of it, you'll only make yourself sick and get Phillips madder at you than he already is." He took another sip of his coffee before dropping the chair back onto all four feet.

"I got the perp's DNA off Gnarly," David said. "If it doesn't match with Lee Dorcas's DNA, then that will prove he didn't kill Katrina. Phillips won't be able to close the case as a murder-suicide."

Travis squinted at him. "Then Phillips will look like a fool and you'll be out of a job."

"That's the risk I have to take," David said. "Katrina was depending on me to save her. I failed her there. Now, she's depending on me to catch her killer."

* * * *

Mac didn't feel like Mickey Forsythe. He sucked in his breath and turned off Spencer Road, passing the No Thru Way sign to take the last leg of their run to a tall glass of orange juice, unless the Point's petty thief had stolen the jug from his fridge. Seeing that they were heading home, Gnarly stepped up the pace to pull on his leash.

In the mid-morning, his neighbors along the cove were in the process of waking up to begin their day living the life of leisure. While Gnarly dragged him down the Point, Mac waved good morning to bed-headed folks clutching coffee mugs in their fists while retrieving newspapers at the end of their driveways.

When Mac neared the end of the Point at a dead run with Gnarly barking all along the way, he ran into the neighbors who lived in the gray cedar house on the opposite side of what had once been Katrina Singleton's home—the Hardwicks.

Gordon Hardwick was taking his newspaper from the box when the German shepherd charged.

"Gnarly! Stop!" Mac bellowed while digging his heels into the pavement and yanking back on the leash with both hands.

Beyond Gordon Hardwick, he saw a tan standard poodle sleeping on a chaise on the front porch. At the sound of Mac's call, his neighbor whirled around to glare at the man and dog. They stopped halfway to the porch. In his anxiousness to get at the other dog, Gnarly reared up on his hind legs and howled.

When the poodle came down off her chaise to trot toward Gnarly, Gordon Hardwick screamed, "Helga, you stupid bitch! Stop! Stay, you idiot!"

By instinct, Mac stood at attention in response to his sharp tone.

"Sit, bitch!" The poodle sat.

Gnarly continued to rear up and bark at the female waiting for him to rescue her from the dictatorship under which she had fallen.

"I'm sorry," Mac gasped out while he yanked again on the leash to drag his dog toward the road.

His face devoid of courtesy, Gordon said, "Your mutt is in my driveway."

"I know," Mac grunted while pulling Gnarly out into the road. He almost backed into the privacy fence dividing the Singleton and Hardwick properties. "He got away from me. I guess he likes your dog." He shrugged. "Go figure. I never thought of poodles as real dogs."

"And I always thought of German shepherds as Nazi canines."

Mac bit his tongue to keep from responding, "And you should know." Instead he ordered, "Quiet, Gnarly." With a sigh of displeasure, the dog stopped barking.

When Helga uttered a mournful whine, Gordon Hardwick yelled over his shoulder, "Shut up, bitch!" The poodle hung her head.

Gordon stepped up to Mac. "That dog is vicious."

Not as vicious as some people I know.

Gordon's pitch-black hair contrasted with his gray face. He framed his scorn-filled eyes with black cat-eyed glasses. Underneath his white shirt, which he had failed to button up past his pot-belly, Mac saw a yellowed undershirt. He wore wrinkled black slacks with penny loafers on his bare feet.

While his neighbor launched his verbal assault on him, Mac wondered if Gordon Hardwick was aware that he stood at least six inches shorter than his intended victim. Though he could easily be the same weight.

Hardwick's voice rose while he continued, "We thought we were finally rid of that damn fleabag. I'd heard they killed him."

"I said I was sorry," Mac said in a low voice. "It won't happen again."

"Helga can't go outside without him chasing her. His barking is so bad that my wife has to close our office door." His loud list of complaints went on. With each item on his list, he stepped in closer to Mac with his index finger threatening to jab him in the face. More than once the neighbor included Gnarly's rape of their poodle.

During the tirade, an elderly man stepped out of the blue home on the other side of the Hardwick house. He leaned against his mailbox and crossed his arms. The smile on his face caused Mac to feel like the straight man in a comedy.

"I'm sorry," he said one decibel louder in hopes of Gordon Hardwick hearing him over his rant. "I'd appreciate it if you got that finger out of my face."

"Not only is that dog vicious, but he's also a rapist!" With the word "rapist", Hardwick jabbed him in the chest.

Dropping Gnarly's leash, Mac grabbed the offending finger and pulled it back. Along with the finger, Gordon's hand and arm followed until he dropped to his knees in anguish. Holding onto the finger and hand, Mac pinned his neighbor face down on the ground with his knee in the small of his back.

"Now that I have your attention, Mr. Hardwick," Mac told him, "let me make a few things clear to you. I did apologize for Gnarly coming into your driveway, but in your fervor to grasp onto the incident to make grounds for a future lawsuit you ignored it. Therefore, I withdraw my apology. I also want to make something else clear. I hate lawyers. I hate nuisance lawsuits. I hate going to court. So, let me warn you, don't even think of using Gnarly to get to any of my money, because if you do, I won't be wasting so much as a second of my time going to court over something idiotic to support an ambulance chasing scumbag like you, nor will I settle out of court. I'll simply kick your ass up one end of Deep Creek and down the other until you look like the scum they find at the bottom of the lake. Have I made myself clear?"

Gordon grunted.

Mac twisted his hand. "I didn't hear you."

"Bastard!" He groaned.

"Is that a yes?"

"Yes." He uttered a sob.

"Good." Mac stood up.

Gasping, Gordon Hardwick rose slowly to his knees.

"Come on, Gnarly." Mac saw that the two dogs had been watching the show from the chaise on the front porch.

At the end of the driveway, Mac discovered that up and down the Point, his neighbors, some in running togs and others in bathrobes, had stopped what they were doing to watch the scene. Now that the incident had ended, a few of them clapped to show their approval of Mac's handling of it.

Hearing the applause, Gordon's face reddened. "I was attacked," he called out, "for no reason whatsoever!" Putting on the mask of a victim, he rose to his feet, limped inside his home, and slammed the door.

Mac picked up the end of Gnarly's leash with the intention of going to his estate on the Point and not leaving in the near future. He wondered if Howard Hughes had become a recluse after too many interactions with a Gordon Hardwick.

"I'll bet you fifty bucks that right now Hardwick's calling the police to file an assault charge against you."

Mac turned around.

The old man who lived in the home next to the Hardwicks stuck out his hand. "You must be Robin's boy. You take after her." Mac guessed him to be in his sixties, if not older. Thick wire-rimmed eyeglasses covered his smiling blue eyes. He wore a hearing aid in both ears.

Mac wiped his sweaty hand on his pants and grasped his neighbor's palm. "You have me at a disadvantage. You know who I am, but—"

"Ira Taylor. We retired and moved here eleven years ago. We were friends with your mother. My wife Francine is her number one fan. She went running out an hour ago to treat Archie to brunch in exchange for the low down on you and that head Gnarly brought home the other day." He cocked a thumb toward his house. "Want some coffee and the scoop on the ambulance chaser?"

"Figures. Archie is eating brunch and I'm being threatened." While Mac led Gnarly across the Taylor's driveway, he gestured in the direction of the Hardwick home. "Why the applause? Are the Hardwicks that unpopular?"

"The word shyster was made up for Gordy Hardwick." Ira opened the screen door and scooped up a pint-sized terrier in one action. "Your dog is nothing more than an excuse to call the police to create a paper trail against you. Granted, Gordy hates the dog. They've had it out for every dog owner whose pooch sets foot on their property ever since they moved in."

"But they have one." Seeing the terrier, Mac took a tighter hold on Gnarly's leash before stepping inside Ira's home.

"They also hate rabbits, bears, and seagull poop. If Gordy could get a hold of Mother Nature's lawyer, she'd be in court. They also hate jet skis." He chuckled. "Robin bought a couple of jet skis to get the Hardwicks' goat after they filed a complaint with the police against some neighbors who got jet skis for their kids. Then she spent a whole summer doing donuts behind their house for hours on end. Gordy had a cow and Robin had a blast."

Ira led the way to a sunroom which provided a three-way view: the corner of the floral garden in front, the woods to the side, and the cove in the back. Along the way, Mac saw that fishing played a big role in Ira Taylor's life. A cap filled with hooks and lures hung from a coat tree next to rods and reels in the front foyer. Fishing trophies hung on the wall in the sun room. A nine-foot-long swordfish filled the wall above the fireplace mantle. The plaque beneath the fish read that Ira Taylor had caught it seven years earlier off the shores of Nag's Head, North Carolina. The rest of the décor in the home included prints and statues of deer, geese, bears, and other woodland creatures.

Ira poured their coffee into sturdy mugs. "While everyone else here on the Point hates the Hardwicks, they must have intrigued Robin because you wouldn't believe what she did." He chuckled when he handed the mug to Mac. "She killed them."

"She what?"

"In one of her books." Ira studied the titles on a small bookcase until he found a hard back. "It came out a couple of years ago. *Rub Down at Four, Rub Out by Eight.*" He handed the book to Mac before plopping down in a recliner. "She blew them sky high." He asked, "Have you read that one?"

"I found out that she was my mother less than two months ago. So far, I'm up to her sixth book." Mac studied the thick black volume in his hands. The cover was of a bare back on a gurney with a pair of strong hands on the shoulders. "Couldn't they have sued her for that?"

"Only if they knew," Ira said. "Robin changed their characters enough so that only those who knew them and their shenanigans would recognize them. Besides, I doubt if the Hardwicks would lower themselves to read a whodunit. They haven't made any friends around here who would care to tell them."

"How many of our neighbors have they actually taken to court?" Mac handed the book back to his host.

Ira squinted thoughtfully. "The only one they actually managed to get into court was Katrina Singleton. They slapped her with a paternity suit over Gnarly knocking up their poodle. The judge laughed it out of court." He chuckled. "Meanwhile, the Hardwicks had to pay their lawyer and they didn't get a dime from the Singletons. Then they ended up with a bunch of puppies that they refused to bring home from the vet. They would have died if it weren't for your mother. Robin loved animals. She paid the vet's bill and brought them home. She and Archie bottle fed them and got them all homes. Robin's fans were more than glad to take home one of her puppies. When Hardwick found out, he tried to sue Robin for theft. The vet told the police that Hardwick had not only abandoned them, but didn't pay his vet bill. The county prosecutor laughed Hardwick's lawyer out of his office."

"They sound like a real couple of characters." Mac smiled.

"Which I guess is why Robin put them in one of her books." Ira sat up in his recliner and leaned forward to make his point. "Gordy wasn't here two weeks when he came over here and screamed at me, like he was just doing to you, about what a horrible neighbor I was because Eustace had peed in their yard." He offered a plate of sugar cookies to his guest.

"Is Eustace your dog?" Mac gestured with the cookie he had accepted at the terrier engaged in a staring contest with Gnarly.

"No, my grandson. He was two at the time. Hardwick declared it a hate crime because he was Jewish. What the hell!

My grandfather was Jewish. That's who I was named after. Idiot!" Ira uttered a hearty laugh. "That was three years ago." He glanced out the window at the house on the other side of his privacy fence. "He yelled at me again about it last week."

"Did Eustace do it again?" Mac asked, mindful that the child would now be five years old.

"No, Gordy was still mad about it from three years ago."

"I'm glad they aren't living right next door to me."

"Don't feel so safe. From what I've heard, they've targeted the Spencer Inn. They caused so much trouble that they got themselves kicked out." Ira bit into his cookie and spoke around it. "Now that you've come into the picture, they probably envision a big windfall."

"Kicked out of the Inn?"

"Your hotel offers private club membership. For an annual fee, members get to use the exercise club, golf course—you know—all of the amenities that the hotel guests get."

"I wasn't aware of that." Mac asked, "Why did Jeff kick them out?"

"The Inn doesn't kick anyone out as long as they can pay their dues. But that pair picked fights with everyone. Jeff got his fill of it, gave them a full refund, and told them not to come back." Spying a white SUV with black and gold trim crossing the bridge to the Point, Ira crossed the sunroom to watch the cruiser slow down as it approached the Hardwick driveway. "Right on time."

Mac recognized David's cruiser. The two men watched David get out of the driver's seat and pick up a valise in which he carried his notepad and folders from the passenger seat. He slung the strap of the valise over his shoulder.

"You're in luck," Ira said. "That's David O'Callaghan. His pappy was Pat O'Callaghan. He used to be the chief of police until he passed away. That was when we had a real police chief. David's just as sharp as he was. He'll set the Hardwicks straight." He chuckled. "They won't like it, but he will."

After thanking his neighbor for the coffee and information, Mac bid him farewell. Ira was still eying the home next door when Mac led Gnarly out the front door to jog past the cruiser and up the driveway to Spencer Manor.

* * * *

"Here." Gordon directed his wife, "Take a picture of these cuts on my knees where he pushed me down." He rolled up his pant legs to expose wrinkled red flesh.

Priscilla Hardwick aimed her digital camera at her husband's knees.

"Do you see that?" Gordon asked the police officer.

David shook his head. "All I see is a pair of ugly knees."

"They're red and sore. It takes a couple of days for the bruises to show." He pointed at his own face. "Guarantee it! By tomorrow this whole side of my face will be bruised where he slugged me for no reason." He pointed at a red mark on his cheekbone while asking his wife, "Did you get a picture of this welt?"

Obediently, she shot a picture of his face.

David stepped forward to study the mark. "Did you clean up after the alleged assault?"

"It's not alleged."

"Did you wash up?"

"No," Gordon asserted. "I know about collecting evidence. I didn't do anything except call you and my lawyer."

David leaned forward to look more closely at the mark on Gordon Hardwick's cheek. It was round—perfectly round. "Tell me again how you got that."

"I told you. Mac Faraday blindsided me. He grabbed me in some judo hold and shoved me face down in my own driveway."

David strolled around the living room while Gordon continued to recount how, after calling out a welcome-to-the-neighborhood greeting, his new neighbor sicced his dog on him before threatening his life.

Their tan poodle was curled up in her bed in the corner of the room. David noted that he had never seen the dog wag her tail. He thought that if he lived in this home, he wouldn't be wagging his tail either.

He found it. A bottled jar of potpourri rested on an end table. Dust covered the surface of the table, except for a clean ring, evidence of where the bottle had rested until someone picked it up to use as a weapon for a self-inflicted wound.

Next to the bottle, David saw a yellow notepad with line upon line of letters, numbers, and symbols written in a feminine hand. Trying to appear casual in his discovery while picking up the jar, David tried to read the writing but couldn't. The letters didn't form words. Curious if they were a foreign language, he picked up the pad to decipher them only to find that they failed to have the necessary spaces to form word breaks.

Priscilla snatched the notepad from his hand. "That's none of your business." She rushed down the hallway to where he knew they had their office.

Holding the jar in his hand, David turned back to her husband. "I don't see any dirt, grime, or scrape marks in the wound on your cheek, Mr. Hardwick. If you received that by having your face pushed down onto pavement, your face would be dirty."

"I washed my face."

David shot back, "You said a moment ago that you didn't wash it because you didn't want to disturb any evidence. As a lawyer you know all about preserving evidence. I believe you had an altercation with Mac Faraday in your driveway, Mr. Hardwick. Based on your relationship with your other neighbors, it was only a matter of time. Since Mac is worth over a quarter of a billion dollars, I'm sure you couldn't wait to find something to lodge a complaint about against him. You started something and he ended it. But you didn't get hurt enough in your greedy eyes, so you either hit yourself in the face with this jar, or had your wife do it for you."

Gordon's face reddened. "Just do your job and take my complaint."

"No."

With an expression of disbelief, Gordon Hardwick glanced at his wife who had come back into the room. She had left her notepad with the strange lettering in their office. He sputtered, "Wh-what?"

"I said no." David crossed his arms across his chest. "We've had it with you, Mr. Hardwick. In the three years that you've lived here, I've answered more calls to this home to take complaints about your neighbors than I have answered in the entire Point for my whole career. I'm sick of it. The county prosecutor is sick of wasting his time and the taxpayers' money on your petty complaints. The circuit judges are sick of seeing you and your lawyer in their courtroom. You're nothing more than the personification of the sleazy lawyer hunting down his next big lawsuit and we're all sick of it. None of us are going to have any part of it anymore."

In order to make his point clear, he stepped across the room to speak into the little man's blotchy face. "Hunting season in Spencer is closed, Mr. Hardwick."

Gordon was still spewing his vulgar-filled response when David let himself out the front door. On the other side of Spencer Manor's stone pillars, he could see Mac playing fetch with Gnarly in the grassy yard leading down to the boulder-lined tip of the Point.

Seeing the cruiser pull around the circle drive, Mac stopped the game while holding the ball that Gnarly was fetching. Not wanting to quit so soon, the dog pawed at his master until he tossed the ball down to the water.

"Are you here to arrest me for assault?" he called out.

"We're not taking any further complaints from the Hardwicks." David leaned against his cruiser. "What happened?"

"Gnarly dragged me onto their property and Hardwick jumped at the chance to escalate it from unintentional trespass to a vicious dog and assault case," Mac said. "I advised him that taking me to court could cost him more physical damage than he could gather monetarily. I guess he didn't take my advice."

"No," David said. "But no one here in Spencer is going to play ball with him. Ben Fleming won't be seen in court with him unless it's with Hardwick playing the role of defendant. Without being able to get a criminal charge filed, he'd have a hard time getting a civil case for assault going. So you have nothing to worry about."

"Do I look worried?"

Gnarly was once again pawing at his master. He had brought back the ball, but Mac failed to toss it. David threw it as far as he could toward the water.

Mac asked, "Did the autopsy report come back for Pay Back yet?"

"Yes, but Phillips won't let me see it. He says I don't have any need to know the results. So I called the ME and got an unofficial verbal report. He was good friends with my dad." David frowned. "Dental records were a match. It's Lee Dorcas."

"Cause of death?" Mac tossed the ball again for Gnarly.

"Gunshot wound to the head," David said. "Forensics found the slug in the mine and it did come from the gun we found."

"But was the fatal wound self-inflicted?"

"Since the body was so badly decomposed, we have no evidence to prove either way. They found gunshot residue on the jacket, which shows that whoever was wearing it fired a gun." David added, "Yet, there's no evidence of any dog bite on the body prior to death. But the jacket had Gnarly's blood on it and showed evidence of being torn up in a dog attack. They also found blood on the jacket that didn't come from Lee Dorcas or Gnarly."

"Gnarly attacked someone else who happened to be wearing that jacket." Mac put the scene together. "That someone else killed Katrina Singleton."

David continued, "Gnarly attacked him when he left the scene. He was wearing the army fatigue jacket. Gnarly bit the killer and shredded the jacket."

Mac concluded, "Then, he killed Lee Dorcas after putting the jacket on him to make it look like Pay Back killed Katrina and then killed himself."

"If that's what happened, then it's not a simple murder-suicide."

"It's just plain murder."

CHAPTER FIVE

"Someone besides Lee Dorcas had to have a reason to kill Katrina," Mac told Archie during what had become their daily morning hike.

Afterwards, she would give him a cooking lesson while preparing breakfast, which they ate together on the lower deck down by the lakeshore. Archie may not work for Mac, but she didn't skimp on sharing her good cooking with him. Besides being a wine connoisseur and fluent in Italian, French, and German, Archie was also a gourmet cook.

In the early morning's solitude, Mac had taken Gnarly off his leash to let him run while Archie led him on a leisurely trail up the mountain toward Abigail's Rock, where his great-great-grandmother founded Spencer and Niles Holt met his end. She explained that Abigail Spencer had taken the longer, less strenuous, route to the rock that had taken on her name.

"It isn't a simple case of murder," Mac said while navigating the path to keep from tripping over exposed tree roots. "First, the killer had to have known about Lee Dorcas's threats against Katrina. Dorcas must have been abducted in order to frame him for her murder and stage his suicide. Katrina's killer went to a lot of trouble. Why did he, or she, go to so much trouble?"

"You're asking the wrong girl," Archie replied when he paused to await her response. "I didn't really know Katrina. No one did except David. They'd known each other since school. He took her death hard."

Holding something that resembled a rope in his mouth, Gnarly charged down the trail toward them.

"What have you got?" Archie called out to him.

Mac recognized the twisting creature fighting to escape its captivity in the dog's jaws. "It's a snake!"

Together, they screamed and ran back down the mountain. Anxious to show off his treasure, Gnarly gave chase. They broke through the woods, across Spencer Court, and toward the lake. When he saw that they were going to be trapped by the dog and reptile, Mac turned to Gnarly with his hand held out in a signal to stop. "Drop it!"

Gnarly stopped. Fiercely, he shook his head before dropping the snake's limp body to the ground.

After examining the dead reptile, Archie uttered a shriek and covered her mouth. "It's a timber rattlesnake!" She pointed at the rattle at the end of its tale. "Gnarly saved us from a rattler." Cooing with affection, she hugged the dog while examining him for evidence of a snake bite. "Did he bite you?"

"I'm not taking you to the vet," Mac told Gnarly.

"He saved our lives," she argued.

As if to confirm her assessment, Gnarly let off a round of barks while pawing at the ground.

"What a good boy you are!" Archie patted him on top of the head.

"What was all that screaming about?" They heard called from the other side of the trees at the lake's edge.

"Gnarly found a snake." Archie made her way down the path to join Ira Taylor.

The old man had set up a minicamp with folding chairs, two coolers, and an assortment of fishing poles and tackle boxes. "Better than another head."

Hearing his laughter, Mac felt foolish. "How are the fish biting today?" he asked while breaking through the trees to join them.

"Pretty good." Ira flipped open a cooler to show that it contained several fish. "Where were you two heading?"

Archie told him, "I was taking Mac up to Abigail's Rock."

"Ah, that's a beautiful spot," Ira said. "Most magnificent view on this mountain. Too bad that nutcase ruined it all."

"Lee Dorcas had an alibi for Niles Holt's murder," Mac told him.

"That wasn't the nut I was talking about," the elderly man replied with a shake of his head.

"What nut were you referring to?" Archie asked.

Ira said, "No one followed them up that mountain. I know. I was sitting right in this very spot fishing when they went past to go up on the trail. I didn't move. The only way to get to either trail up to Abigail's is there across the road. If anyone had been following them, he would have had to go past me. No one did. I was still here when she came running down screaming about someone killing her husband."

"Maybe he didn't use the trail. If they looked back they would have seen him," Mac pointed out. "Maybe he went through the woods to get to the other trail."

"I doubt it. I always said there was something fishy about Katrina's story about how Holt died. I wasn't the only one, either. Robin agreed with me."

Mac asked Ira, "Did you tell the police about what you saw, or rather, didn't see?"

Ira snorted. "Yeah. A patrolman came and took my statement. Then Chief Phillips came out to see me. He said he would question Katrina about it. That was the last I saw or heard anything about it." He chuckled. "His murder case went cold faster than hers."

* * * *

"Hungry?"

Curious about what Mac had been doing since they talked to Ira, Archie took a lunch break from editing the latest thriller of a hot new writer to prepare two ham and cheese sandwiches. Carrying the sandwiches and glasses of milk on a serving tray, she crossed the deck to where she found Mac stretched out on a chaise with Robin's thick, leather-bound journal open in his lap.

Stretched out next to his master's chaise, Gnarly started out of a deep sleep as if in answer to her question. He sat up at attention with his eyes aimed at the food on the tray.

"Did you call David about Ira?" Archie set their lunch on the table.

"He doesn't recall seeing any statement from Ira. He's going to check the case file again." Mac held up the journal for her to see. "I'm looking up Robin's take on Holt's murder. Ira said Robin agreed with him about there being something weird in her statement. Katrina said Dorcas did it. Dorcas had an airtight alibi. Ira was fishing right there at the start of the trail."

Archie handed him a sandwich and sat on the chaise next to his. "Katrina claimed to have been blindsided. She could have assumed it was Dorcas because he had threatened her."

"Why didn't Robin pursue the case?" Mac bit the corner off his sandwich and sat up.

"We both had tight deadlines."

"Are you sure that's it? I can't believe my mother, whose blood courses through my veins, wasn't intrigued enough to find out what went on up at Abigail's Rock."

Archie confessed, "It wasn't like Robin to turn her back on murder, but she did. I don't know why. What did she say in her journal?"

Mac turned a page. "I haven't found her explanation yet."

Gnarly let out a long whine. He stared at the plates as if he could will the food to come to him.

Mac continued eating his sandwich. "Gnarly stole my hot dog right off the plate last night. I took it out of the microwave and turned around to get the catsup. He jumped up, grabbed the dog, and ran outside with it."

"Serves you right for turning your back on him."

Mac accepted Archie's offer of the glass of milk, took a gulp, and set it on the side table next to his chaise. "Have you seen my flip-flops?"

"Not since you took them off and left them here on the deck to dry after jet skiing."

Mac gestured at the empty spot beside the French doors. "I paid twelve bucks for them. Now, they're gone." He looked at Gnarly, who was staring at the ham sandwich in his hand. "There's a lot of thievery here on the Point," he said. "My Blackberry is missing, too. It cost me over seven hundred dollars and I only had it a month. I left it on the table out here on the deck last night and remembered it after I went to bed. I came down to get it and it was gone. From twelve-dollar flip-flops to Blackberries. I'm beginning to think one of our neighbors is a kleptomaniac."

Archie nodded her head. "Robin thought the same thing. I've lost my car keys, every beach blanket I hang out to dry, and a pair of pink pumps with stiletto heels. Anything left on decks or docks gets stolen. It started right after Pay Back showed up. But if Pay Back is dead, then it can't be him."

"Who said Pay Back was dead? Lee Dorcas is dead, but the evidence says he wasn't Pay Back."

Gnarly inched closer to Mac as he neared the last bite of the sandwich.

Archie said, "I had an interesting conversation with Francine Taylor yesterday."

"Ira's wife?"

"They're year-round residents like us. They're both nice," she added, "unlike the other ones down the road. Francine said the Hardwicks went off about Gnarly on a regular basis."

"I've already gotten closer and more personal with the Hardwicks than I care to get again."

Recalling his account about when he first met Gordon Hardwick, Archie smiled. "Don't you agree that they have a tendency to overreact?"

"Yes."

"Francine says they used to get into some real screamfests with Katrina, which leads me to think that they were probably dancing on the Point when she died."

Amused, Mac asked, "Are you suggesting the Hardwicks killed Katrina over a dog?"

"A few years ago a man poisoned his neighbor because he simply didn't like her and her family."

"We're talking about an ambulance chaser," he argued. "The Hardwicks are looking for grounds to file lawsuits so that they can live off of the court settlements. Katrina's death got them nothing." He turned the sandwich around to begin eating it from the opposite corner.

Gnarly stood up in preparation to pounce on it.

"Want to answer all of your questions about Katrina's murder once and for all?" Archie asked with a naughty grin.

"How?"

"Visit the crime scene? See it live and in person?"

Mac answered, "I'd love to, except that the house is locked up tight."

"Where there's a will, there's a way."

Gnarly nabbed the last of the sandwich from his hand.

"Gnarly! I'm going to kill you!" Mac yelled, but the dog was already making his getaway off the deck.

* * * *

Spencer's police station didn't look like a small-town police department. The three-story log building blended in with the woods that surrounded it. With its stone fireplace in the reception area, four speed boats for patrol docked in the back, and fleet of ATVs and dirt bikes parked in and around the garage, it resembled a sports club. The cruisers were four-wheel drive SUVs able to maneuver over the dirt trails that went deep into the woods and up the mountain.

Spencer only had a dozen officers, but the town's founding family and well-heeled residents were willing to invest in the police department responsible for protecting their families and valuables.

Ever since Mac's phone call, David's mind was preoccupied with what Ira Taylor had not seen the morning Niles Holt went off Abigail's Rock. If it had been any other witness he would have questioned the validity of his statement. He would have assumed Niles Holt's killer had managed to slip past Ira without being seen to follow the Holts up the mountain. Not so with Ira Taylor. A retired naval officer devoted to detail, he would have seen the killer.

As soon as he had finished his morning patrol, David hurried to the file room in the basement of the police department. He studied the labels on the file cabinet's drawers until he found one indicating the letters *Hn-Hz.* After sliding out the drawer, he ran his fingers over the tabs until he found the folder labeled *Holt, Niles.*

He scanned Katrina's statement while carrying the folder to the table where he could study its contents in detail.

Tucked under the case and evidence reports, David found Ira Taylor's statement written up on a single sheet of paper. Ira had signed and dated it. The narrative read almost word for word as the same statement that Mac had relayed to him that morning.

Ira Taylor was fishing off the shore on Spencer Point at Deep Creek Lake when he saw Katrina and Niles Holt. Since it was not yet sunrise, Katrina carried a flashlight. The couple wore hiking shoes and sweaters. Ira and the Holts greeted each other. The victims went onto the mountain trail and disappeared into the woods. Ninety minutes later, after the sun rose, Ira heard Katrina screaming for help. He met her when she ran out of the woods onto the road. Her sweater was torn. Her hair was messed and she was bleeding from a wound on her cheek. She told him that a man who had been stalking her had followed them up to Abigail's Rock, hit her in the head with a thick stick, and shoved Niles Holt off the rock and down the mountain. She thought he was going to kill her, too. She told Ira that her attacker said he killed Niles Holt because "Payback is hell." He then disappeared down the mountain.

Ira reported that when he asked Katrina if she knew where her husband was, she answered that he had fallen off the cliff to the rocks below. When Ira asked if he was still alive, she didn't answer. The witness ran to his home and called the police.

David read the signature of the officer who had taken Ira's statement: Officer Arthur Bogart.

"What've you got there that's so interesting?" a deep voice asked from behind him.

Startled to realize he was not alone, David turned around. Officer Art Bogart, who worked as the department's desk sergeant, towered over him. The policeman peered around David to see what case file he had.

Art, called Bogie by his colleagues, had the worn, haggard face and gray hair of a seasoned officer of the law, but the frame of a bodybuilder. Due to his advanced years, many a rookie dared to take him on in a hand-to-hand match, and ended up face down on a mat in a matter of seconds.

One of Pat O'Callaghan's most trusted patrolmen, Bogie had become David's confidante since the police chief's death.

Stepping aside, David showed him the folder. "Niles Holt's case file."

Bogie put on his reading glasses and bent over to see that he had been reading Ira Taylor's statement. "Why are you suddenly interested in the Holt case?" He frowned.

David responded, "Almost two years ago, you took a statement from a witness who said that he was fishing at the entrance of the trail leading up to Abigail's Rock the morning Niles Holt died. He saw no one else go up on that trail. If no one was following them, then that means the killer had to have been waiting up at the rock for them. Why didn't you pursue it?"

Sighing heavily, Bogie leaned against the table and draped a leg across the corner. "David, you've known me most of your life. Do you think I would willingly let a murder go uninvestigated?"

"That's why I'm so surprised about this."

Bogie's eyes narrowed. "Spencer's first major crime since Phillips became chief is the Niles Holt murder. I took Taylor's statement to Phillips. He said that he would check it out." His chuckle held a wicked tone. "Check her out he did. He questioned Katrina Holt and the investigation ended there."

"What are you saying?"

"Phillips let the case go cold and he let it go cold for a reason."

"You could have fought him."

"I tried." Bogie gestured up the stairs to the reception area. "How do you think I ended up up there? When I challenged Phillips, he took me off patrol and reduced me to clerk." He laughed again. "But Phillips is stupider than I first gave him credit for. From where he put me, I see every piece of paper that comes into this department, including a certain contribution check to the department that Phillips used to renovate his office right after he dropped the Holt case. Katrina Holt signed it."

David's face flushed. "Why would Katrina pay off Phillips? Her husband was murdered." He felt a shiver go down his neck and his spine.

"And she inherited about forty million dollars from his death." Bogie peered down at him. "Right after she gave Phillips that check, she left town."

"That doesn't make sense," David said. "She was being terrorized. He killed her husband. If the case hadn't gone cold, she'd still be alive."

Bogie agreed that it didn't make sense.

A look of determination crossed David's face. "Phillips may be too incompetent to know what to do with evidence, but I'm not." He flipped through the pages of the case file. "We've got his DNA—"

"Which isn't worth anything without a suspect to match it up to," Bogie said. "Besides, the DNA you got was from Katrina's murder. Without evidence to connect the two murders, your perp ain't going to do any time for doing her husband. That's assuming you can catch him."

"I guess I have my work cut out for me." David removed the forensics report from the file and leafed through the stapled pages.

Bogie tried to read the contents over his shoulder. "If Phillips gets wind that you're looking at this again he's going to have your head."

David froze.

"What? Did you find something?"

David pulled back two pages bound with a single staple in the corner. "Look at this." He scraped the upper corner with his fingertips and extracted two torn tabs of paper. "Someone removed a couple pages from the forensics report." He flipped through the pages before and after the missing section. "It was the pages after the preliminary exam and before the ME's conclusions."

"Phillips did find something and removed those pages to cover it up." Bogie told him, "I'll call the medical examiner and request they send us another copy." He gathered up the folder and tucked it under his arm. He fell in behind David when they left the file room. "Don't bother checking your e-mail. We have a virus."

David paused with his foot on the first step of the stairs leading up to the police chief's office. "A virus? How? We have one of the best firewalls there is."

"The whole network's down and our server is crashing. I called in some techs and they're trying to save what they can. Someone managed to get a new virus in through the Internet." Muttering, Bogie turned around to go to the lounge to get a cup of coffee. "I hate hackers."

Sucking up his courage, David returned to his office, where he picked up his private case file for Katrina Singleton's murder. It contained bootleg copies of crime scene reports and his notes from unofficial interviews with witnesses. Then he went up to the third floor and down the oak hallway to Chief Roy Phillips's office.

David recalled that a short four years ago the walls in the reception area and chief's office had been decorated with an assortment of commendations and pictures. The décor consisted of a hodgepodge collection of mementos accumulated during Pat O'Callaghan's distinguished career, including a two-foot-long trout caught while on a fishing trip with his son.

Roy Phillips had gutted the space to have the office reflect the new chief. The furniture changed from government issued to oak and brass. Expensive modern artwork took the place of the commendations.

"Chief Phillips, I've run into some problems verifying your military background," David heard a feminine voice say to the chief during a conversation that floated into the outer office from his private office.

"Why are you checking into my military background?"

"It's background research for Travis's book about Katrina," the questioner explained. "Since you're the chief detective for the case, your character will be very important to the plot." Her tone challenged the commanding officer. "The V.A. doesn't seem to know who you are."

Curious to hear Roy Phillips's response, David stepped into the open doorway.

Red blotches covered the chief's face.

Without seeing the face of the woman seated in his office, David identified the interrogator as Betsy Weaver, Travis Turner's assistant. Rolls of fat from her buttocks and hips spilled over the arms of the chair too narrow for her wide bulk. Focused on getting an answer from the police chief, Betsy didn't notice the witness to her interrogation. With her pen poised to record the chief's response, she glared at the man behind the desk.

"David, I'm glad you're here." Roy Phillips gestured for him to take the empty chair while turning his attention to the woman demanding answers from him. "I'm sorry, Ms. Weaver, but I have an appointment. If you would like to continue this interview, you can schedule an appointment with Officer Bogart."

Her expression lacked the chief's congeniality. "I'll do that." She slapped her notepad shut and picked up her tattered handbag. Clutching her belongings to her chest, she rose from the chair, only to find that her bottom had become wedged between the arms. Before David could act, she plopped down and jumped back up to her feet. The quick action freed her.

She scurried from the room with a hard expression on her face.

"What's Travis's secretary doing running background checks on me?" the police chief demanded to know.

David sat in the chair opposite the one that had trapped Betsy. "Archie would often run background checks for Robin when she was researching a case. Take comfort. If Betsy had found something fishy, Travis would be here interrogating you personally."

The chief's hand went from his mouth where he had been chewing on his thumb to his lap. He sat up straight and smoothed his hair. "Well, I have plenty of time since the computer system is down. What do you need, O'Callaghan?"

David opened the folder he had picked up from his desk. "It's the Singleton case."

"When are you going to let that go?"

"The DNA from the body we found in the mine doesn't match the DNA found on Katrina's German shepherd. That proves he wasn't at the murder scene."

"Where did you hear about the DNA?" The smile evaporated from the police chief's face. The splotches on his face turned a brighter red.

"I've been a cop in Spencer since high school," David said. "I have a lot of friends."

"You have no authority to investigate this case." The chief's thumb flew to his mouth. He made a conscious effort to pull it out from between his teeth before biting it. "Listen, David, I tried to do you a favor. I tried to help you. If you don't back off, you're going to get yourself into trouble and I won't be able to do anything to get you out."

"What the hell are you talking about?" David asked. "Why have you been shutting me out of this case? Afraid that I was going to find conclusive evidence that Katrina wasn't murdered by some run of the mill psycho, and prove you blew it when you didn't find out who really was terrorizing her?"

Roy's eyes darkened. He looked him up and down. "Since you insist on going forward with this, I guess we have a murder investigation on our hands."

"You've had a murder investigation on your hands."

Roy Phillips stuck the tip of his pinkie finger into his mouth before removing it and crossing both arms across his chest as if to pin his hands down to keep them out of his mouth. "H-how well did you know Katrina Singleton, O'Callaghan?" he asked with a stutter in his voice.

"If you must know, we knew each other most of our lives."

"Then she was a friend. H-how good of a friend?"

David could see where the discussion was going. "We dated back in high school."

"Do you want to re-think that answer?" the police chief asked. "You see, I did look into Ms. Singleton's murder and—and I found that you had reason to kill her."

"Me?"

"Did you or did you not spend nights—?"

"She didn't like being alone in her home. Her husband was rarely there. You certainly didn't do anything to help her."

"Were you intimate with her?"

David opened his mouth to argue, but decided not to say anything.

Chief Phillips said, "I-I tried to do you a favor by closing this case as quietly as possible, but you just couldn't leave well enough alone."

David blurted out. "You never wanted to do me any favors. You've been trying to run me out of this department for months."

"You didn't answer my question, O'Callaghan," the chief replied. "Did you sleep with Katrina?"

CHAPTER SIX

The Singleton's back yard showed signs of once having been meticulously landscaped. Remnants of the previous year's plantings struggled to survive in spite of neglect since their mistress's death. Sand mixed with dirt along the lake's shore made up what had once been a private beach. Shaded by the second-level deck, a stone patio extended out into the back yard.

With the copy of the case file that Ben Fleming had given him tucked under his arm, Mac followed Archie over the stone wall separating Spencer Manor from the Singleton home, and jogged across the back yard to the patio. He peered through the French doors into what had once been Katrina Singleton's family room while Gnarly went to work digging in the corner of the patio where the cobblestones, grass, and garage met. The foot and a half deep hole appeared to be an ongoing project.

"Gnarly!" Mac swatted in the dog's direction. "Get away from there!"

Whining, Gnarly backed away two paces before charging back at the hole.

"There must be a rabbit in there. Leave him alone," Archie told Mac. "No one will know that we've been here." She threw open the French door, stepped inside, and punched a security code into the console on the wall.

Uncertain about the wisdom of snooping around a crime scene that didn't belong to him, Mac stepped across the threshold into the vacant family room. "How do you know the security code?"

"You don't want to know."

"Since the killer didn't trigger the security system the night Katrina was murdered," Mac pointed out, "you knowing the code makes you a suspect."

"The security system wasn't deactivated or triggered the night of the murder." She grinned widely. "That's one of the mysteries. The killer managed to bypass the system every time all the way up to the murder."

Outside, she gestured at an oblong ceramic flower container next to the door. It contained soil, but no vegetation. "That's where David found Gnarly. He had crawled in behind the pot. The pot and roof from the deck above protected him from the blizzard."

Mac knelt next to the pot. There were brown splotches of what he concluded to be a mixture of Gnarly's and the killer's blood. The German shepherd had put up a real fight for his owner.

Once again, Gnarly was digging at the corner of the garage.

"Stop it!"

The dog uttered a pleading bark.

"You're going to get us arrested for breaking and entering."

"We're not breaking anything," Archie argued.

"He's breaking their yard." Mac rose and searched the trees and privacy fence separating the Singleton property from the Hardwicks. He spotted the camera perched on a rod extending up from the corner of the Hardwick's back deck. It was aimed at the Singleton property. He saw a bright green light lit on top of the unit. "David said the Hardwicks claimed their security camera was broken at the time of the murder. It looks like it's working to me."

"Maybe they got it fixed since the murder." She stepped back inside.

Mac followed her through the door. The room contained a fireplace and bar, behind which a mirror stretched across the rear wall. Unlike the stone floors in his home, the Singletons' floors were hardwood. Since his first wife's death, Chad Singleton had removed all the furnishings to put the house on the market.

The click-clack sound echoing throughout the empty room startled both of them. Ready to run when caught trespassing, they whirled around to the open door. His nose to the floor, Gnarly made a sweep of the room before coming to a stop near the bar. With his snout following the scent of his dead mistress, he circled the area before lying down with a whine.

"This is where she was killed." Archie knelt next to the dog.

Doubtful, Mac compared the crime scene pictures to the placement of the patio doors and the floor next to the bar where Gnarly rested his head between his front paws.

It proved to be the spot.

Mac continued to examine the rest of the pictures in the folder while imagining how the murder happened.

"We can assume that there's no evidence left since Chad had the place professionally cleaned," Archie said.

"The first rule in investigating is to never assume anything," he said. "If there's nothing left, how did Gnarly lead us here by her scent? I thought he was outside when the murder happened."

Archie went to the patio door. "Maybe he saw the murder through the door, which would have been locked. When he wasn't able to get in to save her, Gnarly ambushed the killer when he left."

Mac opened and shut the patio door. "Did Katrina give the pass code to anyone besides David? Her husband had to have had it. Who else could she have given it to?"

"David told me that Katrina changed the code after almost every incident," she said.

"How did you get the pass code?"

"Hacking," Archie confessed. "But if you go to the security company, they'll have record of the alarm being deactivated just now when I punched in the code. The night of the murder, the security company claims the only break in the system was when she let Gnarly outside. There is no record of any break, deactivations, or trip in the system after that."

Once again, Mac opened and closed the door while studying the lights on the panel for the security system. He glanced over his shoulder to where Gnarly marked the murder spot.

Referring to the pictures of Katrina's dead body and the overturned recliner, he crossed the room. Mentally, he uprighted the recliner and stood where it would have been. Standing over the spot Gnarly marked for them, he shuffled through the photos until he came to one of Katrina's body sprawled on the floor. "Okay, Archie, I want you to lie down here and play dead for me."

"Why me?" she objected.

"Because you're a girl. The murder victim was a woman. If it was a guy, I'd play dead but—" He stopped when he saw her pointing to where Gnarly was lying on his back with his paws up in the air.

"There," she said. "Gnarly's playing dead for us."

"I wasn't talking to you," Mac told him.

The cell phone in her pocket interrupted Archie's laughter. She whipped it out and pressed it to her ear.

"Hello." Hearing laughter in her tone, she sucked in her breath. "Yes, this is Archie Monday." She paused. "Yes, he's here." She held out the phone to him. "It's Jeff Ingle. He wants to speak to Mickey Forsythe."

"I'm not real," Mac took the phone from her. "This is Mickey—I mean Mackey—I mean—How are you, Jeff?" He listened for a moment before saying, "No, I'm glad you called. I'll be right there. His drinks are on the house. Try to get him to eat something."

* * * *

The outdoor café seemed to be serving twice as many customers as it had the previous week when Mac made his first appearance at the Inn. In the short time since moving to Deep Creek Lake, Mac noticed that more boats and jet skis populated the lake with the migration of seasonal residents returning to their summer homes in the resort area.

Staring out at the landscape off in the distance, David sat alone at a table in the corner.

Mac retrieved a bottle of beer from the bar and took the seat across from him. Immediately, he noticed that David's badge was missing from his uniform's breast pocket. "What happened?"

"Lee Dorcas's and Katrina Singleton's deaths have now both been classified as murder."

"That's good."

David tore his eyes from the landscape. "I'm Phillips's prime suspect."

"Why? Why would you have wanted to kill them?"

David closed his eyes and slowly shook his head. He swallowed. "She was scared. She asked me to stay with her while her husband was in the city. So after Mom went to bed at night, I would go over, and one thing led to another..." He left the rest up to Mac's imagination.

"You were having an affair with her!" Mac sounded as if he were speaking to one of his children rather than a stranger who happened to be his brother. "What were you thinking?"

"That no one knew."

"If nobody knew then how did you become a suspect?"

"Phillips has to be guessing. I kept it a secret, but not because of that." David corrected himself. "Yes, because of that. I thought if no one knew I was staying there, then Pay Back would make his move and I could catch him."

"How long did this affair go on?"

"Mid-summer into fall. About five months." David told him in a firm tone, "I had no intention of sleeping with her. I was going to stay in one of the guest rooms. But, after a while, we got to talking about back when we were in school and it just happened."

Mac blurted out, "Affairs don't just happen between grown-ups."

"My career is officially shot! Isn't there anything you can do to help me besides lecture me on everything that I've been telling myself since Katrina died?" David's face was pale with fear. "Do you think I've not been afraid that this would happen?"

"Why didn't you tell me to drop it? If I had known—"

"Would you?" David laughed. "Get real. We only just met and I already know that once you pick up the scent of murder nothing will shake you off the trail. You're as bad as Robin."

Mac sucked in a deep breath. "I certainly didn't want you to become a murder suspect."

"Put yourself in my shoes. If someone you loved got murdered, wouldn't you do everything you could to get their killer? I couldn't sit back and let Phillips do nothing."

"So you pushed for a murder investigation at the risk of being a suspect."

David reiterated, "I didn't think anyone knew about us."

"Someone knew. Otherwise, how did Phillips find out? He isn't smart enough to have figured it out on his own."

David went to the bar for another beer.

Mac considered calling Archie to tell her that he wouldn't be home for dinner until he remembered that she wasn't his wife. She had returned to the guest cottage to work on an editing assignment. She would be eating dinner alone whether he came home or not. He didn't need to check in with her.

David returned with two beers. He set one bottle down in front of Mac. "Travis and Sophia knew."

"Did you tell them?"

"Didn't have to." David paused to take a gulp from his bottle. He continued after swallowing. "Travis was there when she asked for my help. Last Fourth of July weekend, I stopped in to have a drink after work. The place was packed. I ran into Travis and Sophia in the lounge, and we had a drink together in the sofa area. The bartender brought me a drink. Katrina had sent it over." He sighed. "I hadn't seen her in a dozen years, at least."

Mac asked, "Was that what Travis was talking about when he said she told you guys about how Dorcas had murdered her husband?"

"Exactly." David explained, "I was overseas. Archie and Robin had written me about him getting killed. I sent Katrina a sympathy card and she replied. Before that, we hadn't communicated since school."

"But then you saw each other here last July and she bought you a drink."

"I asked her how she was holding up since Niles's murder." After another sip from the bottle, he recalled, "Travis and Sophia knew nothing about it. They had been in Europe that summer. That was the first time I heard the whole story about how Dorcas accused her of stealing his inheritance and about him sneaking into her dressing room on her wedding day and telling her that he was going to kill Niles, and about how Niles died."

"But Dorcas had an alibi," Mac reminded him.

"She knew that. She thought that maybe since the killer hit her in the head, she got confused and assumed it was Lee Dorcas." He drained his beer while signaling to a server for another one before continuing. "Whatever the case, she told me that someone was stalking her, and she was terrified. He had followed her back from Washington and was now threatening her here in Spencer. I had to help her."

"Did she report this to Phillips?"

"She said Phillips was an incompetent."

Mac smirked. "Perceptive lady."

"I didn't straight out offer to go sleep with her right then and there," David insisted. "I started by offering to check the security in her home. After we had finished our drinks, I left with her. I checked out her house. It seemed secure. We had another couple of drinks and I went home."

"Did Travis and Sophia hear the part of the conversation about you staying with her?"

David paused to think. "They left after their table was ready." He sat up. "Actually, I hadn't agreed to spend nights with Katrina at all at that point. When they left, I had only offered to let her call me personally when anything happened."

"When did you start sleeping there?" Mac asked.

"It was a good week later. The day after I ran into Katrina, she called me. Pay Back pinned a note to her front door with a knife. He threatened to throw her off Abigail's Rock the same way he had Niles. I went to her house and checked out the scene. The next day, she called me again. This time, he had broken into her house and written 'Bitch' on her dressing room mirror with her lipstick."

"Was the security system on?"

"Yes, but it didn't go off," David said. "I checked with the company and their records show that someone had used her code to deactivate it. Katrina swore that she never gave her code to anyone. After that, she changed it. She kept changing the code, but that never seemed to do any good."

"When did you start spending nights there?" Mac wanted to know.

"After that," David said. "Katrina was pretty shaken so I spent the night, but we didn't get intimate until a couple of days after that."

"Did Pay Back show up while you were there?"

"Ten days later," David told him. "Katrina had invited me to dinner. We had a bottle of wine and both of us passed out in the living room."

"Wait a minute," Mac interrupted him. "You passed out after only one bottle of wine?"

"The wine had to have been drugged. Afterwards, we both felt like death warmed over for several days." David said, "It had to have been Pay Back because while we were unconscious, he came in and wrote 'Pay Back is hell' and 'This time you live! Next time you'll die!' on all her mirrors with her lipstick. He also slashed her bed. He could have killed us both, but he didn't. This time the security company said there was no break in the system. No one entered the code to deactivate it, nor did they set it off. As far as the security company is concerned, no one came in at all." He sighed. "It was the Ford case all over again."

"What's the Ford case?" Mac wanted to know.

"Milo Ford," David said. "During his career, Dad had a couple of cases where he didn't catch the killer. The Ford case was one that he couldn't figure out how the killer did it. It's exactly the same as Katrina's case. Milo Ford had built Katrina's house back in the mid-1980s. He was a pompous ass. He owned one of the biggest real estate agencies in Deep Creek. Dad found out that Milo was the local drug connection to the rich and famous. No one would testify to bring down the local power brokers' candy man and Dad had no evidence to prove anything. When Dad managed to get warrants to search Milo's house he would never find anything. Not one thing. Dad could never bust him."

Mac reminded him, "You said this was a murder case."

"One Sunday night, Milo's wife and kids came home from a weekend away and found him shot to death in the family room. The security system was on and there was no sign of any forced entry. Nothing. Even Robin Spencer couldn't figure it out."

"A locked door murder," Mac smiled. "I've never had a case like that."

"That's what Katrina's murder is," David said. "The security system was on when I found her body. I had the code and turned it off when I went in. The security company had no record of any break in the system since the evening of the murder when she had let Gnarly out."

"How did your affair with Katrina end?"

David said, "It wasn't any torrid love affair. Not the type Phillips will present to Fleming. I knew Katrina wanted money and status. After everything that had happened, she couldn't wait to get out of Deep Creek, and I made no pretense of going with her. She planned to leave Deep Creek Lake for good the Monday after Valentine's Day and put the house on the market."

"Were you at her place that night?"

"No. Chad was supposed to be coming back. Besides, once she got Gnarly she didn't need me to protect her."

Mac sat back and propped a foot up on the empty chair next to him at the table. He watched the boats out on the water. Fishermen were making their way onto the lake after the jet skis and speed boats had turned in.

He asked David, "Where was Gnarly that night Pay Back knocked you and Katrina out?"

"Katrina didn't get Gnarly until the month after that. Chad had a client who was a dog trainer and he had this retired police dog. Chad bought him and shipped him out here."

"Retired police dog?" Mac was puzzled. "Gnarly can't be more than two years old."

Preoccupied with his problems, David nodded his head. "Yeah, Gnarly does have a lot of puppy in him."

"Do you believe the Hardwicks about their security camera being broken the night Katrina was killed?"

"No, but we don't have any evidence to prove otherwise."

"Even if the killer was able to get around the security system," Mac mused, "how did he get around Gnarly?"

"The only thing I can come up with is that Gnarly was outside. There's no break in the system for her to let him in," David replied. "That's where I found him."

"If she was killed after letting Gnarly out, then how did the killer get inside without Gnarly catching him?" Mac wondered.

"You got me."

"Were any dog bites reported at the time of the murder?"

David cocked his head at him. "I'm not an amateur. I checked with the hospital and all the clinics and doctors' offices in the area. There were none."

* * * *

Two hours later, customers packed the Spencer Inn.

"David, I think we should go home."

David's reaction confirmed Mac's suspicion that he was unable to drive. "Yeah, you're right. Mickey Forsythe is always right, just like Dad was. He always does the right thing, always gets his man, and never makes a mistake."

Mac wondered if the bitterness in David's tone was rooted in Mac's connection to Patrick O'Callaghan. "I know how it feels to have your whole life turned upside down." Mac told him, "A year ago, I came home and found my wife of over twenty years in bed with the assistant district attorney. Did you know that?"

David shook his head.

"Did you know that even though she was the one cheating, because her lover had so many influential friends, I was the one taken to the cleaners? I lost everything. I had an appointment scheduled for the next day to meet with a bankruptcy lawyer when Ed hunted me down," Mac recalled. "I thought Ed was one of my ex-wife's friends. I wouldn't return his phone calls. He'd come in one door at the police station and I'd go out the other. I had no idea I was running from a man wanting to give me a check for two hundred and seventy million dollars."

David laughed loudly. The customers at the next table turned their heads to look at them.

"Goes to prove that none of us is perfect."

"Not perfect?" David asked in a sarcastic tone. "You live on the Point, damn it! You own this town and you don't even know it."

"There's a difference between being rich and powerful, and being perfect. If rich meant perfect, Katrina wouldn't be dead."

"You're Mickey Forsythe."

"Mickey was a figment of Robin Spencer's imagination."

"Hell! You even drive his car!"

"I read the description of his car in her first book and thought it was cool," Mac said. "I decided to buy one. It was the first piece of luxury I ever indulged in."

"You were the top homicide detective in Georgetown," David reminded him.

"I may have been, but my boss treated me as badly as yours does. He'd take credit for my work. He'd blame me for his mistakes. The brass upstairs didn't like me because they wanted cases closed fast, even if it meant putting innocent people in jail. I asked too many questions. That's why I never made chief."

David leaned across the table and whispered, "Mickey is always accused of asking too many questions. After inheriting his mother's millions, he quit his job because his bosses hated him for not playing the game."

"What game?"

"The kiss your boss's ass game." David sat back. "Mickey doesn't care who the bad guy is or who his friends are. If you're a bad guy, you're going down." He finished off the bottle in one gulp and slammed it down. "You're Mickey Forsythe."

Mac ended the conversation with a suggestion that sounded more like an order. "Let's go home."

David accepted his hand on his elbow to lift him to his feet in order to guide him around the deck to the parking lot.

"Hey, buddy, how ya doing?"

In the parking lot, Mac made out Travis's muscular shape in silhouette under the bright lamp. He was stepping out of his red Mercedes convertible. His black sports jacket matched his slacks.

In a low, threatening tone, David asked, "Did you tell Phillips that I was spending nights at Katrina's place?"

Travis looked from David to Mac.

"You were here when Katrina told us about how scared she was sleeping alone since her husband had left," David reminded him. "I was trying to catch the guy."

"Was he the only thing you were trying to catch?" the novelist asked with a smile. "Hey, I'm not the one who slipped between the sheets with a married murder victim."

"So you did rat me out!"

Travis stepped back with a shake of his head. "Phillips asked and I answered. That's all."

Mac grabbed David by the waist and forced him over the hood of his Viper when he lunged for the author.

"You've got a problem, O'Callaghan," Travis said. "You don't know how to use your head. I would have handled the whole thing differently. Too bad. I had hoped we could still be friends."

Mac said, "I don't think you two ever were friends."

Chuckling, Travis climbed the steps to the Inn.

"Get in the car," Mac ordered.

"He ratted me out," David muttered while climbing into the passenger seat of the Viper.

Mac started the engine. "Do you know what this means?"

David shook his head. "I've had too much to drink to know what anything means right now."

"Travis and Sophia knew you were over at Katrina's place while her husband was out of town."

"And he told Phillips."

"You had kept it a secret that you were over there because you wanted to catch Pay Back when he made his move. But Travis blew your cover—pardon the expression. Pay Back probably knew, too."

* * * *

"What's wrong with him?" Violet demanded to know when Mac called to report that David was spending the night at his house.

"He's sick to his stomach."

He turned away to escape Archie's green eyes peering at him from where she sat in front of the flames in the outdoor fireplace. The fire reflected off the golden tone of her bare arms and silky white lounging pajamas.

With his head hanging over the edge of the deck, Gnarly was stretched out on his back on the top step leading down to the beach. He also seemed to be watching his master.

Mac would have called Violet from inside the house, but it wasn't like Archie wouldn't notice David there the next morning. He'd learned early on that she didn't miss a thing.

"But he has to work tomorrow," Violet objected.

"He's not going to work tomorrow."

"Why not?"

"Because he's sick." After soothing her with assurances that David would be home in the morning, Mac hung up and poured a glass of chardonnay from the bottle Archie had placed in the center of the table.

She took a sip of her wine before asking, "David's in a lot of trouble, isn't he?"

"Oh, yeah!" Mac sat back in his chair and propped his bare feet up on the table top between them. "Did you know that he was sleeping with Katrina?"

"No, but I'm not surprised," she said. "David is very popular with the ladies. He's easy on the eyes and really sweet. There's nothing he wouldn't do for you."

"Especially if you're a woman," Mac quipped. "So I've found out."

"Why did Travis blow the whistle? He was David's friend." Archie gazed at him through the darkness. His skin, which had turned bronze since his move to the lake, glowed in the light created by the flames.

"I don't think Travis Turner is into friendship."

"They all knew each other their whole lives," she said. "Katrina, David, Travis. You'd think he'd want to help find Pay Back."

"Travis is an opportunist. Probably has been all along. Look at how fast he got over here when Gnarly found Dorcas's head."

"Probably as fast as he would have been over here when Katrina was killed if he'd been around."

Mac asked, "Where was he?"

"Hollywood," Archie said. "Sophia was there making some reality show about modeling. They only came back a couple of weeks before you got here. As soon as Travis found out about Katrina's murder, he was all over the case for his next book."

"What did he gain by ratting on David?" wondered Mac.

Archie asked him, "Haven't you ever met someone who stirs things up just for the thrill?"

"Maybe Phillips didn't make the decision to blacklist David on his own," Mac said. "When Travis ratted on David, he became Phillips's good buddy and confidante for the big murder case. Think of the hook on that novel if Travis can write himself in as the great amateur detective who breaks the big case wide open."

"Sounds like you have Travis figured out." She reached out and touched the bare foot he had propped up on the table. "Is there anything I can do to help?"

Smiling, he replied, "Oh, I can think of a lot of things you can do to help me."

* * * *

With David sleeping off the beer in one of the guest suites down the hall, Mac turned in at one o'clock in the morning.

As was his routine, Gnarly burrowed under the bed after Mac petted him good night. Within moments, he could hear the dog snoring. He hadn't known dogs snored until he had met Gnarly. Sometimes the dog sounded like a chainsaw.

Instead of reading one of Robin's books, Mac leafed through her journal until he found her entries around the time of Niles Holt's murder. Archie's claim that Robin didn't get involved in his murder because they both had tight deadlines sounded lame. The mother he was getting to know would have dug into the case and not let go until she uncovered the truth.

He found her first reference to the Holts two-thirds of the way through the book.

Betsy, Travis's assistant, came over for a cocktail today. She's such a nice girl. Reminds me of a writer I used to know who committed suicide. I hope Betsy ends up better. Strange bird, though. Seems obsessed with Travis's books. She's spending the summer alone at the Turner place working on his next book. He's in Europe for some film festival. He won't be back until after Labor Day. Last month, he was in New York for two weeks for the Edgar awards. These young writers nowadays. They spend more time networking to promote their writing careers than writing their books. Maybe that's why there are so few good ones anymore.

Now, I'll get off my high horse.

After Betsy left I went out for a walk and had quite a surprise when I met my new neighbors. The husband, Niles Holt, is a retired investment broker. He's about my age. Very distinguished looking. His bride of a month is named Katrina, used to be Dunlap. She used to be David's high school sweetheart. Get it? He's my age and she's David's. She thought I didn't recognize her. She was wrong. I remember her very clearly from when David brought her around. Niles Holt looked at her with the same puppy dog eyes that David had for her. Her diamond necklace made his devotion clear. Five carats worth of diamonds. Not the type of jewelry I would wear around my neck while working in the garden. Maybe she'll get more practical as she gets older. Maybe not. She hasn't changed a bit.

A few pages later, Mac found the entry for the day of Niles's murder:

Murder has come to the Point. This morning, someone shoved Niles Holt off Abigail's Rock. Of course, Katrina is taking this all very hard. She told us that an old client of hers attacked her. After knocking her down with a big stick, he killed Niles. She said he had been threatening her for months and, after murdering her husband, told her "Payback is hell." How tragic. I feel so bad for her. I sent David a letter.

The next day, Robin reported that the police located Lee Dorcas, who had an alibi.

...Now, the police are trying to find out who killed Niles. After watching Katrina on the news with Yvonne Harding, I decided to go up to the Rock and look around. I went down to the bottom of the cliff where they had found Niles's body. It was hard for an old girl like me, but I found a necklace hanging from a tree branch below the Rock. You should have seen this old lady climbing up that pine tree, at least ten feet from the ground, to get that necklace. But I did it. It has to have at least five carats of diamonds on that gold chain. I called Chief Roy Phillips to tell him, but he called me a nosy old biddy before I could even tell him what I found. I put the necklace in my safe.

* * * *

Of all the rooms in the manor house, Mac felt most comfortable in Robin's study. Here, he felt the essence of the woman who had given birth to him.

Robin Spencer's famous mysteries had been penned in the most cluttered room in Spencer Manor. Built-in bookshelves containing thousands of books collected over five generations took up space on every wall. Robin had left her son first editions of all her books. First editions of famous authors personally inscribed to her, and books for research in forensics, poisons, criminology, and the law also lined the shelves. With every inch of bookshelf space taken, the writer had taken to stacking books on her heavy oak desk and tables, and in the corner.

Portraits of Spencer ancestors filled space not taken up with books. Mac didn't know their names. Some appeared to be from the eighteenth century. Others wore fashions from the turn of the nineteenth century and on throughout. The most recent portrait was a life-sized painting of Robin Spencer, dressed in a white strapless formal gown from the 1960s. When he had first seen the picture, Mac had been taken aback by how much Robin resembled his grown daughter Jessica.

The portrait of the demure-looking author filled the wall between two gun cases behind the desk. One case contained rifles and shotguns, while the other had handguns. Some of the guns had been handed down through the Spencer family. Others, Robin had purchased for research.

Robin had acquired other weapons during her career of writing about murder. The coat rack sported a hangman's noose and a Samurai sword hung on the wall.

In a chair in the far corner of the room, Uncle Eugene watched all the comings and goings. A first aid training dummy, Uncle Eugene had been stabbed in the back, tossed off rooftops, and strangled on numerous occasions, all in the name of research. When he wasn't being victimized, he sat in an overstuffed chair in the corner, dressed in a tuxedo with a top hat perched on his head. With one leg crossed over the other and an empty sherry glass next to his elbow, Uncle Eugene looked like he was taking a break while waiting for the next attempt on his life.

On the day of Mac's arrival at Spencer Manor, Archie had shown him the fireproof safe built into the wall behind the portrait of his mother. He didn't need to write down the combination: right 6, left 27, right 63. It was his birth date, further proof that Robin had never forgotten him.

Mac almost gave up his search for the necklace she had found up at Abigail's Rock. *Maybe*, he thought, *Robin decided to get rid of it to protect Katrina for David's sake*. Then his fingers landed on a small envelope tucked under heavy business folders and papers in the safe's far corner. Its contents made a scratching noise when he slid it toward him.

Holding the business folders and papers up to allow room, he extracted the small envelope and emptied its contents into his palm. The string of diamonds burst with light in his hand when they caught the morning sun streaming through the window.

The gold chain contained no less than five carats of diamonds. The clasp claimed the only imperfection. The link that would have held the missing part was broken, as if the necklace had been ripped from its owner's throat and tossed off Abigail's Rock along with her husband.

CHAPTER SEVEN

Searching for the journalist who had interviewed Katrina after her first husband's murder, Mac strolled around the small Morgantown, West Virginia, television studio, when a shapely blond with legs that didn't quit rushed from a corner office to grab him by the arm. "Excuse me, but are you Mickey Forsythe? Are you really him? You look just like him. I saw you on Oprah."

"No, I'm not Mickey Forsythe. I'm Mac Faraday." He extracted his arm from her grasp while asking for Yvonne Harding, which prompted a loud gasp followed by a bombardment of questions.

"That's me! What do you want to know? Stuff about your mother? I knew her since I was just a little girl. David O'Callaghan—his dad was Spencer's police chief—he introduced us."

"How about Katrina Holt Singleton? I'm looking for information about her."

"Katrina? Well, we went to school together, but we didn't keep in touch."

Yvonne led Mac into a lounge furnished with a sofa that had seen better days, if not years, and a stained coffee table. She took two bottles of water from a portable fridge and offered one to him.

"David would be more help than me," she said. "He dated Katrina for almost a year."

"Girls aren't as open with boyfriends as they are with their girlfriends."

"Katrina didn't know the meaning of the word friend." She squinted at him. "Why are you interested in her?"

"I'm trying to find out who killed her."

Suspicion crossed her face. "I heard that a crazy ex-client did it."

"Evidence suggests otherwise." Mac sucked in a deep breath. "Now they think David murdered her."

Scoffing, she sat on the arm of the sofa and crossed one long leg over the other. "David would never kill anyone, especially Katrina."

"Why did you say that she didn't know the meaning of the word friend?"

"Katrina wasn't anyone's friend. It took me a long time to figure that out. Even after…" her voice trailed off.

"After what?"

"It's ancient history."

"I love history." Mac urged her to continue.

"It was schoolgirl silliness." Yvonne shook her head with a laugh. "Okay, here you go. Back in school, Katrina and I worked at my father's sporting goods shop in McHenry. A couple of guys came in all the time, and I had a huge crush on one of them."

"Who was that?" Mac offered a guess. "Travis Turner?"

"No, not him," she answered. "I loved David O'Callaghan."

"David?"

Blushing at the memory, she rolled her eyes. "I'd turn to mush every time I saw him. He hung out with Travis and they drove around the lake in Travis's black Jag convertible. They came in pretty regularly, so we knew they liked us. Finally, one day, we arranged to get together after the shop closed. I prayed all day that David would couple up with me."

Mac surmised, "But that didn't happen." When she paused to swallow a gulp of the water, he could see that the memory still hurt after what had to be over a decade.

"Since we were going in Travis's car, Katrina and I assumed he would be driving. So David would be in the back. David opened the passenger side door and held back the seat for me to get in, but Katrina pushed me out of the way and I ended up sitting in front with Travis." She sighed. "That seemed to write it in stone. I was with Travis from then on, until Katrina dumped David and our foursome broke up. Then we all went our separate ways."

"Did Katrina know that you liked David?" Mac imagined how she felt when her best friend started dating the object of her infatuation.

Yvonne answered in a firm tone. "Of course she did. She used to tease me after he left the shop about my screw-ups in front of him. Katrina loved nothing more than something that belonged to someone else."

"So," he concluded, "you had a crush on David and Katrina basically stole him from you. Then, you ended up with the rich playboy in the hot car." He chuckled. "Have you interviewed your former boyfriend since he hit the big time?"

"I interview Travis on our show every time he comes back to the area. We always joke about the irony of it all," she said. "Back in high school, I wrote his term papers. Who would have thought? Now, he's a Pulitzer Prize–winning author. Last summer, when he came on the show to promote his latest bestseller—I forget the name of it. He's been churning out one a year. He brought some pictures from when we were in school to show the audience. We had a good laugh." Her mirth took on an irritated note. "He also brought Sophia Hainsworth. Gorgeous, but touched."

"Why do you say that?"

"I made the mistake of kissing Travis hello on the cheek and she about scratched my eyes out. She told me to keep my claws off him. He was hers. She can keep him." She cocked her head at him. "I thought you wanted to talk about Katrina."

Reminded of his reason for seeing her, Mac started. "According to my mother's journal, she saw Katrina on your show after her first husband's death."

"I remember that interview," she said. "It was your average plea-for-justice type report. Katrina told about how she and Niles went up to Abigail's Rock—"

"I know the story," he interrupted her. "Can I see that interview by any chance?"

After some time rummaging in a portable pod filled with shelving that served as the news station's archives, Yvonne took Mac to her office where she loaded a DVD into a player for them to view. She perched on the corner of her desk with her legs crossed. He was so interested in the news report that he didn't notice her bare knees inches from his shoulder.

For the first time, Mac saw Katrina in life. He could see what attracted David to her. She wore her black flowing hair loose. Her flawless sun-kissed skin with an olive tint added an exotic touch to her beauty. For her television appearance, the new widow displayed her slender figure in a black sleeveless dress with a plunging neckline.

Katrina reminded Mac of someone, but he couldn't put his finger on whom.

"What are you looking for?" Yvonne whispered.

"Something Robin saw and thought was important enough to make her climb up the face of Abigail's Rock."

"What was that?"

"She didn't say."

He turned up the volume.

"It was our last week at Deep Creek," Katrina told Yvonne and the audience in a soft voice. "I remember as a child, climbing up to Abigail's Rock with my friends. Once—it was such a happy memory—a former boyfriend and I climbed up there to watch the sunrise. It was the most beautiful and romantic thing that ever happened to me."

On the screen, Mac saw Yvonne flinch at the reminder of Katrina's relationship with David. He wondered if the dig had been intentional.

"It was my idea that we go up to the rock to see the sunrise before going back to the city. But when we got up there—" Katrina choked. "It happened so fast."

The reporter patted her hand. "That's okay."

"No, I want to go on…He blindsided me. We came out into the clearing at the rock. It happened so fast. Suddenly, I was on the ground with blood on my face. Niles was screaming and—" Uttering a sobbing noise, she dabbed her eyes with a tissue. "He was gone!"

After a moment, Yvonne announced, "The man originally suspected of attacking you and killing Niles has been eliminated as a suspect."

"He's been threatening me. But I have to admit I never saw my husband's killer. I didn't really see anything."

Mac squinted.

Seeing his questioning look, Yvonne asked, "What is it?"

"She didn't see anything," he replied.

On the television, Yvonne asked, "Did he say anything to you? Do you know why he killed your husband?"

"No, he didn't say anything."

Mac turned off the television.

"Did you see what Robin saw?"

"Yep." He handed her the remote. "Thank you very much."

"You're not going to tell me, are you?"

"Nope."

CHAPTER EIGHT

After seeing Yvonne Harding, Mac rushed back to the manor, grabbed the next Robin Spencer book on his reading list, and lay out on the deck next to the shore to enjoy the sunny day. Gnarly's moan when he stretched out in a sunray next to the chaise reflected his master's joy.

Mac recalled numerous beautiful days that he had spent in stuffy rooms with self-serving supervisors or murder suspects. With a sigh, he leaned his head back, embraced the touch of the sun on his face, and opened Robin Spencer's seventh book. He noted the copyright date on the first page: the same year he had started school.

He had read less than one page when Archie jogged up the path from the gazebo. She wore a long powder blue skirt and blousy top. Her earrings and bracelets around her bare ankles matched the shade of blue in her clothes. "Hey, Mac, have you seen my phone?"

"No," he replied. "Have you seen my Blackberry?"

"I guess the petty thief snagged them both."

"The cell service claims no one has used my Blackberry since it disappeared." He marked the last word he read with his finger. "Why would someone steal a Blackberry if they didn't intend to use it?"

"The same reason someone took my cordless phone. It doesn't work if you're out of range."

"When did you last see it?"

"Last night, down at the gazebo. One of my writers had called for a progress report. I suspect she really wanted therapy. She's quite neurotic. After we hung up, I tossed the phone onto the bench and got into the hot tub."

"Did you look there?"

"That's where I just came from." She groaned. "I hope it didn't fall into the lake."

"Either that or the Point's klepto got it." Mac returned to his book.

She stood over him. "What are you going to do about David?"

"I'm going to find out who really killed Katrina."

"I was thinking…" She went on to suggest that they visit the local power brokers on their turf: the Spencer Inn.

"Why?" Using his index finger for a bookmark, Mac closed the book.

"You can help David by exercising some of your inherited influence in the political arena here in Spencer."

Sucking in his breath, he disagreed. "I'm not cut out for politics. Ask my old bosses if you don't believe me."

Archie sat at the foot of the chaise, which forced him to bend his legs to prevent her from sitting on his feet. "Robin used to tell me when I was struggling to get someone to even read my stuff, that it isn't what you know, but who you know." Threatening to press her breasts against his knees, she leaned toward him. "David needs help and you're the only one with the influence to give it to him."

"The root of David's problem is that he had sex with a woman he wasn't supposed to be having sex with."

"The way I see it, that's the only ammunition Phillips has in his conspiracy to get rid of him. Phillips has been out to get him ever since he came to Spencer, because David's twice the investigator, and man, he is."

"No matter who you know," Mac said, "sleeping with a victim or witness is always an issue."

"Now that Dorcas's death has been ruled a murder, what is the first thing Phillips needs to do to railroad David into jail?"

"Find evidence against him. That is, after his case against David is blown out of the water when they compare his DNA to the DNA that they collected off Gnarly and see that it's not a match."

"Mac," Archie asked, "who collected that DNA from Gnarly?"

He sucked in a deep breath while she pointed out that in addition to David being the first officer on the scene after Katrina's murder, he was also the one who insisted on forensics collecting the blood and tissue samples from Gnarly's fur for evidence.

"It's like one of Robin's plotlines," Archie said. "The victim's killer just so happens to be a cop. He makes sure he's the first one on the scene and plants someone else's DNA on her dog to throw suspicion somewhere else."

Mac chuckled. "Now you sound like one of those slimy defense attorneys that used to get my collars off by throwing unbelievable scenarios out for the jury to chew on."

"Is it really that unbelievable?" she asked. "In your whole career, you never saw or heard of a cop planting evidence in order to frame someone or maybe seal a case against a suspect?"

The smile dropped from Mac's face.

"Phillips is going to do all he can to make a circumstantial case against David. As soon as he can do that, then he's going to the county prosecutor to get an indictment." So far, Archie hadn't said anything that Mac didn't already know. "We need to get someone bigger than Phillips on our side who can keep David out of jail until you prove he didn't do this. Now, who is bigger than Chief Roy Phillips?"

"County Prosecutor Ben Fleming."

* * * *

When Violet's nurse offered to take the elderly woman to the beauty salon and lunch in McHenry, David grabbed the opportunity for a nap. His mother's frail health made occasions of being alone in his own home a rare and treasured occurrence.

The room was dark. Naked, David gazed out across the lake from the bedroom window. The wind roared in his ears. Born and raised on the water, he wasn't frightened by storms, but this one scared him.

"Darling, come to bed." Her voice was pleading.

David turned from the window.

Katrina lay beneath the sheet that outlined her naked body. Her black hair glistened in the soft candlelight. Candles covered every surface. "Hold me." She reached out to him. "I need you to make me feel safe."

He took her into his arms. Overcome with desire, she pushed him down onto the bed. The wind roared in his ears while she made love to him.

Someone was watching them. He could feel their eyes on them.

"No! Stop!" He shoved her away.

"I want you."

"Stop!" Pushing her away, he sat up.

In the darkness, David made out the silhouette of the intruder.

"Oh, no!" She screamed while pointing. "It's alive!"

David saw the gun aimed at her.

With one blast Katrina was dead at his side.

Too late, David dove for his gun.

"You're a dead man, O'Callaghan!"

The gun went off again.

With a shriek, David bolted up out of his bed. He gasped out a sigh of relief when he realized the shooting was only in his dream—until he heard it again. He dove from the bed to the floor.

Searching for the gunshot's mark, he removed his personal gun, a nine millimeter Berretta, from its case in the closet and loaded it. His heart pounded in his chest while he tried to determine from where the shots were fired: the front of the house, or the back. Conscious of the dozens of windows that afforded a view of the lake, David made his way through the house looking for what the shooter could have hit. The shots sounded so close. He went outside to examine the exterior of the house.

When he went around to the front, a police cruiser pulled into the driveway. Bogie stepped out of the SUV. "Getting some sun?"

David had been so distracted by the shooting that he didn't notice he was still in his boxer shorts. He stepped back around the corner of the house to get out of sight of passersby.

"Are you checking out a report of gunshots?" he asked.

The officer shook his silver head. "What gunshots?"

"They woke me up." Now fully awake, David remembered that Hazelhurst, a small community on the opposite side of the lake from Spencer, wasn't in Spencer police's jurisdiction. The state police answered calls for the rural area too small to warrant its own police force. "It must have been a dream."

Bogie checked his watch to see that the time was early afternoon. "I guess if you're on suspension you should take advantage of the time off to rest up."

"I didn't have a good evening."

"So I heard." Bogie added, "You're not the only one. Phillips canned me today."

"You're kidding."

"Nope," Bogie said. "When I went in this morning, Phillips called me into the office and asked if I had any plans to work tomorrow. I said yeah. He said don't bother."

"He can't fire you without cause."

"As a favor," Bogie said mockingly, "he said he'd give me early retirement."

David swallowed. The elder police officer was like an uncle to him. "I'm so sorry, Bogie. This has to be because of me."

"It's not your fault."

"What are you going to do?"

"Go fishing with my son and grandkids." Bogie flashed him a smile before adding, "I didn't come here looking for sympathy. I came to offer my support. You got screwed. Phillips is afraid of you, and me, as evidenced by how fast he got me out of there after finding out that you were reopening Katrina's case. If there's anything I can do to help you or your mother, just give me a call." He winked. "I may not have my badge anymore, but I do have my gun."

"Turner ratted me out about Katrina, didn't he?"

Bogie answered with a single nod of his head.

"Why? What did he have to gain?" David asked

"What do you think? A cop on the inside being the killer? All the better twist and turns for his next big book. Turner has been pouring it on and Phillips has been lapping it up. Turner promised to make him technical adviser on the movie after selling the book to Hollywood. Phillips thinks he's on his way to Tinsel Town to sleep with supermodels." Bogie clasped his shoulder warmly. "Keep your chin up, Dave." With another offer to help him or his mother with anything they needed, he climbed back into the patrol car and drove off.

David continued to scan the trees that surrounded his home for a clue to who had taken shots at his house. They had sounded so real. They couldn't have been a dream.

* * * *

"There's the man I'm looking for," Mac announced suddenly during Jeff Ingles's tour of the grounds at the Spencer Inn.

Carrying shotguns, Benjamin Fleming and four companions were hiking down a trail leading to the woods. Upon seeing the prosecutor, Mac jogged across the lawn. "Hey, Ben!"

Generally, the Inn's guests dressed in upscale fashion. Ben and his friends looked as if they had been costumed for a skeet shooting scene in a movie. In contrast, Mac's wardrobe had monetarily failed to catch up with his bankroll. The owner of one of the country's most luxurious resorts had neglected to put socks on his feet which were encased in worn loafers, which were the same age and condition of his jeans and blue t-shirt with "POLICE" emblazoned across the back.

Seeing Jeff's sidelong glances at him during the tour, Mac made a mental note to invest in a better wardrobe. Unfortunately, having a budget beyond his wildest dreams did nothing to change Mac's distaste for shopping.

Since his inheritance, Mac had invested in one suit from an Italian tailor who his daughter had learned designed the clothes for her favorite movie star. Mac suspected she dragged him to the designer in hopes of casually meeting said actor. Now all he had to do was find an occasion appropriate for wearing the suit, which he hesitated to put on for fear of ruining it after paying thousands of dollars for it.

At the sound of Mac's voice, Ben turned from where he was about to descend the path to an area designated for skeet shooting. His friends halted to see who could be so forward as to dare interrupt them. "Mic—"

"Mac."

"Mac," Ben said, "Forsythe."

"Faraday," Mac corrected him again. "Mac Faraday."

"Good to see you." Ben looked from him to Archie and then to the manager, who was jogging at a more dignified pace behind them. He introduced Mac to the rest of the men in the group. At the mention of his name, each of their expressions changed from perturbed to welcoming, even encouraging, him to join them.

"I heard about you moving into Spencer Manor." One of Ben's friends stepped forward and grasped Mac's hand in both of his. "I'm Pete Mason, Spencer's mayor. I loved your mother's books. Most everyone here in Spencer did. She was the unofficial queen of Spencer."

Tanned and athletic looking, Pete Mason resembled a 1940s movie idol. His facial features lacked any flaws. As if to avoid betraying a hint of human frailty, not a strand of his silver hair, mustache, or goatee dared to stray out of place. Even his fingernails were trimmed and polished to perfection.

Mac held onto the mayor's hand after their greeting. "Excuse me." His brain nagged at him. "Have we met?"

Pete Mason chuckled. "I don't believe so." Glances at his friends encouraged them to join in his amusement. While the others in the group did, the prosecuting attorney did not.

"Listen, Mick—" Mayor Mason slapped Mac on the back. "Mac."

"Mac, most of us on the town council have a private cocktail party here in the lounge every Friday during the season. Usually I invite my friends for a round of golf beforehand. Since it's your club—"

Mac caught Archie's eye.

Archie had filled him in about the mayor's private parties where political deals were made and broken. She had also informed him about the mayor being instrumental in getting Phillips appointed to police chief after Pat O'Callaghan's death. He boasted that Roy Phillips served as a general in the army, trained at the War College, and worked for several years at the Pentagon.

After accepting Pete Mason's invitation, Mac joined the group of men on the range.

Meanwhile, Archie went to the lounge to dig up what she could on Katrina Holt Singleton, who had belonged to the Inn's private club during her marriage to Niles Holt. She never renewed her membership after returning to Spencer with her second husband.

Archie spied a familiar face sipping a glass of wine. She and her red-haired companion wore tennis whites so clean and wrinkle-free that Archie wondered if they were wearing them for sport or show. Their hair and makeup didn't reveal any signs of the physical exertion that comes from the use of their clothing as it had been intended. Concluding that they were in the lounge for the sport of being seen, Archie stepped over to the women's table. "Well, hello, Sophia. What a pleasure to see you here."

Startled in the process of reapplying her lipstick, Sophia looked up at Archie who smiled down at her and her companion. "Excuse me. Do I know you?"

"I'm Archie. We met here a few nights ago. I was with Mac Faraday, Robin Spencer's son."

With a bored expression, Sophia snapped her compact shut.

"Who's Mac Faraday?" the redhead asked.

"The illegitimate son of that has-been mystery writer." Sophia flapped a hand in Archie's direction. "This is his secretary, Andy."

"Archie," she corrected her. "And Robin Spencer, who had won *two* Pulitzers during her career, was never a has-been."

"Has-been since Travis came along. He's only just started."

Choosing not to fight this battle, Archie moved over to take a seat at the bar where she could see Mac when he came back up the path from skeet shooting. The bartender wasted no time in filling her order for a white wine.

A cell blasted a rap tone somewhere in the lounge.

Recognizing the signal as hers, the redhead snatched the phone from a strap on her purse. "I'm having cocktails with Sophia Hainsworth. Why are you bothering me?" After hearing the caller's answer, she uttered a loud curse. "Well, you tell her that I said..." She spewed an unending string of vulgarities while gathering her belongings. Blowing a kiss in Sophia's general direction, she rushed out with the cell phone pressed against her ear.

More interested in repacking her lipstick and compact, Sophia kissed her friend in the air before turning to a table in the corner of the lounge. "Betsy, don't forget to pick up my dress at the cleaners on your way home. Do be careful with it. The last time it got wrinkled before you put it away."

Until she heard Sophia speaking to Betsy, Archie hadn't noticed Travis's assistant sitting alone at a small table in a remote corner of the lounge. A plate with bread crusts and a catsup smear indicated that she had eaten lunch. While sucking up the last drops of her milk shake through a straw, she made notes in her writing tablet. Archie wondered if Betsy sat in the corner out of a desire for privacy or because Sophia didn't want to be seen with someone so beneath her.

"Betsy," Sophia snapped when the other woman didn't respond to her demand.

"I heard you."

With a glare, Sophia concentrated on paying her bill until something else caught her attention.

Archie followed her eyes.

Outside on the deck, a waitress was mopping up a spilled drink off the white ensemble of Travis Turner. In spite of her embarrassment over the mishap, the server giggled at the celebrity's quips while she wiped down his body with a linen napkin.

Sophia's eyes darkened before she rushed out onto the deck and grabbed the cloth from the woman's hand. "What do you think you're doing?"

While apologizing, the server threw up her hands to protect her face from the napkin which Sophia used to slap her.

Laughing in a situation that Archie would have found mortifying to have any part in, Travis grabbed his cursing wife into a bear hug.

Even with the distance between them, Archie could see tears rolling down the server's cheeks. Manager Jeff Ingles appeared on the scene to aid his employee. Between the two men shielding the server while throwing peace offerings at Sophia, the scene disintegrated. Jeff led his sobbing employee away in one direction, while Travis ushered his wife, still firing verbal abuse over her shoulder at the other woman, in the other.

"My, my, my," Betsy said. "Betcha didn't know super-models were such high maintenance."

"People are like dogs," Archie said. "The beautiful, poofy ones always need grooming, while the working dogs are happiest when you let them lie."

"I never thought of it like that." Betsy seemed intrigued by her analysis.

"How's Travis's restaurant, Turner's, doing?" Archie picked up her glass of wine and crossed the lounge. She moved a chair from another table to join Betsy in the corner.

Turner's was an upscale restaurant on the opposite side of Deep Creek Lake at the foot of the Wisp, a ski resort. Since its opening soon after Travis's second bestseller was published, the restaurant had become popular with well-heeled tourists and fans of the writer.

"Fine." Betsy slipped her notebook into her stained and torn oversized shoulder bag. "Why?"

Archie gestured with her head in the direction of the deck where the author had been moments earlier. "Why is Travis hanging out at the Spencer Inn? One would think he would be patronizing his own restaurant."

"You're very perceptive," Betsy said. "It's better for Travis's career if he's seen with the in-crowd. The A-list don't hang out at tourist spots, which is what Turner's has turned into. That's why he's been casing the Inn."

"Casing?"

Archie's mind raced. The Spencer Inn was as much a part of her life as Robin Spencer had been. Mac had confessed that owning such a prestigious place overwhelmed him. If Travis offered to take it off his hands, he might accept. For Archie, it would be like losing Robin all over again.

"A couple of months ago, Travis bought seventy acres on the south end of the lake from Chad Singleton. He's planning to move Turners there, and build a hotel and bungalows. He's going to call it Turner Village."

"I didn't know the Singletons owned seventy acres on the south end of the lake."

"Katrina's first husband bought it before he died. He organized this group of investors. They called themselves the Eagle Group. Their goal was to get rich developing everything that could be developed on Deep Creek Lake."

"Really?" Archie asked. "And they continued after he died?"

"Was killed." Betsy glanced out the window at the view of the lake. "Have you ever met a true femme fatale? A real live one, I mean?"

"A couple. Have you?"

"Yes," Betsy said. "They make such a big deal about prejudice in this country. Equal rights for blacks and women. What about equality for the fat and ugly? If you're beautiful, not only can you get away with murder, but the chief of police will take you out for dinner. People like me haven't got a chance."

Archie challenged her. "Have you tried?"

"Yes," she spat out. "I sent my books to everyone. No one would even read them. But then Travis sends a book to Robin Spencer and within a year he's got a feature in *Publisher's Weekly*."

Archie told herself that it had to be difficult for Betsy to take orders from the likes of Sophia Hainsworth-Turner. "I admit, Robin read Travis's book because she's known him since he was a child and it's easier if you know people. It's unfortunate, but that's the way the world is. Very often, it's not how talented you are, but who you know. But her reading Travis's book and it ending up on the bestsellers list had nothing to do with how good-looking Travis is. Robin would never endorse a book that she didn't love. If she didn't like his book, she would have told him. But she loved it. Robin said his first book was the best mystery written by an unpublished writer that she had ever read."

Betsy's face turned pale.

"Are you okay?" Archie asked her after a long moment of silence. "What femme fatale are you talking about? Is it Sophia?"

"Did you know that Travis's stepmother was murdered?"

Archie reacted with surprise. She would have thought Robin would have told her about that, or at least David.

"She was young—skinny and gorgeous, of course." Betsy recounted, "She sold real estate. One morning, she went to her office and there was a fire. They found her body after they had put it out. She had been shot in the head."

"Did they catch whoever killed her?"

"No."

"Does Travis have any ideas about who killed his stepmother?"

Betsy's eyes met hers. She whispered, "His father."

"Why? Was she cheating on him?"

"Yes…with Travis. She was his first love. He said it broke his heart."

When she found her voice, Archie asked, "Did Travis ever tell anyone back then about his suspicions? He could have told his friend David or maybe Katrina."

"Katrina wasn't his friend. She wasn't anybody's friend. She pretended to be my friend, but she wasn't."

"I didn't know that you knew Katrina," Archie said.

Betsy replied, "I interviewed her about her husband's murder for a project I had been working on. She thought I was going to make her famous. That's the only reason she even spoke to me."

"Did you interview her before or after Pay Back came to town?"

"Before." Betsy frowned when she took a sip from her milk shake and found the glass empty. "Wasn't that the name on the jacket of the body they found in the mine?"

"Yes," Archie said. "They positively identified the victim as Lee Dorcas, but his DNA doesn't match that found at Katrina's murder scene. So he didn't kill Katrina. Do you know why someone would go to so much trouble to kill her?" She grinned at her. "Come on. You edit mysteries. You have to love them yourself. Don't tell me that you haven't been thinking about who killed her."

"You should be asking Travis," Betsy said. "He's been researching Katrina's murder for his next book."

"And you were researching Niles Holt's murder."

"I abandoned that project."

"Why?"

Betsy shrugged. "I didn't have time to finish it."

Archie could see that she didn't want to talk about it any further. "Do you know what Travis has found out in his research? What has he written so far about her?"

In silence, the famous author's assistant gazed out across the landscape.

"Betsy?"

She blinked. "You'll know when everyone else does." Announcing that she had to go, Betsy picked up her handbag. "Sophia needs her dress to wear to her next fancy party with

Travis." She leaned over to whisper to Archie. "He really hates these parties. He only goes because she makes him."

What a strange girl, Archie told herself after Betsy left. She was the outcast, but seemed to be a wealth of information. *Is it because nobody notices her lurking?* Archie dismissed that thought. From what she had observed, Travis Turner lived for the party scene. She couldn't see him being made to go to any party where he could rub elbows with high society.

"Archie!"

She heard her name called out so sharply that she almost spilt the last drop of wine on her way to the bar.

"Is that you?" Francine Taylor rushed across the lounge in her direction. "I thought it was." Inquiring if she had come for a local women's group luncheon, Ira's wife plopped down in the seat Betsy had vacated. "Want some company?" Francine explained that she would prefer to have a last cocktail before going home to the chore of cleaning her husband's morning catch.

After ordering a second glass of wine and one for her guest, Archie gave Francine an update on the Singleton case. "Evidence proves Lee Dorcas, Katrina's disgruntled client, didn't kill her. So it had to be someone else. Can you think of who that someone would be?"

Francine thought over the question in silence. After the server arrived with her glass of wine, she answered, "Maybe Roy Phillips. Katrina played him for a fool."

"The police chief? How?"

"Roy made a play for her before Niles's body was even cold. It was quite laughable. Phillips is a dolt. You do know that he had served in the army with Mayor Mason, don't you? That's the only reason he got the job of police chief."

"Did he just make a play for her, or did they actually become lovers?" Archie asked in a breathy voice. She couldn't envision a beautiful woman like Katrina with the unattractive police chief.

"It was over before it began," Francine said with a wave of her hand. "Katrina played him along, got him completely hooked, and then ran off to Washington in the dead of night. It had to be humiliating for him."

"Humiliating enough for him to want her dead?"

As if struck with a sudden thought, Francine announced, "If anyone hated Katrina enough to want to kill her that would be Pete Mason."

"The mayor?" asked Archie in disbelief.

"He always swore Katrina cheated him," Francine told her, "and no one cheats Mayor Mason and gets away with it."

"How did Katrina cheat him? The same way she cheated Lee Dorcas?"

"Pretty much. Katrina was his financial advisor until she lost him a bundle. It isn't like he lost his lunch money. He comes from money. But all the same, you don't cheat Pete Mason. He blacklisted her. I'm sure that's one of the reasons she went back to Washington. No one who mattered in Deep Creek would have anything to do with her."

"If she lost so much of his money, why didn't he sue her?"

"Maybe because he got more pleasure out of making her wish she was dead."

* * * *

"Pull!" Mac shouted.

Two clay pigeons simultaneously took to the air. He aimed his shotgun and fired two shots that took them both out. The group of men behind him applauded.

Mayor Pete Mason slapped a hundred dollar bill into Mac's palm. "Where did you learn to shoot like that?"

"In my line of work, being able to shoot was a job requirement." Mac handed the shotgun back to the attendant and pocketed the bet. Their session was over and he had shot a perfect score.

Ben Fleming and Mac fell in step behind the group of men on their way to the lounge for a round of drinks. "I find it interesting that you showed up here looking for me the day after David O'Callaghan is suspended from duty and becomes a suspect in two murders. Is that a coincidence, or does it have something to do with your mother's relationship with his late father?"

"I'm interested in knowing what you're going to do about the case."

"Order me a drink and we'll talk about it."

When Mac and Ben went into the lounge, Archie looked up from where she and a silver-haired woman sat at a table in the corner. Both women had a glass of white wine set before them. Mac winked at Archie before following Ben Fleming to the opposite end of the bar where he ordered two beers.

"David O'Callaghan is in deep trouble," Ben said.

"How deep?" Mac felt his first gulp of beer go down his throat and cool his churning innards.

"According to evidence he gave Phillips—"

"Which Phillips failed to find himself."

"Phillips found it, but David became the prime suspect. Phillips made the bad decision to save the police department scandal since one of their own was the only suspect who could have done it."

"What's David's motive for killing Katrina Singleton?"

"She dumped him for another guy when they were in school. She comes back to town and seduces him into an affair. He thinks this time they'll make it, but she dumps him again." Ben took a sip of his drink. "Screw me once, shame on me. Screw me twice, shame on you."

"Let's say David slept with Katrina," Mac suggested. "Let's say she dumped him a second time. Is there any real evidence to prove David killed her and Dorcas? Do they have anyone to put him at the scene? Do they have any evidence to prove he crushed her throat? Do they have the murder weapon with his fingerprints on it? Do they have any evidence that he shot Dorcas in the head and dumped his body in the mine? Has anyone bothered asking David for his DNA to compare with what forensics got off Gnarly?"

"Why was the one cop who happened to be sleeping with the victim the first one on the scene?"

"David didn't do it." Mac asked the question that had brought him to the Inn that afternoon. "What do you intend to do about him?"

Ben shrugged. "Mac, I have a certain loyalty toward David, his father, and your mother. They have all saved my reputation more than once."

"Then you owe him."

"I know," the lawyer said in a low voice, "but I can't turn my back on a killer."

"He's not a killer, and Phillips is no police chief," Mac said. "He doesn't know the first thing about investigating a murder case."

"But if he brings me enough evidence to take to a grand jury—"

"If there's no real evidence, then he can't bring it to you," Mac said.

"What do you propose? I'm straight, Mac. I won't be a party to anyone destroying or tampering with evidence."

"I'm not going to destroy evidence—I'm going to find it. All I want from you is to hold off on indicting David with whatever circumstantial evidence Phillips brings you until I find out the truth about what happened. Think about it. If you indict an innocent man and then I bring in the real killer— which I will do—you're going to look like a fool. Won't it be bad enough when I make Spencer's police chief look like an idiot? Do you want to be in that company?"

"You sound so much like your mother, it's scary," the prosecutor said. "How much time are you talking about?"

"How much time are you willing to give me?"

"Not much." Ben groaned softly. "Don't look now but Chief Phillips just walked in."

Mac wished he had eyes in back of his head. "Is he heading this way?"

"Straight for me." Ben whispered hurriedly, "I'll give you as much time as I can."

Phillips stepped toward the prosecutor with his hand out.

"Hey, Roy, how are you doing?" Ben greeted him.

"As well as can be expected with two less officers."

"So you told me this morning."

Ben directed him to a table away from the bar on the other side of the lounge. "Let's have a round and talk about what we should do."

With a glance over his shoulder, Mac headed for the exit at the opposite end of the bar. He saw Archie sitting with her back to Ben and Roy's table.

"Excuse me, but I need to—" Before Archie could finish excusing herself, she saw three people come into the lounge.

She recognized Prissy and Gordon Hardwick. Their unpleasant demeanor contained an overabundance of smugness. Their companion was plump to the point of obesity. She wore her black hair in a bluntly cut bob. After leading the couple to the bar, she tapped Jeff Ingles on the shoulder.

"Hello, Jeff," their female companion said. "As the manager of the Spencer Inn, I believe these should go to you." She extracted a folded bunch of papers from her purse and slapped him in the chest with them.

The Hardwicks smirked at the customers in the lounge.

"How much?" Jeff asked their lawyer.

"Seven million dollars."

Jeff laughed. "That's an awful lot of money to sue a group of people you hated to begin with for expelling you from their club."

"We hated you because you hated us," Gordon said. "You're all a bunch of anti-Semitics."

"Now you're reaching. Nowhere on the membership application does it ask anything about religion. To tell you the truth, I thought you were a couple of atheists. You certainly acted like it." Jeff scoffed, "You joined this club to get expelled in order to file this suit." He dropped the papers onto the top of the bar. "It's not going to work. I won't let you use my establishment to support you in the high life."

"We'll see you and Mr. Faraday in court, Mr. Ingles." The lawyer urged the Hardwicks to leave before engaging in any more sparring of words.

"What do you intend to do about them?" Ben asked the manager.

"What else? I intend to get rid of them."

CHAPTER NINE

"The more I get to know people, the more I like my dog," Mac told Ed Willingham in Jeff Ingles's corner office off the Spencer Inn's reception area. "And he stole my breakfast this morning."

Ed Willingham had requested a meeting to discuss the Hardwicks' lawsuit against the Spencer Inn. Again, Jeff Ingles dressed better than the Inn owner in a tailored suit made of a material Mac couldn't identify. He had thrown on a red t-shirt, black jeans, and loafers without any socks.

Mac's lawyer explained the Hardwicks' agenda in simple terms. "They are willing to accept, and expect, a hefty out of court settlement to make this whole nuisance go away. Otherwise, they'll drag it out as long as need be and drag the name of the Spencer Inn through the mud along the way."

"But I—we've—done nothing wrong," Mac argued.

"Of course not," Ed said. "If it's dragged out, then most likely they'll lose the case. They're banking on you paying them so you don't have to be bothered."

"I'm already bothered," Mac said. "What do you mean 'most likely'? I thought you said they didn't have a case."

"My firm handled the restaurant from whom they won the multi-million dollar lawsuit," Ed told him. "The server tripped over Gordon Hardwick's briefcase, which he had left on the floor where anyone could trip over it. None of us expected the jury to come back on the side of the plaintiff. You can never tell what a jury is going to do."

"The Hardwicks were begging us to kick them out," Jeff Ingles grumbled.

"Of course," Mac said. "That's why they joined the Inn the same week it hit the news that I inherited Robin Spencer's estate. They're banking on me rolling over and playing dead to avoid the hassle? They're in for a big surprise."

"This could get expensive," Ed warned him.

"I once went to arrest a child killer who refused to be taken alive. He shot my partner before cornering me in a warehouse. My backup was nowhere to be seen and I had to turn off my radio so he wouldn't know where I was. It was dark and I couldn't see him." Mac grinned. "He's now six feet under. When I was broke I refused to go down without a fight. Now that I'm rich, I don't plan to start."

Ed slapped his notebook shut. "Then I guess I have to get to work."

The manager said, "I can give you a whole list of witnesses who will testify to the Hardwicks' shenanigans since being admitted into the club."

"Thank you, Jeff." The lawyer rose and shook the business manager's hand.

With effort, Jeff stood up. In spite of his young age, he moved like an elderly man.

"Back giving you trouble today?" Ed asked.

"Rain must be on the way."

"What ever happened with the woman who did that to you?" Remembering Mac's presence, Ed explained, "A couple of years ago Jeff was on the wrong end of a hit and run. He spent a month in the hospital."

"That's terrible." Mac now understood the hotel manager's slow and sometimes painful movements.

Jeff said, "It happened right out here in the parking lot during the off period between Labor Day and autumn leaf peeper season. I came out the side entrance after locking up and heard this couple fighting in the garden. I remember hearing a woman running across the parking lot on the way to my car. Suddenly, this Ferrari came out of nowhere. The lights came on right in my face. I think she was as surprised to see me as I was to see her. She swerved and hit the brakes, but it was too late. She clipped me. I landed on the trunk of my car. Broke both of my legs and back. The doctors said that the pain in my back will be with me for the rest of my life. I have pins all through me."

"Did they ever prosecute the woman driving the Ferrari?" Ed repeated the question that had started the conversation.

"No, they didn't." Jeff rubbed the scars on his hand and wrist. "But you know what they say. Pay back is hell."

* * * *

"I'm both surprised and saddened to learn that Patrick O'Callaghan's son is a person of interest in these murders," the voice identified as one of the leading members of Spencer's town council announced over the radio while Mac raced along the curving road around the lake. "I never knew David very well. He always seemed polite—"

"He's talking like I'm dead. Come on, Bill!" David objected from the passenger seat.

"—but then, you have to admit, there's a lot of pressure living in the shadow of a dead man," the councilman David knew as Bill Clark continued. "Ol' Pat put a lot of pressure on his son to be aggressive. You have to be when you're a cop. I used to worry that maybe Pat was teaching Dave to be too aggressive."

"Bull!"

Mac punched the button to turn off the radio. "That's enough of that."

"Bill Clark and his cronies on the town council have tried and convicted me." His passenger didn't appear to be enjoying the wind blowing through his blond hair while racing through the Maryland countryside east of McHenry. Instead, David stared through the windshield without seeing the scenery.

"They're the ones who're going to look like fools."

Mac pulled the Viper into McHenry's airport. The small airport consisted of a building that resembled a warehouse and an assortment of private jets and planes used to shuttle the resort area's privileged residents in and out of Deep Creek Lake at a moment's notice.

David asked, "What are we doing here? I thought we were driving to DC."

"We are driving." Mac climbed out of the car. "But there's more than one way out of Deep Creek. Lee Dorcas could have made it back and forth between Washington and here if he flew."

David threw open the car door. "Wouldn't that have been expensive? He was a struggling musician."

"Who inherited a fortune." Mac stepped through the hangar doors into the airport office.

In contrast to the sparse appearance of the airport, the office and lounge contained a sofa, love seat, fully stocked bar, and television. Busy, high-powered clients could conduct business at a desk next to the window looking out across the runway while waiting for their private flights.

A pilot rushed in from the hangar to greet the potential passengers. "Hello, gentlemen, welcome to McHenry airport. Where would you like to fly today?" With his slender build and smooth face, he looked barely old enough to drive a car. The gold pilot wings pinned to his breast pocket above a nameplate that read "Jackson" confirmed that he was a pilot. He told them that the private airline he owned and operated had been in his family for three generations.

Introducing himself, Mac shook the pilot's hand.

Jackson's face broke into a wide grin. "Robin Spencer's son?"

"Yes. I was wondering—"

"I flew your mother!" Jackson interjected with youthful enthusiasm. "She interviewed me for some of her books. She mentioned me in *Flight to Death*." He extracted a hardback from a bookcase in the corner that contained an assortment of reading material for waiting passengers. With pride, he opened the book to the acknowledgements page and held it out for

Mac to read. "See? Jackson Langevoort. That's me. She said I was an excellent pilot and thanked me for my wealth of information that helped her to write this book. I told her how to fake an alibi on a chartered flight. The killer booked a private flight for before the murder in his name and then had someone else show up and say it was him. I couldn't believe it when she gave me one of the first copies hot off the presses and showed me my name in the acknowledgements. A big star like her." He took the book back from Mac. "Of course, this isn't my autographed copy. I keep that one at home and never lend it out." He took a breath before asking again, "Where would you like me to fly you?"

After explaining that he and David were investigating a murder in Spencer, Mac asked if Lee Dorcas had ever booked a flight with him to or from Washington, DC.

Jackson shook his head. "Never heard of the guy."

Mac's description of Lee Dorcas caused a different reaction. "Oh, yeah, I remember flying a guy that looked like that right after the blizzard. I flew him to Houston. Real odd guy. To look at him you never would have guessed he had money."

"How did he pay?" David hoped he had paid with a credit card, which could easily be traced back to the passenger.

"Cash. Up front. I remember him because he was so weird. The army jacket and wild hair. He smelled, too. Like a hospital."

"He smelled like a hospital? Could it have been disinfectant or antiseptic?" Mac asked the pilot while looking at David. "Like maybe ointment to prevent infection from a dog bite?"

"Katrina's killer."

Jackson gasped. "Do you mean he's wanted for murder? You don't think he stole that money, do you?"

Mac asked, "What name did he use to book the flight?"

Jackson flipped through his reservation book while saying, "Oh, I remember that all right. Between what he looked like and the name, I wondered if I was going to make it back alive. P. B. Cooper." He pointed at the line in his reservation book.

"Get it? D. B. Cooper was the famous hijacker. This guy went by P. B. Cooper."

While David studied the information in the log, which didn't tell much, Mac wanted to know if the passenger had mentioned his reason for going to Houston or where he would be going from there. Jackson replied that the passenger wasn't talkative at all. With thanks, Mac took Jackson's business card and the two men resumed their drive to Washington.

After the Viper raced out of the airport onto the road leading to the freeway east, a Spencer police cruiser and a white sedan fell in behind them.

Mac yelled above the roar of the engine. "Here's what I think happened. Our perp kills Katrina and Lee Dorcas to make it look like a murder-suicide. Then, he takes a private flight out dressed up like Pay Back to mix things up." He glanced in David's direction. "What did you find out about Ira's statement when you looked at the Holt case file?"

"What makes you think I bothered looking at the case file?"

"You're a good cop, David. How long did you wait after I called you before reading Ira's statement? What happened? Why wasn't anything done about it?"

David said, "Chief Phillips gutted my dad's old office to build a new one, all paid for by the widow Holt."

Mac fought to keep the Viper on the road while looking over at him to make sure he wasn't joking. "Who took Ira's statement? Phillips?"

David shook his head. "No, Bogie took it. He's a good guy. My dad trained him. Bogie took the evidence to Phillips, who personally questioned Katrina. Then, he ordered Bogie to drop the case. Bogie fought him and ended up being demoted for it. Katrina made a contribution to the police department and went back to Washington." He added, "Phillips forced Bogie into early retirement after he found out that I was still on Katrina's case."

Mac asked, "What was Katrina hiding worth bribing a police chief for?"

"I'm still trying to find that out. Two pages from the forensics report are missing from the file. Bogie ordered a copy of the full report, but Phillips forced him out before he could get it. I called my contact in the lab again and she said that she sent it the same morning that Phillips ousted Bogie. He must have intercepted it. So I asked for another copy. But my bud said that when she went looking for it, the folder was missing. Not only that, but so is the evidence box."

"Phillips is covering his butt," Mac said. "Robin tried to look into the case, but he stonewalled her. She went up to search the crime scene and found a necklace that she had seen Katrina wearing a couple of months before."

"Was it a diamond necklace?"

"Yes."

David said, "Katrina told me that Niles had given her a five and a half carat diamond necklace. She had it less than a month before it disappeared. She believed Lee Dorcas stole it."

"Don't look now, but we're being followed."

David checked the rear view mirror. "That's Chief Phillips in the cruiser. The white sedan is a state trooper. He's a buddy of mine. At least he used to be. I guess not anymore."

"I don't like being followed." Mac pressed his foot on the accelerator.

"Cops love giving tickets to rich guys in sports cars."

"They have to catch me first."

Mac raced around a curve on Garrett Highway to take him over the top of a steep hill before pulling over and coming to a halt. When the two cruisers crested the hill and saw the stopped Viper, they pulled up behind it. The police chief got out of his cruiser. Mac waited until Phillips got to the bumper of his car then he hit the gas. Once he was on the road, he stomped on the brakes and did a one-eighty before racing by them. He threw the wheel to the left to take the Viper onto a side road that went down into a gully.

Chief Phillips ran back to his car while the trooper backed up to give chase. Both cars turned on their lights and sirens.

David clutched the sides of his seat. "Oh, yeah, this is going to get me into less trouble."

They raced along a twisting wooded country road. Without warning, Mac screeched to a halt, forcing the cars to either stop or hit him. While the cars skidded off the road into ditches, he threw the Viper into reverse and bypassed them before swinging the roadster around to head in the opposite direction. Upon their return to Garrett Highway, two county sheriff cruisers fell in behind the string of police cars.

"Now we've got the whole police department coming down on us," David said.

"For what?" Mac asked with a laugh.

"Resisting arrest for one."

"What am I resisting arrest for?"

"Speeding."

"Was I speeding?"

"You are now."

"In that case I'll go back." Mac hit the brakes and swung the steering wheel. The Viper did a donut to speed back toward the cruisers. "Ever play chicken?"

"No."

Unprepared for the sudden assault, two cruisers went off the road to avoid a collision. Mac turned onto a side road, then turned off again to hide the car along an abandoned hiking trail until the remaining patrol cars drove past in their pursuit.

Once they were safe, Mac backed the car out and quietly headed east toward his old stomping grounds in Washington DC.

* * * *

The sound of a car racing through the manor's stone entrance told Archie that the next couple days alone weren't going to be quiet ones.

Gnarly jumped off the sofa he had been sleeping on in her studio and jumped up at the window. Barking, he ran for the door as if to run through it.

Archie heard her name called out from the front door. Leaving Gnarly locked inside, she stepped out in time to see Chief Roy Phillips press his finger on the manor's doorbell.

"May I help you?" She silently prayed that he hadn't come to report that something had happened to Mac and David.

"Excuse me, Ms. Monday." He took off his hat and smiled broadly at her while stepping down the walkway toward her cottage. "I hate to interrupt you, but may I speak to Mr. Faraday?" He brought his thumb up to his mouth before seeming to think better of it and shoving his hand into his pocket.

"I'm sorry, but he's not here. Would you like for me to have him call you?" She made no move to invite the man instrumental in David's suspension inside her home.

"Where is he?" the police chief asked.

"I can't say exactly."

His thumbs inserted inside his utility belt, he stepped forward. "Why won't you tell me where Mr. Faraday is?" He gazed down at her.

Archie refused to back away. "Because you have no need to know where he is. He's not under investigation for anything."

"He just led me and the state police on a high-speed chase around Deep Creek Lake."

"Then I'll be sure to have his lawyer call you."

"That may not be necessary if you can tell me where he was going in such a hurry."

Tired of the circular conversation, she gestured toward his cruiser in the driveway behind him. "If you don't care to leave a message then I suggest you leave."

The police chief didn't move to follow her suggestion. "Ms. Monday, your boyfriend may be rich, but he's not too rich to go to jail. Maybe if he'll talk to me, we might be able to come to an understanding that can help David out of this situation."

"You couldn't care less about helping David." Archie turned away. "Now leave."

"Don't give me a hard time, Ms. Monday." He grabbed her by the arm. "If you don't convince Mr. Faraday to trust me, then people could get hurt." His fingers dug into her flesh.

Archie pulled back but he tightened his grip. "Let go of me!" She could hear Gnarly barking from inside the cottage. The door shuddered when the dog threw himself against it. "I'm calling—" She started to threaten to call the police, but remembered that he was the police.

Uttering a scream from the depths of her gut, Archie jerked up her leg to crash her knee into Police Chief Roy Phillips's groin. Yelling in agony, he released her arm to clasp his privates with both hands. At the same time, Archie threw open the cottage door and released the hound of Spencer Manor.

Before Chief Phillips could collect his wits, Gnarly hit him full force in the chest with a hundred pounds of fur and teeth. Both the dog and the police chief went over the porch railing and landed in Robin Spencer's rose garden.

As quickly as Gnarly's attack began, it ended, with Roy Phillips flat on his back among the thorns. Gnarly straddled him with his teeth at the police chief's throat. With wide eyes, Phillips gazed up at the German shepherd daring him to give him reason to rip out his throat.

"Help!"

Dog drool dripped from Gnarly's mouth onto the police chief's nose and chin. His hot breath felt moist on Chief Phillips's face.

"Call him off!" Remembering his gun, Phillips moved his hand toward his holster.

Snarling, Gnarly lunged.

Instinctively, the chief held both hands up where Gnarly could see them.

"How fast are you on the draw, Roy?" Archie yelled from the front porch over Gnarly's growling.

If her question lacked sense, the .44 Magnum she had aimed at Police Chief Roy Phillips brought her point home.

"Come, Gnarly." She called the dog to her side.

Releasing his prey, Gnarly stepped backwards to stand at her side.

Her weapon aimed between his eyes, Archie stood over the unwelcomed guest. "Here's the way I see it, Roy. I have you in my sights and my finger is on the trigger. So does Gnarly. We can take you out in less than two seconds. Your gun is in its holster. I estimate that it will take you three seconds to draw it—if you can do so before Gnarly rips out your throat—take aim, and fire on whichever one of us you decide to shoot first. The way I see it, the one you don't get first will have two seconds to spare to take you out before you fire on them. Now, if you feel lucky, give it a shot. If you don't feel lucky, I suggest you leave and don't come back without a warrant." She grinned. "So, I ask you again, Roy, how fast are you on the draw?"

His eyes narrowed. "You're making a big mistake, Ms. Monday." The police chief rose to his feet and backed toward the cruiser. "Tell Mac Faraday that this time he's messing with the wrong people."

CHAPTER TEN

"If it isn't Archie Monday. What a pleasure to see you here."

At the mention of her name, Archie turned around from where she was admiring the early evening's view from the Spencer Inn. She had stopped in for dinner only to be reminded that it was Friday, the night of the mayor's weekly cocktail party. Dressed in casual summer wear, she felt out of place among cocktail dresses and summer suits. With her plate of appetizers, Archie had moved away from the crowd to the edge of the deck when she heard her name called.

The county prosecutor stepped away from Mayor Pete Mason to take Archie's hand. "Did your new roomie bring you as his guest?"

Roy Phillips grasped the lawyer's arm from behind. "I need to talk to you." Seeing Archie, his eyes narrowed. "You! What do you think you're doing here?"

Archie smirked. "I'm here as a guest of the owner. What are you doing here?"

Roy hissed in Ben's direction, "Did Ms. Monday tell you that she threatened to shoot me this afternoon after ordering her dog to attack me?" He held out his arms in his short-sleeved shirt to display deep scratches that ran up his arms and on his throat. "He almost ripped my throat out. I barely escaped with my life."

"Calm down, Roy. I'm sure this is all a misunderstanding." A red cast came to Pete Mason's tanned face.

Archie said to the police chief, "You started it."

"I'm an officer of the law and you, Ms. Monday, pushed your luck too far this time." Seeming to suddenly remember the party guests in earshot, the police chief cleared his throat. "Needless to say, Ben, I'm going to be needing a warrant." He chewed the skin on the side of his index finger.

"A warrant?" the mayor gasped. "Now, Roy, we should talk about this."

Archie turned away. "I'll leave you gentlemen to discuss this issue alone. If you decide to arrest me, you'll find me at the bar."

Ben watched Archie climb onto a bar stool and order a drink before turning to the chief of police. "Phillips, why did you go to Spencer Manor?"

"I went to see Mac Faraday. This morning he led me and a state trooper in a high-speed chase."

Pete suggested, "You can't blame him for having some fun. He's just come into a huge fortune and he has that hot car. Who wouldn't want to make out like a big man on campus?"

Ben brought his point home. "Why did you go chasing after him in the first place?"

"He was speeding."

The prosecutor chuckled. "Speeding?"

The mayor's stern expression showed that he failed to see any humor in the situation. "Don't go messing around with Mickey Forsythe."

"He isn't Mickey Forsythe," Roy Phillips said.

"Even so, Faraday is a direct descendent of this town's founder and there're still a lot of people here in Deep Creek who haven't forgotten the Spencer legacy. With Forsythe's—"

"Faraday," Roy corrected the mayor.

"Whatever." Pete continued, "With his money and lineage, if he decided to make some changes in Spencer, then there won't be anything any of us can do to stop him."

The prosecutor added, "Including run for mayor."

Pete Mason tugged at his shirt collar.

"In other words, Faraday's got a license to make his own laws here in Spencer," the police chief said.

"Cut the bull, Roy. You weren't enforcing the speed limit. You were chasing Faraday because of David O'Callaghan," Ben said.

"Who happened to be in the car with him."

Ben lowered his voice. "I'm not going to be made a fool of prosecuting an innocent man. I don't suppose you compared O'Callaghan's DNA to that found on the dog?"

"The lab doesn't have it yet."

"O'Callaghan went to the lab yesterday to give it to them voluntarily. Why would he do that if he was guilty?"

"He was alone with that dog," Roy replied. "Who's to say he didn't plant someone else's DNA on the mutt to throw us off the trail?"

Ben argued, "He may be good, but he's not that good. If he killed the Singleton woman and got attacked by her dog, his DNA would be all over that mutt. Not only that, but O'Callaghan would have bite wounds on him. He's clean."

"Maybe the dog didn't attack the Singleton woman's killer," Pete suggested. "Maybe he attacked someone else who happened to be there. The dog wasn't found until the next day. They could have been two separate incidents that have nothing to do with each other."

Ben turned to the police chief. "Have you got anything solid to prove O'Callaghan killed the Singleton woman?"

"He slept with the victim and she dumped him," the police chief declared. "That's motive."

"I won't even be able to get this case beyond a preliminary hearing with that." The prosecutor ordered, "Move on to other suspects."

"What about Monday and her dog?"

"In my professional opinion, you should stay away from Archie Monday and leave her alone…and that goes for her little dog, too."

Chief Phillips resumed chewing the middle finger on his left hand when the county prosecutor walked away.

Mayor Pete Mason snatched Roy's hand from his mouth. "You idiot! Back off Mac Faraday."

"Why, Peter? Is he a possible investor?"

"I wish," the mayor said. "Faraday was one of the best homicide detectives in Washington. Nothing could get past him, or can. Now he's picked up a scent of something rotten here in Spencer. If that scent leads him to my door, then you're going to find yourself wishing that dog had ripped your throat out." Mayor Mason signaled a passing server for a refill of his drink.

"How's it going, chief?"

Startled, the two men whirled around.

Travis Turner smirked at them. "You look like you're having a bad day." He gestured across the room in the direction of the county prosecutor. "I guess Fleming refuses to prosecute David O'Callaghan."

Chief Phillips said, "He who has the biggest friends with the biggest wallets wins."

"Too bad." Travis's smile broadened. "Did you ever find out where they were going this morning?"

Pete Mason picked up on the satisfied expression. "Out with it, Turner."

"Lucky for you, O'Callaghan's mom is friends with my aunt, who happens to be a busybody with a big mouth. They're in Washington visiting Faraday's cop friends."

"What for?" the mayor asked.

"Come on," Travis said. "Faraday's a cop, retired or not. Cops may retire, but they don't quit. I learned that while researching my third book." He lowered his voice. "They're checking out Katrina's old clients to see if she cheated anyone else. Weren't you one of her clients, Peter?"

"No."

"I could have sworn one of my sources—"

"Your source is wrong, Turner," the mayor told him. "I never met Katrina until she moved here."

"I guess my source meant someone else," Travis said.

"Must have."

"Lucky for you. Faraday and O'Callaghan's suspect list is the last place you'd want to end up."

The mayor led Roy Phillips away through the crowd. Chuckling, Travis turned around and almost knocked over Archie Monday.

"Excuse me." Travis grabbed her arm when she turned to return to the bar. "Where are you going in such a hurry?" He brushed her arm with his fingers. "I heard Faraday went back to the city. So happens I'm free this weekend."

"I'm not," Archie said. "I have a tight deadline."

"But we all need a break." He brought his face close to hers. "How about if we go someplace quiet?"

She backed away. "What about Sophia?"

"She's in New York." His expression resembled that of a wolf about to devour its prey. "We'll have the place all to ourselves."

"No, thank you." She turned away, but he tightened his grip on her arm.

"Maybe you don't understand." The usually smooth tone in Travis's voice roughened.

Archie looked down at his hand on her wrist. She looked back up at him. "I believe I understand fully." She yanked her arm to free his grip, but he held on. "Move your hand or lose it."

His tone turned menacing. He peered into her eyes. His grip tightened. "The most beautiful women in the world have begged me to make love to them—and you—some little nobody—you think you can say no to me? I'm—"

Before he could finish, Travis's legs buckled. Abruptly, he was on his knees with his throat in Archie's free hand. Her grip made it difficult for him to speak.

"I said no thank you."

In his struggle to take in a breath through the windpipe held in her grasp, Travis released her arm. Beneath his golden tan, his face reddened from lack of oxygen.

She glared down at him. "When a woman says no, she means it. Remember that."

When she released her grip, Travis, gasping for breath, slumped to the floor. The surrounding guests applauded the entertaining scene.

As he climbed to his feet, Travis hissed at Archie, "You bitch. I'm going to kill you for this."

Deciding to leave the Inn before encountering any other conflicts, Archie snatched up her handbag from the bar and headed for the lounge.

At the edge of the crowd, Archie caught sight of someone else who hadn't dressed for the occasion. She wore cream-colored polyester slacks with food stains on her thick thighs. Instead of sandals, she bore old athletic shoes on her sockless feet. On the warm spring night, while the other female guests broke out sleeveless dresses to show off their tans, Betsy opted for an oversized top that resembled a maternity tunic.

Not being one to spend time in the sun, Betsy's complexion was pale. But when Archie approached her, she saw that the blood had drained from her face. Tears spilled out from under her thick glasses to flow down her cheeks.

"Betsy," Archie felt compelled to say, "I'm sorry, but Travis brought that on himself. I told him no." She didn't know if Betsy heard her. Without saying a word, Betsy ran down the stairs.

Over the railing, Archie saw Betsy run towards the garden. Mayor Pete Mason and Chief Roy Phillips were engaged in a serious conversation when she stumbled into the mayor, which caused him to spill his drink on the police chief. She offered no apology for the collision before disappearing into the garden's maze. The two men looked at each other before following her.

* * * *

Archie arrived home from the Spencer Inn in time to enjoy the last bits of sunlight spilling across the lake before it set behind the mountains. She sipped her white wine while resting her head on a cushion on the chaise.

After returning from his evening patrol of the Point, Gnarly stretched out at the bottom of the steps within striking distance of any duck that dared to near the dock. His groan of pleasure matched hers.

"Hello? Archie?" She heard called from around the corner of the house.

Francine Taylor turned the corner of the house and waved to her. Every evening after dinner, the older woman would get her exercise by swimming in the cove. She had combed out her wet silver hair and wore a terry cloth bathrobe over her swimsuit. "I guess it's time for an after dinner drink."

"Care to join me?" Archie held up her glass.

Francine wasted no time in pouring a glass of wine from the bottle Archie had opened and taking a seat in the chaise next to hers. "I have a case for you. I want you to find a hacker." She corrected herself. "Maybe you shouldn't. Because if you do find him, I'll kill him and end up in jail. But then, considering that he's a hacker, the jury will probably refuse to convict."

In a tone that was stating more than asking, Archie replied, "Have you been the victim of a hacker?"

Francine growled before sipping her drink. "He sent me an e-mail with your name on it. It said that it was pictures Robin wanted me to have. I opened one, and the virus swooped in and turned my hard drive into a zombie. Can you take a look at it and see if you can fix it?"

After Francine reported that her computer would turn on, Archie assured her that she would be able to sweep the virus from her hard drive and could recommend a better firewall for her system. "I wonder if your hacker is the same one that's been trying to get a worm into my system," Archie observed. "My firewall has been working overtime lately."

Noting that recently another neighbor's computer had crashed, Francine declared the mystery a case for Mickey Forsythe. "And when he's not tracking down hackers and murderers, maybe he can squeeze in identifying the Point's petty thief."

"Has our thief struck again?"

"Just now. I went for a dip in the lake and when I came back my robe was gone. It's at least five years old. Why would someone steal an old bathrobe? I liked that robe. I had it all broken in. Robin would have caught him by now."

Archie said, "If our petty thief is a kleptomaniac, which I think he is, he's bound to eventually blow his cover or at least get help."

"Couldn't he have gotten help before stealing my robe?" After taking a sip of her wine, Francine asked, "Has Mac tracked down Katrina's killer yet?"

Archie smiled slyly. "You'll have to wait and see."

"I have to tell you that I couldn't believe it when I heard David was a suspect," Francine said. "The ladies at the Hair Hut asked me if I'd seen him here looking suspicious and I told them no. From what I saw, David was trying to help her. It isn't like there weren't enough other people wanting to break her pretty neck." She refilled her glass. "Oh, Gordon Hardwick and Katrina used to get into terrible screaming matches. They called Gnarly a rapist for knocking up their poodle and accused him of getting into their garbage." She laughed. "Gnarly didn't do it. Everyone who lives on Deep Creek knows that the bears like garbage. That's why we get dumpsters. But the Hardwicks refused to get a dumpster. They decided instead to shell out four times more money for a security camera to catch Gnarly." She smirked. "What did they get? Tape of two bears getting into their garbage. But did they ever admit they were wrong about Gnarly? No."

Archie said, "Too bad their camera was broken the night of the murder. They could have recorded Katrina's killer."

"They're lying about that camera being broken," Francine stated with certainty. "They got the bears on film five weeks ago—after Katrina's murder. They lied to the police about their camera because they don't want to do anything to help catch her killer. That would be decent of them and they'd rather burn in hell than do anything decent."

"Did the ladies at the Hair Hut recall Katrina getting into screaming matches with anyone else besides Gordon Hardwick?" Archie asked.

The beauty shop was a fountain of information about goings-on along the Point. Through Francine, Robin could find out what the ladies at the beauty shop were talking about without setting foot in the shop herself.

"Sophia Hainsworth-Turner, for one."

"What about?"

"I never found out what it was about." Francine cocked her head at Archie when she saw that she had missed this piece of information. "One day, I was lying out on the dock and heard a cat fight. Katrina and Miss Calm-Cool-and-Collected herself were screaming at each other. It almost turned physical."

Recalling the scene she had witnessed at the Inn, Archie said, "Sophia does have a temper."

"That's for sure. Sophia isn't all that she seems to be." Francine smirked. "Did you know that she had a police record? She was arrested for assault and attempted murder. She copped a plea in exchange for anger management counseling."

"From what I've seen, it's done a lot of good," Archie said with a note of sarcasm. "How do you even know this?"

The neighbor answered, "One of the girls had read it in one of those gossip magazines. It came out after Sophia got that big contract with the cosmetic company. They even had a picture of her mug shot. She looks horrible without makeup." Francine recounted, "Sophia was making a name for herself as a model when her boyfriend—Do you remember that guy who starred in that television series about vampire hunters? The one with the curly blond hair? He took his shirt off at least once in every episode?"

Archie recalled the hunky actor.

Francine continued, "They dated for a while, but then he dumped Sophia for that actress that plays the bitchie lawyer in one of those legal shows. The blond that wears her skirts up to here." She pointed at her neck. "The new girlfriend started getting threatening phone calls. Her house and car got broken into and trashed."

"Sounds familiar." Archie noted that the incidents Francine listed sounded similar to the harassment Katrina had suffered in the months before her murder.

"One night, Sophia broke in and attacked her. The boyfriend saved her." While clinking her wine glass against her host's, Francine finished, "And that, Ms. Monday, is the skeleton in Ms. Sophia Hainsworth-Turner's closet."

"And what a scary skeleton it is indeed," Archie said.

CHAPTER ELEVEN

"How long will this take?"

Through the crack of the penthouse door, a blue eyeball trimmed in long lashes threatened not to allow Mac and David to enter. They were intruding on Rachel Adams-Singleton's evening out with her new husband.

When she hesitated to keep their appointment, Mac considered being equally rude by informing her that her groom had set the time. Instead, he promised that they would only take a few minutes of their time.

She shut the door. A few minutes later, she permitted them entrance to the top floor penthouse in Crystal City, Virginia. The high-rise condos provided a view of the Potomac River and the planes taking off and landing at Reagan National Airport.

Chad Singleton had wasted no time on mourning since his first wife's death had left him with a forty million dollar estate. Not only did he remarry and quit his job as an associate at the law firm where he had met Katrina, but he also traded up from Niles Holt's brownstone in Georgetown.

Tall and model slim, his trophy wife's red hair fell to her shoulders. Her pale skin made her look like a porcelain doll. Her turquoise dress hugged every curve of her body on its way down to her shapely legs.

She escorted them into the living room and ordered them to wait while she fetched her husband. Mac was admiring the view of the Washington Monument on the other side of the Potomac River when their host made his entrance.

"Good evening, gentlemen." Shorter than Mac imagined, Chad Singleton had the sleek build of a cat. The color of the shirt he wore under his suit matched his wife's dress. "You're lucky you got here when you did," he told them. "My bride and I were about to go out for the evening. We've got reservations at Michel Richard Citronelle," he said as if the name of the restaurant meant something to both of his guests. While it did to Mac, it meant nothing to David.

Chad motioned to the sofa next to where David sat and ordered Mac in a tone disguised as congeniality, "Do sit down."

"No, thanks. I'd rather stand," Mac replied.

Chad directed Rachel into the recliner across from David and stood with his hand on her bare shoulder. "As I told you on the phone, I'm not obligated to speak to either of you."

"And I thank you for taking the time to see us," Mac said.

"What do you want to know?"

Mac began. "What did Katrina tell you about this man tormenting her?"

"That he was Lee Dorcas." Chad let out a chuckle. "The police insisted it wasn't him. She said he looked like him. He had the dreadlocks and beard and wore an army jacket. To tell you the truth, I think you guys are chasing your own tails. You found Dorcas's body in Spencer, didn't you? He blew his brains out after killing Katrina. Face it. You guys blew it. You would have saved her if you had locked Dorcas up after he killed Niles Holt."

Grasping her husband's fingers, Rachel interjected, "We're lucky he didn't decide to do in Chad, too."

David said, "It's hard to disprove an alibi when there are dozens of witnesses swearing that the suspect was hundreds of miles away someplace else."

"Have you ever heard of a plane?" Chad scoffed.

Before David could respond, Mac asked, "Did you ever see Lee Dorcas threaten Katrina?"

"Everyone at Ingram and Henderson saw it," Chad said with a nod of his head. "I'm surprised he didn't shoot her then. Katrina tried to calm him down, but he wouldn't have it. Security finally showed up and hauled his ass out of the building."

"What was he ranting about?" Mac asked.

"He insisted Katrina stole his grandmother's money."

"Had she?" Mac ignored David's glare at the suggestion.

Chad's expression became more smug when he replied, "I wouldn't know any of the details pertaining to how Katrina conducted her accounts. She told me that the old lady spent it."

Mac suppressed a grin. He could see that Chad had all the slimy qualities it took to be a lawyer. He had his suspicions about his late wife, but he knew better than to own up to them. It was to his legal advantage to claim that he had been misled.

Mac resumed the interview by asking, "That day Dorcas came to see Katrina at the law firm, did he threaten her?"

"He threatened to kill her. And now she's dead and you have his body with a self-inflicted gunshot wound. As far as I'm concerned this case is closed."

"The gunshot wound was not self-inflicted," David told him. "That's why the case is still open."

Mac asked, "Did you hear Dorcas threaten to kill Niles Holt?"

Chad shook his head. "Katrina told me he threatened to do that on her wedding day. He showed up in her dressing room."

"When did she tell you that?"

Chad sucked in a deep breath before shrugging his shoulders. "I don't remember."

"Was it before or after Niles died?" Mac inquired.

"After. She told me after we started seeing each other. I do remember that."

David wondered, "If Dorcas had killed Katrina's first husband, weren't you concerned about becoming her second husband, especially when he was still terrorizing her?"

A questioning look crossed his face at the suggestion that marrying Katrina could have put his life in danger. Finally, Chad replied, "I figured Dorcas considered them even."

"Suppose he wasn't the one harassing her," Mac suggested. "Did Katrina have any idea who else it could have been and why he had targeted her?"

"Why do most crazies target anyone? They're nuts."

"Did you ever see him?" Mac asked.

"Never. Like I said, he never showed up when I was around."

David wanted to know, "If he never showed up when you were around, why didn't you stay with her? As her husband, you should have protected her."

"Because I had to be here in the city. Katrina chose to stay at Deep Creek. She was courting the county commission to change the zoning on some land Niles owned," Chad explained. "She was afraid that if she didn't babysit it that the zoning would fall through. It did as soon as she was dead."

"Really?" Mac responded to the new information. "What happened to the land?"

Chad smirked. "I sold it for a nice profit. Now it's someone else's headache." He stroked his new wife's shoulder. "Since I married Rachel, I don't want to spend as much time wheeling and dealing the way Katrina liked to. She wanted the power that comes with money. I intend to enjoy the luxuries it affords."

With his eyes on Rachel, David asked, "How long have you two been seeing each other?"

She glanced up to Chad.

He answered, "We've been friends for a long time."

"Katrina knew about your affair," David said. "She had an appointment scheduled with her lawyer to change her will and file for divorce. Fortunately for you, she was murdered three days before that meeting took place."

"I didn't kill her," Chad said. "The police already checked into that. I had an alibi." He grinned down at Rachel. "A very lovely alibi."

She extended her hand, on which she wore a sapphire ring surrounded by diamonds. "My Valentine's Day present. Chad gave it to me the night of the blizzard after we got stranded together."

Chad said, "I thought what the heck."

David asked, "Before or after your assassin confirmed your wife's death?"

"I resent that."

"Dave?" The expression on Chad's face told Mac that the interview he wasn't obligated to grant them had ended.

David ignored Mac's warning. "Come on. You married Katrina for her money but you also wanted Rachel. You could never have asked her to marry you as long as Katrina was alive."

"If I was going to hire a hit man to kill Katrina, don't you think I would've simply had it done instead of having it dragged out for months?"

"David has a point," Mac said. "You would never have divorced Katrina. Monetarily, you had too much to lose. You couldn't have married Rachel while you were married to Katrina. That's bigamy. Why would you ask your mistress to marry you the same night your wife got killed if you didn't know that she wasn't going to be around to end the party?"

"This interview is over."

After Chad slammed the door behind them, David apologized to Mac. "I guess I blew it."

Mac punched the signal for the elevator to take them down to the garage. "He's right. If he had paid to have Katrina killed, his assassin wouldn't have tormented her for all those months."

The elevator doors opened and they stepped inside.

"If it wasn't a professional hit, then it had to be personal." Mac watched the numbers indicating their descent ten floors to the underground garage where he had parked the Viper three levels below ground.

The doors opened to let them out into the parking garage. When they passed the handicapped parking spaces next to the elevator, the back of a van opened. Three thugs dressed in black baggy clothes with caps pulled down over their ears spilled out. Two more joined them from the front seats on either side of the van.

Mac and David rounded the corner to take them to the back of the garage. When he turned the corner, Mac saw that instead of getting onto the elevator, the five men were sauntering several feet behind them. "Have you got your gun?" he asked David in a low voice.

"Yes. Do you?"

"Always."

David tried to glance over his shoulder. The youths had picked up their pace to close the distance between them. "Are they after us?"

"Do you see anyone else for them to come after?" Mac stopped, whirled around, and yelled, "Are you crazy, man?"

His abrupt action caught the brute about to jump him by surprise. Before his attacker could regroup, the former cop grabbed him and the gun he had pulled out of his waistband. Mac whirled the youth around to use his body as a shield when his cohorts opened fire. Mac returned their fire with both fists; the gun he had taken from his own holster and the assailant's gun still clutched in his hand.

In a matter of seconds, three young men lay dead on the cold gray pavement.

Meanwhile, David dropped back behind the Viper and fired three shots into the chest of a fourth shooter who charged directly into the police officer's open fire. The kid dropped to the ground without one of his shots hitting its target.

David felt a rush of air and a sharp pain hit his bicep. Gripping his arm, he fell back behind the sports car.

All was quiet except for running feet and what sounded like a child's laughter.

David looked up from his bleeding arm to see a boy smiling down at him. In the oversized clothes of his generation and the darkness of the parking garage at night, he looked like a man. Up close, under the glare of a nearby light, the boy's baby face made him resemble a child playing dress-up in his daddy's clothes. His gun too big to hold onto, he held it in a clumsy grip with both hands.

The boy pointed the gun into David's face.

Braced to kill some mother's child, David aimed his gun at the boy.

The blast of gunshots echoed throughout the garage.

David waited for the darkness of death to overtake him.

The boy's eyes filled with surprise. His mouth dropped open. Blood spilled onto David's pant leg. When the boy collapsed, instinctively David held him and patted his back as if to soothe the child in his death.

He looked up at Mac who was standing over the boy. He was ready to fire again if need be. "He would have killed you."

"He isn't even old enough to shave," David objected.

"Those are the worst ones. They get enough practice killing to become pros by the time they do."

CHAPTER TWELVE

Less than two months after retiring from Georgetown's detective squad, Mac Faraday returned. After a visit to the emergency room to mend David's arm, they had a few hours' sleep before meeting Detective Sam Groom at the Georgetown precinct about killing five members of a street gang called the Tarantulas.

Even though Georgetown was out of the Crystal City, Virginia, jurisdiction where the shooting took place, Mac called his former colleague to uncover the motive behind a DC street gang's attempted hit on a retired cop.

Mac had made it a point to wear the suit that his daughter had forced him to have tailored. He also parked his Viper next to Lieutenant Harold Fitzwater's broken-down Dodge. He hated to admit that he wanted to rub his former boss's nose in his windfall. In addition to the suit and car, he brought two boxes of donuts and a carafe of Starbucks coffee for the detectives—the way to his former colleagues' hearts.

In the detectives' squad room, Mac was mobbed by the old gang. After a discussion about the good life of a multi-millionaire, Tony, one of the older detectives, announced, "Hey, Mac, you should have seen Harold this morning. Sam made the mistake of telling him about you taking out five Tarantulas."

"Costello told me that one of them didn't have any diamonds on his back, yet," said a chubby cop. His fellow cops called him Buddy because he was everyone's friend.

Tony said, "Guess last night was his initiation. Lucky thing for us he failed."

"What do you mean about diamonds on his back?" David asked.

Mac explained, "The Tarantulas mark their members with tattoos of a black spider on the back of their neck. The gang member gets a red diamond on the back of the spider for each of his kills."

"If the kill is a cop, then the tarantula gets a white diamond," Tony said without humor.

Mac went on, "If the gang accepts you, then you get the tattoo of the spider. All you get to do is hang out without them killing you, but you aren't a full member until you earn your first diamond."

"By killing someone," David said. "That kid last night—"

"He had no diamonds. He was looking for you to get him his first one. It would have been white."

"That would have made him a real big man on the streets," Tony said. "That's what every Tarantula dreams of: for his first diamond to be a white one."

David asked, "How did they know we were cops? We weren't in uniform."

"Someone had to have told them. Crystal City isn't their turf," Tony said. "Word on the street is they were looking for someone. It had to be you."

"Which makes it self-defense," Mac said.

"And Harold is cussing a blue streak because it didn't go down on his turf so that he could hang you out to dry," Buddy said.

"Even if it was," Tony said, "he doesn't have enough political pull anymore to make it stick since his good friend Steve is on the fast track to hell."

"Steve is on the fast track to hell?" Mac tried to keep from smiling about the misfortune of the assistant district attorney who had caused his divorce.

"He screwed up royally," Buddy told him. "He slept with the defense attorney for the Garland case. While he was in the shower, she went through his drawers, and not the drawers he wanted her to go through. She got information on the case that he didn't want her to have and Garland walked." The big man laughed. "Now Steve spends his days working night court and his lap dog Fitzwater lost his pull in the DA's office."

Mac said, "What goes around comes around."

"Hey, Faraday, you're here early," a bald-headed man with a bushy mustache yelled through the crowd from the doorway. "After getting me out of bed after midnight, you better have saved one of those donuts for me."

Mac reached into the box and found that he was lucky. They had left one chocolate cream-filled donut, Sam's favorite. He held it up to show the detective. "This one has your name on it."

Mac and David followed the wave of Sam's hand out into the corridor and down the hall to an interrogation room. For the first time, Mac found himself sitting on the opposite side of the table, facing the two-way mirror. The position felt odd.

While Sam opened up his folder and notepad, David asked, "Have they IDd the victims from the shooting last night?"

"They got IDs," the detective answered. "Each one was a Tarantula. One of the guys in the gang unit says they got orders last night to take out a couple of off-duty cops."

Mac asked, "From who?"

"Someone on their board," Sam said. "It had to be done last night or today. They were told that you would be driving a red Viper."

"How many red Vipers were there in that parking garage? They simply searched until they found your car, and then they waited for the guys that went with it." David asked the detective, "What did you mean when you said that the order came from someone on their board? They're a bunch of kids playing with real guns. They certainly aren't incorporated."

"Gangs are becoming sophisticated and enterprising. The Tarantulas have backing from a mob in Philadelphia, the Marlstone family."

While the detective continued, Mac sat up straight in his chair.

"The feds have been after the Marlstones for years. They're small but growing. They run drugs, prostitution, and illegal arms. People are afraid of street gangs. So the mob puts the gang on the payroll to do their dirty street work while they pull strings from their corporate offices, kind of like the board of directors giving orders to their minions on the assembly line." Noticing Mac sitting up in his seat, Sam asked, "Did you ever have any cases against the Marlstones?"

"Peter Marlstone," Mac said. "Nine years ago, his wife, Brianna, was found dead in the tub in their penthouse overlooking the river."

"Peter was the nephew of the CEO, Reginald Marlstone," Sam told them. "He was fifth in line to run the empire after his uncle and three cousins."

Mac recalled, "We discovered that Brianna's father was Hector Sanchez, Marlstone's partner in crime. They're from the Southwest."

"Texas?" David asked.

"Houston, I believe," Mac said.

"Pay Back's destination after killing Katrina," said David.

"Small world," Mac replied. "Peter called his wife's death an accident. When I revisited the case a couple of years later, I found physical evidence with technology we didn't have before that proved she was murdered. But when I went looking for him, Peter Marlstone was gone. Right now, there's an outstanding warrant for his arrest."

"I can do you one better on that." Sam grinned. "Information from the feds says that Hector Sanchez put out a contract on Peter Marlstone. The Sanchezes and Marlstones are no longer partners. They're enemies, thanks to Peter, who disappeared after embezzling millions of dollars from the Sanchez family. If he isn't dead, he's hiding deep in the underground."

"And what a better place to lay low than on a lake in a small town in the woods," Mac said.

David said to Mac, "You can't be talking about Pete Mason."

"Cosmetic surgery. Cheek implants. Nose job. He must have lost about thirty pounds and pumped himself up. I knew I'd seen him before, but couldn't place him." Mac asked David, "When did he show up in Deep Creek Lake?"

"Maybe five years ago." David corrected himself. "He's been mayor for four years and lived in Deep Creek a couple of years before that. More like six."

Sam said, "Marlstone calls in his old gang."

"If Peter ordered the Tarantulas to kill us, then that means he still has connections to the family business," Mac said.

Realizing that he was right, Sam sat back in his chair. "He's working behind the scenes. Easy to do nowadays between computers, blackberries, and the Internet."

"Is there anybody else on that contract Sanchez put out on Marlstone?" asked Mac.

Sam squinted at him. "Who do you have in mind?"

"Pete Mason brought in a friend that he made police chief in Spencer." Mac laughed. "How better to run an illegal business than to have a good buddy be the chief of police? Any thoughts on who he might be?"

Sam chuckled. "Tall skinny guy? Real nervous type?"

David and Mac nodded their heads.

"Marlstone had help stealing that money from the Sanchez family. Their accountant, Roy Herman. One night, Herman had taken one too many Valium with one too many drinks and got behind the wheel. He killed a couple of teenage girls. Marlstone bailed him out. Forty-eight hours after that, they were gone with fifteen million dollars of Sanchez's money."

"So they are wanted by both the police and the mob." David sucked in a deep breath. "And Spencer has been depending on a pencil-pushing mob accountant for our safety and security. No wonder Katrina got killed."

Mac asked Sam, "Did the Holts have any connection to the Marlstone or Sanchez family?"

"I'll put in a call to our connection with the feds to find out. Marlstone probably ordered the hit because you recognized him."

"Someone killed both Niles Holt and his wife," Mac said. "Peter Marlstone is a killer. He's worth taking a closer look at."

The door to the interrogation room opened so abruptly that all three men instinctively reached for their guns.

The slender man in the doorway wore a gray suit that had seen better days. He would have appeared much taller if he didn't slouch.

Mac felt his stomach tighten at the sight of his former boss, Lieutenant Harold Fitzwater.

Sam pursed his lips to conceal a chuckle—in anticipation of what, Mac was not sure. The detective's thick mustache wiggled up and down and side to side in a comical fashion while its owner directed his attention to a report in a folder.

"Faraday," Lieutenant Fitzwater snapped. "I want to talk to you." Leaving the door open for Mac to follow, he disappeared down the hallway. His demeanor made Mac wonder if he had forgotten that the retired detective no longer worked for him.

Sam and David mentally waged a bet. Would Mac follow or would he not?

As if the lieutenant's order had never happened Mac asked Sam, "What does the DA in Arlington say about the shootings last night?"

Fitzwater stepped back into the room. "If you have a minute?" A note of courtesy found its way into his tone.

His face void of emotion, Mac looked up at him.

"Please."

"I guess I can give you one minute." Mac strolled out into the corridor.

The chief of homicide's office consisted of a cubicle in the corner of the squad room. Its thin walls contained windows that looked out over his domain.

Once inside, Harold slammed the door so hard that his office walls shook. His eyes narrowed to slits. "Did you make a visit to Internal Affairs on your way out of here?"

Mac chuckled when he answered, "No."

"You're lying, Faraday!" The lieutenant slapped his inbox from the corner of the desk to the floor. Mac sensed that he wanted to hit him instead of the papers.

"I don't lie, even when my career is being threatened, as you surely know." Mac fought the urge to smile. "What happened, Harold? Internal Affairs catch up with you and Steve about the Gibbons case?"

"You did rat me out!"

"As much as I wanted to, I kept my mouth shut and trusted that they would get wind of you and a certain assistant district attorney helping a serial rapist escape prosecution." He laughed. "They're not stupid. Everyone knew that something dirty happened. It wasn't a coincidence that the Gibbons kid got on that plane when he did. They caught up with you, didn't they? What are they going to do?"

"The DA is prosecuting me for accepting a bribe." He added in a low, threatening tone, "When I find out who ratted me out…"

Mac looked out into the squad room. He had been tempted to go to Internal Affairs. He spent months putting the Gibbons case together. He wondered at the time why the lieutenant kept urging him to look for the Rock Creek Park serial rapist somewhere other than where the evidence led him. Until Archie connected the dots between Steve Maguire, Harold Fitzwater, and Gibbons's father, it never occurred to him that his boss was dirty. He had been too close to see it.

Mac watched through the window as Sam and David returned to the detective's desk in the squad room.

Mac said, "Don't you remember? Even the media speculated that someone on the inside must have given Gibbons the heads up."

While the other detectives glanced curiously at the closed office door, Sam didn't look up once. Mac recalled that Sam had transferred to homicide from uptown less than a month after Freddie Gibbons Jr. got away.

"You're a dirty cop, Harold."

"I'm not dirty." The lieutenant said, "I was simply playing the game—the same game everyone else plays."

"Bull! Haven't you figured it out yet? Your political game-playing with Steve put a bullet in your career. Even if you manage to get out of this, none of them—" Mac gestured at the detectives on the other side of the office walls, "are ever going to trust you again. They aren't going to be watching your back because you didn't watch mine." He grinned. "I wonder what Freddie Gibbons is doing right now. How many European girls has he raped since you let him go?"

"You son of a bitch," Harold hissed, "standing there in your five thousand dollar suit. You brought me down for what? Revenge?"

"I didn't bring you down, Harold. You brought yourself down when you cut the deal." Mac opened the door. "By the way, this isn't a five thousand dollar suit. It's a fifteen thousand dollar suit. I paid more for this jacket than your car is worth."

David stood up when he saw Mac leave his former boss's office. "Ready to go?"

"I am if you are." Mac offered Sam his hand. "Thank you for all your help." Gripping his hand, he whispered into the detective's ear. "You're IA, aren't you?"

Sam answered with nothing more than a grin.

* * * *

"Okay, Bogie," David said into his cell phone. "Let us know if they do anything suspicious. And be sure to tell the guys not to do anything to let Herman and Marlstone know that we're onto them." He flipped the phone shut and turned to Mac.

They were waiting for Ron Goldstein, Katrina's estate lawyer, at an outdoor café nestled between two high-rise office buildings on a corner of M Street.

By Saturday afternoon, patrons would crowd the downtown eateries to fill each other in on the week while planning for the weekend ahead. There was so much to do, and so little time to do it.

Two tables away, a party of young women drank Bloody Marys while gaily recounting the events of happy hour the night before. One with short dark hair and huge eyes laughed with delight when David accepted a Bloody Mary that she had sent to him.

After snagging a table at the eatery, David called Bogie with the news about their mayor and police chief. Detective Groom and Mac had warned that they couldn't arrest the fugitives until the police were positive that Mayor Mason was indeed Peter Marlstone and Roy Phillips was Roy Herman. Pete Mason didn't resemble Peter Marlstone enough for Mac to make a positive identification. While waiting to get the proof they needed, David enlisted his friends on the Spencer police force to keep an eye on both of them to ensure they didn't escape.

When he turned to report on his conversation with Bogie, David found Mac staring into space. "What are you thinking so hard about?"

Blinking, Mac's thoughts snapped back long enough to answer him. "Everything."

Their server refilled Mac's coffee while David paused to sip his Bloody Mary.

"Who's Pay Back? Why did he pretend to be Lee Dorcas? Did Dorcas play any role in this other than patsy?" He seemed to be muttering more to himself than David. "Niles's murder. That wasn't a professional hit. Pros don't leave witnesses. If Peter Marlstone was behind Niles's murder, Katrina would have been tossed off Abigail's Rock along with him."

He sat up straight when he spotted a man with thick curly hair craning his neck to search the faces of the customers. His clothes were so wrinkled, he looked as if he had worn them to bed. Seeing Mac, he scurried toward their table.

"Here's Ron Goldstein to give us the goods on Katrina and Chad." Mac stood to shake the lawyer's hand and introduce themselves.

"Nice to meet you," the attorney said. "I'm glad you called." He sat across from them while straightening his clothes. "These last few weeks have not been easy ones." He tucked his shirt into the waistband of his pants.

Mac asked, "Were you close friends with Katrina?"

"Lawyers don't have friends. They have connections." Ron caught the server's attention and pointed at Mac's cup to signal an order for coffee. "I was Katrina's connection until she married Holt's millions."

The server had finished filling the lawyer's cup, which he snatched to gulp. After letting out a sigh, Ron said, "I guess you came to the right place if you're looking for someone who knew her. I knew both her and Chad before, during, and after they scored their respective fortunes."

"Then let's start with the obvious," Mac said. "Who had the most to gain by Katrina's death?"

Ron replied, "That's easy. Chad. He charmed Katrina into changing her will to make him her beneficiary before the ink dried on their marriage certificate."

"I assume they had a pre-nup," Mac said.

"That, too. In the case of divorce, Chad would have gotten one hundred thousand dollars for every year they were married."

David said, "But Katrina had an appointment scheduled with you to change her will and file for divorce."

"Katrina wasn't as stupid as Chad liked to think," Ron said. "Everyone knew about Rachel. They've been together since forever."

"If she knew about Rachel, why did Katrina marry him?" Mac wanted to know.

"Because Katrina wanted him," Ron answered. "Katrina liked to have things. They started at the firm at the same time. Chad is a good-looking man. Katrina liked good-looking men. She pursued him, but got nowhere because he already had a gorgeous, but poor, girlfriend."

Mac started to ask, "If Rachel and Chad were an item—"

"Chad wanted money," the lawyer interjected. "Rachel had everything except that. They have both been digging for gold since they hit Washington. You should have seen some of the rich widows and divorcees Chad courted. Rachel knows first-hand which congressmen and senators are unfaithful to their wives. Chad finally struck gold with Katrina after she became Niles Holt's widow. He seduced her into thinking that he was always in love with her. I guess she wanted it enough to believe him—until after the nuptials."

Mac sat forward in his seat. "Is it possible that Katrina and Chad started seeing each other before Niles Holt died?"

"Only casually," Ron answered without hesitation. "I'm sure Katrina got off on screwing around with Chad behind Rachel's back. But he had no intention of making a commitment to Katrina until after she became a rich widow."

"Do you recall Chad being there when Lee Dorcas had that altercation with Katrina over the money missing from his grandmother's estate?"

"I couldn't swear to it."

David asked, "Did you witness it?"

Ron nodded his head quickly. "The whole thing. I thought Dorcas was going to kill her then and there."

"Did Ingram and Henderson investigate his claim of embezzlement?" Mac asked.

"We had no choice. He sued us." The lawyer signaled the server for more coffee. "We settled out of court."

After the waiter refilled their cups and moved on to another table, David told him, "Katrina told me that the judge threw the case out due to lack of evidence."

"That's not the first lie Katrina told," Ron laughed. "We threw Lee Dorcas a bone to go away and he did."

Mac asked, "How much money did Katrina steal from his grandmother?"

"I didn't say that she did."

"Ingram and Henderson has the biggest, baddest lawyers in DC working for them. If Katrina didn't do anything wrong, then you would have fought the suit to protect the firm's reputation."

After glancing around to ensure no one could hear, Ron confessed, "We did find evidence of wrongdoing. Like you said, we have the highest-paid attorneys with the most impeccable reputations working for us. We could have dragged his suit out in the courts until Lee Dorcas was old and gray. But he wanted money for his music career and he wanted it now. So we settled."

"For how much?" David wanted to know.

"We gave him back what Katrina had stolen, plus a hundred thousand dollars for restitution. He got half a million dollars. That's a pretty big bone, if you ask me."

"But you didn't file any charges against Katrina for embezzling his grandma's nest egg," Mac noted.

His eyes wide with fear at the suggestion, Ron shook his head. "That wouldn't have done our firm's reputation any good. Katrina resigned and the case was quietly settled."

David wondered, "Was Lee Dorcas satisfied with the settlement?"

"He got everything he lost and then some," Ron reminded them. "What more could he want?"

"Maybe he wanted a pound of flesh," Mac suggested.

Ron stared down into his coffee mug. His eyes took on a faraway look.

"What are you thinking about?"

"After Dorcas filed his suit, I was assigned ass-kissing duty." Ron chuckled. "I actually managed to get Dorcas to bring his accounts back to Ingram and Henderson as long as I handled his money."

"You must kiss ass with the best of them," Mac said.

"A couple weeks after Niles Holt died—less than a month for sure," Ron recalled, "Dorcas came into my office with a cash deposit. One hundred thousand dollars."

David interrupted him to ask, "Why'd he bring it to you and not a bank?"

"Good question," Ron said. "The most obvious answer is that it came from a less than up-and-up source. You take a hundred thousand dollars in cash up to a bank teller and eyebrows will raise, tongues will wag, and questions will be asked. By bringing it to me, the money was quietly deposited into his account without a lot of questions."

Mac asked, "Where did the money come from?"

"He never told me," Ron answered, "but he had the biggest grin I ever saw."

"It couldn't have been a payoff for killing Holt," David said to Mac. "Dorcas had an alibi."

Mac pointed out, "Unless he had chartered a private plane to get him to Deep Creek and then to his singing gig. Jackson's not the only pilot in the world. But I doubt if he would have done Katrina any favors by killing her husband so that she could inherit forty mil."

Ron held up his hands. "I'm only telling you what happened. The guy was a no-talent musician living off his inheritance. Money always went out of Dorcas's account. It never went in except that one and only time. That's why it stood out in my mind."

They drank their respective drinks in silence while considering the possibilities.

Ron broke the silence. "Katrina never ran for Miss Congeniality. Other people probably wanted to kill her for reasons besides money."

"Who else would want her dead?" David asked.

"More than one associate at the firm," Ron said. "Katrina stole other people's ideas, as well as her clients' money. She'd charm new associates to do her work for her and then take the credit. She screwed over more than one lawyer to move up." He added, "Niles Holt was my client. She wined and dined him—stabbed me in the back a few times—until Niles switched his account to her."

"How long ago was that?" Mac asked.

"Four years ago." Ron laughed. "Don't go looking at me. In spite of Katrina's crap, I'm now a partner, thanks in part to cleaning up her messes after she left."

When Mac inquired if Katrina had any clients connected to the Marlstone syndicate, Ron bristled. "We don't knowingly represent drug dealers or anyone involved in organized crime. We didn't know what Peter Marlstone was until Katrina had us in deep."

David asked, "Did Katrina steal from them?"

Ron's face flushed. "After the Dorcas case, our book-keeping department went over her accounts with a fine-tooth comb. Peter Marlstone had already withdrawn his money and disappeared by the time the feds came looking for a paper trail. Two years ago, when bookkeeping went through Katrina's accounts from then, they found half a million dollars missing from his account. It's weird. He never filed a complaint about it."

"Probably because he didn't have time to stick around to litigate." Mac went on, "What about Chad? Where did he fit in the firm?"

"Chad kissed butts and stabbed backs, but he wasn't that good a lawyer. He knew how to look more important than he really was." He added with a small grin, "Rachel may be gorgeous, but she is nowhere near as smart as Katrina was. She believes everything Chad says and does. I can't believe she stood still to let him marry Katrina, even if it was only supposed to be temporary."

David asked, "How did Rachel expect him to end his marriage if he was only going to get one hundred thou per year?"

Ron cleared his throat. "To tell you the truth, I don't think Rachel is smart enough to think that far."

"Do you think she would have married Chad if he was planning murder?" Mac asked.

Ron shrugged. "You got me."

"Do you think she's capable of arranging to have Katrina killed to free Chad to marry her?"

The lawyer paused. "I don't know. Rachel isn't very bright, but now that you mention it, it could be an act."

David saw Mac sit up straight.

Ron seemed to see it, too. "What did I say?"

"An act," Mac muttered. "It could be just an act."

* * * *

"Oh, this is such a lovely home," Debra Gerald gushed to Archie while gazing across the grounds from Spencer Manor's front porch. "I would love so much to work here."

According to her resume, this applicant fit the bill. Debra was clean, well-spoken, polite, and had experience both as a cook and housekeeper in some of the finest homes in Charlotte, North Carolina. She also claimed to like dogs.

Unfortunately, Gnarly didn't like her. Soon after Debra arrived, he began barking and pawing at the oversized handbag she clutched under her arm. He became such a nuisance that Archie had to lock him in her cottage before giving the applicant a tour of the house.

Other than Gnarly, the interview went well. All Archie had to do before offering Debra the job was to check her references and schedule an interview with Mac.

"I'll call you tomorrow with a time that Mr. Faraday can see you," Archie said while she escorted Debra to the car.

Suddenly, Gnarly tore around the corner of the house. Somehow, he had escaped the cottage.

"Gnarly! No! Stop!" Archie shrieked when the large dog charged toward the prospective housekeeper.

In mid-air, Gnarly grasped the corner of Debra's bag in his jaws.

"Stop it!" Debra pulled on the bag by the straps.

Growling, Gnarly held onto the bag for all it was worth.

"I don't know why he doesn't like me," Debra called out to Archie. "Most dogs love me."

"Drop it, Gnarly!" Archie hit him with her open palms. "I don't know what's gotten into him."

"Let go of it, you dumb mutt." Determined to win the tug of war, Debra whacked the dog's snout with her fist.

Gnarly twisted his head and shook the bag until it tore to spill its contents.

When she saw what had scattered in the driveway, Archie screamed.

The bag had contained an array of personal mementoes, jewels, watches, silver, knick-knacks, and other priceless memorabilia—all taken from inside Spencer Manor. Debra had grabbed everything she could lay her hands on during the job interview and tour of the house.

"You're a thief. That's why Gnarly doesn't like you."

Debra dropped the bag and ran for her car. Leaving tread in the driveway, the thief drove off between the stone pillars and on up the Point.

"That's another applicant I need to cross off our list."

* * * *

After lunch, Mac and David stopped at the Old Ebbitt Grill on Fifteenth Street in downtown Washington. Piquing their curiosity when she asked that they not tell her husband, Rachel Singleton had scheduled the meeting that morning.

She was nursing a gin and tonic at a booth in a dark corner. Looking like a model belonging on the cover of a society magazine in a jade suit with matching jewels, Rachel stood out even in a restaurant that catered to the city's most beautiful people.

"Thank you for seeing me," she said. "You got Chad so mad last night that he threatened to call his lawyer if you try to question him again. I thought maybe if you knew the truth about Katrina that you'd understand why he walked away from her the way he did."

When the server appeared, she told them to order anything they wanted. She was buying. Mac ordered a beer on tap while David ordered a mineral water.

Wordlessly, they eyed the server until he left before Mac asked, "What truth do you want to share with us?"

"Katrina was nuts." When the two men responded with silence, she rattled on, "Yes, Chad married her for her money. She chased him for years but he loved me. Then, after her first husband died and she inherited all that money, he thought what the heck. Who wouldn't?"

"And you didn't mind your boyfriend sleeping with another woman for her money?" David asked doubtfully.

"Katrina cheated, too," Rachel said. "She had a lover in Deep Creek after she married Chad."

David's cheeks took on a shade of pink.

"Did Chad tell you that?" Mac asked her.

Silently, they waited while the server delivered their drinks. They didn't resume their conversation until he was out of earshot.

Rachel told them, "Less than two months after they got married, Chad smelled another man's cologne on his bathrobe when he went to the lake. Katrina said it was her perfume. She lied."

"Did Chad ever talk to you about Pay Back and how he hurt Katrina?" David's tone betrayed his disbelief of Chad's compassion for his wife's terror.

"It wasn't what you think," she argued. "At first Chad did believe that someone was after Katrina. But then, when no one could catch the guy, and when she started really losing it, we started to wonder."

David suggested, "Maybe she was losing it because no one could help her."

"Maybe if she told the truth once in a while someone would have wanted to help her."

"Wait a minute," Mac interjected, "what did she lie about?"

"First, she said this crazy client killed Niles," Rachel recalled. "After the police said that it couldn't have been him, she said the killer looked like him. Then, she said that she was being attacked in Deep Creek while Chad was working here during the week. The police interrogated Chad. They told him that she said that she was being harassed while she was living here, before she went back to Deep Creek, and that the stalker had to have followed her from Washington to Deep Creek." Shaking her head, Rachel's face contorted with contempt. "Nothing happened to her here."

Surprised by the announcement, David looked at Mac, who asked, "Are you talking about the time period between Niles Holt's murder and when Katrina returned to Spencer after marrying Chad?"

"Yes," she answered. "Katrina told the police that someone had been after her all along since this Dorcas guy threatened her the first time. But I was here in the city that whole winter after Niles died. Chad was with her all the time. Nothing happened. Check with the police. She never reported anything because nothing happened."

David seemed to ask both of them, "Why would Katrina lie about something like that?"

"That's something you need to ask a shrink." Rachel reached into her purse and slapped a micro cassette recorder in the center of the table. "She would get drunk and make really weird phone calls to Chad saying all this wild stuff. After this one he decided that she didn't have enough money to make him stick around. That's why he went ahead and gave me the ring. He figured that if he could hold on until June, then it would be one year and he would get a hundred thousand dollars and get out."

Mac picked up the recorder and hit the Play button.

They recognized the smooth male voice from the night before. "Katrina, what do you want me to do? I'm four hours away. Why don't you call the police when this guy shows up?"

"I have." Her high-pitched voice was choked with tears. "It's always the same. They come out here, check the security system, and say it's working fine. They can't find how he gets in here. He knows."

"Knows what?" Chad asked with an impatient tone.

"He knows!" she sobbed. "He's like some demon that appears out of nowhere and knows everything. Pay Back is hell!"

"Eventually, he's going to slip up and the police will catch him."

"No, he won't."

"Of course he will."

"You just don't understand. The police *can't* catch him because he's Pay Back."

"What does he know, Katrina?" Chad begged, "Tell me what he knows."

"What I did!" She sucked in a shuddering breath and let it out. "He's Pay Back! He's hell personified!"

"Katrina, how much have you had to drink?"

"Not enough."

He ordered, "Go to bed."

"You know, Chad, you aren't completely innocent either. We're both cut from the same cloth. I've done nothing that you're not capable of doing yourself."

"I hate talking to you when you're like this, Katrina."

"I know about Rachel."

"And I know about your lover. I may not know his name, but I know he's been wearing my bathrobe."

"That means we're both cheats," she said. "So tell me, Chad, how much does Rachel love you?"

"Good night, Katrina."

"Does she love you enough not to kill you after you get all my money?"

"You're crazy."

"Do you even know, Chad? Or do you know and you're afraid of the answer?"

"I'm hanging up."

"I wouldn't go up to Abigail's Rock with her if I were you, Chad."

Click.

Rachel turned off the machine.

Mac looked over at David. His cheeks were no longer pink. Now his face was white.

"See?" Rachel asked them. "Katrina was crazy. That's why Chad wanted out. After this phone call, he wanted to get as far from her as possible. That's why he never went back to the lake."

"Can I have this tape?" Mac asked.

"You certainly can. It's a copy. Chad's lawyer has the original to use if something ever happened."

"Something did happen," Mac reminded her. "Someone killed her."

CHAPTER THIRTEEN

Mac checked the time on his watch while turning the Viper onto Spencer Point. Instinctively, he wanted to keep his eyes averted when he passed the Hardwick home, but curiosity overcame his bitterness toward the neighbors.

A van with a cockroach huge enough to take up the whole side panel rested in their driveway. The name splashed on the door indicated that it belonged to a pest exterminator.

Carrying what resembled an oxygen tank, a man in white overalls jogged out the front door and across the driveway. His long ash-colored hair, fashioned in dreadlocks that looked more like a bird's nest, hung down to the middle of his back. He made a failed attempt to cover up the nest with a white ball cap pulled down over the top of his head. Dark reflective sun glasses concealed his eyes.

The exterminator jumped into the front seat of the van and slammed the door shut.

Mac didn't know if he found the man with the tank so interesting because of the contrast between the stark white overalls and the bushy hair, or maybe because the Hardwicks had bug problems.

When he saw Archie sitting on the front steps, he recalled his reason for hurrying home. Hoping that she was waiting for him, he gunned the engine to take him up to the front door.

Gnarly's non-stop barking punctuated his elation. Archie claimed it had started before Mac pulled into the driveway. She assumed that the dog's sensitive ears had picked up the sound of the Viper's engine and Gnarly was excited about his master's return home. She appeared to be wrong. Becoming increasingly agitated, Gnarly threatened to charge through the stone entranceway at whatever was upsetting him.

"Gnarly, will you shut up?" Mac ordered when he couldn't hear Archie tell him about the events of her weekend.

As if to answer him, Gnarly jumped up to plant his paws on Mac's chest. He then whirled around and once again perched between the pillars to resume barking.

"What's wrong with you?" Archie asked Gnarly. "The thief is gone and she won't be back."

Whining, Gnarly hung his head and turned in a circle before plopping down in the driveway.

With a shake of her head, Archie followed Mac inside the house.

* * * *

"Where's the bologna?"

Mac swore that he had left an unopened pound of bologna in the refrigerator before he went to Washington. Now it was gone.

Archie hadn't eaten it. She didn't like processed meat. He learned this fact when she screwed up her nose and uttered an "ugh" noise after he had offered her a hot dog.

He became distracted in his search for the missing lunchmeat when, through the kitchen window, he spotted Archie in the hot tub out at the tip of the Point. Soft blue lights under the water along the walkway and around the gazebo cast the spa in a dreamy air. She had warned him that sometimes she would soak naked in the hot tub. Mesmerized with visions from the depths of his imagination, he stared at the tub until he recalled his manners, stepped back from the window, and returned to preparing dinner.

With the lunchmeat missing, Mac settled for a peanut butter and jelly sandwich with a glass of milk.

"Light dinner?" he heard Archie ask while he was returning the ingredients for his meal to the fridge. She had slipped into her red robe to cover up.

Fearing that she would see him trying to determine if she wore anything under the robe, he kept his back to her. "Someone stole my bologna."

"Don't look at me." Screwing up her nose at the mention of the lunchmeat, she sat at the kitchen table. "Maybe Gnarly did it."

"Oh, yeah, I can see him opening the fridge, stealing my food, and then closing the door behind him."

She smiled up at him when he crossed the room with his plate and glass. "Gnarly nabbed that thief pretending to be a job applicant."

He sat across from her. "I never said he wasn't smart. He is. Like a fox." He took a bite of his sandwich.

"Did you know he had an identity chip? The vet found it when David took him in after the murder," she told him. "Chad Singleton never changed his registration. This weekend, I went online to register him and guess who Gnarly was registered to. The United States Army."

"The army? What was he trained for? Stealing food from the enemy?"

She shrugged. "They wouldn't tell me. But they did tell me that he was dishonorably discharged."

"How does a *dog* get dishonorably discharged from the United States Army?"

"You got me. They refused to talk about it. This rude woman said that it was classified and then started interrogating me."

Mac looked at the sandwich in his hand. The bologna, along with the butter and bacon, was missing. On the surface, Archie's theory that Gnarly was stealing food from his fridge was laughable. Mac swore that more than once the dog distracted him so that he could steal food from his plate. But could Gnarly really take food out of the fridge and close the door behind him? If so, that would explain why food he swore he hadn't eaten disappeared.

"Where is Gnarly?" Archie asked.

"Sulking someplace. He wouldn't stop barking until I whacked him on the snout. The last I saw him, he ran downstairs to crawl behind the sofa." Mac raised his voice. "Gnarly!"

She joined in the call. "Gnarly! Come here, boy!" She called for the dog out the deck door.

Within moments they heard the familiar jangle of Gnarly's tags and the click of his paws on the stone steps leading up from the home theater on the ground floor.

With a thick cloth handbag clutched between his jaws, the German shepherd emerged at the top of the stairs. Purple flowers decorated the torn and discolored bag that hung from threadbare shoulder straps.

Archie said, "That isn't the same bag he took off the thief."

"Let me take a look at that." When Mac reached for it, Gnarly jerked his head away and turned to escape with his prize. Anticipating the move, Mac blocked his path and grasped one corner of the bag. It contained something thick and heavy. After a tug-of-war, he extracted the bag from the dog's jaws.

"Where did he get this?" Mac turned to Archie. "Could it be Robin's?"

"I thought I threw away all of her old handbags."

He asked Gnarly, "Where did you get this?" Sitting at his feet, Gnarly answered by looking over his shoulder through the French doors to the outside.

The bag contained a large brown sealed envelope. Two labels on the front indicated that it had been mailed special delivery with a signature required. Both the return address and the addressee were the same: Betsy Weaver in Los Angeles, California.

"Betsy Weaver?" Mac looked across the table at Archie. "Why do I know that name?"

"Travis's assistant," she reminded him. "You've never actually met her. She was at the bar that night we took David and Violet out to dinner."

"Why would she mail a package to herself special delivery with a signature required?"

Gnarly charged before she could answer. With a single bound, he captured the bag out of Mac's hand and ran back down the stairs to the play room and home theater.

"Follow him," Mac ordered.

Leaving the package on the kitchen table, they ran down the stairs in time to see Gnarly burrow behind the leather sofa.

"Why do I think my Blackberry is back there?" Mac asked. "Grab an end."

They moved the sofa out from the wall.

Surprised by the intrusion, the German shepherd sat up from his nest of treasures: towels, beach blankets, women's handbags, wallets, keys, shoes, cell phones, and empty food wrappers. The most recent addition was a pack of bologna.

Archie broke into a round of giggles. "Someone has been a very busy doggie."

"Someone has been a very naughty doggie." Mac picked up a chewed-up wallet that still contained cash and credit cards. He read the name to find that it belonged to a neighbor from the other end of the Point. "David said the petty thefts started shortly after Pay Back arrived on the scene. Shortly after Pay Back showed up, Katrina got Gnarly for protection. The thief wasn't Pay Back. The dog protecting her from Pay Back was the thief."

Spying a pair of chewed-up pink pumps with stiletto heels, Archie shrieked. "My shoes! Bad dog!"

Gnarly darted between them and escaped up the stairs with the cloth handbag still in his possession. They let him go to dig through his treasures. The loot included Mac's Blackberry and Archie's phone.

"Now do you believe me that Gnarly is smart enough to open and close the refrigerator door?" she asked.

With both hands, Mac held up fistfuls of empty food wrappers. "I think this evidence makes him a strong suspect."

He picked six wallets and eleven purses from the nest of stolen goods. The handbags contained cosmetics, cell phones, keys, and wallets. Gnarly appeared to be more interested in chewing on the outside than the goods inside. Archie knew the victims of the thefts. They all lived on the Point and across the cove.

"Do you have any idea how difficult it is to replace lost credit cards?" Mac picked up a wallet that she had discarded.

"Oh, lighten up. It isn't like Gnarly went out and bought a home theatre with them."

Covered in dirt and food and grease stains, one wallet appeared more worn than the others. The discolored and mildewed leather had been chewed to bits. Along with thirty-seven dollars in cash, the pockets contained credit cards and identification.

Mac dug his fingers inside the card section to extract the driver's license that had been pierced by Gnarly's teeth. He observed the expiration date first. Issued by the Commonwealth of Virginia, it was scheduled to expire in four years. After studying the photograph and name of the wallet's owner, he did a double-take. The long, bushy, ash-colored hair was twisted into dreadlocks.

"Look at this." He handed the license to Archie.

Her eyes squinted while she studied the image. When the image registered with her, they grew wide. "No way!"

"He kind of looks like the bug man I saw coming out of the Hardwicks' place this afternoon." Mac studied the license again. It had been issued to Lee J. Dorcas.

Archie wondered, "Do you think that maybe Gnarly had dug this up in the mine after finding his body?"

"Dorcas disappeared in February. Cash, credit cards, ID. Nothing appears to be missing. Look at all these teeth marks. Gnarly must have had this for months." Mac scratched his head while he thought. "The killer dumped Dorcas's body in the mine, a popular spot for hikers. He had to know that the body would be found eventually."

"Long after he took off on a chartered flight to Houston," she said.

"Why would his killer pretend to be Dorcas on the flight to Houston? Why not someone else? Someone completely off the radar?"

"To throw the police off his trail," Archie answered. "If Phillips thought he had left the area, then the police wouldn't be looking for him here."

Mac stood up. "I'm calling Fleming."

* * * *

"What are we talking about here? Immunity from prosecution for theft in exchange for Gnarly's cooperation in identifying Dorcas's killer?" Ben Fleming found it impossible to keep the amusement out of his voice when Mac phoned him about the chewed-up loot stashed behind the sofa. "Considering what you just told me, I think Gnarly is a canine of interest in this case."

Once again, Mac was gazing down at the gazebo where Archie waited for him. She had been wearing her red swimsuit under the robe.

"Hey, Ben, what do you know about Pete Mason?"

"He's a pompous ass."

"Did you know that Katrina used to be his investment lawyer?"

"No," Ben said, "but now that you mention it, Mason never did welcome Katrina into Spencer society. I wondered about that."

"Her firm says a half a million dollars disappeared from Mason's accounts, but he never filed a claim or charges against her."

"Maybe Mason decided to take care of it himself," Ben suggested.

After promising to talk more the next day, Mac hung up and went upstairs to change into his swim trunks. There, he found Gnarly on his bed ripping Betsy Weaver's bag into tattered pieces.

"What are you doing?"

Leaving the shredded handbag behind, Gnarly jumped off the bed and crawled under it.

"Unbelievable." He picked up the bits of slimy cloth and cotton filler from the comforter. "A dog burglar living under my own roof." He tossed the handbag into the trash on his way into the walk-in closet.

In the privacy of Spencer Point, secure behind a line of trees, Mac and Archie relaxed in the hot tub against the jets pulsating their bodies.

After he had slipped into the water next to her, she asked, "Did you find out anything in Washington?"

He shrugged while pouring a glass of wine from the bottle she had opened for them to share. "We met Chad Singleton and his new bride."

"What's she like?"

"Very beautiful."

Archie cocked her head at him. Her eyes narrowed. "How beautiful?"

"She's blindly in love with her husband," Mac said. "She claims no one bothered Katrina while she lived in Washington after Niles died." He felt her foot brush against the inside of his leg. He wondered if it was an accident. Considering that the tub was large enough to hold ten people, he doubted it. He kept his leg still.

"Maybe Katrina was but didn't tell Rachel. It isn't like Katrina would have confided in her."

"Maybe," Mac said. "Where did Pay Back come from?"

"Everyone wondered that."

"Someone said something about putting on an act. That got me thinking. Pay Back was all just an act," he said. "He had to learn enough about Lee Dorcas to know what he looked like and how he behaved. Then Pay Back put on an act, impersonating a man who had a score to settle with Katrina. That would answer the question about where Pay Back went when he wasn't terrorizing Katrina. Where did he go? Home to change out of his Pay Back costume to re-emerge as fill-in-the-blank."

Mac was on a roll. "And then when he made his escape on the chartered plane after killing Katrina, he did so wearing his costume. He could have gone anywhere from Houston. He could even have taken the next commercial flight right back here. Round trip in one day and no one would ever have known he left." He concluded with the question, "Why did he choose the name Pay Back?"

Thoughtfully, Archie wondered, "If he had his own score to settle with Katrina, why not settle it in his own name?"

"To get to her," Mac suggested. "Finding out that it wasn't Dorcas, but knowing that someone was after her and not knowing who. That's mental torture."

"If you're right, then Katrina's killer was a vigilante and Pay Back was a symbol of his motive?"

"Pay Back is hell," he muttered. "Who did I hear say that?"

She asked, "Is Chad a viable suspect? He killed Niles to free Katrina for him to marry, and then decided to get rid of her to have it all to himself. I told you about the Eagle Group."

Mac recalled, "That's Niles Holt's investment group." He pressed his leg against her foot. She responded by rubbing the underside of his calf.

"Before he died, Niles Holt quietly bought seventy acres on the west side of Deep Creek Lake," she said. "Last summer, Katrina courted the county commissioners to change the zoning from residential to commercial in order to build a retail development complete with condos and jet ski rentals right on the lake."

"Chad says that was why she hung around Deep Creek." He draped his arm across her shoulders.

Archie moved in closer to him. "Maybe Pay Back really had to do with Katrina raping the land." She wrapped her arms around his shoulders and looked into his eyes.

The lights from inside the hot tub cast them in a golden glow.

"Mac?"

"What?" He sucked in a nervous breath.

Her eyes locked on his. "When are you going to kiss me?"

"Uh?"

"Yes?"

"I guess…" Mac licked his lips. "Now."

He brought his lips to hers. He could feel her warm breath on his face.

She brushed her fingers against his cheek.

The silence of the night exploded. The ground shook while the sky filled with red, orange, and yellow hues.

CHAPTER FOURTEEN

After the explosion, Archie wasted no time in running to her cottage to call Ira and Francine Taylor, who owned a police scanner.

While Archie changed out of her swimsuit, Mac ran upstairs to the master bedroom balcony in hopes of seeing the source of the excitement on the Point. When he threw open the bedroom door, Gnarly went flying off the bed and under it.

"Now what have you done? Blown up the Schweitzer's safe?"

Gnarly's tail wagged where it stuck out from under the bed.

With no time to lecture the dog, Mac rushed out onto the balcony and craned his neck to catch a glimpse of the happenings on the other side of the stone wall and pine trees that separated Spencer Manor from the rest of the Point. He cursed the boundary that obstructed his view. With no such solitude when he lived in Georgetown, he had cherished the privacy the trees and wall provided until now.

He could spy two fire trucks speeding across the bridge onto Spencer Point to extinguish the blaze on the other side of Katrina Singleton's home. The flames licked the treetops with menace.

"It's the Hardwick house," Ira told Archie on the phone. "We saw both Gordon and Prissy pull into their driveway about a half an hour ago. They were gone most of the day. Prissy was bragging to Francine about them winning a day at some spa in Cumberland."

"Do the fire fighters know that they're in there?"

"I doubt if it will do any good. We saw it go up. There's no way they could have survived that explosion. It smells like a gas bomb to me."

"What about Helga?" Archie tried to keep from choking at the thought of the Hardwicks' poodle dying in the explosion.

"I doubt if she made it out either," Ira answered.

As if on cue, the phone rang when Archie stepped through the deck doors into Mac's living room. Before she could report her findings, he answered the instrument to discover Violet O'Callaghan on the other end of the line.

"Where's David?"

Assessing that her demanding tone stemmed from concern for her son's well being, Mac told the elderly woman that he hadn't spoken to David since he dropped him off at their home that afternoon.

"Someone set him up," Violet said. "He got a call right after dinner from some woman he called Rosie. She told him that she had some report, and he went flying out of here like a bat out of hell. I told him to pick up milk on his way home. That was four hours ago. He's not answering his cell phone."

Mac felt a lurch in the pit of his stomach. After taking down the name of the grocery store in McHenry, he hung up the phone

Through the living room window, Archie peered down the road. The sound of multiple sirens indicated that on the other side of the manor's stone wall the fleet of emergency vehicles battling the blaze was growing. Next to her, Gnarly stood on his hind legs with his front paws on the window sill to monitor the action.

"David is missing." Mac grabbed his car keys from a hook next to the door.

"How did he disappear?" After slamming the door in Gnarly's face to keep him inside, Archie jogged behind Mac to the garage.

When Mac told her about David getting a phone call from a woman named Rosie, she grinned. Head of the forensics lab, Rosie was one of their best sources. Archie punched a speed dial number into her cell phone and placed it to her ear. After a short conversation, she hung up. "David's been there, picked up a forensics report from her, and left four hours ago."

"From there he was going to pick up milk and go home," Mac said. "Since when does it take four hours to pick up milk?"

*　*　*　*

The General Store on Route 28 didn't close until midnight. Mac and Archie found David's truck parked in the corner of the store's parking lot.

"At least he made it here," Mac said.

"Why do you flat out assume something bad happened to David?" Archie asked.

"Five unsolved murders. That's why."

At the checkout next to the entrance, a gray-haired woman in a yellowed white smock read a celebrity magazine borrowed from the book and magazine rack.

"Excuse me." Mac reached for his badge in his back pocket to flash at the cashier only to remember that he had retired from police work. "We're looking for a man. He would have come in shortly after seven o'clock this evening." He went on to describe David as mid-thirties, athletic build, with blond hair and blue eyes.

Without answering, the clerk looked from him to Archie.

"Hi, Flo. Did you see David O'Callaghan come in here this evening?"

Mac's face flushed at the reminder that Deep Creek wasn't the big city of strangers that Georgetown had been.

"Yeah," Flo said, "he bought a gallon of non-fat milk."

"Did he talk to anyone?" Mac asked.

"Sure did." She grinned to reveal a mouthful of rotten teeth. "Yvonne Harding. She's the lady with the news show. I remember when she was in all those beauty pageants. They were back in the dairy section so long that I about told them that they were going to have to start paying rent. While they were checking out, he told her that there was no sense in taking two cars. So she offered to drive."

Archie told Mac, "That explains why David's truck is still here."

Mac suspected Flo knew the answer before he asked the question. "Did you hear where they were going?"

"The Spencer Inn."

"How long ago did they leave?"

With a weary sigh, Flo checked the time on the clock over the check out. "They had to have been in here for close to an hour. Maybe three hours ago."

*   *   *   *

"Why are you assuming the worst?" Archie clutched her seat while Mac raced up the mountain road to the Spencer Inn. "Flo told us how David and Yvonne were acting. He met a woman and decided to go have a drink with her."

"I'll feel better if I can see with my own two eyes that he's okay."

"David got along fine without his big brother for over thirty years," Archie said. "He's a trained police officer. He knows how to take care of himself."

She hurried to keep up with Mac's pace across the deck and back to the lounge where soft music and lights created a romantic ambiance. The sound of a couple's laughter gave away their whereabouts. They found the lounge's only customers in a corner booth giggling over a joke between lovers—or soon-to-be lovers. An ice bucket and two champagne glasses took up one end of the table.

"Ready for a refill?" David asked her.

"Sure." She held out her glass to him. When she saw Mac, Yvonne covered her mouth to conceal a gasp. "Mac Faraday!"

David looked up from where he had drained his champagne while reaching for the bottle. "Mac, what are you doing here?" He saw Archie trying to contain her amusement. "Archie! Fancy meeting you two here!" He gestured at the empty side of the booth. "Why don't you join us?" He grasped Yvonne's shoulder. "Archie, you know Yvonne Harding. She interviewed Robin quite a few times."

After ordering a bottle of Dom Pérignon from Robin's, now Mac's, special reserve, Archie slid into the offered seat.

"Your mother is worried about you," Mac told him in a low voice.

"Of course she is," David replied.

"Someone blew up the Hardwick house tonight."

His smile dropped. "Were they inside?"

Archie said, "The Taylors saw them go in minutes before it went up."

"From the smell, I suspect a gas bomb did the job," Mac said.

David sucked in his breath. "It was only a matter of time. They made a lot of enemies."

"Were they friends of yours?" Yvonne reminded them of her presence.

"No," David said. "They were just a couple of lawsuits waiting to happen."

"Still," Mac said, "they didn't deserve to be blown up."

David agreed before changing the conversation. "Hey, guess what Yvonne told me."

"What?" Mac didn't know whether to be relieved or angry that David had let him worry. Reminded that David wasn't obligated to report to him, Mac became mad at himself.

"Katrina and I got together because she jumped in the back seat of Travis's car with me when the four of us went out on that first double date," David said. "It turns out Yvonne wanted to pair up with me. What a kick! Travis and I had it planned to be me and Yvonne, and him and Katrina. But when she shoved Yvonne out of the way to get in the back seat with me, I thought Yvonne didn't want me."

The server arrived with the champagne that Archie had requested.

After Archie approved it and the server left, David grinned at his date while caressing her hand. "I remember telling Travis before that date that I didn't think Yvonne would be interested in me, but he didn't seem to think it would be a problem."

Mac noted, "Except Katrina jumped into the back seat to be with you instead of next to Travis in the front seat."

"Maybe she assumed that a rich playboy like Travis wouldn't be interested in her," Archie suggested, "which doesn't fit with her character profile."

Yvonne said, "Katrina had no self-esteem issues."

"It seems very odd that neither you nor Katrina wanted to be coupled with Travis Turner," Archie told her. "I had the impression that he's been a stud since way back."

"Travis had looks, a hot car, and lots of money," Yvonne said. "Those things always turned Katrina on; but, for some reason, she was never interested in him. Ironic, ain't it?"

Mac leaned across the table in David's direction. "What was in that forensics report that you got from Rosie tonight?"

"How did you know about that?"

Archie said, "When Violet called us, she said that you left after getting a call from Rosie."

David sighed. "The forensics report in our case file for the Holt murder was missing a couple of pages. The file at the state lab had also disappeared. Rosie found the report in the computer database and printed it up for me."

"There must have been something in there that someone didn't want anyone to see," Mac said.

David removed two folded sheets of paper from his jacket pocket. "It doesn't make sense." He handed the report to Mac. "Forensics found cashmere fibers under Niles Holt's fingernails. They also found fibers on his jacket that are consistent with the cashmere sweater Katrina was wearing when they went up to Abigail's Rock. Her sweater was stretched and torn when she came down from the rock."

Mac said, "Plus Robin found Katrina's necklace hanging from a tree branch below Abigail's Rock."

Yvonne interjected, "What does all this mean? It sounds like you're saying that Katrina killed her first husband." She let out a quick breath. "That's why you wanted to see her interview on my show," she said to Mac. "Did she say something to incriminate herself? What did I miss?"

"Katrina changed her story from her original statement," Mac said. "Robin wrote in her journal the day of Niles's murder that Katrina said she saw Dorcas and spoke to him. He told her that pay back is hell. But then, two days later, on your newscast, she said that she was blindsided. She had been knocked down senseless and only caught a glimpse of the guy. He looked like Lee Dorcas, but never said anything."

"Why would she change her story?" Archie wondered.

Mac explained, "She had to offer some sort of explanation for identifying someone who was hundreds of miles away."

Yvonne said in a soft voice, "I can't believe Katrina would have killed anyone. I know she was self-centered, but murder…" She gazed at David. "We all grew up together."

David frowned. "There's nothing in the evidence that proves anyone else was on the scene. Even Ira Taylor says no one else went up to Abigail's Rock that morning. Katrina paid Phillips off to make this report disappear because she killed her husband. I don't know if she had planned it, or if it just happened."

"Sounds like a murder of opportunity to me," Mac said. "If it was planned, she did a bad job doing it. In either case, Lee Dorcas had drawn so much attention in threatening her that Katrina decided to accuse him of killing her husband. Unfortunately for her, he ended up having an airtight alibi, which she found out about after she had already pointed her finger at him. Then she was married to that statement. She could only wiggle out of it by changing her story and saying that she had been hit in the head and was disoriented."

Yvonne recalled, "She did have a bruise on her cheek."

"Holt probably hit her in self-defense while she was shoving him off the rock," David said. "He had to grab onto something to save himself and in doing so got her sweater fibers under his fingernails."

"He also ripped off her necklace," Mac said. "Robin was right in the first place. Katrina killed her first husband and she lied about Dorcas harassing her."

Archie disagreed. "But we all saw Pay Back."

"And someone murdered Katrina," David reminded them.

"But not the same person who killed Katrina's first husband," Mac said.

* * * *

Mac suspected Gnarly of wrongdoing. The dog was waiting for him when they got home from the Spencer Inn, but instead of nudging Mac's hand for a greeting or begging for a biscuit, Gnarly raced upstairs to the bedroom. Mac noticed his tail tucked between his legs.

Interpreting his posture to be guilt, Mac called out, "You better not have messed on the floor."

Normally, Gnarly would follow Mac and sprawl out on the floor at the foot of his bed until his master turned the lights out. If Mac failed to tell him goodnight with a pat on the head, the German shepherd would nudge him until he petted him, or preferably scratch him behind the ears. Only after a proper goodnight would the dog crawl under the bed and go to sleep.

There was no nudging or begging for a goodnight that night. Gnarly dove under the bed and stayed there.

At six o'clock, Gnarly jumped on the bed to wake Mac up, the German shepherd's morning wake-up routine. Feeling like he was sleepwalking, Mac staggered downstairs to open the back door to let the dog out and then went back to bed. He refused to open his eyes all the way for fear of waking up beyond the point of returning to sleep.

One hour later, Gnarly barked below his window to be let back in.

Mac shuffled back down the stairs and opened the door. Still in a sleep-filled fog, he sensed rather than saw Gnarly come inside. Groping the counter, Mac felt his way to the coffeemaker and punched the button. He was on automatic pilot when he opened the cabinet and dished the dog food into

Gnarly's bowl before pouring coffee into his mug. After downing a half a cup of the caffeine, Mac sucked in a deep breath and turned to the animal gulping down pellets from his blue ceramic bowl.

He blinked.

Sucking in another breath, he gulped another mouthful of coffee to clear his vision.

The vision remained the same.

After another gulp of caffeine, Mac woke up enough to know that he was seeing what he thought he was seeing.

Two dogs were eating from one dog dish. One was a German shepherd. The other was a purebred standard poodle.

"You're a dognapper, too!" Mac's outburst prompted both dogs to gallop from the kitchen and up the stairs to his bedroom. "I don't believe it! Gnarly! I'm going to kill you!"

A scream stopped him from giving chase.

At first, Mac thought the scream came from Archie at her cottage. When he heard it again, he realized that the screamer was further away. He threw open the door and ran out onto the deck.

Clad in a slinky pink nightgown, Archie ran up the steps from her cottage. "What's going on?"

Another cry made them realize that it came from across the cove. They ran down to the lake's edge. There, they could see Travis holding Sophia in his arms while she cried into his shoulder.

Sirens signaled the oncoming police.

"What's going on?" Archie asked as if Mac would know.

Even if he knew, he wasn't available to answer. He had jogged back inside. The phone was ringing when he ran into the kitchen. Mac snatched it from the base and checked the caller ID.

"What's going on at Turner's?" he asked.

"DB," David answered. "Sophia found Travis's assistant dead."

"But Roy—" Mac started to remind David that their police chief was an embezzler and bail jumper hiding from the mob.

"I'm on it. Meet me at Turner's in fifteen minutes."

CHAPTER FIFTEEN

"Okay, men, we know what to do." Even though officially he was still suspended and a murder suspect, the officers on Spencer's police force listened to David O'Callaghan as if he were wearing his late father's shoes. "We need to contain this crime scene."

Mac and David arrived poolside at Travis Turner's estate anticipating a scene with the police chief, only to have Roy Phillips, aka Roy Herman, be a no-show.

Assigned to keep Chief Roy Phillips under surveillance, Bogie called David to announce that the police chief had disappeared during the night. His cruiser was still in the garage where he had parked it after returning home from the explosion at the Hardwick home, but Phillips was nowhere to be found.

Grabbing the reins, David ordered the officers to rope off the patio and pool area where the dead body of Travis Turner's secretary was sprawled out face down in a chaise.

While David directed the investigation, Travis leaned against the outdoor bar warming his hands on a mug of hot coffee. He wore a cardigan sweater over jeans.

"How's Sophia doing?" Mac asked him.

"She'll be okay." Travis sighed. "I should have known Betsy would do something like this. She's suffered from

189

depression since I've known her. She went off her meds and has been drinking a lot."

"What meds?"

"Anti-depressants. I don't know what ones. You'll find them in the guest house."

When the pool area was sealed off with crime scene tape, the officers proceeded to snap pictures of Betsy Weaver's body from every angle. David knelt next to the chaise to study the scene closely.

Face down, the woman's bulk, clad in cream-colored polyester pants and a tunic-type top, resembled a beached sea mammal. An overturned patio table surrounded by glass from a broken goblet and bottle rested in an alcoholic puddle next to the chaise.

"Was she drinking the last time you saw her?" Mac asked Travis.

"Probably," he replied. "I went swimming in the pool last thing before leaving to pick Sophia up at five o'clock yesterday and it was nothing like this." He indicated the dead body and mess. "Sophia's plane came in about six and we went to my place, Turner's—Have you been there yet?"

Mac said that he hadn't.

"Really? You should come as my guest. It's very popular with the out-of-towners looking for a good time…Anyway, we went there for dinner. Since I own the place—you know, celebrity and owner of the establishment—I had to mingle with the guests and the next thing I knew, it was closing time. We didn't get back here until after one and went straight to bed." He shrugged with a shake of his head. "Betsy stays in the guest house and I didn't see her at all yesterday. I assumed she was working on my next book. The deadline is the end of this month. For all I know, she was over there swilling away." He held out the mug to Mac. "Coffee?"

While his host fetched the coffee in the kitchen, Mac took in the home of the famous author.

From across the cove, the Turner home appeared to be the same size as Spencer Manor. When he had arrived that morning, Mac realized that it was noticeably bigger. The living room equaled the size of his living and dining room combined. Like the manor, granite made up the floors. The artwork and furnishings were so impressive that Mac felt as if small cards reading "Do Not Touch" should be displayed.

Travis arrived from the kitchen with the fresh mug of coffee. "Try this. It's a private blend I get from a man living in the hills of San Luis Obispo, California."

Mac cupped the warm mug in both hands and sipped it.

"How do you like being an innkeeper?"

Mac blinked while digesting the question. "What?"

"The Spencer Inn," Travis said. "How do you like the sudden awesome responsibility of running one of our country's most prestigious resorts and restaurants?"

"Not as overwhelmed as I do now that you laid it out for me like that."

"I'd be glad to take it off your hands," Travis grinned, "at a very nice price I might add."

"No, thanks."

"I wouldn't be so fast to turn me down if I were you. You haven't heard my price."

"I don't need to." Mac took another sip of the coffee. "For the first time in my life, I have a legacy. You can't put a price on that. Granted, I wasn't raised with it, but now I have it. It's something that my ancestors built for their descendants and I intend to pass it on to my children."

He saw displeasure with a hint of anger on Travis's face.

This is a man who doesn't hear no very often.

"Do you know who may have wanted to kill your secretary?"

"What?" Travis scoffed. "She was a secretary. She had no friends. She's never dated in all the years I've known her."

"How long is that?"

Sneering, Travis shrugged. "I don't know." After a pause, he answered in a questioning tone. "Seven years? She was my agent's admin assistant back when I was an actor. When my first book sold, I hired her away from him." He said, "Listen. I'm not going to let you or David blow this whole thing out of proportion. Betsy either killed herself or had an accident."

191

"And in either case, her death has to be investigated. Any death determined to be from other than natural circumstances has to be investigated by the police."

Mac had had this conversation more times than he could count. Someone dies either by his own hand or in an accident and the victim's family and friends assume that a couple of forms are signed and the investigation ends there. They don't realize that the police need to answer how said accident or suicide came about.

Travis's face turned red. "Figures that cow would turn this place into a circus."

"I'm sure David and his crew will do everything they can to stay out of your way." Mac drained the coffee mug.

The writer sucked in a deep breath. "Want another cup?" After Mac accepted his offer, he took the mug.

Mac followed him into the kitchen. The pantry included a walk-in refrigerator. The top-of-the-line appliances and utensils shone like they had never been used. He assumed Sophia wouldn't lower herself to common household duties such as cooking. Travis poured Mac's coffee into the mug from a technically intimidating coffee maker.

"I suggest you look at the police chief, Roy Phillips." He handed the mug back to Mac. "If that's his real name."

"What makes you think it isn't?"

Travis leaned against the kitchen counter. He crossed his arms over his chest. "Betsy was a frustrated writer. Since we got here, she's been spending her free time working on her own book. I offered to recommend it to my agent after she finished it. She got this idea for a story about a small-town police chief who was really a murderer hiding from the law. For the last year, she's been following Roy around. Somehow she got under his skin. I saw them at the Inn a few days ago and he told her in no uncertain terms to stay away from him. He shook her up pretty bad. By the time I got home, she was drunk and babbling that he was going to kill her." He cocked his head at Mac. "You don't think that maybe she found out something and he killed her, do you?"

"Hey, Mac?" David called from the hallway before entering the kitchen. "There you are. The state police are here and the cottage is open. Are you coming to check it out?"

* * * *

Betsy Weaver's home had one bedroom, a bathroom the size of a walk-in closet, a kitchenette, and a great room with a dining area. The great room served as her office. She had a small patio area that, judging by the lack of furniture, she didn't take advantage of. The smell of musty carpets, dirty laundry, and rotting garbage assaulted Mac's and David's nostrils when they stepped through the door to search for the cause of her death.

Notepads like the type Mac had seen her writing in filled every flat surface available: kitchen counter and table, end tables, coffee tables, crammed in among the books on her bookshelves, sofa, and floor. Not a page was left unmarked.

"Steve realizes the sheriff killed his missing wife. He tricks him into leading him to the body by making him think he had already found it," David read a paragraph from a notebook on top of the stack on the kitchen table. Bills in unopened envelopes rested next to the notepads.

"Travis says Betsy was a frustrated writer." Mac went to the sofa. An empty prescription pill bottle rested on the floor under the coffee table. Not wanting to touch it for fear of disturbing evidence, he pointed at it with his hand encased in evidence gloves that David had given him. "Pill bottle, but it doesn't have a pharmacy label on it."

"Maybe she was self-medicating." David snapped a picture of the bottle on the floor, as well as the empty wine bottle next to a water glass with residue of red wine crusted at the bottom. He recognized the label on the bottle as being a cheap wine available at the local store. "Pills and booze." He shook his head. "What a way to go."

"What was here?" Mac had noticed rust-marked indentations in the carpet in the corner of the room. The marks formed a rectangle next to a minute computer desk that held a laptop computer and printer.

"File cabinet." The answer came from the open front door. Travis leaned casually in the doorway with his arms crossed over his chest.

"Where is it now?" Mac asked.

"Don't know," Travis answered. "It was locked. Betsy lost the key a long time ago and couldn't get into it. When Sophia and I came back from California a few weeks ago, the cabinet was gone. She must have gotten rid of it."

When David demanded to know what had been in it, Travis shrugged while replying, "Manuscripts. Contracts. Whatever it is people keep in locked file cabinets."

The author looked around the cluttered room. "If you won't be needing me, Sophia and I have appointments with our hair stylists. Can you be sure to get that body out of here before you leave? We're hosting a party tomorrow."

Stunned by the order, Mac glanced at David, who paused long enough for Travis to read the glare in his eyes before responding. "Betsy Weaver will be moved after, and only after, the medical examiner has completed her on-scene examination. I'm sure if Betsy was aware of how inconvenient her dying next to your pool was going to be to you, she would have chosen someplace else to expire."

Travis uttered a noise that sounded like a "humph" before sauntering back to his house.

David muttered, "Did fame make him that self-centered or has he always been like that?"

"You tell me." Mac went into the bedroom. House cleaning-wise, he found it to be the same as the rest of the cottage. The closet overflowed with two piles of laundry. One pile smelled clean, the other didn't.

Water glasses with varying amounts of water littered the nightstand too small to hold everything on it. It also contained an alarm clock, lamp, and cordless phone crammed to the side closest to the bed.

Why does she have everything crammed to one side? Mac knelt to study the set up. *What was on the far side of the stand?*

When he opened the door on the front of the nightstand, an avalanche of notebooks spilled out. Like the others, notes filled the pages, front and back. The nightstand also had a drawer that contained one notepad that appeared to have been started recently and a pill case, which Mac recognized to be birth control pills.

"Travis told me that Betsy didn't date," he called out into the living room.

"As long as I've known her, I've never seen Betsy with anyone." David came into the bedroom where Mac held up the pill case.

"How long have you known her?"

"Since she moved back here with Travis after he hit the big time," David answered. "She's been living here in the guest cottage for years." He paused before adding, "Come to think of it, she probably spent more time here than Travis."

"Anyone stay here with her?"

David shrugged his shoulders. "Someone could have. I know she stayed here by herself that whole summer Travis and Sophia got married and honeymooned in Europe. We should ask Archie. Betsy was a big fan of Robin and used to visit her."

"Robin did mention her in her journal. No boyfriend? Are you sure?"

"None that I know of." David suggested that some doctors would put women on oral contraceptives for medical reasons other than birth control. For example, to control their menstrual cycle.

Mac was half-listening. Something sharp had punctured his knee. He rose up to find that he had put a hole in his pants. Blood seeped from a small wound. Imbedded in the carpet where he had been kneeling, he found the cause of his injury: a shard of glass.

"With all those glasses on the nightstand, she must have knocked one off," David suggested.

Mac studied the clear piece of glass. The water glasses were thick and rounded. This four-inch-long piece was thin, flat, and clear. One edge was a clean and straight cut.

He held the broken glass up on the vacant portion of the nightstand. "What do you think?" he asked. "Picture frame?"

David glanced around the room. The trash contained no broken glass. "Where's the picture now?"

"Maybe the boyfriend knows."

One of the town's police officers stuck his head in through the doorway. "The ME is done. Want to talk to her before they haul away the body?"

* * * *

The body bag rested open on top of the gurney. It took two troopers and two Spencer officers to lift Betsy's body to put on it. Along with the medical examiner, David and Mac examined the body before they zipped the bag shut to take her to the morgue.

Betsy stared up at them with cloudy gray eyes.

"Any idea how long she's been dead?" David asked the medical examiner, an attractive middle-aged woman with her long blond hair pulled up and clipped to the back of her head.

"The blood had settled in her back, but she was found face down. The body has definitely been moved." The medical examiner explained, "Plus, her body temperature doesn't jive with the outside temperature and the condition of her body. In my opinion, she's been put on ice."

CHAPTER SIXTEEN

"This is the smartest dog I've ever seen in my life—and I've seen a lot of dogs in my life."

A lot of dogs, Bernie O'Reilly had seen.

While Mac was at the Turner home getting the low-down on the body next to their pool, Archie found Priscilla Hardwick's sister, Bernie. The dog trainer and breeder had sold Helga the poodle to the late couple. After some negotiation with animal control, Archie got permission to turn Helga over to Bernie, who lost no time racing to the Spencer Manor to collect the dog.

Big boned and taller than her sister, Bernie wore khaki shorts, work boots, and a dusty safari hat on her head. Her long salt-and-pepper hair flowed down her back.

Upon her arrival, Bernie took the poodle into a hug and kissed her snout. By the time the two left, the passive dog felt comfortable enough with Bernie to return her affection with a lick on the cheek.

Sitting on the porch steps between Helga and Gnarly, the dog trainer recounted how her sister had stolen the poodle from her.

"Prissy got it in her head that she and Gordon wanted a show dog." Bernie appeared to be talking to the canines as well as Archie. "So I sold them the pick of the litter from one of my dogs, a grand champion. Helga was worth well over a thousand dollars. When the check bounced, Prissy promised to make good on it. After waiting a good year, I filed a suit against them for payment. I'm in business. I can't be giving away grand champions. The day after they got the papers, the computer network at my kennel got hit by a virus and everything was wiped out, including thirty-two thousand dollars from one of my bank accounts."

Archie asked, "Do you think Prissy did it?"

"I know Prissy did it. I couldn't prove it, but I know she did." After Gnarly knocked her hat from her head for the third time, Bernie set it on the step. "She was a hacker and identity thief. She spent all her time on the Internet stealing everything she could get out there. Anyone who pissed her off, even by looking at her cross-eyed, she'd send them a virus, and then go in and rob them blind."

"You don't seem that broken up about her death."

Bernie hugged the poodle again. "Dogs never mess with you. You always know where you stand with animals. I'd trust a wild lion before I'd trust a man."

"Since you know so much about dogs, can you answer a question about this one?" Archie pointed at Gnarly, who had his tongue in the trainer's ear.

"What kind of question?" She giggled like a schoolgirl flirting with a new beau.

Archie told Bernie about Gnarly's thievery, his nabbing the thief posing as a job applicant, and his dishonorable discharge from the army. Doubtful about the information's validity, Bernie took the German shepherd out into the yard to perform a battery of tests: giving him commands, timing his reactions, and other experiments. She was still testing Gnarly when Mac's Viper rolled between the stone pillars.

"What's going on?" He sat next to Archie on the porch steps.

"Gnarly is being tested."

"Betcha a hundred bucks he cheats."

Archie let out a laugh before noticing the hole and blood in the knee of his pants. He told her about the broken glass and birth control pills in Betsy's bedroom. Like David, she shook her head at the suggestion that Travis's frumpy secretary had a boyfriend. "I never saw her out with anyone. She never mentioned a man in her life. She never mixed with anyone here in Spencer. I always saw her alone in the corner watching everyone. Robin once said that Betsy reminded her of a writer she knew a long time ago who lived through the characters she created. Robin thought she lived in this fictional world that she had created because it made her feel safe. Writers have complete control of what they put on the page, and no one ever really gets hurt." She concluded, "Robin worried about Betsy because that writer she knew ended up killing herself."

"That's what Travis says happened." Mac recalled the notebooks that filled the cottage. "He said that she wanted to be a writer."

"The world is full of writers who've never been published. Some writers never even try to get published." She explained, "Some people get their entertainment watching television all day long. Others listen to music. Others write, if only for themselves."

"But someone put Betsy next to that swimming pool after she was dead," he said. "Certainly not some made-up character from her notebooks. David said Betsy used to visit Robin."

"She felt sorry for Betsy. I had some problems with her," Archie confessed.

"What kind of problems?"

"She always had some excuse to come over here to bounce book ideas off Robin or ask her advice," she said. "I got the impression that she wanted my job, and I didn't like that at all."

"Why would Betsy want your job? Travis Turner is one of the hottest writers out there right now."

"But Robin Spencer is a legend," Archie said. "A hundred years from now, people may not know who Travis Turner is. He hasn't been around long enough to prove that he has staying power. For all we know, he may be the flavor of the month. Robin Spencer had a track record proven over four decades and eighty books. She'd won every book award out there, plus two Pulitzers, two Oscars for best screenplays, and a Tony for a play that's still running on Broadway. Any editor or aspiring writer like Betsy would have given their right arm to work with Robin Spencer."

"Did any of Betsy's ideas include an escaped murderer posing as a police chief?"

The suggestion startled Archie. Recalling that the last time she had seen Betsy, Chief Roy Phillips was following her into the gardens at the Inn, she asked, "Why?"

"Travis claims Chief Phillips threatened her," Mac said. "Maybe during her research, Betsy uncovered something that she wasn't supposed to find out."

Gnarly galloped up the steps to greet Mac with his tongue in his face. Archie introduced Mac to Bernie, who was scratching her chin.

Mac asked the trainer, "Did he pass your tests?"

Bernie announced, "This is the smartest dog I've ever seen in my life—and I've seen a lot of dogs in my life."

"But he got a dishonorable discharge," Archie said. "If he's so smart—"

"Probably because he's smarter than any of those generals," Bernie quipped. "There's smart as in being able to follow commands. That's the type of dogs they want in the army and on police forces. Gnarly is smarter than that. He's smart enough to come up with his own commands. He's able to look at situations, analyze them, and come up with what to do on his own without a human telling him. Plus, there's the added element that he knows he's smart. If someone tells him to do something he knows in his independent mind isn't the thing to do, or if he just plain doesn't respect the one giving him the order, he won't do it."

Archie recalled, "Like when that thief was here for that interview. I told him to stop barking at her and behave, and he wouldn't. He knew I was wrong. That's why he disobeyed me."

Bernie agreed. "A less intelligent dog would have obeyed you, and she would have gotten away with all the loot."

Mac chuckled. "Are you saying Gnarly got a dishonorable discharge for failure to obey a superior officer?"

"Better than it being treason." Archie smiled.

"You've never seen a dog like this before?" Mac asked the trainer.

"Yes, I have, but none on the same level as Gnarly." Bernie patted the German shepherd on the head. "If there's a category of genius for dogs, he's in it."

Mac and Archie exchanged glances, each trying to form the next question. Mac blurted it out, "If he's so smart, why is he going around stealing stuff?"

Crossing her arms, Bernie propped a foot up on one of the deck steps. "Mr. Faraday, you were a cop for how many years?"

"Twenty-five."

"And how many times did you have cases where the bad guy was some smart young kid with too much time on his hands?" She gestured at the subject of their conversation. "Gnarly is a German shepherd. He comes from a long line of working dogs, plus he's smart. Now all he has to do all day is lie around in the sun and fetch a ball once in a while. He's bored. He likes to work his mind and he's got a good one. He's an unemployed veteran with nothing to do. He needs a job."

Gnarly gazed up to his master with a pleading look in his big brown eyes.

"Do you know how to cook?" Mac asked him.

* * * *

"Surprised to see me?"

While the sun was bright and warm, breezes sweeping across the outdoor café at the Spencer Inn held a chill that raised goose bumps on guests' naked arms. Clouds traveling in from Washington threatened to dump rain upon their arrival at Deep Creek Lake. On the other side of the tennis courts, golfers raced the oncoming storm to finish the course.

Before meeting the county prosecutor for cocktails, Mac stopped at Mayor Pete Mason's table on the deck overlooking the tennis courts to flaunt the Tarantulas' failure.

Pete Mason slipped an arm across the shoulders of his companion, a red-haired woman dressed in a purple, backless dress with a plunging neckline. They were sharing shrimp cocktails and champagne. "Why should I be surprised, Faraday? This is your joint."

"That's right," Mac said. "It's my joint, and I have the right to refuse service to anyone, most especially people who try to have me killed. Enjoy your last meal, Marlstone."

The mayor smirked. "You must have me confused with someone else."

"I don't think so. Good-bye."

Mac crossed the deck to where Ben Fleming was already drinking a martini. Having spent the afternoon playing tennis, the lawyer wore tennis whites while his host had thrown on jeans and a t-shirt.

They waited until Mac had ordered his own martini before launching into the business of murder. Reminding himself that the Hardwick home blew up only the night before, Mac asked if the Hardwicks had been killed in the blast. So much had happened in the last two days, it seemed like the explosion on Spencer Point had happened days earlier.

"Both of them. They probably didn't know what hit them." Ben continued, "Here's something for our side. David's DNA doesn't match that collected from Gnarly. Plus he doesn't have a mark on him. He's not the one that Gnarly attacked."

"I knew that," Mac said.

"But Phillips is arguing that David was alone with Gnarly when he took him to the vet. Plus, he was the one who called forensics to collect evidence from the dog. He's speculating that David planted someone else's skin and blood on Gnarly to throw us off the trail."

"That's so impossible, it's laughable," Mac argued. "There's no way he could have removed every speck of his blood and skin from the scene and replaced it with someone else's. What do you really know about Roy Phillips?"

"He's an idiot."

"David told me that Mason and Phillips supposedly knew each other at the Pentagon." Mac said, "But that's not true. Pete Mason was never in the military. Mason isn't even his real name."

"Who is he?" Ben demanded to know in a low voice.

Casting a quick glance in the direction of the mayor's table, Mac whispered, "You'll find out later."

"How much later?"

"Soon." Mac said, "Katrina not only knew who our mayor really was, but she had once been his business lawyer and embezzled money from him the same way she did Lee Dorcas."

Intrigued, Ben looked over his shoulder and across the café at the table in the opposite corner. Spying the redheaded beauty whispering into the mayor's ear, he said, "I've never seen her here before."

"You clumsy bastard!" the mayor yelled when the server knocked over his glass, spilling the champagne.

"Excuse me, sir," the server apologized. "I'll get you a new glass."

"Looks like someone is having a bad day." Mac turned around when he saw the server pick up the glass with a linen napkin and hurry away with it.

Jeff Ingles rushed to the table where the mayor was wiping away the champagne that had spilled into his lap. "I am so sorry, Mr. Mason. Accept our apologies. Our wine steward will serve you another bottle of champagne on the house."

The mayor continued cursing the server who was now long gone.

"He won't be waiting tables here at the Spencer Inn anymore. I assure you."

"That's for sure," Mac muttered under his breath.

"What did you say?" the prosecutor asked him.

Mac shifted the conversation back to their original topic. "My source told me that Katrina and the police chief got close soon after she became a widow."

Ben forced himself to stop studying the mayor who was other than who he said he was. "Who told you that?"

"Their affair lasted only long enough for Katrina to make a contribution to the police department to cover renovating the chief's office, after which two pages from a forensics report disappeared from her husband's case file, after which she dumped the police chief like a hot potato and ran back to Washington."

"Where did you learn all this? What report?"

"The report proving that she killed Niles Holt."

"You're kidding."

"I'm not," Mac said. "Robin visited the crime scene. She found Katrina's necklace hanging high up in a tree below Abigail's Rock. Forensics found cashmere fibers under Niles's fingernails. They match the sweater Katrina was wearing at the time of the murder. She wasn't disoriented after being knocked down by an attacker. She was the attacker, and Niles ripped off the necklace and clawed up her sweater while fighting for his life."

Ben sighed. "That means our police chief is dirty."

"As dirty as a pig in a pig pen." Mac sipped his martini.

Ben took a sip of his martini and sucked in a deep breath. "Where do the Hardwicks fit into all this?"

"I think they were lying about not getting any evidence to prove who really killed Katrina. Their security camera isn't broken. I don't think it ever was."

"Now tell me something I don't know," Ben said.

Mac replied, "The man I saw coming out of the Hardwick home the afternoon before it blew up fits Pay Back's description."

The prosecutor blinked. "Witnesses saw a van belonging to an exterminating company in their driveway. The company swears they didn't service the Hardwick home."

"The man I saw also resembled Lee Dorcas's picture on his driver's license.

"That's why Katrina kept saying that it was Dorcas and the police kept questioning him," Ben said. "Speaking of Dorcas's driver's license, did you bring his wallet?"

Mac flushed. He had searched the house before leaving to meet the prosecutor, but couldn't find it.

"I guess Gnarly stole it back," Ben chuckled.

"Since the killer looked like Dorcas or Pay Back, I wonder if maybe the Hardwicks got something on their security tape that would have told us who Pay Back is and how he got into the Singleton home without activating the alarm. But, instead of turning that evidence over to the police, they decided to use the opportunity to collect monetarily on it." Mac asked, "What kind of bomb was it?"

"A gas bomb. It was detonated remotely. They were gone all day at a spa in Cumberland. The spa said the Hardwicks had a two hundred and fifty dollar gift card. Unfortunately, they don't keep record of who buys their gift cards."

"The killer sent them the gift card to get them out of the house in order to plant the bomb," Mac said.

The prosecutor agreed. "Did you know that Robin Spencer used the same MO in one of her books?"

"Really?"

"When I told Catherine about how the Hardwicks were murdered she said that it sounded like *Rub Down at Four, Rub Out at Eight*. The killer lured a couple of shyster lawyers from their home by sending them a gift certificate for an all-day pampering at a spa. While they were gone, he planted a bomb in their house. When they came home all refreshed and renewed, he blew them up."

Mac shook his head. "My mother's books sold millions upon millions over the course of four decades. At least a million people read that scenario."

"But none of those million got into a wrestling match with Gordon Hardwick shortly before they were killed; nor were the Hardwicks suing any of them."

"I intended to fight that lawsuit," Mac said.

"Now you don't have to." Ben suggested, "There could be another reason for someone wanting them dead. Did you know that Prissy Hardwick was a hacker? She'd been charged a couple of times. I discovered that during a background check."

Mac said, "Her sister told us that she was also an identity thief."

"The Spencer police department recently got hit by a virus that managed to get into their network. It took out scores of their records." Ben shook his head. "In reconstructing their financial records, the police found a hundred thousand dollars missing from their operating fund."

"The same thing happened to Prissy's sister after they had an argument," Mac told him.

"Well, in this case, the feds managed to find the money. Thank, God. It was an online transfer executed the same day the department got hit. The money went from the police department's operating fund to a bank in South America. That account was traced back to Gordon Hardwick."

"They sent the virus to cover up the theft. Interesting," Mac muttered. "What was the motive for their murder? Put an end to a frivolous lawsuit? Blackmail? Or was it simple revenge for stealing someone's identity and screwing up their credit?"

"And then there's—What's her name?" Ben asked, "Travis's secretary?"

"Betsy Weaver. They're now called admin assistants."

"Travis called me this morning. He's concerned that you and David might intend to drag out the investigation into her suicide."

"Who? Me?" Mac asked. "I'm nothing more than your average millionaire playboy. I don't even work for the police."

Ben chuckled at his mock innocence. "Travis's next book comes out next month. The media is predicting that it will be his fifth bestseller in four years. He's afraid that if this simple suicide is blown out of proportion that it will adversely affect his book's release."

Mac smirked into his drink. "Heaven forbid death steal his thunder. Contrary to what Travis Turner told you, Betsy Weaver's death is not a simple suicide."

"He said she was mixing pills and booze. She was depressed."

"Her body had been put on ice and then dumped by that pool during the night."

"Damn." Ben sighed heavily. "Where does she fit into all this?"

"I have no idea."

* * * *

When Archie saw the array of appetizers for the women's cocktail party, she wished that she had opted to have cocktails with Mac and Ben instead. Then, she could have ordered a decadent platter of raw oysters and an obscenely expensive glass of white wine from Robin's private reserve.

Why do women assume that every woman is on a diet?

"Looks scrumptious, doesn't it?" Sophia Hainsworth-Turner whispered to one of her companions before reaching in front of Archie to grab a plate to load up with vegetables.

Sighing, Archie put one green vegetable after another, and one fruit slice after another onto her plate. She'd run over to McHenry for a hot fudge sundae on the way home.

Dressed in a blue off the shoulder sun dress with her hair falling in dark waves to the middle of her back, Sophia didn't portray any sign of mourning the death of her husband's assistant. She urged Archie to move down the buffet table so that she could return to a table filled with other beautiful wives of influential Spencer residents.

While spooning yogurt onto the corner of her plate, Archie told her, "I'm sorry about Betsy. It must have been such a shock finding her this morning. Were you two close?"

"She was such a dolt pulling a stunt like that at the worst time." Grabbing the spoon from Archie's hand, Sophia put a dollop of yogurt onto her plate. "Travis's next book is due at the publisher by the end of this month."

Abruptly, Sophia paused. Archie could see her mind working. Her expression morphed from arrogant to congenial. "Andy—"

"My name is Archie," she corrected her.

"Whatever," Sophia responded. "You wouldn't be looking for editing work by any chance, would you? I'm sure Travis will pay you a nice bonus if you can help him make his deadline." She offered her a spoon for the gelatin.

Rejecting the spoon with a wave of her hand, Archie reached for the salad dressing ladle. She put an extra spoonful of ranch on her plate. "Spencer has certainly turned into a regular Peyton Place. First, Katrina, then the Hardwicks, and now Betsy."

"Betsy killed herself. I mean, who would care enough about a pathetic thing like her to want her dead?"

"I felt sorry for her. I remember when she used to visit Robin. It sounded like her whole life revolved around Travis and his books."

"Which is nothing worth anyone killing over," Sophia declared. "Big difference between her and Katrina, who had a gift for making people want her dead."

"Are you thinking of anyone in particular?"

"Not really."

"How about someone who got into such a cat fight with her that the neighbors called the police?" Archie turned to go back to her table.

Sophia froze.

The model followed Archie across the room. "It wasn't the first time that someone called the police on you, was it, Sophia? You're not the type of woman that someone would want to get mad." Archie took her seat.

Narrowing her eyes to slits, Sophia looked around to see if anyone heard them. Instead everyone directed their attention to the chairwoman at the podium. After taking the seat next to Archie, she replied in a low voice, "Katrina was a slut. One night I came home from a day out with the girls and do you know what I found? That bitch was lying on the sofa with my husband on top of her. As soon as she saw me, she ran like the coward that she was."

"And you went after her."

"She told Travis that she would sleep with him if he could convince his friends on the county commission to approve her zoning request."

"I bet that got you really mad," Archie said.

"Travis married *me*."

"But he was on top of Katrina."

Sophia insisted, "He was fighting her off."

"While lying on *top* of her?"

Archie could sense that Sophia's fury was near the boiling point. Her jealousy came from more than insecurity. "I heard that Travis was quite a lady's man in his day," Archie said. "It must have been pretty difficult for him to put his old ways behind him. Maybe impossible."

"How well do you really know my husband?" There was an accusatory note in Sophia's tone.

"Not well at all. Most of what I know I heard from a friend of mine who grew up with him." Archie asked, "Was it simply a one-time thing, or was Travis having an affair with Katrina?"

Sophia's dark eyes bore into her. Archie gave up on getting an answer from her by the time she responded, "Travis has a mistress."

"Someone in Spencer?"

"I don't know who. I thought it was Katrina, but he's been with his mistress since she was killed." Her fury simmered near the surface. "Whoever she is, she'd better hope I never find her."

"Or what? She'll end up like Katrina?"

"I'm not a killer."

"Katrina made a pass at your husband. She was terrorized to death the same way you terrorized that actress in Hollywood after she stole your boyfriend."

Under her golden tan, Sophia's face turned white.

"Research is a vital part of my work," Archie said.

"Is that what they call it?"

"Am I wrong? Were you not arrested for assault and battery a few years ago? You're threatening a woman who you can't even identify because Travis is sleeping around."

Sophia sat up to her full height and glanced around the room as if to judge if now was the right time and place for her to present her side of the story. "Archie, how old are you?"

Archie wondered where this conversation would lead. She guessed to a confession, but a confession of what? "I'm thirty-five."

"You're still considered a young woman. As long as you can do whatever it is you do, you'll be ageless. But I'm twenty-nine. My youth and my looks are my livelihood. My next birthday, I will become old. The roles won't come anymore, and I'll have to find another way to be supported in the lifestyle to which I have become accustomed. Now I have Travis, who the critics are calling the next Robin Spencer. Two movie producers are fighting over *A Death in Manhattan*. One of Travis's conditions for the sale of the movie is that I play Naomi."

Archie recalled that the main character in Travis's first novel was a plain, overweight woman brushed off by the police when she witnesses a murder. "I'm sorry, but I can't see you as Naomi."

"Neither can anyone else," the supermodel admitted. "But that's the trend nowadays. Beautiful starlets putting on weight and dressing down to earn their Oscars and credibility. After that, Travis and I will be Hollywood's power couple." Sophia glanced around. "That's our plan and I'm not about to let anyone get in our way. I'll do whatever I have to to protect my future."

Archie told her, "Ambition is one of the top five motives for murder."

* * * *

"Did you hear the good news?"

Jeff Ingles had the widest grin on his face since Mac had first met him. "Ed called. He said that since the Hardwicks are dead, so is their lawsuit." He crossed his office to clasp Mac's hand and shoulder. "Just like my mother always used to say, 'Pay back is hell'."

In a flash, Mac recalled where he had heard that phrase. "Didn't you say that before?"

"Pardon me?" was Jeff's response.

"The woman who hit you with her car," Mac reminded him. "She drove a Ferrari, didn't she?"

"Yes."

Curious about Jeff's reaction, Mac lied. "I heard that Katrina Singleton drove a red Ferrari."

The joy in Jeff Ingles's face evaporated. "I saw her face behind the wheel of the car. She paid off Phillips."

Before Mac could think of what question to ask next, Jeff had returned to his desk. "Do you know that for a fact?"

"She had to," Jeff said. "I signed a sworn statement saying that after midnight I saw her driving the Ferrari that ran me down. But Chief Phillips produced a police report proving that Katrina Holt had reported her car stolen six hours before. The next morning, they found the Ferrari in the state park." His voice rose in anger. "That woman lied and our police chief helped her get away with almost killing me. Why? I can only imagine. If her car had been stolen that night, then what was she doing having dinner here with him the same evening?"

"They were here having dinner? Together?"

"They were here—together—having dinner," Jeff said. "Then she runs into me with her car and her boyfriend refuses to arrest her." He sucked in his breath. "But I know the truth and she paid for it."

"Who made her pay for it?" Mac asked in a quiet voice.

The manager hesitated a moment before gasping, "You don't think—"

"Someone calling himself Pay Back terrorized and harassed Katrina Holt Singleton for months before killing her. When talking about the hit and run, you told Ed and me that pay back is hell. That's what Pay Back did before he killed Katrina. He made her life hell. She left you for dead. Now she's dead. Some would call that pay back."

"You're putting words in my mouth," Jeff shouted.

"Did you terrorize Katrina?"

"No!"

Mac could see that Jeff wanted to order him out of the office, but he couldn't forget that he was the boss. "You said she paid. How did she pay?"

211

"I meant because she's dead and I'm not. That doesn't mean I had anything to do with it. I saw her here all the time. That night she ran me down was less than a week after her husband had died, and I tell you," he swore, "she wasn't in mourning."

Mac paused to consider Jeff's observation. He had also seen Katrina's lack of remorse in the recording of Yvonne Harding's program.

Concern leaked into the manager's voice. Rubbing the scars on his hand and wrist, his voice crept up an octave. "You're not seriously thinking that I killed her, are you?"

Mac recalled, "Didn't you say that you heard a couple arguing when you came out of the Inn that night before you were hit?"

Quickly, Jeff nodded his head. "Yes, I did. I told the police about it."

"Was Katrina the woman you heard?"

"She had to be. The argument stopped right before she came running out of the garden."

"Was Chief Phillips the man she was arguing with?"

Jeff shrugged before nodding his head. "She was having dinner with him."

Mac asked, "Were they guests at the hotel?"

The inn manager replied with certainty that they weren't.

"You said this was an hour after the restaurant and lounge had closed."

"I had to count the receipts and lock up," Jeff explained.

"If the restaurant and lounge were closed and they weren't guests of the hotel," Mac asked, "then what were they doing for the hour before Katrina came running out and hit you with her car?"

Jeff scoffed, "They were in the garden. It was dark. Use your imagination. We're chasing couples out of there all the time."

"But you said they were fighting," Mac said. "You were hit one week after Niles Holt was murdered. Katrina may not have been a guest here at the Inn, but maybe the man she was fighting with was. I want to see the guest log for that night."

CHAPTER SEVENTEEN

The temperature dropped at the same rate that the wind picked up to form waves on the lake. The mist finally drove Mac inside from the back deck, which had become one of his favorite spots. He was starting his first fire in the stone fireplace under the portrait of Mickey Forsythe when Gnarly leapt up onto the loveseat to enjoy the warmth of the flames.

"What are you doing up there?" Mac demanded to know. "You don't belong on the furniture."

Gnarly lay down and gazed into the fire.

"Now you listen here. I don't care if you are a canine genius. You're a dog and you don't belong on the furniture. Now get down."

Gnarly sucked in a deep breath, which expanded his broad chest.

"I'm the boss here. If you don't get off that loveseat, I'm going to get you off." Mac grabbed him by the collar.

Gnarly growled.

Releasing his grip, Mac held up his hands as if the German shepherd had pulled a knife on him. "Okay. We'll drop this for now." He picked up the next book in Robin's series and took a seat on the sofa. "Not only are you a dog, but you have dog breath."

"Oh, great! You built a fire."

He had been so engrossed in his argument with Gnarly that Mac hadn't noticed Archie, armed with a food tray, come in through the French doors and up the stairs from the dining room to join them.

She wore blue jeans and a sweater. In spite of the cold, her feet remained bare. Mac wondered if she bothered with boots when it snowed.

He smelled chili. So did Gnarly, who jumped off the loveseat to pursue the bowl across the room.

When Mac took the tray from Archie, he revealed a sheet of paper clutched in her hand underneath. She had run a background check on Betsy Weaver. Licking the soup spoon like a lollipop, Mac scanned the printout.

Archie perched at the other end of the sofa to sum up her findings. "No surprises except that she's dead. She wasn't into anything. No debts. No substance abuse. No scandals. Nothing. So I made a couple of phone calls. That's where things got interesting."

"Who'd you call?"

"Robin's literary agent, Brad Zimmerman. Robin had introduced Travis to him. I thought maybe if Betsy was a writer that maybe she had talked to him about representing her. Turns out, she called him at home on Saturday night."

"The same night she was last seen alive," Mac said.

She agreed. "Now Brad told me that he didn't really know Betsy. They have never really talked, but she insisted that he see her. So they made an appointment to meet in his office first thing Monday morning."

Mac noted, "That would be today."

"He didn't even know she was dead until I called him. He thought she blew him off."

"Did she tell him about the book she was writing about Chief Phillips?"

Archie slid across the sofa until she ended up next to him. "Brad Zimmerman is an ass—Robin's assessment, not mine…though I do agree. He's a wonderful agent but a terrible human being. He wouldn't talk to Betsy Weaver about any book she was working on until she had finished it and it had Travis's seal of approval. That's the way he is. He only agreed to meet with her because she was Travis Turner's assistant and she sounded upset—so upset that he called Travis to ask him what was going on. Travis told him that she was drunk."

Mac set the papers aside. "If Phillips threatened her because of her book—"

"Phillips and Mason were the last people I saw her with, or rather following her," she told him. "Maybe they killed her and dumped her body by the pool to warn Travis not to finish her book. Since he told you about it, he must know about them. Maybe they're afraid of ending up in his next bestseller."

"That's a lot of maybes." Mac picked up the bowl of chili and ate a couple of spoonfuls. "Travis told me that he had met Betsy back when he was an actor in Hollywood. He hired her away from his talent agent after his first book sold."

"That had to be over five years ago."

"It still might be worthwhile hunting this agent down," Mac said. "He could give us insight into Betsy's and Travis's lives back in Hollywood."

"Would that be relevant?" Archie asked. "That was a long time ago."

He agreed. "Five years is a long time to know someone, but Travis doesn't seem upset about Betsy's body being in his back yard, other than the possibility that her death may overshadow his next bestseller."

"That tells me that Travis is a jerk, which isn't exactly news," Archie said.

Aware of her eyes on him, Mac stopped eating.

Her green eyes searched his face. The corners of her lips curled.

Setting the bowl aside, Mac slipped his arm across her shoulders. "Now where were we?"

"Talking murder." She moved in closer to him.

"I don't want to talk about murder." He pulled her closer. "I want to talk about last night."

She didn't fight his embrace when he asked her to recall what they were doing before the explosion interrupted them.

"I loved working for Robin, but I have to admit, you living here brings a whole new dimension to life in Spencer Manor." She wrapped her arms around his neck.

"Every home a bachelor acquires should come with a woman." Mac leaned toward her. "All that came with my last house was a dishwasher that died four months after we moved in."

The phone rang. He snatched it from the base and checked the name displayed on the caller ID.

"Hold that thought," he told her before connecting to the caller on the other end of the line. After hearing the caller's news, he smiled broadly. "I'll meet you there." He hung up.

"Looks like we got some good news for a change," Archie said.

"We certainly did," Mac said on his way to the front door. "We're going to catch a killer."

* * * *

Pete Mason lived in a million-dollar home tucked in the trees at the end of Mickey Forsythe Court. Two state police cruisers, two Spencer police cruisers, and one unmarked car with Detective Sam Groom and David O'Callaghan inside were waiting at the entrance to the court when Mac pulled up in his sports car with Archie.

"How did you like that little trick with spilling the wine into his lap?" Sam asked Mac. "No judge would give us a warrant until we got proof positive that Mason is Marlstone. He may have changed his weight and face, but he couldn't change his fingerprints." The detective pulled an envelope from his pocket. "The warrant for Peter Marlstone's arrest." He patted his breast pocket. "I also got one here for Herman."

"First, we have to find him," David said. "He must have found out that we fingered him. He disappeared during the middle of the night."

"Herman may have gotten away, but at least we got Marlstone." Mac got back into the car to follow them down the court to the stone home at the end. Lights inside and out lit it up like a showplace.

They stood off to the side to ring the doorbell and waited. When they didn't get a response, Sam rang it a second time.

A small woman with a weathered face trotted across the foyer and pulled open the door. She started when she saw a group of men and a woman on the stoop.

Sam flashed his badge. "Is Mr. Mason home?"

Her eyes widened more. "Yes, but he can't be bothered right now. He's got company."

Before she could finish with her objections, the officers charged into the house with their guns drawn. The elderly woman shrieked. "What do you want? You have no right. What do they want with Mr. Mason?"

Before Archie could explain, a trooper called from up the stairs. "We're too late."

Mac cursed. "He got away again."

"No, he didn't run," the trooper said. "Someone else got him first."

Upstairs, Peter Marlstone was lying spread-eagle in his king-sized bed. Black and silver fur covered his chest down to his pelvis, which he had squeezed into a pair of red silk bikini briefs that matched the sheets on the bed. The ice bucket on the nightstand contained an empty bottle of champagne and two crystal flutes. Marlstone's head rested on a blood-soaked pillow. Blood had overflowed from his open mouth into his goatee.

He had a bullet hole between his eyes.

The maid screamed and ran from the room.

"Looks like I wasn't the only one who found Marlstone," Mac said.

"Where's the woman?" Sam asked.

One of the state troopers stepped into the doorway. "Marlstone's Mercedes is gone."

Mac picked up a black jewel-cut stone resting in the dead mayor's open palm. "You won't be finding the woman." He handed the jewel to Sam. "A black diamond. The trademark of the mob's top assassin. She leaves a black diamond on the scene to signal her hits. The Sanchez family spared no expense in finding Peter."

"The Black Diamond," Sam admired the dark stone. "Damn!"

*   *   *   *

One week before Memorial Day, residents returning for the summer season filled every table at the Spencer Inn's restaurant. Patrons on the waiting list crowded into the lounge. Neighbors catching up on the latest scandals around the lake caused a dull roar that replaced the Inn's usually elegant ambiance. Four murders in two days right in their back yards and their missing police chief made the top of the list on the gossip circuit.

Refusing to let Jeff evict a party from his table, Mac, Archie, and David sat at the bar for drinks while deciding if they wanted a late dinner, or to turn in and get a fresh start in the morning.

After the bartender delivered a glass of wine from Mac's private stock, Archie said, "At least you got the Black Diamond's descript—"

"Mine to add to a long list of descriptions," Mac interrupted her. "That's what's bizarre about this woman. She doesn't care about witnesses seeing her because she's a chameleon. She's tall. She's short. She's skinny. She's voluptuous. She's fair skinned. She's olive skinned. She's got delicate features. She's ethnic looking. She's a brunette. She's a blond. Today, I saw a redhead." He concluded, "The only thing consistent in witnesses' descriptions is that she's drop-dead gorgeous—and I mean drop dead."

David nursed his beer while thinking out loud. "So Peter Marlstone was a mob hit. Roy Herman is most likely dead, via the Black Diamond or another mob hitman. Their killer or killers will probably never be caught."

"I'll bet money that they're long gone." Mac agreed.

Archie smiled when she asked, "How much?"

"That leaves the Hardwicks and Betsy Weaver," said David.

"Could Betsy's death be a suicide?" Archie asked.

David answered, "The medical examiner told me today

that she had been dead twenty-four to forty-eight hours before her body was dumped by Travis's pool. Plus, forensics found fish blood on her clothes. Tuna, to be exact."

"What was the cause of death?" Mac wanted to know.

"Drug overdose. Pills mixed with booze." David added, "But she didn't take them on her own. She had bruises on her neck and jaw. Someone pried her mouth open and forced the pills down her throat. Why would someone want to kill a mousy loner like Betsy? I can understand the Hardwicks. We have enough suspects who wanted to see them dead to fill this whole place." He gestured to indicate the Inn's spacious lounge.

Archie proposed, "Have you checked out those notes that Betsy wrote?"

Mac chuckled, "It would take a year to read all those notes. Betsy was obsessed with writing them. Why?"

"Writers make notes," she explained. "The rest of us have our real world to deal with, which gets complicated enough. Imagine if you had the real world, plus a fictional world. Robin would be in the middle of writing a shootout between Mickey Forsythe and a street gang, and suddenly, right when Mickey runs out of bullets, her publicist would call about a speaking engagement. She couldn't completely switch her mind from directing Mickey in a getaway. So, she'd write a note on the notepad next to her laptop, put the call completely out of her mind, and keep writing away until he had made his escape. Then she'd refer to her notes."

David wondered, "What good would an unknown writer's scribblings be in helping us to find out who killed her?"

"Betsy was always lurking," Archie said. "People never noticed her. There's no telling what she saw. Maybe when she bumped into Peter Marlstone and Roy Herman the other night, she overheard something they didn't want her to hear."

David recalled, "I walked in on Betsy questioning Herman at the police station. She told him that she had been doing a background check and it didn't add up."

"Maybe Herman disappeared because he killed her when she found out who he really was," Archie suggested.

Mac said, "If Betsy found out who they really were, she could have told Travis, who has already been pointing the finger at Herman."

"If she's a frustrated writer like Travis says," Archie asked, "why give him all the good stuff?" She gasped before they could respond.

"What's wrong?" Mac asked her.

"Three Witches incoming."

Sucking in a deep breath, David sat up straight. "Are they coming this way?"

Mac turned around on his barstool. "Who are the three witches?" He spied two men and a woman crossing the lounge in their direction. Dressed to kill, they projected the arrogant air of success and power he had come to spot with ease when he worked in Georgetown.

"Ol' Pat used to call them that," Archie explained in a low voice. "The town council members who hired Pat were cool. They were from Spencer and understood the way things were. Then they died off and these bozos from the city retired out here and got into local politics. They were all corporate CEOs making like fifty million dollars a year to stab backs and throw their weight."

"They hated Dad," David said. "He'd never let them tell him what to do. They can't stand people who aren't afraid of them."

"Here they are," Archie hissed when the Three Witches stepped up behind David's stool.

"David?" The taller man with a muscular build removed his mirrored sunglasses to initiate the conversation. "Jeff told us that you happened to be here."

Mac recognized his voice from the radio. He was the town councilman whom David had identified as Bill Clark.

With a glance in Mac's direction, David picked up his beer glass and turned around to face them.

It was an even match with three against three.

"We heard that you inserted yourself into investigating the events of this past weekend," the woman standing between the two men said. She had plump cheeks, a flabby neck, and middle-aged spread. Her silver-blond hair fell to her jaw line in a bob cut.

"Only after I discovered that the police chief you hired was a bail-jumping member of the mob who killed two girls while drunk driving, Nancy," David replied. "I guess where you come from, you trust the little people to run background checks on potential employees. If any of you had, you would have discovered that, according to the Social Security Administration, Roy Phillips died forty years ago."

The Third Witch objected, "We trusted the mayor—"

"Are you talking about the same mayor wanted for murder?" Mac asked.

The three witches responded to Mac's dig with a glare. He hadn't been invited into their conversation.

Yep, they're from Corporate America.

"Excuse me," the third witch told Mac, "but this is a private conversation about town business."

"Then, as a resident of this town, I'm most interested in listening. Looks like you have a town with no mayor or chief of police, which may or may not be bad considering that the ones you had hired were unqualified criminals."

"Now look here—" Bill Clark took a step toward Mac, who rose to challenge him.

David stepped between them. "It is what it is, Bill. No spin—exactly the way you don't like it. Now, if you don't mind, the three of us were having a private conversation and if you don't have anything of importance to tell me, then I suggest you leave."

Nancy replied in a smooth tone, "We do have something important to ask you, David. Like your friend said, we don't have a mayor or a chief of police. Word is spreading like wildfire about how Pete and Roy misled all of us. Confidence in the town council—"

"In other words, you three," Archie interjected.

"—is very low. Summer residents are talking about changing their plans—"

"Summering someplace else and taking their money with them," Archie translated.

Nancy glared at her before continuing. "We need to do something to instill confidence in Spencer. We need a police chief, one with a name that says 'You're safe with us.'"

David replied, "So you want to hire a police chief and call him Pat O'Callaghan?"

Bill Clark sneered. "Cut the BS, David."

"I'd watch it if I were you, Bill. My father taught me to be overly aggressive at a young age. Growing up in his shadow, there's no telling what it's done to my psyche."

The councilman's face flushed.

"I've had a lot of time to listen to the media," David said.

Mac asked, "'How much are you talking about?"

Bill Clark's smile contrasted with his arrogant tone. "Frankly, I don't believe that's any of your business, mister."

"It's mine," David countered.

Nancy began, "Considering that you don't have the same experience your predecessor had—"

"*He* had none," Archie, Mac, and David interjected in unison.

All Three Witches flushed.

The third councilman suggested, "I guess we could match his salary."

Before David could respond, Mac said, "I'll match that offer plus up it ten percent."

The Three Witches turned to him with angry expressions.

Mac smiled at them. "I happen to be looking for a vice president in charge of security for the Forsythe Foundation, and I would love to have a vice president by the name of O'Callaghan. Like you said, the name instills confidence."

The council members looked from one to the other.

"Maybe I should order another round of drinks while you chew on that." Archie whirled around on her stool to gesture for the bartender. "Put our drinks on their tab."

CHAPTER EIGHTEEN

Mac couldn't sleep after encountering four murders and a missing police chief in two days. Even when he worked homicide in the city, four murders in two days was pushing it.

They ended up closing the Spencer Inn after the Three Witches caved in to David's demands for accepting their offer to become Spencer's police chief. The sweet deal included a generous hiring bonus.

Mac had let Gnarly outside when he returned home in the middle of the night. The dog disappeared into the fog. Too keyed up to sleep, Mac warmed his hands on a hot mug of decaf coffee and stretched out on the chaise to wait for Gnarly's return. He almost spilt his coffee when he awoke with a start.

In the dim light of early morning, he saw a silhouette with tall pointy ears at his feet. It resembled the superhero Batman. With a shriek, he sat up.

"Gnarly! I'm going to kill you!"

Swinging his legs around to sit on the edge of the chaise, Mac checked his watch to see that he had been asleep for over an hour. The dog laid down on the vacant end of the chaise to rest his head in his master's lap.

"What did Gnarly do now?" Clutching her own mug and a sheet of paper, Archie called from the top of the steps leading down to her cottage. Like Mac, she was in the same clothes she had worn the night before. His assumption that she had gone to bed to get some sleep was wrong.

"I couldn't sleep so I decided to check my e-mails." She shook the sheet of paper at him while sitting in the chair across from him. "I never expected it, but I got a reply from Victor Morgenstern."

"Who's Victor Morgenstern?"

"Only one of the top talent agents in Hollywood," she said.

"Thinking of becoming a movie star, Arch?"

"No, but you reminded me yesterday that Travis Turner went to Hollywood to become a star."

Now awake, Mac remembered Travis telling him that Betsy had been his agent's assistant.

"Victor never represented Travis Turner. He wants to make that abundantly clear," Archie said. "Betsy Weaver was Victor's Girl Friday."

Mac took the e-mail. He saw that Victor had written a long narrative in reply to Archie's message informing him about Betsy's murder and asking what he could recall about his former employee.

She continued. "Victor couldn't stand Travis. He says he was all gloss and schmooze, but no talent. Travis didn't want to act. He wanted to be a movie star, which Victor explains are two different things. Then, suddenly, Plain Jane Betsy was dating. Guess who."

He sat up straight. "Travis Turner."

She nodded her head. "Victor says it's not unusual for ambitious actors to try to get in with top agents by dating their employees in order to have a good word put in for them. Victor tried everything he could to warn her, but she was in love with Travis. Suddenly, out of the blue, Travis signed a book deal that made history, and she quit her job to help her fiancée with his blossoming career as a famous mystery writer."

"Fiancée?" Stunned, Mac repeated the word. "I only saw Betsy once, but from what I saw they weren't anything other than boss and admin."

"I saw them together more than you and thought the same thing." She stood up. "I can't see Travis—"

"He referred to her as a fat cow." He gasped. "He had to have been using her. But for what?"

"Editor," Archie said. "Not to blow my profession's own horn, but good editors play a vital role in a writer's career. There's more to a hot book than a good story. There's the boring technical stuff." She concluded, "If Betsy hadn't edited his books, I guarantee Travis would never have gotten where he is today."

"If they were romantically involved, why did Betsy stay on after Travis married Sophia?" Mac had to think a moment. His conversation with Travis the day before seemed so long ago. "I don't get it."

She said, "You'd be surprised how many women think a cheating man is better than no man at all. I'm willing to bet Sophia knew nothing about it. She told me yesterday that she knew Travis was cheating. Can you imagine what she'd do if she found out that Betsy Weaver was the other woman? Maybe she killed her."

While reading the e-mail Mac sipped his cold decaf coffee and sat back on the chaise. With Gnarly at the other end, he couldn't stretch out his legs. When Mac tried to urge the dog off by pushing against him with his feet, Gnarly growled. Eventually, the dog permitted Mac to warm his feet under him.

After a long stretch of silence during which they both turned over the case again and again in their minds, Archie stretched her legs until her feet rested under the edge of his chaise. "What are you thinking so hard about?"

"Where does a frumpy, overweight book editor fit into this? What connection does Betsy have to Katrina? Who was Pay Back?" Mac sighed. "I have this feeling that if we can figure out what he was paying Katrina back for, then we'll know everything." He made a circling gesture with both hands. "It will all come together."

Archie reached for his hand. "Maybe we need to step back and look at the whole picture. When Robin would get to this point in a case, she'd go work in her garden."

"The security system was never deactivated. It never went off. How did he bypass security?" Mac turned in his seat to study his house.

Archie wondered at the puzzled look on his face. "What's wrong?"

"Which brings us back to the original locked room murder." Mac stood up.

"What original locked room murder?" She followed him across the deck and down into the back yard.

"Pat O'Callaghan's unsolved murder case," Mac said. "David told me about it. It happened in the Singleton house."

"Two murders in the same house? Don't let that get out. Chad will never be able to sell the place."

They turned the corner of the stone wall to enter Katrina's beach and trekked up the back yard.

"Someone shot Milo Ford. Neither Robin nor Pat figured out how the killer entered the house, shot the victim, and got out without tripping the security system—the same way Katrina was killed." Mac paused at the patio to study the house's outside wall. "How did Pay Back get in to drug the bottle of wine without anyone detecting it?"

"What are you looking for?" Archie asked him.

"A way into the house that will bypass the alarm."

"Do you mean like the way a cat burglar breaks into the bank through the ventilation system in the dead of night to get away with the big heist?"

"Something like that," Mac said. "If Katrina changed her code regularly, and the system shows no record of being deactivated with the code, then it must not have been used. But he—"

"Or she."

"—still got in. They must have had a way into the house that went around the system."

Gnarly's whine interrupted Mac's concentration.

Like before, the dog dug away at the corner of the house. The hole he had been working on the last time they visited the crime scene had grown more than two feet to expose the house's foundation.

"Gnarly, you're going to get us all in trouble," Archie said. "Get out of there!"

The dog clawed at the siding connecting the corner of the garage with the house.

"Stop it, Gnarly!" Mac pulled him away from the house by the collar.

Seeing what the dog had uncovered with his digging, Mac released Gnarly, who resumed clawing at the siding.

Archie knelt next to the hole. "Gnarly has been working at this for a long time. Looks like he' been digging up the house."

"Most dogs dig up gardens." Mac ran his fingers along the side of the house. "There's a seam here."

She studied the spot he marked with his fingertips. Instead of the cedar panels that covered the house overlapping each other, the planks rested flush next to each other.

"I wonder…" Mac peered closely at the grain. "Could it be?" He pressed his fingertips into what appeared to be a knot-hole in the plank.

Click!

A three foot wide, six foot tall section of the siding along the wall of the house popped open.

Before Mac and Archie could get over the shock of their discovery, Gnarly stuck his nose in the opening. After squirming his body through, he charged inside. His bark resembled a battle cry.

"Gnarly, wait!" Archie hurried into the darkness after the dog. "The killer might be in there!"

Mac ran in after them.

The room was no more than three foot wide and approximately twenty feet long.

When he darted into the dark room, Mac collided with Archie who had stopped when she found what appeared to be a window looking into the home theater.

"Look!"

Recalling the mirror behind the bar, Mac told her, "It's a two-way mirror." His eyes adjusted to the darkness. The room was bare with no paint or wallpaper. Plain wooden planks made up the walls. A ladder led up to the next floor of the house.

Gnarly clawed at the wall at the opposite end of the room.

"What did you find?" Archie knelt next to the dog. "Is there another room behind this wall?"

They squinted to see what held the dog's interest. One of the panels appeared to be broken. Like the door leading into the secret room, the edges were flush with the wall.

Mac forced his fingers into the hole, grasped the edge of the board, and pulled. The board came out of the wall and dragged a drawer behind it. The drawer contained a canvas bag.

The movement created a cloud of dust.

Gnarly sneezed before pouncing on the bag, which caused more dust.

Archie covered her nose and mouth. "What is it?"

Waving the dust away, Mac opened the bag. Before he could search the contents, Gnarly thrust his head inside. After Mac pushed him away, he extracted a plastic bag containing a white powder from the canvas bag.

"Is that cocaine?" Archie asked.

"Maybe." Mac set it aside. "Supposedly, a drug dealer built this house." Yanking the edges of the canvas bag to open it wider, Mac peered inside. "Now I know definitely what this is." He pulled out his hand to show her a bundle of hundred dollar bills. "It's time we call our new chief of police."

* * * *

In spite of his success in negotiating a winning deal for his late father's job, David didn't sleep well. Once more, he was in Katrina's bedroom. Again, she called him to her bed and in the midst of making love, he realized they weren't alone.

Katrina pointed her finger at the intruder. "Oh, no! It's alive!"

"No!" David screamed when the intruder aimed his gun at her and pulled the trigger.

He dove for his gun, but it was gone.

The killer aimed his gun at him. "You're a dead man, O'Callaghan." He pulled the trigger.

His heart pounding, David sprang up in his bed.

* * * *

"Milo Ford dealt in drugs," Mac explained to David. "He needed to hide them where the police couldn't find them. So he must have built this room when he designed the house."

While Bogie and Archie counted the bundles of hundred dollar bills on the patio, Mac and David searched the series of secret rooms. After his appointment to police chief, David called Bogie to offer him the position as his deputy chief. The position came with a substantial raise, a condition for his accepting the position of chief.

The ladder led up to the second floor where the passages branched out into a maze of narrow hallways. The secret rooms went up to the attic. Peep holes permitted spying in every room.

"This is really creepy," David breathed when he found the tiny window into the bedroom where he had been intimate with Katrina.

"Pay Back knew everything she did. He came and went without activating the security alarm," Mac told David. "This is how he did it."

With their flashlight beams, they scoured the wall of the room on the ground floor, where they found a small door no taller than three feet and not much wider. The oblong knob looked like it belonged on a medicine cabinet.

"Where does it lead?" David called out to Mac once he managed to fit his shoulders through the opening.

Mac felt around. Ahead, he could hear water running. Feeling his way in the darkness, his fingers made contact with a wooden surface that felt like a door on a hinge. Pushing the door open, he plunged toward the light.

After over an hour in the dark caverns of the house, Mac's eyes were still adjusting to the light when he heard Archie shriek, "Where did you come from?" She had been washing her hands at the sink when he fell out of the bathroom cabinet behind her.

"You wouldn't believe what's in this house," Mac told her.

With no towel to wipe her hands on in the unoccupied home, Archie wiped her wet hands on the seat of her jeans. "Oh, I'd believe it. You won't believe what we found in that bag."

On the patio, Bogie was completing an inventory form of the bag's contents when David and Mac followed Archie outside. "We have seventy-five thousand dollars in hundred dollar bills," he reported. "The dates on the bills aren't any later than the 1990s."

"Which puts it around the time someone murdered Milo Ford," David noted.

"Yep," the older officer agreed. "Your daddy was convinced he was a drug dealer and this proves it." He held up one of the bags of white powder. "Two kilos of heroin. But that's not all." He reached into the bag. "We also have this." He extracted a revolver.

David took the gun. "I wonder if that's the weapon used to kill Milo."

"Leaving it in the secret wall that the police don't know about would pretty much ensure no one found it," Archie said.

"But why not take the money?" Mac asked. "Or the drugs? My guess is that the drugs, money, and gun belonged to Milo and he was killed before he could use it."

With the gun, David gestured at the secret panel. "Assuming this bag belonged to Milo and his killer didn't know about it, then how did Katrina's killer know about this door? Dad interviewed everyone."

"If anyone knew about Milo's secret hiding place, they would have taken this stash a long time ago," Bogie agreed. "His widow and kids certainly didn't know about it. She could have used this money. It turned out Milo was up to his eyeballs in debt."

"What about Milo's drug friends?" Mac asked Bogie.

The older officer shook his head. "Milo made the mistake of cheating the wrong people. We assumed that got him killed."

"Maybe the killer knew about the secret hallways, but not where Milo had hidden the money," Archie suggested.

"Or maybe Milo's murder had nothing to do with drugs or money," Mac said.

* * * *

At Spencer Manor, Mac made a fresh pot of coffee and warmed breakfast pastries in the oven for Archie and David. Bogie took the bag they had found, along with its contents, to the station. Forensics would run tests on the gun to see if it had been used in any reported crimes.

"Now we know how both Pay Back and Milo Ford's killer did it." Archie took a cautious sip of the hot coffee.

"The question is," David asked, "are they two separate killers or one? The only connection I can see between Katrina and Milo Ford is that they lived in the same house. Katrina didn't use drugs and had no drug connections."

"They were both into real estate," Archie pointed out.

"Katrina inherited her real estate," David countered. "Milo dealt more in drugs than real estate. Emma Turner ran his legitimate business."

"Turner?" Mac whirled around from the oven where he was removing the hot cookie sheet filled with cheese Danish. "Is she any relation to Travis?"

David nodded his head. "His stepmother."

Recalling an earlier conversation, Archie asked in an excited tone, "Wasn't she murdered?"

"Travis's mother was murdered?" Mac dropped the hot tray onto the granite counter.

"Stepmother," David corrected him. "And yes, she was murdered. Travis and I were sophomores in high school. She managed Milo's real estate office. One morning, she went in to open up the office, and someone shot her in the head and set fire to the building."

"Betsy told me that Travis thought his father did it." Archie accepted the roll Mac offered to her.

With a knife, David stabbed the butter in the tub on the kitchen counter. "My father said Milo did it." He buttered his pastry. "He just couldn't prove it."

While drinking his coffee and eating his breakfast, Mac looked from one of them to the other like a spectator at a tennis match.

Perched at his master's feet, Gnarly favored the food more than the conversation.

"Did you know that Travis was sleeping with her?" She cocked her head at David.

He laughed.

Offended by his laughter, she asked, "Why do you find that so funny? Travis is a hound. He even cheats on Sophia Hainsworth."

"You never saw Emma Turner," David said. "Every boy who saw her had fantasies about sleeping with her. Believe me, if Travis had slept with her, he would have shouted it from the rooftops."

"Except for the fact that she was his father's wife," Mac reminded him. "What would Travis's father have done if he found out that she was being more than motherly to his son?"

David flushed. "Travis's dad did have a temper."

Mac responded with a "Hmm," before popping the last of his pastry into his mouth, much to Gnarly's disappointment.

"What about Pay Back?" Archie reminded them about the recent murder. "What was he paying Katrina back for?"

"I have no idea." After refilling his coffee mug, Mac checked his watch. It was only seven-thirty. "I hate to speak ill of someone you cared about, David, but Katrina lived a high-risk life. So far, we've discovered that she cheated, lied, stole, and murdered. Any of her victims had reason to kill her. In order to find out which one, we have to figure out who was so enraged that they would go to so much trouble to kill her."

CHAPTER NINETEEN

"What's this?" Mac held a potted plant out to Archie.

"That's a chrysanthemum." Giggling, she emptied the contents of the pot into her bare hand. "You really don't know anything about gardening."

At her urging, they sat on their knees in the flower garden that filled the driveway's inner circle. Archie had suggested that by taking his mind off the murders with gardening, Mac, like his mother before him, could come to a solution to the case.

Rolling in the flower bed, Gnarly seemed to enjoy working with potting soil more than Mac, whose gardening consisted of handing stuff to Archie. He felt near collapse from boredom.

Relief came when David raced his cruiser through the stone entrance. Dressed in his crisp uniform with the shiny gold chief's badge pinned on his breast, he climbed from the driver's seat. "I didn't know you were into gardening."

"I'm not." Mac jumped to his feet to take the sheet of paper that David held out to him. "What's this?"

"A confession." He responded to Mac's questioning expression by clarifying, "That's a copy of it. The original is in evidence at the station. It came in today's mail. It was post-marked yesterday."

Wiping her hands on her jeans, Archie scanned the letter in Mac's hands. "Who's it from?"

"Betsy Weaver," David told them.

Archie objected, "But she was killed Saturday or Sunday."

Mac reminded her that she had last seen Betsy Saturday evening. "If this was mailed Saturday night, then it wouldn't have been postmarked until two days later."

David summarized the contents of the letter. "Betsy fell in love with Travis the first time she saw him. When he started having an affair with Katrina, Betsy harassed her until she became so consumed with jealousy that she killed her. The Hardwicks saw her leaving the scene and started blackmailing her. She didn't have any money to pay them off, so she had to kill them."

"I didn't see Betsy Weaver coming out of the Hardwick home," Mac objected. "That perp was slender and taller."

"I'm simply telling you what she says in her letter." David held up his hand.

Archie took the copy of the letter from Mac. "What about Lee Dorcas? What about this whole Pay Back routine?"

"She says she lured him out here pretending to be a promoter with the promise of a singing engagement. She killed him and dumped his body up at the mine where she knew it would be found come spring. She assumed Chief Phillips would call it a murder-suicide and close the case."

Archie's doubt matched Mac's. "I can't see Betsy being strong enough to walk up that trail to the mine, let alone lug a body up there to dump."

"All she had to do was put it into the back of an ATV and drive it up there," David said.

"Don't tell me you actually believe this." She shoved the letter into his hands. "Who wants lemonade?" She went inside to prepare the refreshments.

"Whoever dumped Dorcas's body would have had to have carried the body through the barricade at the opening in the mine," Mac pointed out, "which is a tight fit for a thin person. Doing that requires both strength and dexterity. Betsy Weaver didn't have either."

"This confession also makes no mention about a man matching Lee Dorcas's description taking a chartered flight to

Houston," David said. "It can't be a coincidence that the Monday after the blizzard someone looking like Dorcas flew out of here."

"Maybe because our killer doesn't know that we know about that flight." Mac grinned. "We now know for certain that Betsy's murder is connected to Katrina's." He climbed the steps.

David followed him around the house to the back deck. "I had that dream again."

"What dream?" Mac sat at the table under the umbrella. After working in the hot sun, he yearned for the shade of the deck.

"This awful nightmare I've been having ever since her murder. Pay Back kills Katrina. Only he doesn't look like Pay Back."

"What does he look like?" Archie returned to the deck with a pitcher of lemonade and sugar cookies.

"I don't know. It's dark." David lowered himself into a chair. "Katrina and I are together in her bedroom. He's there. Katrina yells. What she yells doesn't make sense."

"What does she yell?" Mac asked.

"'Oh, no! It's alive!' He shoots her and then he shoots me. That's when I wake up."

Mac grimaced. "That's a really odd thing to say when someone breaks into your bedroom while you're with someone. 'It's alive'?"

"That's what Dr. Frankenstein said when he created the monster," Archie agreed. "If I were writing a scene like that, I wouldn't—"

"This isn't a book, Archie," David said.

"She's right," Mac said. "If someone broke into my bedroom, I would yell 'Get out,' or maybe, 'What are you doing here'—Could that have been—?"

David shook his head. "I remember in my dream that her saying that even surprised me. Every time I dream it, she screams, 'It's alive!' and she's terrified."

"What was alive that she thought wasn't alive? Niles?" Archie looked at Mac. "Could the intruder be Niles?" She turned back to David. "Maybe deep down you knew all along that she killed Niles and felt guilty for sleeping with his killer."

David dropped his head into his hands. "Niles is dead. He wasn't Pay Back and he didn't kill Katrina."

Archie asked, "Did you know that Sophia threatened Katrina?"

David chuckled, "I answered the call when Sophia came over for a piece of her. Believe me, you would never want to get Sophia mad at you. I came very close to cuffing her."

Mac asked, "Why did Sophia want a piece of Katrina?"

"Sophia claimed Katrina tried to seduce Travis," David said. "Katrina told me that it was the other way around and Travis tried to rape her. Sophia caught them. I told Sophia that if I ever caught her over here again that I would arrest her and that wouldn't look good in the tabloids. My warning must have worked. Katrina never heard from Sophia again."

"What about Travis?" Mac asked. "Did you question him about Katrina saying that he tried to rape her?"

"According to him, she offered to sleep with him in exchange for his influence to get her zoning request approved. He said, she said. Katrina refused to press charges. I dropped the case."

Archie said, "Sophia is athletic enough to have committed the murders."

"Plus she is insanely jealous and violent." David smiled at the prospect of finding his killer.

"Wait." She changed her mind. "Sophia was in Europe that first summer. She hadn't even met Katrina until well after Pay Back showed up."

"When was that?" Taking a cookie from the plate, Mac asked David, "When did Katrina first talk to you about Pay Back?"

David sighed. "When I ran into her at the Inn last Fourth of July weekend. I was overseas when Niles was murdered."

"That same summer Travis met Sophia in Europe. They didn't come back here until the next spring," Archie said. "Sophia hadn't even met Katrina until then."

Mac's eyes bore into David's. "Last summer, while Pay Back terrorized Katrina, who would she call for help? The police or you personally?"

"She would call me on my cell. She never called the station."

Archie declared, "Because she didn't trust Chief Phillips."

David agreed. "She said he was an idiot."

Mac turned the printed e-mail Archie had delivered that morning to the blank side. At one end, he drew a line down the page.

"This is two years ago." Mac wrote across one end of the line. "Lee Dorcas threatens Katrina at Ingram's office in Washington. He causes such a scene that they call security. About this same time, Katrina gets engaged to Niles Holt." He made a note about the engagement on the same line.

"Soon after that, Katrina marries Niles." Mac drew another line down the page next to the first line. "Allegedly, Dorcas came into her dressing room at the church and threatened to kill her new husband." He noted the threat along the line. "No reports or witnesses. As a matter of fact, she told no one about this incident until after Niles Holt was killed three months later." He drew another line further down the sheet.

David said, "I know where you're going with this, Mac. It makes sense and doesn't make sense all at the same time."

Archie agreed. "We all saw Pay Back. I thought we'd already decided Katrina killed Niles and tried to make Lee Dorcas the patsy."

"Bear with me for a minute." Mac studied the paper. "Katrina kills Niles and claims Dorcas did it. After his murder, she makes a statement about being threatened for months *before* Niles's murder. But during that time period no one saw anything to confirm that." He looked up at Archie.

She asked him, "Do you mean did anyone see Pay Back that first summer?"

"Or Lee Dorcas? After Niles was killed, Robin wrote in her journal that Katrina said someone had been threatening her, but she didn't act like a woman being threatened. Robin doubted her story so much that she hiked up to the rock to examine the crime scene herself and found Katrina's necklace off the cliff."

"That's right," Archie said.

"And forensics points to Katrina being the killer," David said. "So we can conclude that during that first summer, Pay Back wasn't real. At that point, Katrina had made up the harassment to throw suspicion away from her."

Mac drew another line down the page. "Katrina moves back to Washington." He drew a second line an inch further down the page. "She marries Chad Singleton." He tapped the two lines with the pencil. "Now, Katrina told David that the same man that killed her husband continued threatening her after she went back to the city. But now we know that said man didn't exist. Plus, according to Rachel Singleton, Katrina didn't get any threats that she knew of."

"Rachel isn't a credible witness," David said.

"Maybe, maybe not." Mac drew another line. "Katrina and her new husband return to Spencer. Shortly afterwards, Chad goes back to the city. Katrina runs into a former beau, who is now a cop. She tells him about the harassment going back to when Lee Dorcas first threatened her at the law firm the year earlier. Claiming that she is too frightened to be alone, she invites him to spend nights in her home to watch over her."

Laying down the pencil, Mac looked over at David.

"Are you telling me that I'm an idiot?"

"Same thing happened to me," Mac said. "Once I gave a murder witness my cell phone number to call me if she needed anything. She called me three times claiming the killer had come after her. Each time, she wanted me to spend the night to protect her. I got suspicious the second time. The third time I told her I'd write her up for filing a false report if she called me again."

"Are you saying that Katrina lied to lure David to her house so that she could seduce him?" Unable to comprehend a woman doing such a thing, Archie shook her head.

"It wouldn't be the first time a woman played the damsel in distress to get an attractive cop to come to her aid."

"But we all saw Pay Back," she objected.

"He drugged us one week after I was there," David said.

"But did anyone besides Katrina see Pay Back *before* that night? At the wedding where Lee Dorcas threatened Niles? A threat Katrina failed to mention to anyone until after Niles had been killed. That *first* summer? In Washington, while Chad was reeling her in for her money?"

Archie and David looked at each other in silence.

"I saw Pay Back," Archie said. "So did Robin and the Taylors."

"*After* David started keeping an eye on her."

David blurted out, "I thought you were trying to clear my name!"

"You're not a suspect."

"That isn't the way I'm hearing it."

"First, Katrina tried to frame Lee Dorcas for killing Niles. When he had an alibi, the killer became some mysterious stalker that resembled Dorcas. When she saw you, she used this same fictional terrorist to lure you to her home. Someone decided to make him real. We don't get a third person confirmation that Pay Back exists until after you came onto the scene."

"That's what Katrina meant in your dream when she said 'It's alive,'" Archie told David.

"Katrina had created this monster. Suddenly, it came to life and destroyed her—just like in *Frankenstein*." Mac studied his timeline. "Since no one saw Pay Back until last summer, then we can conclude that Katrina's killer didn't come into the picture until then."

Archie said, "Sophia was here last summer."

"Sophia met Katrina the same night I saw her at the Inn," David recalled. "I remember Travis was excited to see Katrina because they hadn't seen each other since high school. That may have been when it started."

"Sophia's connected to Betsy." Archie smiled. "What a convenient patsy. Killing a nobody like Betsy would have been like stomping out a bug with her shoe."

"We're forgetting about Gnarly," Mac interjected.

David and Archie became quiet. At the sound of his name, Gnarly sat up from where he had been dozing in the afternoon sun.

"Gnarly attacked Katrina's murderer," Mac reminded them. "Our suspect has to have dog bites on him or her."

Archie frowned. "Sophia doesn't have a mark on her. That's for certain. She shows enough flesh for us all to see that."

"Betsy didn't have any dog bites on her either," David said. "That proves her confession is a fake."

Mac countered, "But someone killed Betsy and wrote a confession in her name to point the finger at her. I think we need to go have a talk with Travis."

* * * *

"Do you have an invitation?"

The Turners' butler stopped Mac, Archie, and David at the front door. The combination of his black suit, tie, and humorless manner reminded Mac of Lurch from *The Addams Family*. With unpleasant glances at the party crashers, guests in professionally designed ensembles barged past them to enter the by-invitation-only poolside event.

David pointed at the gold badge pinned to his chest. "How's this for an invitation?"

"Wait here." Lurch went through the foyer and out onto the back deck.

Archie craned her neck to see that many of the guests had changed into swimsuits for sunning or swimming in the pool, next to which their host's assistant had been found dead the day before. "Where's Betsy's place?"

"It's behind the garage." Before David could inform her that the guest house had the decor of a tool shed, Archie jogged across the driveway.

"David!" they heard Travis call out from across the foyer. His royal blue ascot matched the hue of his tailored summer suit. "You're just in time for a private party celebrating my latest book deal. Five million dollars' advance for five books."

His broad smile dared them to ruin his moment of grandeur. "I hope this isn't official business."

"It is," David said.

Travis's smile wavered. "Well, seeing as how you aren't properly dressed, it would be best to meet in my study. Let me go explain to some of my guests."

Mac saw Councilman Bill Clark loitering across the foyer. His expression darkened when Travis whispered to him the cause of the interruption.

"O'Callaghan, what do you think you're doing?" the politician demanded to know. "Do you know who this is?" Behind him, Mac saw a smug grin cross their host's face.

"I am well aware of who Travis Turner is," David replied in an even tone. "But this takes precedence. We have a murder to investigate."

Bill Clark scoffed. "She committed suicide."

"If you can tell me how someone not only rolls over from her back to her stomach, but also moves from one location to another hours after killing herself, then I will gladly leave and go back to writing tickets for all the cars that are illegally parked along the road out there." David gestured at the cars belonging to Travis's party guests. Many were parked along Spencer Drive in plain view of No Parking signs on both sides of the road.

Bill Clark opened his mouth but nothing came out. He glanced over his shoulder at Travis.

"Lividity." David explained, "When someone dies and lies in one position for a period of time—hours—their blood settles at the lowest point. In Ms. Weaver's case, the blood settled in her back. That means she had been on her back for twelve to twenty-four hours before someone dumped her face down by Travis's swimming pool." He looked beyond the councilman to his former childhood friend. "Considering that she was his assistant and her body was found next to his pool, then Travis is the natural first person to question about these inconsistencies."

Travis's broad grin returned. "I'll be glad to answer all of your questions. Anything I can do to help."

When he followed the famous author into his study, Mac sensed before he saw a pair of eyes gazing down at him from over the fireplace. They belonged to a raven-haired beauty. The emerald green drape encasing her bosom matched her eyes, which seemed to invite them to take her into their arms.

"Gorgeous, isn't she?" Travis gazed up at the portrait. "It's a Deloise original, a little Christmas present for my bride. Cost me more than the advance for my second book, but worth every penny. How many men can say they commissioned Antonio Deloise to paint their wives for them? Did you know that he was dying of cancer?"

"No, we didn't." Mac could see David trying to find his voice.

"That's not for public knowledge." Travis smirked. "A year from now, this painting will be worth ten times what I paid for it."

David turned his back on the portrait. "Travis, we're having a couple of problems in closing Betsy's case."

"I was hoping it wouldn't come to this." Travis strode over to the fireplace. "I underestimated you, bud." With his back to them, he stared up at the image above him. "I found Betsy's body in my bed when I came home Sunday afternoon."

"Sunday afternoon?" Mac turned around from where he had been studying the book titles that lined the shelves in Travis's bookcase.

Unlike Robin Spencer, Travis's study contained one bookcase that held bestsellers no older than five years. A massive solid oak desk filled one corner of the author's office. A closed laptop rested in the center of the desk.

"To change my clothes before going to pick up Sophia at the airport." Travis turned to them. "That's why I moved the body. I didn't want Sophia to find out."

"Find out what?" David asked. "What was your secretary doing in your bed?"

"Killing herself. Don't you get it? Betsy flipped out." He plopped down in a leather chair. "She hit on me the first time I walked into Vic Morgenstern's office. She was very attentive and I admit I liked her, but not the same way she liked me. She was the one who insisted that I send *A Death in Manhattan* to Robin Spencer. When I got the book deal, she begged me to take her along with me. I did, but I made it clear that we would only be employer and employee. We worked good together, but things changed after I brought Sophia back from Europe."

Unable to keep the sarcasm out of his tone, Mac asked, "Why would she change after you married another woman?"

"Were you intimate with your secretary?" David wanted to know.

"No!" Travis practically shouted before bursting into laughter. "My wife is one of the most beautiful women in the world. Why would I lower myself to someone like Betsy Weaver? Why would I have to?"

David glanced at Mac before replying, "Are you trying to tell us that Betsy killed herself in your bed as an act of symbolism?"

"Of course," Travis said. "After I married Sophia, she became depressed and started acting weird. When she found out that I was having an affair with Katrina—"

"What?" David exclaimed.

With a quiet laugh, Travis looked up at the painting over the fireplace. "Come on, Dave. Did you really think you were the only one?"

"Katrina said you forced yourself on her."

"I guess we should have gotten our stories straight, but when Sophia walked in on us, she didn't give us a chance." Travis's smile faded. "Betsy couldn't understand how I could have an extramarital affair with Katrina, who I hadn't seen in years, and not her. She took her anger out on Katrina. I saw her following Katrina around." He hung his head. "I should have said something. If I had, Katrina would still be alive."

After giving Travis a moment to suck in a deep breath and regain what little composure he appeared to have lost, Mac demanded that he tell them what had happened that weekend.

"Betsy had been shadowing me for a long time. Frankly, I've gotten used to it. On Saturday, I went to the lounge at the Inn. A woman sent a drink over to me. Of course, I had to thank her. She told me that she was my biggest fan." He chuckled. "One thing led to another and we made a date to get together at her place. On the way to my car, I ran into Betsy and she was hysterical. She accused me of cheating on her. I saw then that I had no choice but to put an end to this. So I told her how it was. The next afternoon, I came home and found her in my bed. You don't have to be a rocket scientist to figure out what happened. I couldn't let Sophia find Betsy in our bed. I tried to carry her to her cottage, but she weighed a ton. I only got her as far as the pool and dropped her." He shook his head with a laugh. "I know all about lividity, but rolling that lard ass over onto her back was like trying to move a whale."

David raised an eyebrow in Mac's direction before asking, "Do you have the name and address of the new friend you hooked up with on Saturday?"

"Yes, but I can't give it to you," Travis said. "She's married, too. You've both seen how jealous Sophia gets. If she found out, there's no telling what she would do." With a grin, he added, "I don't know what it is about me that I pick these jealous types."

David replied, "We understand, but I still need to check out your alibi. I will be discreet."

While Travis scribbled out a name and address on a sheet of the typing paper from the inbox, Mac asked, "Did you ever read any of Betsy's writings?"

"I read a couple of her manuscripts," Travis said. "They were pretty much rewrites of my books."

Mac told him, "Your agent told us that she called him Saturday night and insisted on seeing him first thing Monday morning. Do you know what that was about?"

"No." Travis handed the information about his alibi to David. "I planned to ask her, but never got the chance on account of her offing herself."

*   *   *   *

When Archie found Betsy Weaver's cottage, she sighed with relief to find that her laptop didn't have a password login.

Her relief faded when she found that it also didn't have any pictures, files, or documents.

Someone had taken the laptop back to its factory settings and deleted all of Betsy's files in the process.

They had neglected to take her notebooks.

Scanning random sections, Archie knelt on the floor to dig through the piles of yellow tablets. As she had suspected, the books contained storylines, outlines, and character notes for murder mysteries. She was shuffling through a two-foot-tall pile of notebooks on the floor in Betsy's bedroom when she heard, "What are you doing?" hissed into her ear.

Shrieking, Archie clutched the notebook she was reading to her chest.

Mac laughed.

"Don't you know better than to sneak up on a girl?" She whirled around and slapped his legs with the writing tablet.

He knelt next to her. "Did you find anything?"

"I found something missing. Someone wiped out Betsy's hard drive. Her desk is cleared out. No disks, no flash drives. No nothing."

"So whoever killed her didn't want anyone to find what she was working on," Mac said. "Who?"

"The Black Diamond," Archie said. "Think about it. The Black Diamond is a master of disguise. Who knows more about makeup and changing looks than a supermodel?"

Mac chuckled. "Sophia?"

"Unaware that his new bride moonlights as an international assassin, Travis brings Sophia home. Betsy is here blending into the wallpaper so that Sophia doesn't notice her. But Betsy notices Sophia, who notices Roy Herman and Peter Marlstone. Maybe Sophia even contacts the Sanchez family to negotiate the hit. Betsy thinks she has found the story to make her writing career happen; but, she also becomes a dangerous liability to the Black Diamond, who must eliminate her."

"Sophia was in New York this weekend," he said.

"Do we know that for a fact?" She asked, "What did Travis say?"

"That it was a suicide and he dumped the body by the pool because she died at an inconvenient location."

"Do you believe him?"

"No, someone forced those pills and booze down her throat, and then put her on ice before dumping her next to the pool."

Convinced of her assessment, Archie declared, "Sounds like a mob hit to me. That points to the Black Diamond."

Mac gathered the notebooks scattered around them. "We need to find out what Betsy had been working on that got her killed."

"What are you doing?"

Almost dropping the books she held in her arms, Archie gasped when she saw Sophia behind Mac.

She had tied her wet hair up in a scarlet scarf matching the bikini she wore under a black overwrap. To illustrate her impatience, she tapped the toe of one of her high-heeled sandals while waiting for them to explain their presence in her guest house.

Mac turned around to answer. "We're investigating a murder."

"Murder? Give me a break. Who'd care enough about that dweeb to want to go to the trouble of killing her?"

"We think someone killed Betsy because she uncovered something while researching one of Travis's books," Mac explained. "We need to take the notebooks to read for possible evidence about what she may have found."

She waved her hand in a gesture of dismissal. "Take them. They're nothing but trash. Get them out of here."

Mac glanced at Archie. Sophia was unconcerned about what could be in Betsy's notebooks. While Archie gathered them in a laundry basket, he made conversation with their hostess. "I saw your painting. It's really a masterpiece."

"Painting?"

"The one Deloise did of you that's hanging in the study," he said. "Not every woman can say she was painted by Antonio Deloise."

Her reaction surprised him.

"Augh! That! I wish Travis would burn that piece of crap." She screwed up her face. "It doesn't even look like me."

Mac stepped up to Sophia. "Did you tell Deloise that you didn't like the painting? Maybe he could have fixed whatever you didn't like."

Her lips curled. "Travis wanted to surprise me. He had given Antonio some pictures from my portfolio to paint from." She tilted her head. "What are you looking at?"

"Your eyes," he said.

"A movie critic called them bedroom eyes." She licked her lips. "Do you like them?"

"Mac!" Archie shoved the laundry basket into his back. "I'm ready to go."

* * * *

The sun went down on what Archie had considered to be a productive day. She had spent most of the evening reading through Betsy Weaver's notes. Now, she yearned for dinner and conversation with Mac.

She found him asleep on the back deck. Clutching one of Robin's books to his chest, he leaned back in a chair with his feet propped up on the corner of the table. Curled up in a tight ball, Gnarly was sleeping under his master's raised legs. Archie considered snapping a picture of the scene. They reminded her of Mickey Forsythe and Diablo.

She snapped her fingers next to Mac's ear. "Hey! What's happening?"

Growling and barking at the same time, Gnarly sat up. His head collided with Mac's legs, which knocked his master off balance so that he almost fell from his chair.

With a smile, Archie said, "I came to see if you wanted dinner."

"I don't know." Mac rubbed his eyes. He woke up more to tell her that he was reading.

"Looked like you were sleeping to me." She sat across from him. "I was reading, too. Betsy wrote a lot. Like Travis, she was into murder mysteries. She was good, too."

Mac marked his place in Robin's book and set it aside. "If she was so good, why did she work for Travis?"

"There're a lot of very good writers out there who can't get published, either because of timing, or not knowing the right people. Betsy thought she wasn't pretty enough."

"People don't care what authors look like. Either they like what they write or they don't."

"Betsy had some issues." She sighed. "One of the outlines I read in her notes is a chapter by chapter copy of Travis's second book. Now, I haven't read every mystery out there, but based on that, it's entirely possible that Betsy, while she wrote well, had trouble coming up with original plotlines. I also found notes for a mystery about a series of murders in a resort town. The killer ends up being the mayor, who ends up not being who he claimed to be."

"Sounds familiar," Mac said.

"Makes one think that maybe Betsy had been lurking in the wrong place at the wrong time. The ME believes her time of death was before Marlstone's. Maybe he killed Betsy before the Black Diamond caught up with him. Wouldn't that be ironic?"

Studying the cover of the book he had been reading, Mac didn't hear what she had said. "Why would a writer mail a package special delivery to herself?"

"Proof of copyright." Archie gasped. "That package that Gnarly brought home. Betsy had mailed it to herself. She's a writer. A quick and inexpensive way for writers to prove the date of writing a manuscript is to mail it to yourself special delivery. You file the package away without breaking the seal. The postmark is a legal record of the date the manuscript was completed. Did you open it?"

"I was going to return it to her," Mac said. "It turns out she was dead one full day when Gnarly brought it home."

"Let's go open it." Archie jumped to her feet.

A shot rang out from across the cove. The windows in the French door behind them shattered.

Mac flew out of his chair, plunged Archie down onto the deck, and covered her with his body. Barking loud enough to wake up everyone on the Point, Gnarly raced down to the dock.

"Gnarly!" Archie attempted to get up to save the dog.

Mac pushed her back down. "Stay down!"

Another shot echoed across the lake followed by the roar of a jet ski speeding away.

The voices of neighbors calling out inquiries about the source and cause of the shot, and possible injuries, floated across the cove and down the Point. Moments later, they heard the jingle jangle of Gnarly's tags and the patter of his paws on the deck. Sensing all was safe, Mac climbed off Archie. Immediately, she hugged Gnarly who returned her affection with licks to her face.

"I'm the one who shoved you out of the way of the bullet," Mac objected. "Why are you hugging him?"

"You're not a defenseless dog."

"Gnarly's as defenseless as a rattlesnake."

*   *   *   *

"Someone is very nervous." David knelt to pick up a shard of broken glass from the kitchen floor.

The report of shots fired brought out David and Yvonne Harding, with whom he was having dinner. David excused himself to use the bathroom to clean up after Mac discreetly pointed out lipstick on his cheek and collar.

Bogie had been teaching a women's self-defense class in McHenry. The muscle-bound deputy chief arrived in sweats with protective padding.

"The Black Diamond," Archie said. "That's who's nervous."

"Who's the Black Diamond?" Yvonne wanted to know.

"A high-priced assassin."

"This isn't her MO. The Black Diamond always hits her mark." Mac gestured at the broken window and glass scattered inside the kitchen. "This is the work of an amateur."

David quipped, "If he's an amateur, why are we having such a hard time catching him?"

"Maybe because we don't know what this is all about yet. But I think Gnarly brought home something that can lead us to his motive." Mac led them to the stairs in the corner of the kitchen. "It's in my bedroom."

Gnarly seemed to be waiting for them in the middle of Mac's bed. The package he had brought home two nights earlier rested under his front paws. He didn't object when Mac took the envelope from him. Moving to the edge of the bed, the dog appeared to be as interested as the humans in learning its contents.

Mac studied the postmark on the package. "Very interesting."

"What's so interesting?" David wanted to know.

Showing the package to them, Mac pointed out, "Betsy Weaver mailed this to herself a decade ago."

Examining the post markings on the front of the envelope, David said to Mac, "She hadn't even met Travis yet. What could it possibly have to do with her or Katrina's murders?"

With a whine that sounded as if his feelings had been wounded, Gnarly plopped down onto the mattress.

"I don't know. But Travis is in this up to his eyeballs. I think that broken picture on Betsy's night stand was of him."

David laughed. "Betsy wasn't Travis's type."

"Betsy had something that Travis needed," Mac said. "I think he slept with her to get that something. She had it locked up in the file cabinet. After killing her, he couldn't get it open. So he took the whole cabinet to keep us from finding it."

"That something being what? What could little old Betsy Weaver possibly have that rich and famous Travis Turner would want from her?" David asked. "She was a nobody that scribbled junk in notebooks. What would a big fat cow—"

"David!" Yvonne chastised him.

"Travis's words, not mine," David clarified before turning back to Mac. "What in the world could she have that was important enough to Travis for him to lower himself to have sex with her?"

"I don't know, but it had to be something. Maybe she had evidence of something from his past locked up in that file cabinet."

"In other words," Archie translated, "blackmail."

"Very possibly," Mac said. "My gut is telling me that Travis is our killer."

"Mac," David said, "his alibi checks out. He was with a woman he had met at the Inn Saturday night. Believe me, she didn't want to admit it. Her husband was out of town and she says that if it comes to going to court, she'll deny it."

Archie suggested, "Maybe he killed Betsy before going to see her."

"The ME can't be conclusive about the time of death," David agreed. "Even so, we still need a motive."

Yvonne said, "Maybe Betsy found out about Travis killing Katrina."

"His stepmother worked for Milo Ford, who built the Singleton home," Mac reminded David. "Maybe his step-mother knew about the secret entrance and told Travis, which would give him knowledge of the crime scene to be able to get in and out without tripping the security system."

"Travis couldn't have killed Katrina." David shook his head firmly. "He and Sophia flew out of McHenry before the blizzard. I checked with the pilot. There's no way either of them could have flown back before the airport was closed due to the storm. And now we come right back to the matter of motive. Why would he have wanted to kill Katrina?"

Mac said, "He admitted to having an affair with her. He wouldn't be the first husband to kill his mistress."

"No way!" Yvonne laughed heartily at the suggestion. "Katrina couldn't stand Travis. When I interviewed her after Niles died, we got to talking about him. The literary world had crowned him their Golden Boy, but she wasn't the least bit impressed. She said he was a phony in high school, and he was a phony now."

Whining, Gnarly pawed at the package like it was a bag of dog food.

Mac said, "We might as well check out Betsy's literary masterpiece."

Archie grasped his hand before he tore open the envelope. "Once we break that seal, then it will be no good to Betsy or her estate if the manuscript becomes a copyright issue."

"Betsy Weaver is dead," David reminded her.

"What about her estate?"

"You told me that she was incapable of coming up with original storylines." Mac ripped open the package.

As expected, it contained a typewritten manuscript held together with two rubber bands crisscrossing the package. The top page announced the title of the work as *Murder in the City*. The second line listed Betsy Weaver as the author.

"Have you ever heard of this book?" Yvonne asked Archie.

"The title sounds familiar," she answered, "but I can't place it."

*　*　*　*

"Sorry for the mess." Mac slipped some hundred dollar bills into Jackson's palm to pay for cleaning the carpet where Gnarly had expelled his breakfast during the private flight from McHenry to Reagan National Airport.

"He doesn't get car sick." Mac watched the German shepherd stagger down the steps to the stationary ground where a stretch limousine waited for them. "I'll give him air sickness pills before the flight back."

Jackson said, "Good idea."

Struck with a sudden thought, Mac said, "The police told me that you flew the Turners to Los Angeles the day before the Saint Valentine's Day blizzard."

"I've flown them out there quite a few times," the pilot answered with pride.

Mac asked, "Was Travis Turner on that flight?"

"Oh, yeah," Jackson said. "Saw him myself. He was sicker than a dog." Glancing at Gnarly, he chuckled at his impromptu quip.

"Sick? How? A cold?"

"It's not a good idea to fly with a cold, especially a head cold. The pressure can make you feel like your head is going to explode. He had the stomach flu. I suggested that he not go, but Sophia said he had appointments with movie producers."

"She told you that?"

Jackson nodded his head. "He spent the whole flight curled up under a blanket in the back." The pilot glanced back inside and covered his face to block the smell of Gnarly's vomit. "At least he didn't throw up."

After thanking Jackson for the flight to Washington, and promising not to let Gnarly eat anything before the return flight that afternoon, Mac descended the stairs to climb into the back of the limousine that would take him to his appointment.

Reluctantly, Chad Singleton had agreed to see Mac Faraday. The meeting was to take place at an outdoor café along the Potomac River in Old Town Alexandria, Virginia. Sick to his stomach, Gnarly rested at Mac's feet with no interest in stealing food from the other diners.

"You still look green." Mac patted the dog on the head with one hand while drinking his Brandy Manhattan with another. Resting his head against Mac's leg, Gnarly responded to his touch with a long groan.

Archie was a good influence. Mac was enjoying the finer things in life that he had been unable to afford months before. For the first time, he requested the restaurant's best brandy for his Manhattan—no matter what the price.

While waiting for Chad Singleton, Mac admired his new pair of leather shoes, purchased at Neiman Marcus. They cost more than his jeans, which had been bought off the clearance rack while on the verge of bankruptcy. The shopping trip followed the dog throwing up into his old loafers.

Mac never imagined riding in the back of a white stretch limousine. When he had heard the price for an afternoon rental, he felt guilty over spending so much money that he had not earned personally. The pleasure of leaving the pressure of maneuvering his way through airport traffic to a uniformed chauffer overrode his guilt.

Mac enjoyed seeing the café's lunch crowd attempting to peer through the limo's smoked glass to see who the lucky passenger could be. Recalling how he used to do the same thing not too long ago, he chuckled.

The heir apparent to the Holt millions was one of those who slowed his pace to study the symbol of wealth before sauntering over to Mac's table. The insignia embroidered on the breast of Chad's athletic suit announced that he had come from the upscale athletic club down the block. Mac recalled having checked into the cost of a membership years earlier. It far exceeded his cop's budget.

Chad Singleton started their conversation without greeting. "My lawyer advised me not to talk to you." In other words, Mac should chock him showing up as a favor.

"I'm not a cop anymore." Mac gestured at his limo. "I'm a millionaire playboy. Sit down and order a drink."

Chad whirled around. "Why waste my time if you don't have the authority to arrest me?"

"Katrina murdered Niles," Mac declared one decibel louder than his lunch guest would have preferred. "You knew about it."

Chad's shoulders stiffened.

"That makes you an accessory."

Chad turned to glare at him.

"I think you'd like a drink," Mac said.

All cockiness vaporized. Before taking a seat, Chad peered at the other diners as if to determine if any of them were undercover officers. He noticed the German shepherd lying inert under Mac's chair. "Is your dog all right?"

"No." Mac nodded in the direction of the server standing over their table. "What do you want to drink?"

Chad ordered a scotch from the waiter, who refilled Mac's water glass before leaving the two men alone.

"This is Gnarly," Mac told him.

More interested in ensuring that he wasn't about to be arrested, Chad shrugged his shoulders at the introduction.

"Don't you recognize him?"

Chad glanced under the table. His eyes met Gnarly's. Neither of them showed recognition. "Should I?"

Mac said, "He's the dog you gave to Katrina to protect her from Pay Back."

"So this is the mutt that let Katrina get killed."

"He almost died trying to catch her killer. Didn't you check out the dog you bought?"

"What do I know about dogs? A dog is a dog. My buddy said he knew about some dog the army wanted to get rid of. He told me the price was a steal for a fully trained, purebred German shepherd. So I bought him and had him shipped to Katrina, who gave me hell for saddling her with a mutt that kept digging up her back yard. I was trying to do her a favor." He looked suspicious. "I thought you called me here to talk about Katrina's secret, not some dumb dog."

Both men sat back in their seats while the server placed Chad's drink on the table.

"He's not dumb," Mac said after the server left.

He was aware of Chad's eyes on him. His police experience told him that Katrina's husband was nervous about what he had figured out.

Chad masked his nervousness with confidence. "You can't prove that I knew Katrina killed Niles."

"She pretty much said so on this tape."

Mac pressed the button on the recorder he had set next to his glass.

"He knows!" Katrina's sobbing voice came from the recorder. "He's like some demon that appears out of nowhere and knows everything. Pay Back is hell."

Without emotion, Chad sipped his drink while listening to his late wife's anguish. "That doesn't prove I did anything wrong."

"But you're capable of it," Mac said. "You were both cut from the same cloth."

"So tell me, Chad," Katrina asked from the recorder, "how much does Rachel love you?"

"This is where it gets interesting." Mac turned up the volume.

"Does she love you enough not to kill you after you get all my money?"

Chad pointed out, "Notice that I said she was crazy."

Katrina begged for an answer before advising him, "I wouldn't go up to Abigail's Rock with her if I were you, Chad."

Mac turned off the recorder.

"All this proves is that Katrina was very unstable."

"You're right. This recording doesn't prove that you were in on her plan to kill Niles Holt." Mac smirked. "I notice that you haven't asked me where I got this tape. Could it be because you wanted me to get it? Why? What recordings did you make that you don't want me to hear?"

Chad sipped his drink. "Like you said you're not a cop anymore. You can't do anything to me."

Mac rested his elbows on the table. "Katrina went fishing for a rich husband, just like you were fishing for a rich wife. She hooked Niles Holt. Then, she killed him so that she could have his money without having to sleep with an old man. How's that?"

"I had nothing to do with any of it," Chad said in a low voice.

"Pay Back is hell. He was doing what Katrina paid the chief of police not to do—punish her. Maybe her own guilt pushed her over the edge, or she could have been getting pay back for something else and only assumed it was for killing her husband."

"Maybe," Chad said. "*If* she killed him, I didn't know anything about it."

"You knew. Otherwise, she wouldn't have called you for help. Since you didn't report it, that makes you an accessory." Mac chuckled. "That's why you recorded her calls. You wanted her to admit to Niles Holt's murder so you could hold it over her head to get out of the pre-nup and get a better divorce settlement."

"I didn't kill anyone."

"Did you suspect her of killing him before you married her?"

Chad drained his drink. "What if I did? I didn't have any proof."

"When did the thought first cross your mind?"

Chad looked down into his glass. "Katrina had her name on all of his accounts within a week of the engagement."

"What did she say when you talked to her about killing Niles?"

"We didn't talk about it."

"Come on," Mac said. "That's what she meant when she asked you if Rachel would ever kill you. That's what she meant about going up to Abigail's Rock. You knew and she knew you knew."

"She was drunk on that tape."

"What did she tell you? Did anybody besides the chief of police know that she killed Niles?"

Chad studied the faces of the diners gathered at the tables around them.

"Well?" Mac forced him to turn back to him.

"I put it together *after* Holt died. It didn't take a rocket scientist to figure it out. She kept saying Lee Dorcas did it, but he had an alibi as tight as they come. Then she said it was some mysterious stalker. She certainly wasn't in mourning. All I had to do was wink at her and she jumped into bed with me."

"So you jumped into bed with a murderer," Mac said.

"She was filthy rich and wanted me," he said. "Who wouldn't?"

Mac refused to respond. "Does anybody else know Katrina murdered her first husband?"

"Probably the lover she had in Deep Creek."

Knowing that Chad was referring to David, Mac asked, "Who else?"

After a moment of deep thought, Chad answered, "There was that writer."

"What writer?" Mac's thoughts immediately turned to Travis Turner.

"Some author wanting to write about Katrina and make herself famous," Chad explained. "Right after I came back to Washington, she called all excited because this writer thought Niles's murder would make a good mystery, only she would fictionalize it. I warned Katrina that she was playing with fire. I mean, if I could figure out that she did it—For her to go over her story in detail—"

"Her own piece of fiction," Mac noted.

"Exactly," Chad said. "Katrina wanted to be famous."

"Did she tell you this writer's name?"

"Probably, but it didn't mean anything to me. Anyway, I think the writer put it together. They got into a fight. Katrina didn't give me any of the details. I half-expected to hear from the police, but nothing happened, except Pay Back materialized not long after that."

* * * *

"Okay, Mr. Faraday, we've landed in McHenry," Jackson called back from his cockpit. "I hope you enjoyed the flight…considering." The pilot unlatched his seat belt and stood up to check on his passengers.

The German shepherd appeared to have recovered from his air sickness. He was curled up on one of the four lounging chairs in the passenger compartment.

The pilot's sole human passenger was still asleep under the blanket where he had been when the flight began. Wherever he ate lunch, Jackson swore he was never going there. When they met at the airport for the return flight, Mac announced that he had been throwing up since his meeting. He was asleep on the sofa in the back before the private jet taxied down the runway.

Aware that Mac Faraday had been a homicide detective, poison crossed the young pilot's mind when he saw no movement under the blanket.

Gnarly lifted his head from his nap and yawned.

"Mr. Faraday, are you okay?" Jackson pulled back the blanket to reveal a bald head.

"It ain't Faraday. It's Groom." Detective Sam Groom threw back the blanket and sat up.

"What the—?" Jackson leapt back.

"I decided to try an experiment," he heard Mac's voice behind him. The pilot spun around to find his registered passenger in a lounge chair resting with its back to the cockpit. With no other passengers registered for the flight, Jackson had assumed it was empty.

"Experiment? What kind of experiment?" Jackson demanded to know.

Mac explained, "You said that during the whole flight to California, Travis Turner was asleep under a blanket. I wanted to see if someone else could have been under that blanket."

Jackson objected, "I saw you come on the plane."

"But you didn't see me slip on and take his place," Detective Groom said. "Just as easily as I slipped on, Mac could have slipped off. Private chartered flights don't have all the security measures in place that commercial flights have."

"Did you actually speak to Travis Turner after the plane landed in L. A.?" Mac asked,

"He was sick." The pilot sputtered out a comment about how he couldn't remember if he did speak to his passenger.

Mac grinned at the detective. "That's what I was looking for."

"You still don't have motive for him doing it," Detective Groom said.

"That's only one small detail."

CHAPTER TWENTY

"Gnarly! I'm going to kill you!" Mac grabbed the barking dog by his collar and shook him. "Stop it!" While his guests, Sophia and Travis Turner, took cover behind the front door, he slapped Gnarly on the snout. "I'm sorry," he told them. "He's very territorial. I'll lock him in the bedroom upstairs."

Mac gestured in the direction of Archie, David, and Yvonne, who had remained seated in the living room during the attempted attack. "The server will get your drinks. One of the Inn's best chefs is cooking dinner for us."

Ready to make a run for it if Gnarly broke loose, Travis and Sophia joined the rest of the party. Before they could sit, a server dressed in the uniform of the Inn appeared to take their drink orders.

Archie could see Sophia giving her and Yvonne the once over. Judging by the smirk that crossed her face, the celebrated model was conducting her own private beauty contest in her head. Proclaiming herself the victor, she sat on the loveseat without acknowledging the losers.

David clasped Travis's hand. "Hey, buddy, good to see you. No hard feelings?"

"None now that you've taken me out from under the microscope." Travis smoothed the lapel of his suit jacket.

As they did for every public appearance, he and Sophia had coordinated their attire. The blue in his suit matched the hue of his wife's dress, as well as the sapphires in the jewels around her neck, wrist, fingers, and dangling from her earlobes.

"Now that all of our questions have been answered about Betsy's death, we have no choice but to close the case," David explained.

When he took the drink the server offered on a silver tray, Travis's eyes met his friend's. Silently, he thanked him for not mentioning his indiscretion the weekend of Betsy's murder.

David said, "I'm sure you understand why I had to be thorough in my investigation. Naomi said it best in your first book—what was it she said? I can't remember exactly. About how the truth has a way of ending friendships? I'm sure you know the line I'm talking about. Since you wrote it, then you must know how true it is."

Gnarly's abrupt bark startled Sophia out of her seat.

"Gnarly! Back! Shut up!" Mac called from the hallway upstairs.

The dog answered with snarling barks.

They heard a door slam.

"That dog should be put down," Travis said. "He's dangerous. He scared Katrina. That's why she kept him in the garage."

Sophia sat up straight. "How do you know Katrina kept that mutt in the garage?"

"I don't remember who told me. I found out at some point during my research."

"Speaking of your research," Archie asked, "when are you going to start writing your book about Katrina?"

"Don't make me neuter you!" Mac appeared at the top of the stairs.

The barking stopped.

Their host paused to smooth his hair, messed in the wrestling match, and straighten his suit. After composing himself, he strode down the stairs to join the party. The server met him at the bottom with a glass of champagne.

After a short conversation between Mac and his guests about the warm weather and the onslaught of summer residents returning to Spencer, the server returned to announce that dinner was ready.

Mac invited his guests to gather in the dining room where the Inn's staff had prepared the table with the Spencer family's century-old china. "You should be honored to know that this is the very first time I've eaten in this room. I usually eat in the kitchen."

After holding out Archie's chair at the head of the table, Mac sat at the other end. David and Yvonne sat next to each other on one side of the table while Travis and Sophia sat on the other.

The server brought out chilled copper salad plates. While she set one in front of each guest, Mac told Sophia, "We're having salmon for the main course. Jeff told me that you're a quasi-vegetarian. You eat fish, but no other meat."

"Thank you for noting that." She picked up her fork. "The media is always watching my waistline."

Mac turned his attention to the rest of his guests. "I've learned a lot of little things about household chores since my divorce. Today, I learned that fish leaks. No matter how you wrap it, the slime oozes out," he told them with a grin before sipping his champagne. "The Inn delivered the salmon this morning and I thought they had wrapped it up nice and tight. But when I went to make a sandwich for lunch I found that it had leaked onto my baloney. Even Gnarly refused to eat that slimy mess. The slime oozed down to the bottom of my fridge." He asked Sophia, "Does that happen to you?"

Offended by the suggestion that she did such mundane chores as cleaning, Sophia said, "I never paid that much attention to the floor of our refrigerator."

"You have a walk-in fridge," David said. "I saw it. It's huge. I'll bet you could hide a body in there."

"Why would I want to hide a body in the fridge?"

David said, "To slow down decomposition to throw off the time of death."

Sophia turned to her husband. "What are they talking about?"

Travis glared across the table at David.

"We're simply making polite dinner conversation." Mac picked up the pepper mill. "Anyone want pepper on their salad?"

* * * *

After dinner, Mac invited his guests into the study for cigars.

Gasping at the décor in the room devoted to Robin's writing, Sophia clasped her throat upon spying the various weapons, research materials, and memorabilia of murder.

"This room helped to inspire Robin." Archie handed Sophia a sherry glass. "Doesn't Travis have a room—?"

"He wouldn't dare." Sophia gulped down a taste of the liquor.

After draping his suit jacket over the back of the chair behind the desk, Mac removed a box from the bottom drawer. "My mother was a closet cigar smoker."

"Robin loved to smoke one every now and then," Archie explained. "She had an average of five a year."

David hung his suit jacket on the coat rack before taking a cigar from the open box. "I remember sharing a couple of cigars with Robin. Dad loved nothing more than a good cigar after closing a case."

"Then we should have one, by all means, now that we've solved Katrina's murder." Travis took the cigar Mac offered to him.

Archie ignited a crystal cigar lighter and held the flame to the end of Mac's cigar. After it caught flame, she turned to Travis, who had also taken off his suit coat. While she held out the flame to Travis's cigar, she noted his bare muscular arms exposed by the short-sleeved shirt he had worn under the suit coat. His bronzed flesh was smooth and flawless.

"Hey, Travis, do you know what this is?" Mac had removed a book from a shelf behind Robin's desk.

Travis smiled broadly when he saw the cover. He took the hardback and opened it. "It's the first book that I autographed. 'To Robin, My Mentor and Inspiration, With all my gratitude, Travis Turner.' I dated it five years ago this summer." He showed the inscription to Sophia. "I owe everything to her."

"Can you do me a favor?" asked Mac. "I've never known a bestselling author. Can you read *A Death in Manhattan* to me—to us? It would be such a kick." He turned to the rest of his guests. "How about it?"

After David, Yvonne, Archie, and even Sophia voiced encouragement, Travis accepted the invitation and took the book that his wife held out to him. Perched in a chair in front of the fireplace, he cleared his throat.

"A Death in Manhattan, by Travis Turner."

He turned to the first chapter.

"The alarm clock blasted its way through Naomi's dreams to jerk her out of a pleasant slumber to rejoin the world…" By the third paragraph, Travis was enthralled in his role of the author playing center stage to his private audience.

"Preoccupied with the cats circling her feet in search of their breakfast, the old lady was unaware of the killer behind the curtain waiting for the opportunity to steal what was left of her miserable life…" Aware of another voice added to his own, Travis stopped.

Behind his desk, in unison with the famous author, Mac had been reading from a stack of typewritten pages. "What's wrong, Travis? Why did you stop reading?"

Travis closed the hardback. "What do you have there?"

"Do you mean this? Oh, it's just something the dog dragged in." Mac restacked the papers. "Funny thing about this manuscript. Word for word it's the same as *A Death in Manhattan*, except for the title page. This story is entitled *Murder in the City* and the author listed below it is Betsy Weaver."

Sophia sneered. "Betsy was a no-talent writer wannabe."

Mac held up the brown envelope. "We found this manuscript in this envelope, which had been postmarked and sealed ten years ago. Travis met Betsy seven years ago."

"According to the math, Travis," David said, "Betsy wrote your blockbuster three years before you met her."

"Travis?" Sophia clutched her throat.

"It's a scam," he told her. "They're jealous and trying to discredit me." He pointed at the envelope. "They found this while searching Betsy's place. Then they changed the title page and printed up a copy of *A Death in Manhattan* from the file on her computer before deleting everything. Why? Envy. That's why."

Mac slowly nodded his head. "And that would probably fly in the media except for one fact."

"Betsy registered her copyright with the Library of Congress years before she met Travis." Archie handed a copy of a certificate to Sophia. "Betsy registered ten books with the Library of Congress, and they have copies of all of them on file."

Sophia argued, "But is it the same book?"

"It's easy enough to find out. All we have to do is compare what Betsy had submitted to the Library of Congress ten years ago to what Travis sent to Robin three years later," Archie said. "The title sounded familiar to me, so I went through Robin's archives and found the manuscript he had sent to her. This hardcopy manuscript is exactly the same, word for word, right down to the title. Robin suggested Travis change it from *Murder in the City* to *A Death in Manhattan*. She also recommended having Naomi's scoundrel love interest lose everything in the end."

"So Betsy wrote the book. Robin wrote the title and changed the ending. What did you write, Travis?" David asked.

Mac answered, "His name on the cover, contract, and royalty checks."

The set of Travis's jaw told them all that they were on target.

"At one point in my mother's journal," Mac said, "she noted all the parties, personal appearances, and traveling that you did. She actually asked at one point, 'When does he write?' The answer is never." He stood up and leaned over the desk in

Travis's direction. "You were the world-famous author. Betsy was the writer."

Breathless with disbelief, Yvonne said, "Katrina was right. You're a phony."

Sophia sprang from her seat. Without a look back, she left the manor.

"Everything's falling apart, Travis," David said.

Mac explained, "Years ago, when you started dating Betsy to get in with her boss, she fell in love with you. She trusted you enough to show her books to you and you saw how talented she was. So you sent one to Robin, who saw the work of a bestselling author. When opportunity knocked, you locked Betsy in the bell tower, and opened the door."

"Why would she have ever agreed to let him take credit for her work, especially when her books were winning awards?" Yvonne asked Travis, "Did you at least share your fortune with her?"

Archie said, "Betsy told her old boss in Hollywood that they were engaged."

"We found birth control pills in her cottage," David said. "You were sleeping with Betsy to make her think you loved her."

Yvonne declared, "You're nothing more than a common gigolo."

"Do you think I enjoyed having to whisper sweet things into that cow's ear to make her write for me?" Travis glared at her.

"You're more than a gold digger, Travis," David said. "You're a murderer."

Reigniting his cigar, Mac leaned against the corner of the desk. "Betsy had very low self-esteem. I can only imagine how Travis sold this crazy charade to her. She was ugly and he was gorgeous. The public loves beautiful people. No one would want to buy her books if they saw what she really looked like. But if the public thought her books were written by a hunk, then together they would go to the top."

"And Betsy bought it." Archie shook her head. "You must have done a real number on her."

Chuckling, Mac said, "But then, two things happened. Niles Holt was murdered in Betsy's back yard and she decided to write a murder mystery about the case. She started interviewing Roy Phillips and others in the community. Last summer, when Katrina had returned with her second husband, Betsy invited her to her cottage so that she could interview her. Seeing how hard Betsy worked on Travis's books, and how little time and effort he put into them—"

"And knowing how he got through school making girls in love with him do his homework," Yvonne interjected.

"—Katrina figured out his secret," Mac said. "At the same time, Betsy, being the real murder mystery writer, began to suspect Katrina of killing her husband, just like my mother did, and told Travis about her suspicions."

David picked up the story. "Now we have two people, each holding something over the other's head. Katrina wanted Travis to use his influence to get the zoning changed on her investment property. Meanwhile, Travis wanted Katrina to…What?"

Yvonne asked, "What?"

David cocked his head at Travis. "Are you going to tell them what you were paying Katrina back for or should I?"

Travis laughed. "This is where you are all off base. Yes, Betsy wrote my books. I paid her very well for it."

"With sex," Archie noted.

"They were great books and she was very satisfied with me," Travis said with a wicked grin. "But I didn't kill anyone. I was with a lady friend when Betsy went off the deep end and took all those pills."

David told him, "Your lady friend crumbled like a house of cards when I threatened to arrest her for accessory to murder. She admitted that you asked her to lie. You didn't get to her place until twelve thirty and left before dawn."

"Betsy finally saw you for what you really were," Mac said. "She called your agent and demanded to see him. She then packed up her sealed copy of *Murder in the City* to show him as proof that she was the real mystery writer. Perplexed by her insistence, your agent called you and you realized that the goose that laid the golden eggs was flying away. When your charm failed to work anymore, you cut your losses and killed her. What little you knew about murder, you knew that cold slows down decomposition. So, you put Betsy's body in your walk-in fridge, getting fish blood on her clothes. Lividity caused the blood to settle in her back while you met with your woman friend to set up an alibi." Mac continued, "I suspect by the volume of notepads around her cottage that Betsy was a writing machine. In order to keep your career going with her dead, you had to collect as many of her unpublished manuscripts as possible from her laptop and file cabinet, which she kept locked. So you had to haul the whole thing out to break in. Then, you went to pick up your wife at the airport. That night, after Sophia went to bed, you dumped Betsy's body by the pool for her to find."

Travis laughed, "Your story is nothing more than that. For one thing, I was in Hollywood when Pay Back murdered Katrina. Sophia and I flew out the day before. Betsy was here. She confessed to killing Katrina."

"I checked with your pilot," Mac said. "He had filed a flight plan that had you and Sophia flying from McHenry to Los Angeles the day before the blizzard. Only the pilot is less than positive about you being on that plane."

David said, "Somehow, you manipulated Betsy into taking your place on that flight while you stayed behind to kill Katrina. That's premeditation."

Travis shouted, "You can't prove that!"

"I believe we can," David said. "We were looking for evidence that the killer had left after the murder. But when we looked in the opposite direction, we found that Betsy had taken a commercial flight from Los Angeles to Dulles the Monday after the murder. How did she get from here to Los Angeles, Travis?"

"Meanwhile," Mac said, "you were on a private chartered flight to Houston in your Pay Back costume under the name of Cooper. We found the pilot who flew you from Houston to Los Angeles. That's the downside of fame. People have a tendency to remember you. You even autographed a copy of one of your books for him."

David said, "You were so careful to cover your tracks out of Deep Creek, but not to California. You had everything so well planned. All so you could kill Katrina."

"That vicious dog of hers attacked whoever killed her." Travis held out his arms to show them his smooth skin. "Look. Do you see any dog bites?"

"The pilot who flew you to California also remembers that you were wearing a heavy cap over your head, scarf, dark glasses, and gloves, even when you got to California where the temps were in the seventies," Mac said. "You then spent the next eight weeks in Los Angeles."

"Negotiating a multi-movie deal with one of Hollywood's top producers," Travis said. "It's going to make me millions."

"Would you still make those millions if Betsy went public about writing your books in exchange for regular rolls in the hay?" Archie asked. "Sounds to me like a motive for murder."

"During those two months, you'd been making regular visits to a top cosmetic surgeon," Mac said. "I've been talking to him. He couldn't violate doctor-patient privilege, but he did tell me that, hypothetically, if he had a dog bite victim for a patient, after three months he would be sufficiently healed to the point that makeup—like the kind his supermodel wife wears to cover up her flaws, would conceal his scars." He took a linen handkerchief from his pocket. After dipping it into a pitcher of water, he held the wet cloth out to Travis. "Care to prove to us that you haven't recently been bitten by a German shepherd?"

Travis backed away from the cloth. "I refuse to dignify this crap."

"You don't need to dignify it," Mac said. "Your DNA will."

"I'm not giving you my DNA, either."

"We already got your DNA," David told him.

Travis spun around to glare at him.

Mac said, "You just ate dinner here in my home, off my utensils, which are all on their way to the lab. Once they get

269

your DNA profile, they'll compare it to the killer's DNA that forensics had taken off Gnarly. That will be all the evidence we need to prove that you killed Katrina."

Yvonne asked him, "Why did you kill her? What did she do?"

Travis grabbed his suit coat and slipped it on.

Travis's handsome face hardened while David told him, "You've been fixated on having her since the beginning. All those years ago, when you were supposed to pair up with her on the double date and it didn't happen, you acted like it was nothing. But really, that wasn't the way it was. You were obsessed with her and have been for a very long time."

"Get real."

"You even had Antonio Deloise paint her for you," David said.

Travis laughed loudly.

David insisted, "As soon as I laid my eyes on that portrait I could see that it was Katrina."

"That painting is of Sophia," Travis said. "I admit Sophia bears a resemblance to Katrina."

"Katrina had green eyes!" David yelled over his objection.

Travis fell silent.

Mac said, "Sophia's eyes are dark brown."

David picked up a book from the center of the desk and flipped it open to show a page to Travis. "Our high school year book. I recognized that picture immediately. The green drape she wore. Katrina searched high and low to find the perfect color for her senior picture. She wanted it to match her eyes. Sophia didn't pose for Deloise. You had sent him this picture of Katrina." He tapped the picture he held out to him. "You had him paint Katrina, the woman you could never have."

"You stole her from me." Travis removed his hand from his suit coat to show a small handgun.

"No, Travis, I didn't steal her." David closed the book. "She chose me over you."

"Then, last summer, you took her from me again!"

He aimed the gun at David's chest.

"Drop it, Travis!" Mac drew his gun from where he'd had it concealed behind his back before getting up from behind the desk.

Travis yelled, "I've had the most beautiful women in the world begging for me to make love to them! But Katrina— even when I threatened to blow the whistle on her for killing her husband, she spit in my face—because of you!"

"It's over, Travis!" Mac shouted.

"It's your fault I killed her!" Travis pulled the trigger.

David ducked behind Robin's desk.

The shot hit Uncle Eugene in the chest. The doll went flying out of the chair.

With David out of range, Travis aimed his gun at Mac, who grabbed his arm to send the shot up to the ceiling. Mac tackled him in the mid-section and they fell back into the bookshelves. Both men dropped their guns when they crashed to the floor.

Behind the desk, David grabbed the pistol he had concealed in an ankle holster.

After ducking behind the sofa, Archie and Yvonne tried to make their way out of the study to safety.

"Yvonne! Archie! Get out of here!" Mac pulled Travis back to keep him out of reach of his gun.

"What do you think we're trying to do?" Archie yelled.

Travis rolled over onto his back and kicked Mac in the stomach. When he doubled over, the killer snatched up his gun. Spotting a hostage, Travis grabbed Yvonne by the hair. He pressed the muzzle of his gun against her temple. "I'm going to shoot her! I mean it!"

"Hold your fire!" David yelled at Mac who had retrieved his gun.

Travis grinned at Mac. "You knew it was me all along. What gave me away?"

Mac glared silently at him.

"You've been taunting me ever since you got here," Travis said. "Don't think I haven't noticed you staring at my house, willing me to give myself away."

"I haven't been staring at your house," Mac said.

"Yeah, right! And you haven't been taunting me with Dorcas's wallet. I throw it away and you drop it on the seat in my car. I bury it. You dig it up and leave it on my doormat with the newspaper. You've been slapping me in the face with it for weeks."

"I haven't—" Mac muttered before he realized what had happened to the wallet he found behind the sofa. "Gnarly," he breathed.

Keeping his pistol aimed at him, David ordered, "Give it up, Travis."

"You'll have to catch me first." Twisting Yvonne's arm up behind her back, Travis backed his way out of the study using his hostage for a shield.

With the phone pressed to her ear after dialing emergency, Archie took the stairs two at a time to let Gnarly out. The German shepherd was nothing more than a golden brown blur when he shot out the door.

"We can't let you go, Travis." David followed him and his hostage into the living room.

"One more dead body on my hands isn't going to make any difference."

Mac had darted out onto the deck to come up behind Travis to block his escape. He threw open the dining room's deck doors. "Don't do it, Travis!" He aimed his gun at him.

"You're not leaving me any choice." Travis pressed the gun against Yvonne's head.

Gnarly's growl filled the room. Before anyone could discern where the noise had come from, the dog flew over the railing of the upstairs landing. Seeing a hundred pounds of fur and teeth descending down on her, Yvonne dove in David's direction. Gnarly struck Travis in the chest and took him down to the floor.

Mac stood over the groaning killer with his gun aimed at his head. "It's over, Travis."

"It's not over until I say so." Abruptly, he rolled over and fired a shot at David.

Mac pulled his trigger, but nothing happened. His gun had jammed. During his entire career, his gun had never jammed.

Meanwhile, Travis shot out the door into the darkness.

Gnarly scrambled to his feet to give chase.

Yvonne sobbed while holding David in her arms.

"Paramedics are on their way," Archie told them.

Mac knelt next to him to examine the hole in his shoulder.

"It's not bad," David grimaced.

"I've never seen a good gun shot," Mac tried to joke.

"Don't worry about me. Get him. He killed Katrina." David thrust his pistol into Mac's hand. "Here. It's Dad's gun."

Mac caught the glimmer of a knowing look in David's eyes. He wanted to know if David was trying to tell him what he thought he was, but there wasn't time. Travis was getting away and Gnarly was on his trail.

Outside, Mac could hear Gnarly's call on the other side of the stone wall. He found the German shepherd digging at the secret door in the corner of the neighboring house.

"Quiet, Gnarly," he ordered before hitting the button to open the secret door into the passageway.

The dog slipped through the opening.

Sucking in his breath, Mac followed with the pistol ready to fire. In the dark confines of the narrow room, with no obstacles to hide behind, he listened for the jingle jangle of Gnarly's tags. With a human partner, they would have a system worked out between them to keep from shooting each other by mistake. He couldn't predict his partner's actions with Gnarly.

Mac listened while waiting for his eyes to adjust to the darkness. Had he and David found all the secret ins and outs in the house?

Travis had to have known about the door and rooms for years. His stepmother must have told him. He could be hiding anywhere to ambush him. He could even have escaped through another exit that they hadn't discovered.

Mac felt a nudge against his thigh followed by a wet snout pressed against his hand. He grasped the dog's collar while holding his gun ready to shoot with the other hand.

Gnarly led him down the narrow corridor. Mac tripped around the ladder and several feet further until the dog stopped. With a whine, Gnarly scratched at the wall.

Kneeling next to him, Mac felt around until he found a door handle, not unlike the one they had found that led into the bathroom. He pried his fingers under the crack and pulled it open.

Gnarly charged.

On his hands and knees, Mac followed. The entrance was identical to the other one. It went through a cabinet and came out behind the bar in the home theater. Mac guessed that this was the way Travis had entered the room without Katrina seeing him the night he killed her.

A light over the sink dimly lit the room. Mac crawled out of the cabinet to find Gnarly tearing into Travis's suit coat left on the floor in the middle of the empty room.

By the time Mac stood up, the dog had become aware of the trick. "Very clever." He held up the jacket to show the dog. "He took off his coat to throw you off his scent."

Enraged, Gnarly erupted with a round of barks. Charging the bar, he planted his front paws on the counter and growled at his mirrored image behind it.

Mac searched for places that Travis could be hiding. With no furnishings, there weren't any.

Behind the bar, he could see his own image looking back at him. It was the same two-way mirror Pay Back had used to watch Katrina's every move.

The two-way mirror!

"Get down!"

The mirror exploded.

Mac plunged Gnarly to the floor.

A rain of shattered glass fell on them.

"Stay!" Mac jumped up to his knees and braced the dog against the bar while firing his father's pistol into the darkness of the secret room.

When it was over, all was quiet.

They could hear the sirens of the police and paramedics racing to Spencer Point.

Mac rose to his feet. Freed, Gnarly shook to send the glass dust in his fur flying before planting his front paws on the bar to observe the damage. He uttered a whine.

Falling forward onto the bar, Travis laid face down in the broken glass. A pool of blood formed under him.

Mac took the gun from his hand. "Travis?"

"Mac," he gasped, "don't worry about me. I'm world famous. I'm going to live forever."

With that, bestselling author Travis Turner gasped his last breath.

EPILOGUE

Ironically, Travis Turner's killing spree didn't shock the media as much as the motive behind it: to conceal the identity of who had really written his books. The police found twelve completed manuscripts in the famous author's study. Each had Betsy Weaver's name written on the title page.

They also uncovered Katrina Holt Singleton's wedding ring along with a dreadlock wig splattered with Travis's and Gnarly's blood.

A DVD that Travis had hidden in his safe proved his motive for killing Gordon and Prissy Hardwick. The disc contained a security recording filmed from their back deck the night of Katrina's murder. It showed Gnarly ambushing Travis when he left Katrina's home via the secret door. During the attack, Gnarly pulled the wig from Travis's head to reveal his face before he beat the dog senseless with the bat he was carrying.

A search of Travis's bedroom closet turned up the baseball bat. Police found traces of Gnarly's blood and fur on it. Forensic evidence also revealed it to be the weapon used to crush Katrina Singleton's throat.

The publishing industry reeled for weeks in response to the news about America's hottest mystery writer being a fraud. While deciding what course of action to take, Travis's publisher yanked Travis's, or rather Betsy's, fifth bestseller from publication, losing millions of dollars on hardbacks already printed with Travis Turner's name on the cover. In the end, they set a new publication date to release what they predicted to be the most awaited book of the year: a re-release of *A Death in Manhattan* with Betsy Weaver's name on the front cover.

Meanwhile, Sophia Hainsworth dropped the Turner name before her chartered jet touched down in New York. A self-proclaimed victim of Travis Turner's con, she went on the talk show circuit telling and re-telling how the man she loved had misled her.

Truly believing he was a writer, she had been duped into helping him set up a phony alibi for Katrina's murder. She claimed Travis had told her that he was testing out a plotline for one of his books. Also, he explained away the dog bites with a dramatic story about saving a lost child from a pack of wolves during the blizzard.

Within a week of the news breaking, Sophia accepted a multi-million dollar book deal to pen her memoirs about her marriage to the famous bestselling author who had conned the world.

Archie turned down Sophia's request to ghost write the piece.

With all the sensational coverage of Travis Turner's scandal, the residents of Spencer forgot about their phony police chief until a Mercedes registered to their mobster mayor turned up at the bottom of one of Deep Creek Lake's coves. Roy Herman's body was in the trunk. He had been shot in the back of the head and had a black diamond tucked in his pants pocket.

In celebration of the Fourth of July, Mac Faraday hosted his first official party as master of Spencer Manor. Cocktail hour would be followed by a cookout of steaks, chops, chicken, and grilled lobster. After sunset, Spencer was going to be treated to the biggest fireworks show it had ever seen.

To introduce himself to Deep Creek society, Mac had invited all of his neighbors and gifted each of them with a party goodie in the form of new leather wallets and purses to make up for what his dog had stolen.

Taking up camp near the outside bar, Violet kept the bartender hopping to keep her martini glass filled. David watched her from a few feet away while sitting with Yvonne, Mac, Archie, Ben and his wife Catherine, and Bogie. Jeff Ingles lingered nearby while ensuring his employees were on top of things. Three cooks from the Inn scurried inside and out in preparation for the grilling. Gnarly cruised the guests and staff for snacks and pettings. Between munchies, he helped himself to cookies that Violet had stashed in a pouch hanging off the arm of her wheelchair.

"If you didn't keep returning Lee Dorcas's wallet to Travis, then who did?" Bogie asked Mac while sipping his beer.

Mac laughed, "The only one I can think of is Gnarly. Remember when the police came here after he brought home Dorcas's head?"

"Gnarly was going nuts," David recalled.

"He also freaked out when the Hardwicks' killer was planting the bomb at their house," Archie said. "It was Travis."

"But he didn't go nuts when Roy Phillips came out to see Archie until he attacked her," Mac said. "Nor did he react that way when I was interviewing housekeepers. The only one he tried to attack was Travis. Looking back, like Travis playing Pay Back to get back at Katrina for rejecting him, I think Gnarly embarked on his own campaign against Travis to make him pay for getting away with murdering his mistress."

"Kind of sophisticated thinking for a dog, don't you think?" Ben chuckled.

"So is petty thievery to alleviate boredom." Mac shrugged with a smile. "Gnarly stole or found that wallet. He brought that sealed manuscript to us. I doubt if he knew the significance of it, but he did sense that it had to be important." He patted the dog on the head. "Circumstantial evidence points to Gnarly." Mac's touch startling him; the German shepherd yanked his head out of the pouch of cookies.

Jeff stopped by their table with a bottle of wine. "Who was Katrina arguing with that night that she hit me with her car? Was it Phillips or whatever his name was?"

Mac answered, "It was Lee Dorcas. He had checked into the Inn one week after Niles Holt's murder, the same night as the hit and run."

"What was he doing here?" Archie asked. "Was he stalking Katrina after all?"

Mac reminded David, "Do you remember Dorcas's lawyer telling us that shortly after Holts's murder, Lee Dorcas deposited one hundred thousand dollars into his account? He never said where he got it."

"It couldn't have been a payoff for killing Holt," David said. "Dorcas had an airtight alibi."

"Even so, if I was accused of murder, especially by someone I already despised, I'd start nosing around. After the police talked to Lee Dorcas, he came out here to see what was going on."

"He blackmailed Katrina," David concluded.

"Look at it from Katrina's side," Mac suggested. "She married Niles Holt intending for him to have a simple accident, but he fights back. She ends up with a bruise on her face, a torn sweater, and a missing five carat necklace. She has to come up with another story. So she used Lee Dorcas, banking on him not having an alibi. Then, to make matters worse, the chief of police comes up with not only a witness, but physical evidence against her. She has to keep him in line. At the same time, she has the man she accused of killing her husband threatening to blow the case wide open." He chuckled, "She was between a rock and a hard place. Dorcas had to have been following her and saw her having dinner with the chief of police. They met in the garden afterwards to discuss a settlement in exchange for his silence. She paid him to go away."

Jeff said, "What I heard was not a negotiation, it was an argument."

Mac explained, "First, Katrina stole from him, and then she tried to frame him for murder. Dorcas had to have been furious with her."

"That's why it cost her so much for his silence." Seeing that everyone had finished their appetizers, Jeff whispered into his transmitter for the busboys to clear the tables and the chefs to prepare the grill for the main course.

Catherine asked, "Did any of these murders have anything to do with Emma Turner's or Milo Ford's murders?"

David said, "The gun we found in the bag in the secret room turned out to be the one used to kill Travis's stepmother."

"Emma Turner was an informant," Bogie revealed. "She was into drugs and Milo was her supplier. When Ol' Pat caught her with some cocaine, she struck a deal to snitch on Milo. A few weeks later, she got killed."

"Dad was convinced Milo did it."

Bogie told them, "A few months later, Milo got killed off."

"Travis had to have found out about that secret entrance into the Singleton house somehow," Mac said. "His stepmother must have told him."

Catherine asked Mac, "When did you first suspect Travis in all this?"

"When it came out that he had ratted David out, I knew Travis wasn't what he appeared to be."

"I thought he was a jerk," Yvonne said, "but never thought he was a killer."

Mac agreed. "Just because someone is a phony doesn't necessarily mean that he's a murderer."

Ben asked him, "When did it occur to you that he was a murderer?"

"One hint was when he killed Betsy," David answered.

"If he hadn't killed Betsy, he may have gotten away with everything," Mac said. "The mistakes he made in covering up her death revealed how little he knew about the very thing he supposedly wrote about: putting her in the fridge on her back, and then dumping her face down next to the pool. Sloppy."

"Still, Travis was very clever," Ben countered. "The Hardwicks' murders and the way he set up his alibi for Katrina's murder wasn't the work of a dummy."

Mac said, "He stole both of those crimes from my mother's books: setting up the flight to California with Betsy pretending to be him, sending the Hardwicks a gift card to the spa. He put a lot of work into those murders. He didn't have the luxury of time to plan when he killed Betsy."

"If he was in love with Katrina why did he kill her?" Catherine wanted to know.

David explained, "Travis was hot for Katrina, but he wasn't in love with her. He had plenty of other women, but Katrina rejected him." He sighed. "I really don't think she meant to. I think, like I thought Yvonne would never be interested in a guy like me—" He kissed Yvonne's hand. "I think Katrina, being from the same side of the tracks, assumed Travis wouldn't be interested in her."

"Travis could have any woman he wanted," Mac said, "except Katrina. It must have bothered him someplace in his psyche. Maybe he saw Katrina as the one he could never have and became obsessed with having her."

"That was twelve years ago," Yvonne said. "What about last year?"

Archie explained, "When Katrina ran into David and Travis at the Inn, she naturally directed her attention at her first love, David, who happened to be available. Once again she rejected Travis, even after all his success. His ego couldn't handle it."

Catherine asked Mac, "But when did you come to actually suspect him?"

"Something my mother observed in her journal clicked with me. She noted that Betsy was always working so hard while Travis was playing. Then, Yvonne mentioned that she wrote his papers in school. Between that, and seeing how close he stuck to the case, I started thinking, 'If he isn't a writer, then why is he so interested in this case?'"

Yvonne asked, "If Katrina killed Niles Holt, and the evidence showed that she did, then why did she come back here? If she hadn't, then Travis wouldn't have seen her and thought that she rejected him for David again." She gasped. "If she had stayed away, she would have gotten away with murder!"

Mac said, "Quite simply, Katrina thought she could get away with murder."

Having wheeled over to listen in on the conversation, Violet interjected, "She was stupid with beauty."

"Think about it." Catherine noted, "Katrina married Niles Holt and killed him for his money. Then, Chad Singleton married her for her money and let Travis kill her. Now, he's living high on the hog with Niles Holt's money. Where's the justice in that?"

"Oh, but there is justice." Archie smiled at Mac.

He said, "Archie has been a very busy girl. She went digging through galaxies in cyberspace where she didn't belong and found out that Niles Holt fathered a daughter twenty-eight years ago."

"She's a single mother of two living on food stamps in Florida," Archie told them. "Ed Willingham is going to represent her in an inheritance suit and the Forsythe Foundation is picking up the tab. Robin wouldn't have it any other way."

"Since Katrina inherited Niles Holt's estate by illegal means, as in murder, then she had no right to his fortune," Mac explained. "As a result, Chad Singleton has no claim to all those millions he had inherited from her."

"Excuse me." David went down to the dock.

A silence fell over the table.

Mac went to the bar, got two beers, and joined David on the dock.

"Sorry." Mac handed one of the beers to him.

"She trusted me," David said. "I saw a side of her that she was afraid to show anyone else. She was very insecure."

"She was also a murderer," Mac said.

"I know." David shrugged. "What are you going to do now?"

"Be a rich playboy."

"Whose hobby happens to be murder," David laughed. "Robin made her fortune off Mickey Forsythe chasing killers."

"I'm not Mickey Forsythe."

"Sure, you're not. Next thing you'll be telling me is that Gnarly isn't Diablo."

Smiling, Mac turned away to look up at his guests on the deck, patio, and inside the house—all around him. He still had to remind himself that it was all his. He glanced down at his suit, which he had tailored for close to twenty thousand dollars. This time writing the check was painless.

As if he were reading Mac's mind, David grinned at him.

"Okay," Mac whispered, "but let this be our little secret." He sucked in a deep breath. "David, there's something we need to talk about."

"Dad told me about you years ago."

"Really? You've known all along?"

"But he didn't know where you were," David explained. "When Robin found you and told Dad, he told me."

"All these years, you knew where I was?"

"I knew everything about you."

"And you didn't mind my moving out here?"

David laughed. "Mac, I showed up on your doorstep within hours of you racing into town in that Viper."

"You were waiting for me," Mac said.

"Weren't you curious about me?" David asked. "I'm sure Robin mentioned me in her journal."

"Now that you've gotten to know me, what do you think about having a brother?"

Looking out across the lake, David sipped his beer. "Mac, since meeting you, I've been fired from my job, accused of murder, and shot twice." His shoulders shook with laughter. "I haven't had so much fun since the police academy."

Carrying her glass of wine, Archie came out onto the dock. "What are you two talking about?" In contrast to her white lace cocktail dress, she was barefoot, as always.

"Who stole my cookies?" Violet loudly demanded to know. "Our waiter is a thief!"

David could see Yvonne looking for his help while Violet picked a fight with Jeff Ingles. "I believe I'm being summoned." He jogged up to the deck.

"What are you two up to?" Archie asked Mac.

"Shenanigans." Mac pulled her to him. "Now, where were we?"

"Where were we when?"

"You name it." He wrapped his arms around her waist. "I've been trying to kiss you for the longest time, but it seems like every time I get you this close—"

"Somebody interrupts us." She wrapped her arms around his neck.

"Why is that?"

"Can't we talk about that later?" She pressed her lips firmly against his. She sighed when they parted. "Finally."

Their romantic bliss ended when screams erupted from up on the deck.

"Gnarly! No!" Jeff was yelling.

Partiers scattered in an effort to escape. Servers carrying trays of glasses collided, spilling drinks and breaking glasses. One of the buffet tables overturned. Spilt guacamole and salsa caused a slippery escape route for the stampeding guests.

To Mac's and Archie's horror, they saw the source of the chaos.

Carrying a tray covered with thick steaks, the chef ran to and fro, trying to escape the host's dog. Seeing his only escape, he raced toward the lake. From the deck above, Gnarly took a flying leap and hit the cook in the back to send him and the steaks flying.

Oblivious to the screams, Gnarly plopped down in the midst of the meat to feed on his kill.

"Gnarly! I'm going to kill you!"

The End

About the Author

Lauren Carr fell in love with mysteries when her mother read Perry Mason to her at bedtime. She wrote her first book after giving up her writing career to be a stay-at-home mom. The first installment in the Joshua Thornton mysteries, *A Small Case of Murder* was named a finalist for the Independent Publisher Book Award 2005. Her second full-length book, *A Reunion to Die For* was released in June 2007. Her new series, The Mac Faraday Mysteries, is set in Deep Creek Lake, Maryland, where she and her family often vacation.

Lauren is a popular speaker who has made speaking appearances at schools, youth groups, and on author panels at conventions. She is also an active member of Sisters in Crime. She lives with her husband and son on a mountaintop in West Virginia.

Visit Lauren at her blog http://writerlaurencarr.blogspot.com or her website: http//laurencarr.webs.com for more information.

6219710R1

Made in the USA
Charleston, SC
28 September 2010